THE SPARE MAN

This is a work of fiction. All of the characters, organizations, and events portrayed in this novel are either products of the author's imagination or are used fictitiously.

THE SPARE MAN

A Tor Book
Published by Tom Doherty Associates
120 Broadway
New York, NY 10271

www.tor-forge.com

Tor® is a registered trademark of Macmillan Publishing Group, LLC.

Library of Congress Cataloging-in-Publication Data

Names: Kowal, Mary Robinette, 1969– author.
Title: The spare man / Mary Robinette Kowal.
Description: First edition. | New York : Tor, 2022. |
"A Tom Doherty Associates book."
Identifiers: LCCN 2022010487 (print) | LCCN 2022010488 (ebook) |
ISBN 9781250829177 (trade paperback) | ISBN 9781250829153 (hardcover) |
ISBN 9781250829160 (ebook)
Subjects: LCGFT: Detective and mystery fiction. | Science fiction.
Classification: LCC PS3611.O74948 S63 2022 (print) |
LCC PS3611.O74948 (ebook) | DDC 813/.6—dc23/eng/20220303
LC record available at https://lccn.loc.gov/2022010487
LC ebook record available at https://lccn.loc.gov/2022010488

Our books may be purchased in bulk for promotional, educational, or business use. Please contact your local bookseller or the Macmillan Corporate and Premium Sales Department at 1-800-221-7945, extension 5442, or by email at MacmillanSpecialMarkets@macmillan.com.

First Edition: 2022

Printed in the United States of America

0 9 8 7 6 5 4 3 2 1

For the Whiskey Chicks
Crystal, Eileen, Elizabeth, Liza,
Kathy, Nephele, and Susanna,
you make my life measurably better.

ISS *LINDGREN*

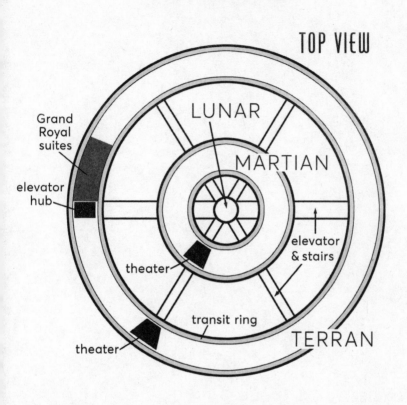

TOP VIEW

Grand Royal suites

elevator hub

LUNAR

MARTIAN

elevator & stairs

theater

theater

transit ring

TERRAN

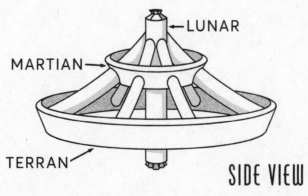

LUNAR

MARTIAN

TERRAN

SIDE VIEW

THE SPARE MAN

Martini

2.5 oz gin
.75 oz dry vermouth
Dash orange bitters
Lemon twist or olive

Stir ingredients over ice for 40 seconds. Drain. Garnish
with lemon twist or olive.

Kneeling on the floor of their suite, Tesla Crane could just feel
the vibrations of the centrifugal ring as it rotated around the interplanetary cruise ship *Lindgren*. Or more likely it was the hum
of the air conditioning. The Terran-level ring was big enough that
even the Coriolis effect was really only noticeable when throwing
things.

"Gimlet, fetch." She threw a chew toy for her Westie, and the
little dog charged in the direction the plush sloth had started to go.

It curved in the air, leaving the small white dog staring in baffled confusion for a moment before she found it and pounced with
enormous ferocity.

Tesla used the reprieve to return to stretching. She put her
hands on the floor, and her new wedding ring caught her eye with
the gleam of platinum-iridium—just like the historic kilogram
standard, because her spouse knew she was a nerd. Smiling, she
lowered her back into the cow position, feeling for twinges as she
raised her head.

The ceiling had a digital sky shading to an Earth sunset. The
simulated clouds changed shape and position in subtle response to
an artificial wind. Not bad for a honeymoon.

On the couch, her joyfrie—fianc—*spouse* watched her over the edge of his embroidery hoop. Shal was compact, with warm brown skin beneath distressingly glossy curls. "What are you smiling at?"

"You." Tesla lowered her head, arching her back as far as she could into cat position. As soon as her head was in reach, she got a faceful of little white dog. Wiggling with delight, the Westie planted tiny dog kisses along Tesla's cheek. Laughing, she tried to dodge. "Gimlet! Not helping."

Gimlet disagreed and swiped her tongue across Tesla's nose.

From the couch, Shal lowered the blackwork he was stitching into the sleeve of a T-shirt. He patted the cushion beside him. "Gimlet, c'mere."

Her dog abandoned Tesla and took a running leap onto the couch. She flopped with her nose on Shal's embroidery hoop and stared up at him with adoration.

"I'm going to need that hoop back, little girl."

She sighed and pushed closer, stumpy tail wagging.

"What's that?" He scratched her ears, grinning. "Yes, Gimlet, I completely agree. We *should* stay in tonight."

"But karaoke is tonight." Tesla returned to cow position, feeling for anything out of alignment.

Or, rather, feeling for anything unacceptably out of alignment. Her spine had its own set of rules about what "normal" looked like. She had her Deep Brain Pain Suppressor dialed all the way down because doing her exercises with the DBPS on was an invitation for more pain later.

"And last night was the Orbit Transfer Party." Shal was trying to ease the embroidery hoop out from under Gimlet, but she seemed to generate her own tiny canine gravity field sometimes. She wouldn't hurt the embroidery, but when she was off-duty she was still a Westie. As they'd said at the training center, "She's a dog, not a robot."

"Be fair, watching the Moon recede was not a bad view. Although the sparkling was questionable . . ."

"Questionable is being kind." He lifted Gimlet's paw only to have her roll over onto her back. "Hey. Kid. C'mon."

"Gimlet, leave it."

Presented with a formal command from Tesla, Gimlet reacted with her service-dog training and pushed back from the embroidery hoop, but she still stared at Shal as if he existed solely to pet her. Which, to be fair, she did with everyone she met and not only Tesla's joyfrien—fianc—*spouse*. Five days into their honeymoon, and it still didn't seem real.

"Thanks." He picked up the embroidery hoop and ran a finger over it looking for damage. "I'm just . . . Never mind."

"What?" She reversed course, slowly edging back into cat position, or as much of it as she could manage with the rods in her spine. "I know that form of 'never mind.'"

"All right . . ." He took his time tying off a knot and snipped it with the pair of scissors she'd given him as a wedding present. The badgers worked into the handles seemed to chase each other as the light played across the hand-forged metal. He set them down and lowered the hoop. "I'm not complaining, mind you, it's only that between the transfer to Low Lunar Orbit, and then to the ship, and then . . . Point is, I thought, maybe, being on a honeymoon, that *maybe* we could get some alone time in."

Tesla wrestled with the five different responses she wanted to make. On the one hand, sexy fun times with her new spouse were always appealing. On the other, she so rarely got to escape celebrity and just be a person.

When Shal had suggested a cruise to Mars for their honeymoon, she had been, at best, dubious. His reasoning was that most passengers would access only the ship's local onboard network, since comms back to terrestrial or Martian databases were hellishly expensive. That meant he could pay the cruise line to reroute ID requests to a fake identity. Her beloved had been right. No one had recognized her yet as the heir to the Crane fortune. So staying in had its appeal, but going out was a limited-time offer. When they got to Mars, these tricks wouldn't work.

But this was also Shal asking. She bent back to cow position. "Sure. If you want to. We can stay in."

He sighed, with an edge of tension. "It's all right. We'll go."

Tesla stopped stretching and looked at him. "I just agreed to stay in."

"Yes. And that was your 'I'm humoring you to do a thing I don't want to do' voice." He ruffled Gimlet's fur, not looking at Tesla.

Tesla lifted her head. "First of all, I don't mind staying in. Honest. It's just the . . . the novelty of being able to go someplace without bodyguards and planning and . . . But it's not like staying in with my shiny new spouse is a hardship."

"Hardship? I should hope I'm a hardship." He grinned and waggled his brows suggestively.

She snorted and went back to stretching. "Nerd."

"Accurate." He pulled a skein of embroidery floss out of his craft bag. "Also, when you put it like that, I can get behind the novelty of going on a date with *my* shiny new spouse without anyone hovering. So let's go out on the town."

"And then come back for sexy fun times." She pushed back to her knees and grabbed the arm of a chair to brace with as she rose to her feet.

He got the goofy sideways grin that sometimes crossed his face and always made her immediately want to take his pants off. "Ready for karaoke, Gimlet?"

"Oh. I don't want to take her."

"Really?" Shal raised his eyebrows. "And I don't ask just because we get better seats when she's with us. Your assistant usually scouts new places for triggers . . ."

"It's karaoke." When she got Gimlet, her therapist told her that her independence would increase because the dog was a tool—medical equipment wrapped in an adorable fuzzy package. But how was Tesla supposed to know if she was getting better if she didn't take a chance occasionally? She crossed the room to Shal and gently pushed the hoop out of the way. Putting one knee on the couch by his thigh, she carefully lowered herself to straddle him. The twinge along the right side of her spine was acceptable. She smiled and leaned down to kiss him. "No one's recognized me yet."

Shal's lips were warm and soft as he answered her. One hand ran down her back, providing stability without being obvious about it. She traced the line of his collarbone, feeling his heartbeat through her palm. Shal's voice had roughened. "Please tell me you picked a short song."

"Mm . . ." She nibbled his earlobe to keep him from fretting about the potential for flashback triggers. It was karaoke. On an interplanetary cruise ship, for crying out loud. It wasn't like they would have pyro there. Breathing into his ear, she said, "Maybe you want to do a duet . . . ?"

"A duet, you say—"

Gimlet suddenly burst into a rolling series of DELIVERY IS GOING TO KILL US ALL barks a moment before a knock on the door finished breaking the mood. Her trainer would not be happy that Gimlet barked like this, but Tesla very, very much appreciated the deterrent that a yappy little dog could be at the door. Better than any intruder alarm. Shal sighed and helped Tesla stand up.

He gave her one more lingering kiss before looking at the door, where the Westie was protecting them from Evil Incarnate. "I'll get it."

Tesla had let him cross the room to the door before remembering that, with Shal's bots, she could have answered it and not had to worry about paparazzi. The deep plum wig and eyebrow reshaping she sported were enough to throw the human eye off.

"Gimlet, come!" Tesla headed into the bedroom to distract the little dog.

Gimlet scurried into the room after her, still huffing with indignation that someone had knocked on the door. In the other room, Shal's voice rose and fell in an indistinct conversation with whoever the villain was. Tesla smiled at her dog. "Door knockers. How dare."

The Westie snorted in agreement.

"You showed them. We are so safe now." Tesla sent Shal a ping to his Heads-Up Display. *::Who is it?::*

A moment later her own HUD flashed a message in her lower-left field of vision. *::Room-service drone. Wrong room.::*

Tesla rummaged through the jewelry she'd dropped on the bedroom vanity and picked out a diamond anklet. It was rather old-fashioned and not worth much, but she liked the way it sparkled.

Sitting on the bed, she tried to cross her leg over her knee so she could reach her ankle. Even pulling on her foot, she couldn't quite get the heel to make contact. A band at the top of her pelvis tightened as she tried.

"I couldn't get it to leave without accepting the delivery or trashing the order." Shal walked into the room carrying a tray covered with a silver dome. "I didn't want it to go to waste. Steak à la Lune."

"Aha! I see your facade of virtue is beginning to crumble." She wrinkled her nose, trying to get the anklet in place.

"First of all, lunar steaks are arguably vegetarian, since they're entirely vat-grown. Second, Gimlet likes steak."

Her dog sat under the tray, looking at it as if she had met her truest love. Tesla laughed. "Gimlet doesn't get people food."

"Fair. But my third point . . ." He whipped the lid off with a flourish. "It comes with *frites à la truffe*."

The scent of fried starch and salt and the earthy joy of truffles wafted from a mound of fries.

"Compelling argument."

Grinning, he set the tray on the side table and grabbed a fry.

Slowly, he placed the fry in his mouth, closing his full lips around the crisp brown morsel. He winked, and his gaze traveled down the length of her leg to the anklet. He did not offer to help, and she loved him all over again for letting her fight her own battles. "So, what song did you pick out?"

"Don't you want to be surprised?" She winked at him. "Or use your superior detecting skills to guess?"

"Retired." He waved a fry at her. "But given what you sing in the shower, I'm betting it'll be either a Mad Guinevere or something by HLX-1."

"Mm . . ." Neither were bad guesses. She grimaced trying to catch hold of the bottom of the anklet and finally gave up. She could use the DBPS or she could accept help from her helpmate. Sighing, she held out the anklet. "Would you mind?"

"It would be my pleasure." Shal knelt on one knee and patted the other.

Tesla rested her foot on his knee as he took the anklet from her. It took him seconds to fasten the gold-and-diamond band. Still kneeling, he ran his hands up her calf, making a circle at the back of her knee. Wetting his lips, Shal looked up at her. "I'm going to make one more pitch for taking Gimlet and then I'll drop it."

"I know what you're going to say." She rested her hands on the bed and pressed down. "Okay, yes, you're right. There's a risk that there will be pyro or some other trigger and I might have a flashback. But if we take Gimlet, people are going to watch us. I . . . I just want one evening where no one stares at me."

Shal smiled at her and bent forward to kiss her knee. "All right then."

"That's it? No fight?" Tesla pouted at him. "And here I was looking forward to makeup sex."

He laughed and beat his chest. "Spouse! You must do as I say, for now we are married and you have no independent mind of your own! Grr!"

Gimlet barked at him.

Laughing, Tesla lowered her foot and leaned forward to kiss Shal on the forehead. "See? We can't take her. She'd eat you alive."

———

There was something magical about being anonymous. Listening to enthusiastic karaoke, Tesla sat nestled in a booth at the back of the R-Bar and scanned for their server. Spotting the distinctive long blue locs, Tesla raised her hand in the universal "I'm ready to order" signal and watched their server continue walking past without looking at her. Again. Anonymity would be marvelous, aside from the fact that she wanted a drink.

On her heads-up display, a message from her spouse pinged for attention: ::*You're going to laugh, but I forgot that your hair was purple.*::

She subvocalized a reply to send via the HUD. ::*Did you lose our booth?*::

Shal had given up on the server before she had and taken another approach. ::*Absolutely not. I'm at the bar—where apparently we are already considered regulars*::

::*And it's just day two of the cruise.*:: She almost opened the calendar in her HUD, but she was on vacation. The urge to check in with the office still itched under her skin, so she pulled Shal's embroidery hoop over and consulted the pattern in her HUD. ::*Well done, us.*::

::*The bartender sends her compliments on your hair*::

::*Which you had forgotten*::

::*And I want you to appreciate the deep and endearing vulnerability that I'm displaying by admitting my shocking mental lapse.*::

Sitting alone in her booth, Tesla laughed, ignored by those around her. Out of habit, she'd picked a table in one of the round booths at the rear of the lounge as a way to have her back to a wall and a buffer between her and the world. She kept looking for Gimlet under the table, skin tightening for a moment every time the little dog wasn't there, before she remembered that she'd done this on purpose. Thanks to Shal's bots, she didn't need to hide behind sunglasses or a courtesy mask; she would have been able to sit anywhere here. All of the cameras and attention were turned to the stage, where a crooner was belting out their karaoke selection with more enthusiasm than talent.

There was still an infectious joy in watching the curvy older passenger, with chartreuse pants around generous hips in the style from their teens, sing a song Tesla had never heard before. Everyone watched the stage. No one was taking a surreptitious snap of her laughter to sell to a gossip column.

Shal sent, *::I heard that::*

::I'm across the bar!::

::There is never a day when I won't recognize the sound of your voice in a crowd. Although . . . I AM used to trying to spot you behind a cluster of admirers—Oh. Got the drinks. En route to you.::

She slid to the edge of the booth to get a better view of the stage. No one "randomly" dropped by the booth wanting her to invest in their start-up or talk about one of her robot designs or magnify her tiny flaws. She was free to try karaoke and have no one care if she failed.

And then her internal radar lit up, needing no online tracker to orient to Shalmaneser Steward.

Or to use his pseudonym for this trip, Mishal Husband. By any name, her spouse.

Tesla crossed her legs, and the diamond anklet she wore glittered in the light as it emerged from the booth.

That sparkle caught Shal's attention as he walked back to their table with a pair of cocktails. His eyes dropped to her ankle, and then traveled appreciatively up the length of her legs, warming her through the core as his gaze continued up and met hers.

His sharp features softened as he slid into the booth next to her. "We could go back to our cabin . . ."

Tesla leaned over, ignoring the twinge in her lower back, and kissed him on the cheek. "Don't be silly. My turn is nearly here, and we've waited this long."

"I could've talked to the karaoke DJ." Shal held out her Manhattan, with a real cherry mind you, and winked at her. She nearly changed her mind about waiting for the karaoke.

"I believe you mean 'bribed.'" She lifted the Manhattan out of his hand. Detectives. They never really broke their habits. "What are you drinking?"

"A bribe *is* a conversation." Shal glanced past her and waved away the close-up magician who had been following them around the ship after Tesla had overtipped him. "Martini. Stirred. New Prussian gin. Dolin Blanc for the vermouth. Two olives."

Tesla rested her hand on his thigh, grateful beyond words for the bubble of safety he enforced around them. "Two olives? I like that you're developing expensive tastes."

"To go with my expensive spouse?" Shal laughed and leaned in to kiss her on the cheek. "Oh! I've just realized that we could shorten 'Mishal' to 'Mi' instead of 'Shal' on the cruise."

"I thought the point of a pseudonym that could shorten to Shal was to make it less likely for me to slip on the name?" That was why they'd settled on "Mishal Husband" as his name for the cruise.

"Sure." He grinned at her. "But this way you can introduce me to people as 'Mi Husband.'"

"My Husband? Really?" She laughed. "You are such an archaic ner—"

"Not what we agreed!" From the booth next to them, a sharp voice cut through a gap in the song.

A balding white passenger with a gamer's belly rounding out a sequined pullover and matching capelet stood facing the close-up magician at the end of the booth's table.

Shal cocked his head to the side, watching. Whenever he concentrated, he got sleuthing face, which had this bright intensity to it, as if he were wringing meaning out of the air.

Tesla slid her hand up his thigh. ::*Are you eavesdropping?*::

The corner of his mouth twisted in a smile. ::*Absolutely.*::

The magician shrugged. His reply vanished into the music so

that only the rhythms of speech said he was annoyed. The bald passenger jabbed a finger at the magician, who took a step back, arms going wide. A moment later, he plucked a card from the air and showed it to the passenger.

Something about it made the passenger's face burn beet red.

::What do you think they're arguing about?::

::Dunno, but none of them know each other well enough to move the conversation to pings.:: Shal set his hand on top of hers and ran a finger across the new wedding band.

::None?:: Tesla could only see two people from where she sat. *::Who else—::*

"Both of you." A third voice, in the husky alto range, interjected from deep in the booth. "We've all—"

Applause buried whatever they had all done as the crooner took a deep bow. A moment later, the karaoke host bounded onstage, all grins. "Let's give a big round of applause again to Annie Smith and that fascinating rendition of 'Who's Laughing Now.' Next up, Artesia Zuraw!"

Shal nudged her and slid to the end of the booth. "That's you."

"Oh! Right." She had not recognized her own pseudonym. Tesla slipped out, twisting to stand, and her back spasmed. Her deep brain pain suppressor compensated automatically, slamming into its built-in safeties so the red cords of pain were present but muted.

She steadied herself on the edge of the table and used the motion to look into the booth next to theirs. At the back of the booth, an elegant passenger with bleach-blond hair and a soft, curving jawline watched the other two with obvious distaste.

"Artesia Zuraw? Are you here?"

Tesla raised her hand. "Coming!"

She reached for Gimlet's leash—but she hadn't brought her dog. This was fine. She could do this. Tesla hurried up to the stage, regretting the decision to leave her cane behind as her back tightened with each step. Dammit. She knew better than to twist when she was standing. She had to clutch the rail to manage the stairs.

The KJ met her with a blinding smile and a microphone. "Hello, my happy one! We are so delighted to have you on our stage! And what are you singing for us, Mx. Zuraw?"

She took the offered microphone, nerves overriding any pain. "Tess. Call me Tess, she/her . . ." She wasn't used to feeling nervous. "I'm singing 'Somewhere to Love' by the Isolationists."

"All right, everybody! Give it up for her and make her feel the love in this room!" The KJ bounced offstage as the first syncopated beats of the jaunty swingpunk tune started.

Tesla watched the lyrics pop up on her HUD as the glowing ball slid closer to the first line. Everyone was watching her and cheering with the same enthusiasm they'd shown her predecessor on the stage.

"Ooh-ooh, ooh-woh
I know this place around here—"

A tray of glasses shattered at the back of the room. At the booth next to theirs, the blond who'd been sitting in its depths was on their feet. Shal stood by them, with a hand out as if to prevent a fall. A swath of red stained their white dinner jacket.

For a moment, Tesla thought that they'd been stabbed, but their gaze was fixed on the server with long blue locs. Shattered glassware covered the floor around the pair. The stain was just red wine or an aperitif. As she watched, the garment self-cleaned, shedding the red liquid so the fabric bleached back to brilliant white. Tugging the jacket into place, the blonde stalked out of the R-Bar.

Everyone watched them go. Which was good, because Tesla had totally lost her place in the song. Being anonymous was very, very nice.

Boulevardier

1.5 oz bourbon
1 oz sweet vermouth
1 oz Campari
Orange peel
Cherry

Stir ingredients over ice for 40 seconds, drain. Garnish with twist of orange peel and a cherry.

The doors to the exclusive Yacht Club portion of the ship hissed open on the concierge lounge. Shal waggled his finger at her, his craft bag bouncing with the motion. "I object to being called biased. You're wounding my professional pride."

"First of all, you're retired. Second, being a detective has nothing to do with karaoke. Third, you're biased by definition. You're married to me."

"Pish! Tosh! Tut-tut!" He made outrageous hemming and hawing noises. "Your Honor, I would note that you are the only person who got an encore."

She laughed in his face. "That was not an encore. I was interrupted and they let me start again."

Behind the concierge desk, Auberi leaped to their feet, tailcoat flapping behind them, with an alertness that gave no indicator of it being two a.m. ship's time. Their aubergine surfer's forelock arced over their left brow like a wave. "Mx. Zuraw! Mx. Husband! Oh, pardon for this." They gestured behind themself to the concierge office and the cadence of their Lunar French accent intensified with distress. "I have here your petite dog."

Tesla went to instant alert. "Is she okay?"

"*Oui!* Yes! Oh, yes, she is well, but she has in some sort of way escaped of your stateroom. I have found her here in the lobby."

Shal squeezed Tesla's arm. "I'll go clear the room." He hesitated and handed her the craft bag. "Would you mind?"

"It's not a . . . No problem." She took the bag, because she couldn't honestly say that the opened door wasn't a problem. She'd had stalkers get into her hotel rooms before. Even traveling incognito, even traveling in the most expensive, most exclusive part of the ship, someone could still get in if they bribed the right person. "Thank you!"

She flashed a smile at her spouse's back as he walked down the ridiculous "Golden Promenade" to the hall where their stateroom was. Encased in an amber resin floor, yellow LEDs sparkled on embedded crystals that looked like discards from a New Vegas chandelier. It was the sort of thing one did to impress new money.

Sighing, Tesla crossed the lobby to Auberi's desk. "I hope Gimlet wasn't a bother."

"Not at all! I used the matter printer to make a leash for her safety. She is very loved." Pirouetting, they rushed to the office door and opened it. "Oh!"

A little bark was all the warning that Tesla got, and then her dog burst out of the office and around the corner, trailing a leash. The Westie's entire back end was wagging as she ran.

Gimlet jumped onto her hind feet, stretching her forelegs up onto Tesla's thighs. Everything from the wideness of her eyes to the frantic half-twists spoke of anxiety.

"Don't worry. I've got her." Crouching with a straight back, Tesla gathered her little white dog in her arms. "Oh, sweetness. Hello. Hello, Gimlet. Yes, yes . . ." The wiggles and kisses from the little dog made Tesla regret leaving her. Gimlet was trained to go *everywhere* with Tesla. Being left behind probably made her feel like she'd done something wrong. She eased Gimlet to the ground, rubbing her ears with both hands. "Hello, perfect girl. Mommy is very stupid. It's not your fault."

"This must be an error with our housekeeping staff." Auberi had reappeared at the desk in their usual spot. "I will—"

Someone screamed.

It wasn't Shal, but it came from the Golden Promenade. "Call for help." Tesla tightened her grip on Gimlet's leash. "Gimlet, heel."

With her dog at her side, Tesla ran toward the Golden Promenade, nearly stumbling to her knees as her back sent a line of white down her right leg. Gimlet got in front of her and put a paw on her calf, signaling her to stop and take a moment. She couldn't. Not until she knew Shal was safe.

"Gimlet, release." Hitting the override on her DBPS to push it past the safeties, Tesla shoved off the wall. "Gimlet, heel." The DBPS gave its standard caution about numbness and other possible side effects of overuse. She had long practice at ignoring that warning.

Overhead, the shipboard speakers said, "Delta, gamma, five-five-niner. Repeat. Delta, gamma, five-five-niner."

Beneath her feet, the Golden Promenade jogged to obscure the curve of the ship and she braced herself on the wall as she rounded the corner. The sparkle floor gave way to carpet and a subdued hall lined with weird cruise art. At the end, it turned to her left again and she entered the tree-lined hall of the Grand Royal Suites.

And halfway down the hall, Shal was lowering someone to the floor.

A red shock of blood coated the front of their white dinner jacket. Even at this distance, the difference between blood and red wine was painfully clear.

Shal looked up as Tesla knelt next to him. "Stay with them. I saw someone."

It was the blonde from the karaoke bar. A knife stuck out of their chest, buried up to its wooden hilt.

As Shal bounded to his feet, she didn't have time to ask him who he saw and her focus needed to be on the passenger. He shoved the service door open and she sent *::Be careful!::* after him, knowing he would ignore it.

"Gimlet, down. Gimlet, stay." What little she remembered from Child Guides told her that taking the knife out would make the bleeding worse. She couldn't tell the passenger that everything would be okay, so she settled for narrating everything she was doing as a way of trying to be reassuring. "Hey, so I'm going to try to stop the bleeding, okay?"

Tesla dumped the contents of Shal's craft bag on the floor. The bag had a hydrophobic self-cleaning overlay, and theoretically, she hoped it would be impermeable to blood too. She wrapped the blue linen around the wound, trying not to jostle the knife. As she did, her skin brushed the passenger's and at the intimate contact, their online systems did a handshake, offering identification, which she accepted in exchange for her fake ID. *::George Saikawa, she/her::*

Saikawa's eyes were rolling in her head. Her mouth gaped like a fish.

Tesla grimaced and leaned down to Saikawa. "Hey? George? George, look at me. Look at—good. Terrible way to meet, but I'll be right here with you until the medics come. Hey—hey, look at me. Come on . . . help is on the way."

Doors up and down the hall opened. In her peripheral vision, Tesla felt people step out into the hall and heard the gawking begin. Blood seeped through the field of flowers on the embroidery bag. It stuck to Tesla's hands and trickled between her fingers. Tesla lifted her head, scanning the wealthy fools who clotted the hall for someone helpful. Some people were staring at her, some at the person lying on the floor, and one person was making eyes at Gimlet.

"Jesus, people. Someone get a towel or something." She looked back down to the stabbing victim, whose eyes had closed. "No, no, no . . . Hey, don't you dare die. I will not allow that."

"Coming through!" A service entrance two doors down slammed open and a medical crew burst out, masked and gloved, carrying a full kit and a megamover.

Tesla looked up and shouted, "Over here!"

The one in the lead spotted Tesla—or more accurately the blood—and dropped to their knees next to her. "What happened?"

"I didn't see it—just that she'd been stabbed. That was all I had."

"Candy, prep an X-14 protocol." The doctor peeled the bag away with bright-blue gloves and discarded it in a biohazard bag, while their colleague positioned the orange medkit over the knife wound. "Friend or family?"

"Bystander. Never met."

"Good job—" They did a double take at Gimlet. "What's a dog doing here?"

"She's my service dog." Tesla wanted to rest her hand on Gimlet's back, but her hands were sticky with blood.

The doctor grunted, and it was hard to read their expression behind the mask. As the orange medkit extended a spider's worth of probes, they produced a pair of shears and sliced the tuxedo shirt open. The machine responded to some command and settled over Saikawa, lights flashing. "I need you to move back."

Tesla nodded, but neither of the medics paid any attention to her. "Gimlet, heel." She stood up, and Gimlet moved with her as if the dog were an extension of her own body. Tesla tugged the hem of her skirt down before she remembered the blood coating her hands. Well. It wasn't as though she'd kept the blood off of the skirt up to this point anyway. And naturally, this one was too expensive to have self-cleaning fibers. She'd have to have it cleaned.

Bracing on the wall, Tesla scanned the hall for Shal, knowing he wasn't there. At her feet, Gimlet put a paw on her calf and Tesla nodded in appreciation of the reminder. A panic attack right now wouldn't help anything. She inhaled for a count of four, held it, and exhaled on a four count. Keeping her breathing slow, she studied the corridor again. About a dozen people stood in the hall, not quite willing to abandon the spectacle and return to bed. Three wore courtesy masks, either due to germs, fashion, or to protect themselves from cameras. She took snaps of faces with her online system in case Shal needed to ask them questions later. A leggy blond passenger with a full beard and fantastic purple muu-muu. The curvy older crooner from the karaoke lounge. Twins with matching dark shaved heads.

She pinged Shal. *::Update?::*

::Mishal Husband is offline.::

Shit.

The ship was a Faraday cage with spotty connections half the time. He was fine. Just chasing a murderer through the belly of a spaceship. What could possibly go wrong? She shut down the HUD. If she got really worried, she would ping his subdermal again.

A rounded person with a soft blue bob that just brushed their courtesy mask sidled up to Tesla. "May I . . . may I pet your dog?"

"No." Gimlet didn't have her vest on, so it wasn't an unfair question. Tesla softened her response. "She's a service dog. Touching her will distract her from her job." Sometimes Tesla could handle it, but not right now. Right now, it would feel like having a stranger touch *her*.

Before she had to deal with the person's response the service door opened again and a solidly built black security officer stepped through. "Honored passengers. I'm Officer Maria Piper, she/her, with ship security. I'd like to ask you all to follow our team to the concierge lobby."

As she spoke, a half dozen other crew members, wearing bright-orange safety vests over server uniforms, followed her into the corridor. Officer Piper gestured to the hall, and two crew members broke off to begin knocking on the doors that were still closed.

The passenger in the muumuu said, "Someone's been stabbed!"

As if Saikawa weren't lying on the floor with medical hovering over her.

"Which is why we need this area clear." Piper turned and spotted Tesla, then the blood on her hands and clothes and then Gimlet, before focusing on Tesla again. "None of that's your blood, is it?"

Lips tight, Tesla shook her head. Because for all of the officer's polite manner, every single person in this hall was a suspect.

"Then go with everyone else." She beckoned a skinny towheaded crewmember, and there was a brief moment of hesitation as she looked up and to the left with the sort of squinting double-blink that was probably an ID request to the HUD on her subdermal system. "Take Mx. . . . Zuraw to the concierge lobby with our other guests. Auberi will meet you and give you a quiet place to get cleaned up."

Tesla gestured to her cabin door, which . . . which Saikawa was directly in front of. "This . . . this is my cabin. I can just change in there."

Piper shook her head. "I can't allow that right now. I'll have someone bring you clean clothes. For the moment, the best thing you can do to help is to follow instructions and give us space to do our job."

Tesla nodded. "My spouse said he saw someone and went after them."

With a sigh that contained a veritable treatise on "helpful" passengers, Piper pursed her lips. "Which way did he go?"

"Service door."

Piper nodded, with a frown, and her lips moved slightly as if she were subvocalizing something. She pointed down the hall. "Lobby. Please."

Tesla and Gimlet followed the crew member and the other

passengers back to the concierge lobby, where more uniformed crew members welcomed them with trays of cocktails and coffee, as if this were a reception instead of an attempted-murder investigation. Soft music played in an acoustic rendering of "Lost in Flowers" by the Kingston Blues group Bad Sazerac. The ship's staff gracefully herded the sleepy, grumbling passengers to the small café tables in the lounge portion of the lobby. Ficus trees dotted the area, backed by big, sweeping "windows" that purported to show the starfield they were crossing. Except, of course, if you could see the actual stars, the speed with which the ship rotated would just make you nauseous. Tesla did not need help feeling nauseous.

Gimlet barked, pulling Tesla's gaze away from the starfield. Best dog. Her heart was already beating too fast and a flashback would be . . . unhelpful.

A moment later, Auberi arrived and let a brief grimace cross their face. "Everything is porridge! Pardon, but the public restroom is not in order for the moment. But I am told that you may utilize the toilet of the employees."

"That's fine. Thank you." She followed Auberi behind the desk, waiting while they used their wrist fob to key the lock.

"This way, if you please." Auberi held the door, eyes scanning the lobby for anything that needed their attention. "The restroom door is to your right. I must . . ."

"Of course." Tesla slipped into the small office space behind the concierge desk. It was an austere box with lower ceilings than the lobby and was lined with storage lockers. She let go of Gimlet's lead and the bloody splotches she'd left on it vanished as it self-cleaned. "Gimlet, release."

Instead of bounding away to check out the room, Gimlet stood on her hind legs to brace herself against Tesla's knee. Her button-dark eyes studied Tesla for damage, snuffling at the blood on her skirt. Tesla couldn't reach down to reassure her dog, because she still had blood on her hands.

The door to the right opened onto a coffin-sized toilet, with a tiny washbasin built into the wall. Tesla triggered the soap dispenser and then waved her hands under the faucet to activate the water. As she scrubbed, the suds on her hands turned ruddy. Tesla felt the pressure of her palms against each other but not the slickness of the soap or the visible dampness. With the DBPS on override, she'd lost fine sensory feedback.

Outside the bathroom, Auberi said, "Mx. Zuraw? I come to bring clean clothes for you. Officer Piper requests of me to recover your skirt."

Translation: *you are covered in blood, and that is evidence.*

"Thanks. I'll be right out."

Steam rose from the water and Tesla yanked her hands out. How hot was it?

She really needed to put the safeties back on the DBPS. It was easy to do more damage when she turned the pain signals off completely. It had taken her a long time after the Accident to learn the difference between chronic pain and new-damage pain.

Grimacing in anticipation, she tapped the DBPS down a notch. On the other side of a velvet wall, a cobweb of bright-red barbed wire waited along the sides of her spine.

At least she looked less like an ax murderer. The room seemed to recede around her, darkening at the edges. Someone had nearly been murdered. Tesla put her hand on the wall to steady herself as she waited the moment out. Wall. Toilet. Mirror. Post-it with "Friendly Greeters Smile at Three Meters." Motivational poster of sleeping kittens with "Are you ready to be your best self today?"

::*What do kittens have to do with best selves?*:: she pinged Shal.

::*Mishal Husband is offline.*::

Rolling her eyes, Tesla opened the door to the tiny bathroom. Gimlet was sitting with her nose against the door and nudged it the rest of the way open. Her entire body transformed into wiggles of joy and relief. Gimlet circled, tail wagging in a semaphore of concern that she might never have seen Tesla ever again.

"Silly. I was going to come back." She knelt to supply the necessary ear skritches, and Gimlet melted her entire body against Tesla.

Auberi awaited, holding a hanger with a subdued purple number in one hand and in the other a tray bearing a glass containing a cousin of a Manhattan. "I have printed a wrap skirt for you, thinking it most comfortable. Also, a Boulevardier. Josie, of the R-Bar, said that it is your preferred drink. I hope I have not exceeded?"

"You are phenomenal." Kneeling on the floor of the tiny, slightly grubby office, Tesla focused on priorities. She lifted the cocktail and took a sip of the tart sweetness in her glass. The tight muscles of her upper back relaxed a little, and her shoulders lowered with the aromas of citrus and honeyed grain.

She had clothes. She had a cocktail. What she needed next was a plan.

"I'm having trouble connecting to my spouse . . . Mishal Husband. Could you help me find him, so I can let him know where I am?"

The mask of careful consideration slipped and froze. Auberi wiped their hands on their trousers and wet their lips. "Pardon . . . Mx. Husband has been arrested."

WHISKEY SOUR

2 oz bourbon
.75 oz lemon juice
.5 oz simple syrup
Cherry

Shake ingredients over ice for 13 seconds. Garnish with
cherry.

If there was one thing Tesla's daddy had taught her, it was always
to have your lawyer on speed dial.

Her grandma had taught her that, when Tesla's rage turned a
room incandescent red, the best thing to do was to stay very, very
still. The time her elementary school science teacher had marked
her correct answer about the most recent supernova as wrong "because it wasn't in the textbook" had impressed in Tesla's mind
how effective that stillness could be. It was also the first time she
used any version of "I want to speak to the manager" when she
asked to go to the principal's office in a voice that was, in hind-
sight, too cold and flat for a ten-year-old.

So she petted Gimlet and waited until Auberi was out of the
office, even though Tesla really, really wanted to slam things.

She did not wait until the room stopped being red to call her
lawyer, because the round-trip comms time meant she would have
about two minutes to cool down. She also did not wait to find
out if Fantine would answer the phone to start talking, because *of
course* she would.

It was Tesla *Crane* calling. Even if they weren't friends, she would
have picked up. So Tesla started talking as she changed clothes,

laying everything out and keeping her voice from rising because the point of calling her lawyer was to follow her lawyer's advice. She wasn't going to undercut whatever that advice turned out to be by shouting so loudly that everyone in the Yacht Club could hear her.

"What have you don—" Fantine had a sleep mask pushed up on her forehead and gel packs pasted under her eyes. She paused, staring at the screen for a moment as she caught up to Tesla's ranting. "Holy Saint Dymphna's dad. They arrested Shal? Why— Okay. You're answering . . ."

As she listened, Fantine got out of bed and the background faded to a discreet blur behind her, but Tesla had been in her home often enough to tell that she was heading to her walk-in closet. "All right. I'm putting on my battle armor. You'll need to transfer me off subdermal, because we're not doing this on your cornea. Borrow a handheld so the festering chowderheads can see me as I explain to them the error of their ways."

Which, if Tesla knew Fantine, meant that she was going to reach through the cosmos to rip out their entire intestinal tract and use it for macramé.

"Copy that." She tucked her bloodstained skirt in the polyamide bag Auberi had provided and stood. "I'll work on getting a handheld—since they won't let me go back to my cabin. And . . ."

Fantine kept going, talking over Tesla in the two-minute delay. "If anyone balks, cite the Titan Convention, section five, paragraph twenty-three, and if they balk I'll eat their nethers on toast. Now, go find your spouse."

Tesla tried pinging Shal and widened her search to look for his tracker anywhere on the ship.

::Mishal Husband is offline. His last known location is . . . ::

The network showed that he was in the Golden Promenade, but it was probably an artifact. Gripping Gimlet's leash, Tesla pulled the office door open and poked her head out, glancing at the ridiculous "golden" promenade with the vain hope that Shal would magically appear. The entire ghastly length of it was empty, which probably had something to do with the yellow caution tape stretched across the end. "Auberi?"

The young concierge jumped, turning so fast that their aubergine cloud-surfer's forelock flopped to the other side of their face. "Mx. Zuraw!" Their hand fluttered to their smooth chest. "You startled me."

Tesla clamped her jaw shut and took a shuddering breath. This was not Auberi's fault. "I'm sorry. Do you have a handheld I can borrow?"

"But of course!" Poor Auberi seemed positively grateful to have something active they could do. They reached into their pocket and pulled out a compact cylinder.

"Thank you." Tesla wrapped Gimlet's leash around her wrist and snapped the cylinder open to unscroll the screen of the handheld to its full-size tablet configuration. "I'm going to make a call to Earth, which I trust you can charge to my room."

The concierge's eyes widened a mere fraction. "Of course." They cleared their throat. "I am required to tell you, by ship's rules, that such a call has a per-minute rate of—"

"I know." Tesla held up her hand. Her father had designed the network that the entire solar system communicated on, and while in other circumstances she might feel guilty about the assumptions that came with privilege, these assholes had arrested her spouse. "Just bill the charge to my room."

"Of course."

Nodding to the concierge, Tesla patched her subdermal into the handheld. Armed with knowledge and a lawyer, she scanned the room looking for Officer Piper. She stood on the far side of the Yacht Club lounge, jotting notes as she listened to the leggy, bearded passenger in the fantastic purple muumuu.

Tesla paused to grab the blood-skirt bag from the tiny office and stepped back out. Having a helpful excuse to approach the security officer would make things start off smoother, and hopefully she could get what she wanted without having to do a serious escalation.

"Here we go." Tesla led Gimlet across the lobby. The Westie could be a brat when she was off-duty, but she must have known that things were serious, because she fell right into step by Tesla's side without the heel command. As she walked, Tesla drew her head up and put her shoulders back. Her stride lengthened. The wrap skirt became a fashion choice that would be emulated in Paris.

The security officer saw her coming and grimaced. She held up a hand to slow Tesla's approach, and that was fine. Tesla would be gracious enough to let the officer finish her interview with the passenger, but that was all the waiting she was going to do.

Gimlet booped Tesla's leg with her nose, reminding her to take a breath. She visualized golden sunlight filling her from the top of her head, but it kept turning sparkling like the promenade. The longer she waited, the harder it was to stay calm.

The door to the Yacht Club hissed open behind Tesla. She turned, willing it to be Shal walking in. No luck. A person with vivid teal hair stepped into the hall. They weren't particularly tall, but all their height was in their legs and the current high-waisted trouser style made them seem like they were a pair of shoulders on stilts.

Gimlet gave her "hello" bark, which always sounded as if she were saying "yoo-hoo."

The person scowled, dropping their gaze to the little dog's wagging tail, and Tesla immediately knew that she didn't like them. They huffed.

Behind her, Piper said, "Shit. He's here." A moment later she rushed past Tesla straight to the shoulders on stilts. "Mx. Kuznetsova, I'm Officer Maria Piper, she/her, with ship security. May I ask you to come with me?"

"My dear, I'm sure whatever it is can wait until tomorrow." Mx. Kuznetsova was presumably the "he" who was here, although Tesla didn't know why Piper was waiting for him. His words were overly precise, as if he were covering for being drunk. "I've just had a spectacularly good evening in the casino."

Piper blocked his attempt to go around her, holding her hands up in a placating gesture. "I'm afraid this can't wait. If you'd come with me, please."

"Why?" He frowned, looking around the room, and seemed to finally see all the things that were not right.

The passengers in bathrobes and pajamas. The yellow caution tape. His gaze landed on Tesla, and she became painfully aware of the fact that she was holding a clear bag with a bloodstained skirt. Damn fashion and its fascination with "natural wear."

Piper hesitated. "I'm about to give you some bad news, and I think you'd prefer to be somewhere quiet."

He was still staring at the bag Tesla was carrying and almost seemed to be addressing her. "Tell me what's hap—" He took in a quick breath, looking around the room again. "Oh God. Oh. Oh, no."

"Mx. Kuz—"

"No." He raised a shaking finger. His eyes were red-rimmed and it looked like he was having trouble catching his breath. "No. I do not prefer to be somewhere quiet. And don't you dare lie to me. You've got bad news and George is offline! Why?"

By the end of it, he was shouting. All the other conversations in the lobby had stopped. Auberi had come around the concierge desk and stood on their toes with a box of paper tissue in their hands.

Piper kept her voice low and gentle. "I'm so sorry. She is dead."

"Dead? Dead, how?" Kuznetsova's voice was shaking.

Down the Golden Promenade, two white crew members headed their way. One was a wall of muscle and neck and the other, a little bit in the lead, was maybe in their mid-seventies with the tight leanness of a long-distance runner. They slipped under the caution tape, holding it up for the wall of muscle to clamber under.

"Security Chief Wisor is here. Please, let us take you someplace quiet where we can answer all of your questions."

Kuznetsova got around Piper and stalked toward Tesla. "What isn't she telling me?"

Behind them, Piper shook her head, drawing a hand across her throat as she focused on Tesla. If this were Shal's investigation, he'd want her to be quiet, too, to keep from tainting a witness. Too bad for them that they'd arrested her spouse. "George was stabbed—I don't know by whom, but my spouse and I were the first on the scene."

Piper's face went still with the kind of suppressed rage that nearly matched Tesla's grandma's. Tesla straightened her shoulders and pursed her lips slightly as a shield.

The lean officer walked up to Kuznetsova, completely ignoring Tesla. "Mx. Kuznetsova. I'm Security Chief Wisor, he/him. I'm so sorry for your loss."

"Fuck you! How the fuck does someone get murdered on a fucking cruise ship?"

Chief Wisor took the shouting and nodded slowly. "That's a question we all have. We've arrested the man who did it—"

Tesla took a step forward. "You did not—"

He whipped around, and if there hadn't been witnesses, he looked like he might have hit her. "You be quiet."

As security chief, Wisor should know who she really was, and while she normally hated taking advantage of the privilege that came with the Crane name, she would absolutely use it now if he was going to lie to the dead passenger's friend. Tesla pointed at the screen, which showed Fantine, who was crocheting as she waited. "This is my lawyer, in Low Earth Orbit, where your parent company is, and in about two minutes, she will begin explaining to you what's going to happen this morning."

Chief Wisor looked like his teeth hurt and as if he did, in fact, know exactly who she was. He turned back to Kuznetsova. "Sir, I'm very sorry. Please know that while we cannot do anything to make things right, we'll make certain that justice is able to be served."

"Justice?" Kuznetsova started to laugh or weep and then he covered his face, sobs choking out of him.

Wisor turned to the wall of muscle. "Bob. Auberi. Show Mx. Kuznetsova to the concierge office so he can have some privacy."

Trembling, Kuznetsova tried to pull himself up, but his eyes were red and swollen. He nodded, accepting a tissue from Auberi as he followed them to the tiny office. What a dismal place to grieve.

Tesla swallowed, then turned to face Wisor. She held out the blood-skirt bag. "This is the skirt I was wearing. I presume you want to keep the chain of evidence clear, and it has not been out of my hands."

He scowled as he took it. "Next time, try not helping."

"I would say I'm sorry, but you've arrested my spouse." Tesla was being That Person, the one that Shal complained about who turned up on every job as if they owned the place and the solar system revolved around them. It was never a good look. And until she was reunited with Shal, they could just give up any hope of good behavior from her.

The air chilled between them as Wisor regarded Tesla and the screen with Fantine. "All right. What do you and your lawyer want?"

"Thank you for understanding the urgency of the situation."

Wisor snorted. Around them, the other passengers continued to sip their cocktails, chatting as if murder were part of standard cruise activities.

"My lawyer will need a clear explanation of why you arrested my spouse. And after that, you may take me to him."

"Ma'am, I'm afraid I can't do that."

"First of all, did you just ma'am me? Really? Is that level of gendered condescension how things are going to go here? And second, if my spouse is on the ship, then yes, you can take me to him." Tesla had encountered his type before. "Real men" who felt like they had to prove themselves with every second word. "You can also take his lawyer to him, or are you planning to violate interplanetary law, especially the Titan Convention, section five, paragraph twenty-three?"

In all honesty, she didn't know what that was, but since Fantine had included those magic words in her instructions for managing obstructive oafs, Tesla was damn well going to use them.

"Now, ma'—" Wisor cleared his throat. "There's no need for you to go to that sort of expense when we can just—"

"You have to know who I am." Despite Shal's efforts to protect Tesla from the public, hiding the information about her identity from the ship would have meant hiding it from border patrol, and that would have been illegal. It was better to save the illegal shit for the times when you really needed it. A honeymoon wasn't that.

"I . . . I do." His face said that he was unimpressed. "But it's still an expe—"

"So, I'll thank you to not pretend that the cost of a call to Earth is a barrier." When facing someone who insisted on ma'am-ing her—someone who was between her and her spouse—she was willing to use her wealth like a bludgeon. "The only barrier is the fact that you are blocking my calls to my spouse."

Wisor tucked his chin in, making the buzz of his hair flash silver in the lobby lights. "All right. Let's you and me go to my office. We can speak more comfortably there."

Resting her weight on her heels, Tesla gave a smile as frozen as the far side of an asteroid. "I believe I was clear. We are going to my spouse, and any conversation we have will take place there."

Wisor exchanged glances with his colleague. "No. You are either a witness or an accessory to murder. I will not escort you to your husband. Now, you can either go to my office voluntarily or I can put you in cuffs."

"I see." Tesla had to bite down on her impulse to go nova on him.

Gimlet huffed, not even a full bark, just a doggy muttered warning to leave her person alone. The man flinched, as if seven kilos of white fluff were a bigger threat than Tesla.

"Gimlet! Be sweet."

She'd met people like the chief security officer before, and the only thing he was going to respond to was a bully who was bigger than he was. Fine. She'd tried clear and direct. If power was the game he wanted to play, she'd play it. Tesla held her hands out to be cuffed. "I'm sure all these fine people would love to watch you cuff me. And it will make such lovely footage for my lawyer to show to your boss."

"Have it your way. I'll ask my questions here." Wisor crossed his arms and glared at her. "What is your relationship to George Saikawa?"

Rude, to omit the person's pronouns, since it was unimaginable that the security chief wouldn't have access to that information. Based on the chief's age, he'd probably grown up before that was standard etiquette.

Tesla wanted to ask if George had family on board. Instead, she tilted her head and waited.

Wisor tucked his chin in again, in a way that he clearly thought was intimidating. "Ma'am?"

"Oh! You thought I would answer now?" She shook her finger at him. "So naughty, Mx. Wisor. Trying to get me to answer without my lawyer's advice."

"Your lawyer is right there, ma'am."

"Ma'am again . . ." She sighed. "My attorney is in Low Earth Orbit, so what we're going to do is this. You are going to tell me all of your questions, and when she hears them, she will advise me. I assume you have other questions?"

"I could cite you for obstruction."

"That would make sense if I were refusi—"

On her borrowed handheld, Fantine drew in a sharp breath. "Oh, for the love of Saint Ivo. I'm a good two minutes behind, but I'm guessing by this point, based on the doucherocket you have for a brain, that you've attempted to put my client in cuffs for no material reason. This is not yet addressing the fact that you arrested my other client without taking the time it would take for a dog to fart to review security footage or interview witnesses. If you think for one second that I'm going to let this incompetent, illegal, and grossly negligent behavior stand, you'll need to install a shunt in your nethers to see where I put your head."

Wisor's mouth hung open a moment.

Tesla smiled at him. "Go ahead and ask your questions. She'll answer them when they get to her."

Fantine continued her rant: "You've said that my client is a witness to a murder, which means that you should also be aware that my other client had blood on his hands because he was first on the scene. I've put in a request for the security footage from your—"

"There is no security footage." Wisor's space-pale cheeks went splotchy red.

"Parent company. While I'm waiting for that—"

"Someone used a spoofer. So there's a question for your client. Why did she and her husband have a device of the same make and model in their cabin?"

Tesla kept her mouth clamped shut around the answer to that. It was their honeymoon. Shal had installed a device that would show surveillance cameras a looped recording to protect her. Being the heir to the Crane fortune meant that there were tabloids that would pay good money for footage of her having sex. Would and had.

"Footage, you are going to allow me to see my other client—"

"Why did the knife used have his fingerprints on it?"

"So that I can determine that he has been treated in a manner consistent with—"

"And why did a witness identify your husband as the murderer?"

Amal's Hospitality

Half yellow bell pepper, deseeded and muddled

6 oz tonic water

1 oz lime juice

Dash cardamom bitters

Fresh ground pepper

Muddle bell pepper in bottom of rocks glass. Add single large cube of ice, tonic water, lime juice, and bitters. Stir till cold. Grind black pepper for light garnish.

The brig where they held Shal was a tiny closet of a room, without any furniture except for a metal bunk and the toilet. Seeing her spouse in a prison cell made Tesla's rage boil up all over again. Her grip on Gimlet's leash tightened. She kept as tight of a leash on her own fury, because she wasn't going to undo all of Fantine's efforts to get her in to see Shal by turning around and yelling at the security chief.

The door clicked shut behind her with a second, obvious, buzz of an electronic lock engaging. She snorted, trying to blow some of the anger out.

Shal had been lying on the bunk and rolled onto his elbow. His right eye was purpled and swollen, but he smiled. "Hello, gorgeous."

"Is that for me or Gimlet?" Tesla let go of the leash. The Westie looked up at her for permission. "Release."

With a bound she was on the cot, wiggling her joy all over Shal.

Laughing, he lay back and let Gimlet wash his face with sloppy enthusiasm. "She's gorgeous. You're my heart."

She was not going to cry. "I brought Fantine."

Shal's eyes widened. "You called her? Good lord. The rate per minute is—"

"Worth it."

"No, no—doll, it's not—"

"We have been married all of five days, and we are not going to fight about money." She shook her finger at him. Her spouse hadn't quite adjusted to being wealthy. "Please grant that I have a better grasp of my financial empire than you do, and shut up and thank Fantine."

Shal opened his mouth and then sighed and nodded. "Appreciate the help, Mx. Brandt. I look forward to hearing what you have to say."

Given the rate that they were moving away from Earth, Tesla now had three minutes to have Shal to herself before Fantine would start talking. He still wore his dinner trousers, but with an oversized souvenir T-shirt of the Interplanetary Ship *Lindgren*. Shal sat up and swung his legs over the edge of the metal bunk, wincing. He put one hand on his ribs for a moment and stared at the floor with his jaw tight.

Gimlet whined and licked his hand. Still studying the floor, Shal fondled the dog's ears before looking up at Tesla with a forced smile. God, did she know that expression.

"What did they do to you?" She crossed the cramped room and nudged Gimlet aside so she could sit next to him. If it were possible to share her deep brain pain suppressor, she would.

With one shoulder, he shrugged. "Well, I was running through a crew corridor with blood on my hands, so they were . . . enthusiastic about stopping me." He patted her knee. "Don't worry, doll. I've survived worse."

"That is not the reassuring statement you think it is."

He laughed and winced again. "Sorry to put you through this."

"This is *not* your fault." Tesla propped the borrowed handheld against the wall so Fantine would have a view of the room, then leaned carefully against her spouse to wait for their lawyer to catch up. She dialed the DBPS further down, accepting the clenching of her back so she could feel the warmth of her spouse as she nestled her cheek against his shoulder.

They had his subdermal deactivated—not just locking him out of the ship network but fully deactivated, so she couldn't even create a local network for a subvocal conversation. But by God, she was going to speak privately with her spouse and she didn't care how it looked to an outside observer.

She tilted her head and kissed the salty musk of his neck. This close, she could let her voice drop to nearly inaudible. "Now, what can I do?"

Shal's arm went around her waist. He pulled her close, undoing all her caution. "Well . . . that depends on how long you're here."

"A half hour." She played with the button on his trousers. "Fantine will start talking soon."

"Mm . . ." Shal nuzzled her, sending pleasant bright sparks along all of her limbs. "And I suppose the two of you have a plan?"

"I hope—oh." She inhaled as his hand drifted up her leg, away from her knee, into the recesses beneath her skirt, and she was very, very glad that she'd dialed the DBPS down. "Oh my."

In between kisses across her cheek, Shal's whisper tickled the curves of her ear. "They have surveillance in the room."

"Yes . . ." Tesla sighed, hoping that it was clear she understood that everything they said would be reviewed. Fantine had said as much. She curled the fingers of her other hand into the collar of his shirt and pulled him closer. "They have a witness who thinks they saw you do it."

"They told me. Plus, looks like someone lifted that steak knife from our room." He nipped the tender skin at the back of her jaw. "Not worried though. Fantine'll get me out." A line of kisses followed the curve of Tesla's neck down and then back up again to her ear. "But whoever did it . . ."

Heat running through to her toes, Tesla turned her head and

breathed into his ear. "They're still out there." She ran her tongue along the line of his jaw and was rewarded when his hand tightened on her hip.

Shal pulled back a little and met her gaze, smiling around his black eye. "I love how well you know me." Then he dipped his head to pay attention to the skin at the edge of her collar. "Do you know who—"

A fuzzy, wet nose jammed into the space between them. Shal grunted and released his grip on Tesla.

"Gimlet!" Tesla pulled the dog away, masking a wince as she did. When she turned back, Shal's face had grayed beneath his usual olive tan. "Are you—"

"Fine. Ish." He nodded. "Honestly, it's no worse than in my boxing days."

"In college. When you were two decades younger." She rested a hand on his back. "Have they had a doctor in to look—"

"Shalmaneser Steward!" The handheld crackled with Fantine's growl. "Did you actually question your spouse's judgment about calling me?"

"Um—"

"I'm going to assume you're apologizing to her right now and move on. I'll give you a list of what I need. When I finish, you start answering the list. First, since we're evidently going to have to do the job of the blazing pile of poo that they have for a security officer, I need any additional eyewitnesses who might have seen the attack. Second, if you do know the victim, I need to know that because I do not want to be surprised later and—" She did a double take, staring at the video. "What the— They beat you? Oh, for the love of Saint Joan on a stake, I am going to roast their privates into char."

"We love you, Fantine." Tesla smiled and patted Shal's knee even though her lawyer wouldn't see her gratitude for another three minutes.

"Tell me what happened, and yes, I know the frog-brained

pants wetters have surveillance on the room, but they can't use a single fart out of it while attorney-client privilege is in place. So start talking and—Jehosephat's swim trunks. I do *not* need to see the two of you making out, newlyweds or not, so knock that off and tell me what's happened."

"Your own fault for introducing us!"

Shal laughed and winced, rubbing his side. "To be fair, she didn't plan for us to get married."

"Objection! You will never convince me that Fantine does anything without a plan."

"Sustained, although Fantine is going to complain about mangling legal terms. So to her question before she starts yelling . . . Gimlet had gotten out of the cabin, so I was walking back to make sure that . . . you know." He glanced at Tesla, grimacing over a shared memory of her beating off an intruder with a pool cue. "Anyway, the hall does this bend, and I was about halfway down it when someone screamed. I ran around the corner in time to see the service door swinging shut and the passenger who'd been stabbed. Side note: The passenger is George Saikawa, she/her, with Kuznetsova International—"

"Wait. You know her?" Tesla's heart slid sideways in her chest. She had been so certain that neither of them had ever met the victim.

"No, no . . . I investigated her boss ten, twelve years ago on a fraud claim." Shal waved his hand in the air like that was nothing. "Saw her—Saikawa, I mean, with Kuznetsova a bunch of times. Kuznetsova was doing the classic middle-aged 'cheating on his spouse with his assistant' thing. But only saw them from a distance through a telephoto drone."

"And you didn't say something? She was next to us in the bar too."

"In the bar, it hadn't seemed important. After, I was a little more focused on catching whoever stabbed Saikawa in the hall. Soon as you came up, I stopped worrying about her." Shal squeezed her hand on top of his knee. "I knew you had her. Anyway—when I got into the service corridor, there was someone moving fast toward the stairs. Body type was on the male side of the spectrum, around 180 centimeters, 70 kilos-ish, bowl cut, straight black hair. What I could see of their skin from behind was pale. Anywhere from Lunar European to Terran Japanese, but—and here's the interesting thing—gloves. Blue nitrile gloves, one of which had blood on it."

She'd heard him talk about his work often enough when they were dating to make a fair guess about what that meant. "So this was premeditated."

"Bet money on it." Shal turned back to Fantine on the handheld. "We went up a couple of levels, toward the center of the ship, and they lost me as centrifugal gravity got weak. Knew how to move with the Coriolis effect. I overshot the door they went through. By the time I got back to it, there was no sign of them. My guess is they had a spoofer on them."

Tesla nodded. "The security chief said it was the same make and model as ours."

"Huh." Shal rubbed his eyes and winced, pulling his hand away from the swollen one. "No chance that they mentioned who it was registered to? Nah . . . didn't think so."

Their spoofer was an extremely expensive model, even by Tesla's standards, that was compact enough to fit into a pocket. Spoofers left a signature, which allowed law enforcement to identify the device in use and were supposed to be registered. It was, of course, possible to get around that. Hers was registered to her alias, Artesia Zuraw, not Tesla Crane.

She glanced at Fantine. "So it was someone with money, presumably."

Shal shook his head. "We aren't trying to solve this."

"They have an eyewitness who identified you as the killer. Your fingerprints were on the knife!"

"Because I was first on the scene." Shal hesitated and grimaced.

"Although I'll grant that the steak that got misdelivered is concerning."

"See! So it was someone who had access to our cabin."

Shal shook his head again, and she wasn't sure if he was disagreeing with her or trying to stop himself from working the case. "Just give Fantine what she needs to get me out and back to our honeymoon. So, back to the spoofer-carrying stabber . . . when we got separated, security was able to see me, bloody hands and all."

"And the beating?"

Shal grimaced and looked away from Tesla. "It wasn't a beating."

"You have a broken rib!"

"Bruised."

Gimlet barked and put her paw on his knee.

"See! Even our dog knows you're lying. Tell Fantine what happened, or she will eat you." Tesla leaned over and kissed him on the cheek. "And I like you. I don't want you to be eaten."

He laughed, winced, and his hand briefly went to his ribs. "Look . . ." Shal gave Gimlet his attention, rubbing her ears until she lay her head on his knee. "Look . . . the spoofer wasn't active then, so the ship will have footage of that. Fantine can see it, and you don't have to hear about it."

"I'm not a delicate wilting flower." Although, truly what she wanted was to wilt into a therapeutic bath with a glass of single malt, preferably Glenfarclas 17. Also preferably with Shal. "You can tell me and I promise not to faint."

He barked a laugh and grimaced again. "I'm not worried about that. I'm worried about unleashing your wrath."

"My wrath." She kissed his cheek. "Has already been unleashed."

═══════

Exactly half an hour after Tesla entered the room, Security Chief Wisor opened the door to Shal's cell. "Times u—"

Gimlet barked, cutting him off.

In the silence, Fantine continued to talk. "—president of the parent company on the line as soon as we finish here. If that weasel bait hasn't moved you back into your cabin by then, which he won't without prodding, I'll get that sorted."

"Chief Wisor! We were just talking about you." Tesla rubbed the little dog's head and leaned over to kiss Shal on the cheek. "Are you finished in our cabin?"

He shook his head. "It will need to stay sealed until we arrive at Mars as part of the murder investigati—"

On the screen, Fantine looked at the Swiss watch she wore so she could ostentatiously remind people when they were wasting her time. "If I read him right, that gut-griping security chief isn't going to let you have a minute more than the half hour we agreed on, so ought to be back in the room by now. So I can't call him the feces-witted failure that I would like to. If I'm wrong, and he's not in the room, I'll repeat myself when I confirm that he's back and I won't charge you for the extra minutes."

Tesla slid off the bed, holding the handheld so the security chief was centered in the camera. Gimlet hopped down and casually sat in front of her to create a barrier, which was a clear sign her service dog had identified Wisor as a stress point. She wasn't wrong.

He looked down at Gimlet, and Tesla used the time to take a calming breath, before he looked up to frown at her handheld. "You've had that on for the entire time? Do you even know how m—"

"Yes. I know how much it costs." Her company owned the satellites the signal was traveling on. Tesla put a finger to her lips and then pointed at the screen. "Hush. Don't speak."

"Security Chief Wisor. You are holding my client without cause and preventing both he and my client, Artesia Zuraw, from enjoying the honeymoon that they have paid dearly for. I am not concerned about proving his innocence. However, I am concerned that you have interfered with his rights. The Titan Convention states that while a vessel en route has sovereignty to maintain order aboard the ship, that authority may not extend to conducting trials or punitive measures. Ergo, you can put someone in the brig if they represent a danger to themselves or others, but by imprisoning my client in this oubliette without cause, you are in violation of the Titan Convention."

"I can't keep order—"

Fantine talked over him, because she couldn't hear him yet. "There are a few options available to you that will not result in a lawsuit that will bury you in a pile of rotting gizzards. One: You can free my client immediately and apologize for the harm done. Two: You can confine him in his original cabin, allowing Mx. Zuraw free access to her spouse, and provide them with a full refund plus compensation for trauma endured. Three: You can confine him to a cabin of equal or greater value, allowing Mx. Zuraw free access to her spouse, and provide them with a full refund plus compensation for the greater trauma endured. Should you choose option one, my clients are willing to forgo their rights to additional compensation." She leaned closer to the camera and grinned like the shark she was. "You don't want me to go any higher than three with your options, because then we get into compensation that your company is not going to be happy about. I await your answer."

And then Fantine placed a ball of vivid carmine yarn on her desk and began crocheting, looking at the camera.

Chief Wisor's face had turned a mottled red. "You can't just make demands like that. A woman was murdered and I have a witness that names this man as the murderer."

From the bed, Shal raised a hand. "Just to clarify . . . someone specifically said 'Mi Husband is the murderer'?"

With a sigh, the chief glared from Shal to the handheld. "Not that specific sentence—which your lawyer would love to pin down—but yes, they picked Mi Husband out of a virtual lineup."

"Your husband?" Shal's eyes widened in mock startlement. "Doesn't that create a conflict of interest?"

"What?"

Keeping her smile under control took a great deal of effort for Tesla. "You said they picked your husband out of a virtual lineup."

"No, I said they picked Mi Husband—all right. Funny." The chief's face hardened. "In addition to the witness, the murder weapon had his fingerprints on it and my crew found him with the victim's blood on his hands. He does not get to kill someone and lounge around with a butler and all the vodka he can drink."

"I resent that." Shal straightened where he sat on the bed. "Gin, please. Bourbon or single malt. But vodka? I think not."

Tesla smiled at Wisor. "I think you should do what Fantine says and check with Legal about this. She's very good at her job. Or you could just restore Shal's subdermal systems and escort us back to our cabin. It's our honeymoon, and I promise I'll keep him in the bedroom."

"Just the bedroom?" Shal sighed and shook his head. "But we have a sunken tub."

"Mm. And I do worry about your ribs." She turned back to Wisor and let her voice harden to match the titanium screws in her spine. "I will note that not only are you holding him here, not only did your staff beat him, but you have not offered him medical attention."

"He declined. Furthermore, no one beat hi—"

On the screen, Fantine lowered her crochet hook and glanced at her wristwatch. "At this point, I'm going to guess that you've blustered about evidence or maybe about eyewitnesses or some other irrelevant point that ignores the Titan Convention. Your ship has a lawyer. I suggest you check with them before you keep digging yourself in deeper—oh." She glanced at the screen. "There you are. Good. I don't have to repeat myself. You 'can't keep order . . .' That's your concern? Confining him to his cabin while we work this out with your legal representatives will 'keep order.'"

He jabbed a finger at the screen. "There is no way in hell that—" His eyes shifted down and to the left as if he were reading a message on his subdermal. "Shit. Neither of you move."

As he stomped out of the room and slammed the door, Tesla's brows went up. "What was that about?"

On the screen, Fantine continued, unaware that the object of her conversation had left the room. "The next objection that you're likely to make, because your brain is about as efficient as a polyamide bag filled with raw egg yolks, is that my client would be in the lap of luxury while suspected of a hideous crime. Yes. That is true. Because they paid for that cabin. However, you will be preventing him from taking part in any of the other activities they also paid for while restricting his liberty for a crime that he—" She glanced to the side at a screen and smiled. "Ah. Good. The nice thing about being old as Methuselah is that you have time to get to know a lot of people. An old golf buddy works for Legal and is aboard and is *not* a vending machine of toad farts. Expect a call shortly."

And *that* was why you always had your lawyer on speed dial.

MANHATTAN

2 oz bourbon

1 oz sweet vermouth

2 dashes bitters

1 cherry

Stir ingredients over ice for 40 seconds. Garnish with cherry.

The cabin that Wisor had arranged for them was a single room overlooking the promenade level with its effort to re-create a quaint English town. The neon sign of the ice-cream shop lit the room's blue velvet curtains with a lurid pink. Tesla crossed the aggressively patterned tan-and-fuchsia carpet to the window, turning to look for another door. "I thought we were getting a suite."

"This is the junior suite." Officer Piper walked Shal into the room, leaving her colleague outside to guard the hall.

Tesla gestured at the single room. It had a bathroom and curtain that one could draw across the "living room" to make a "bedroom." It was bigger than Shal's cell and had upholstery but was still smaller than her office. On the list of problems, the size of the room was very low, and yet . . . Tesla tried to wrestle her disappointment to the back of her mind, because it really, truly didn't matter that this was supposed to be their honeymoon.

Someone had been killed.

She wanted to either cry or shout and had to fight to keep her voice calm. Taking a measured breath, she felt the muscles of her ribs unclench a tiny bit. The size of the room did not matter. It was the principle of the thing and the fact that Shal shouldn't be punished for something he hadn't done. "A suite usually has multiple rooms."

"There's a bathroom."

Shal looked around the room and pursed his lips, frowning when he saw the window. He held his cuffed wrists out to Officer Piper. "If you'd do the honors."

Gimlet sniffed the corner under the desk, stumpy tail wagging with delight at whatever ground-in dirt she found there. Screw it. Fantine had argued for them to have some approximation of their honeymoon while she worked to explain to the cruise line that Shal was obviously innocent.

All Tesla had to do was to show her the cabin and she would fix it. She raised the handheld to address Fantine. "If you could be so kind as to . . ."

The image on the screen was frozen, one eye half-shut, with her lawyer's crochet hook poised between immaculate nails. Of all the times to lose the connection. Tesla gritted her teeth. Fine. She could handle this herself until the connection was reestablished.

Tesla drew herself up and turned to Officer Piper. "Our agreement was for a cabin of equal value to our own."

Piper shrugged her shoulders, uncuffing Shal. "I got nothing to do with that. You have a problem with the accommodations, you talk to customer service or you have your lawyer do it."

"I will." As soon as she could connect. She tapped the Refresh button, frowning, and had to step to the side to let Officer Piper pass. The room was so small that her shins bumped into the loveseat. Tesla stumbled. Not much.

But enough for Shal to spin and reach for her.

He gasped, blood draining out of his face, leaving his black eye even more livid. Hunching over his ribs, he froze. With his eyes closed, he took tight, shallow breaths.

Tesla tossed the handheld on the bed, dialing her DBPS up so her back wouldn't distract her. "Are you—" He was obviously not okay. She slid a hand under his elbow, careful to stay away from his ribs. Gimlet abandoned her interest in sniffing corners and came to sit at Tesla's feet. Her black eyes were bright with worry.

Shal clutched Tesla's arm hard enough that his nails turned white. His breath shuddered and he turned to brace his head against her shoulder. His voice was no more than a hot breath against her skin. "Surveillance. Window. Careful."

Tesla smoothed his hair and kissed his forehead, using the motion to look at the window. Across the promenade, a maintenance robot scaled the wall like a gleaming spider, its eight legs compensating for the shifting centrifugal forces as it moved up the side of the ship. But it wasn't cleaning. Not really. She'd spent enough time being chased by photographers to recognize the signs of a lens pointed her way.

In the doorway of their cabin, Piper hesitated, eyeing them. Could she tell that they'd spotted the camera opposite? Tesla drew herself up and put on every bit of hauteur she owned. "He needs a doctor."

Piper chewed her lower lip for a moment before nodding. "I'll see what I can do."

"You broke his ribs!"

"Wasn't her." Shal's voice was hoarse and strained. "Also, just bruised."

"I do not believe you." Neither did she believe for a moment that he was just acting. He might have taken advantage of it, but he was also in genuine pain.

Gimlet whined at him, tail down and ears drooping with distress. Shal laughed, breath hitching again. He waved the hand that wasn't clutching Tesla's arm as if he could wipe the moment out of the air. "Just need a sec."

"Lie down." The advantage of the tiny room was that the bed was only four steps away. Tesla tried to steer Shal toward it without hurting him. She shot another look at Officer Piper. "I understand that my spouse's condition is not your fault, but when my handheld reconnects and our lawyer sees the state he is in, it would be best if there were a doctor in the room."

"Officer, I appreciate the help." Shal straightened slowly. His skin was the color of overcooked veal. "I don't need a doctor, but our clothes wouldn't go amiss. Also a martini."

Grimacing, Tesla toggled on her HUD with an eyeblink. If nothing else, she could film his condition while she waited for the connection to reestablish. Since her spouse was too stupid to lie down after he'd been beaten. "Will you please lie down, or do I have to sic Fantine on you?"

"I will lie down if you'll lie down with me." Shal waggled his eyebrows at her, but his movements were overly careful as he lowered himself to the bed. Gimlet hopped up next to him and lay down with her head on his knee. "Surprised Fantine hasn't started yelling at me yet."

"Um . . . yeah." She rotated the handheld a little so that he could see the frozen screen without tipping off Piper.

Shal saw it, nose wrinkling for a moment in frustration. "Good thing the time lag means she hasn't seen me wince yet."

Officer Piper stopped at the exit of the room. "I'll try to get a doctor for you."

"Try?" Tesla could feel the pack of rabid dogs under her skin starting to tear through. She took a deep breath and tried to picture a glowing ball of sunlight floating in the middle of her chest. The meditation routine did approximately nothing. "Try."

"Babe."

"My spouse was injured by officers in the emplo—"

"Tess . . ." Shal looked up at her from the bed and then nodded at the security officer. "Let it go."

With a nod to Shal, Officer Piper stepped into the hall. "I'll be right outside." She shut the door.

Tesla stared at it, mouth a little open. "This is outrageous."

"Yeah . . ." Shal lowered himself, grimacing, to lie on his back on top of the bedspread. "But I declined a doctor. Try not to antagonize the people who are helping us?"

"Helping?!" Tesla pointed her finger at the door and her whole hand was shaking. "She hauled you here in handcuffs."

"Yes, but she cuffed my hands in front of my body to avoid putting strain on my ribs, which she didn't have to—"

"Ha! So they are broken."

"Bruising hurts plenty." Shal's mouth twisted sideways in a smile. "She also brought me an ice pack when I was in the brig. Don't make her an enemy."

Tesla squeezed her eyes shut and took a deep, cleansing breath, trying to shed some of the anger. Shal was right. Officer Piper was doing her job and it was not her fault that her boss was an asshole. She opened her eyes and smiled at him. "Fantine will fix this."

"Parts of it, yeah." Shal patted the bed beside him. "Come lie down."

"I'm still . . ." Tesla let her head droop forward. This was the actual problem. Someone had been murdered, and there was nothing Fantine would be able to do to find the actual murderer. Tesla was only fixating on the stateroom because it was a problem she had the tools to solve. Or would, once she could reconnect to Fantine. Scowling, she raised the handheld, tapping the Refresh button again. "For the love of . . . We have to figure out who murdered that poor person."

"Babe. Leave it alone. Come lie down with me and take a breather, okay? Still our honeymoon, even with all of this shit." Shal raised his voice. "Hey, *Lindgren*. Play jazz. Dim the lights. Close curtains. Romantic."

Prompted by the spaceship *Lindgren*'s virtual assistant, saxophone in five-four time skirled around the room. The curtains hushed closed as the lights dropped to a soft amber glow and faux candles sprang into life above the headboard.

"Sweetheart, I'm not sure I'm in the mood . . ."

"Ouch." He clutched a hand to his heart. "Only five days in, and you're tired of me already."

Despite herself, Tesla laughed. Dropping the handheld back onto the coffee table, she shook her head. "Oh, you think I'm tired of you?"

Tesla sat on the bed beside him, bracing with a hand so she could lean down for a kiss. His mouth was warm as his tongue teased the borders of hers. He slid his hand around the curve of her hip and squeezed, encouraging her to lie down the rest of the way.

"Thank God. I was beginning to think I'd lost my touch." Turning his head, Shal planted a series of kisses along her cheek. His breath was a tickling sigh against her skin. "More cameras. Right side above window. Over bathroom door. Ah . . ."

The pulse in the fine skin of his throat visibly sped up as her hand from moved from his hip downward to draw circles on the back of his knee.

Gimlet lifted her head and pressed her nose to Tesla's cheek. She ruffled the Westie's fur. "Move it, he's mine."

"Sorry, lady"—he looked ruefully at the little dog—"I'm afraid I'm spoken for."

With a snort, Gimlet trotted to the end of the bed and flopped down with her head on Shal's foot.

"I see someone is worried about you."

"Mm." Shal closed his eyes, tilting his head back on the pillow with his lips parted.

She found the closure of his trousers and discovered that he wasn't entirely pretending to be aroused. "I'm beginning to understand why you wanted me to come to bed."

"So many reasons." His fingers smoothed the hair at the base of her skull and edged her closer. "I have questions about the knife."

She nodded and slid her tongue along the length of his neck. "It was the one from the misdelivered steak, right?"

"Maybe. Same type." He nibbled her ear. "Fingerprints could have been from when I caught her in the hall."

"Still. Narrows the field. Room attendant. Concierge. Dishwasher—" She pulled back, tugging the bottom of his terrible

T-shirt up toward his head and stopped. Even in the dim light, the mottling on his right side was clearly visible. She rested a hand as lightly as she could on the worst of it and the skin was overheated. "Shal, you have to—"

"Hush." He pulled her hand up to his lips and kissed the brand-new wedding ring she wore. "C'mere."

Shaking her head, she slid closer so that he could whisper in her ear. "Be careful if you start asking questions. Everyone has a secret, and everyone lies."

"Everyone?" She drew a circle around the circumference of his nipple.

"Yes." He twisted to face her, wincing, and slid his knee up between her thighs.

"So when you say your ribs aren't broken . . . ?"

"If I asked how your back is, what would you tell me?"

She would tell him that her back was fine, which meant that today wasn't a cane day and that the assortment of screws and rods holding her back together were only a dim red glow in the recesses of her consciousness.

He stopped her lie with a kiss, and for a moment Tesla let him distract her. It was their honeymoon and Shal had a way with his hands.

The electricity he ignited warmed her, until his lips worked over to her ear. "I'm lying. Yes. But . . . with the medical suite on this class of ship, that wound shouldn't have been fatal. Was Saikawa still alive when the EMTs arrived?"

Tesla went cold, pulling back to nod.

His smile was sad as he leaned in to kiss her on the forehead and murmur against her skin. "Don't call a doctor for me."

———

Tesla lay in the semi-darkness of the cabin, but her brain kept serving up the curve of Saikawa's jaw as her mouth gaped trying to breathe. Her HUD said it was eleven in the morning, but stress made her body say that it was midnight. For all that, she could not stay asleep even after trying every technique her therapist had taught her in the seven years since the Accident.

Five things she could see: Shal asleep in bed. The sheet draped over his chest. His curls tumbled over his forehead. The swelling around his black eye. Gimlet curled in a fluffy white ball by his knee, her head resting on his shin.

She tabbed through her HUD, seeing if there were messages. *Connection unavailable.*

Lovely. She glanced toward the ceiling camera and stuck out her tongue, which was extremely mature. They'd drawn the curtains across the promenade window, but anything to block the half-dome of the room's AI camera would be obvious. Even if it was supposed to be private and encrypted, there was no way that ship security wasn't keeping tabs on them.

Sighing, Tesla reached for the borrowed handheld on the bedside table and unrolled it to see if it had a connection. In its glow, Gimlet raised her head, watching Tesla. The light would probably wake Shal. She let it roll back into a compact cylinder and levered herself out of bed. Gripping the mattress, she paused on the edge of the bed as her back realigned itself.

She stood, steadying herself with one hand against the cabin wall. Gimlet got up and stretched, pink tongue curling with a yawn. The little dog hopped off the bed to follow Tesla into the bathroom. The system sensed her presence and lit the tiny box of a room with a dim glow. The light still made her eyes sting and her hands felt sticky with the memory of George Saikawa's blood. Grimacing, Tesla ran her hands under the faucet and then washed her face.

Solve one problem at a time. Start with checking messages, then move on to the harder questions.

Like why would someone use a steak knife to kill Saikawa?

She unrolled the handheld to full size and immediately spotted the No Connection icon. "Oh, for fuck's sake . . ."

Tesla grabbed the wrap skirt that Auberi had supplied. The

printed cloth had a nearly indefinable textural difference from a true jersey knit, at once too slick and too coarse. But it was also the only clean thing she had to wear. She slipped it on, tying the belt as if it needed to support a sword.

At her feet, Gimlet cocked her head, wagging her stumpy tail uncertainly.

"Mama has to go talk to someone. Wanna go for a walk?"

Gimlet jumped to her feet, tail speeding up in answer. They had potty pads, but both she and Gimlet preferred to go to the animal relief area rather than stink up the cabin. Especially one this tiny.

Tesla rolled up the handheld and . . . the skirt had no pockets. Wonderful. The leash was hanging over the bathroom doorknob. She grabbed it and knelt to slip the harness over Gimlet's head. A spasm licked yellow and red flames up the left side of her spine. She pressed her hand against the wall, concentrating on the cool paneling beneath her fingertips. She visualized cool blue light flowing down from above and dousing the flames.

Slowly, Tesla breathed out and held the harness up again. When she was off-duty, the Westie was . . . opinionated, but when Tesla was hurting? She was the best-behaved dog and slipped into her harness as neatly as if her trainer were in the room.

Tesla led Gimlet to the door of their room and—

It was locked.

She pressed her key fob against it, and the lock flashed red. Denied. Of course she wasn't allowed out. Tesla bent her head, gritting her teeth. Slow breath. Dragging a smile up from the recesses of her soul, Tesla lifted her head and knocked lightly on the door. A pause, during which someone was probably looking at the camera to be certain that she wasn't standing there with a knife.

The door opened, spilling hallway light into the room. Officer Piper stood in the doorway, brows raised. "Yes?"

"May I come out?"

Piper nodded and stepped back.

In the room, Shal stirred on the bed. "Tess?"

"Taking Gimlet to go potty." Tesla hung on to the door for a moment and then leaned back in. She'd heard him talk about too many cases to not tell him where she was really going. "After that, I'm going to stop by the concierge desk to see if I can get our clothes."

She hurried into the hallway, pulling the door shut behind her before Shal could ask any other questions. Even under normal circumstances, he needed more sleep than she did and was notoriously bad about honoring that need. With luck, he would fall back asleep after she left.

Piper checked the door, making sure that it was locked. She had a chair next to the door and a handheld lay on the seat as if she'd been reading. Or watching them.

Tesla attempted a smile. "I don't have a network connection."

"Not my department." Piper retrieved her handheld and settled back onto her seat.

Even the hall felt cramped here. It was narrower than the ones in the Grand Royal Suites and rather than human housekeepers, a service drone trundled down the long curve. Tesla kept the smile on her face. "I understand that. Could I ask you to point me to this level's concierge?"

"You'll have to go to customer service." Piper looked down and held her hand out for Gimlet to sniff. "Well, hello! You are just too cute to be real."

"Don't touch her." Tesla saw Piper harden again. She shook her head, trying to soften it because Shal had said that they needed to not alienate the security staff. "Sorry. She's a service dog. Her vest is back in our old—"

Piper's shoulders dropped and she held up her hands. "No. That's my bad. I knew we had a service dog aboard. I just . . . she's real cute."

"That's why she's still alive." As the words left her mouth, Tesla wanted to reel them back in. "I mean— It's just that she's— Gimlet, go say hi."

"You sure?"

"Yes. It's a command and—"

Three cheery tones sounded. "Good morning, passengers! Have you made your evening plans yet? Check out the Amazing Nile Silver's Magic Show in the Starlit Theateeeeer! And a reminder that we have the Fine Art of Patrick Windlass available in the Promenaaaaaade!"

Piper ignored the shipboard announcement as if she had become so inured to Excessive Capitalization in a Jovial Tone that no she longer heard it, and leaned forward to scratch both of Gimlet's ears simultaneously. With her face relaxed into a grin, she might have been anyone confronted by the irresistible field of Gimlet's cuteness. "Are you the most neglected? Is it true? Yes, it is. I can tell it is."

"Yes. The solar system's most neglected dog." And this was part of why Gimlet needed to be in her service vest. She was too tempting otherwise. "Why customer service? Is this another part of our unlawful incarceration?"

With a snort, Officer Piper gave Gimlet one last pat and straightened in her seat. "No. There's no concierge for this cabin class. If you need help with something, you go to customer service."

"But we're—" Tesla cut her protestation off. The fact that this cabin class was not comparable to their original one was not something Officer Piper could control. She couldn't make a nonexistent concierge appear. Fine. Tesla could go ask Auberi for help. "Thank you. It's not a pleasant surprise, but the information is appreciated."

Piper grunted in acknowledgment. She glanced at the cabin door and then back at Gimlet. "I put in your request for a doctor. How's he doing?"

Nothing in her tone was threatening, but Tesla's heart went rabbity in her chest. "Oh, he's fine." Before she went to bed, Tesla would have counted Piper's request for a doctor as a triumph. "It does look like it's just bruising."

The other woman raised a single brow. "The way he was acting? That's not a bruise."

"Oh, he can be a baby about pain." Tesla swallowed, aware that her lying wasn't worth shit. "But I do appreciate it. And I'm sorry that I was so . . . rudely imperious earlier."

"I would never say that about one of our guests." The corners of her mouth hinted at a smile as Officer Piper picked up her handheld again.

Tesla chewed her lower lip, twisting the dog leash around her fingers. If a doctor came, that didn't mean it would be one of the same medics who looked after Saikawa last night. Unless, of course, they really had been involved, in which case they would absolutely want to pay a visit to Shal.

"Do you know when the doctor was coming?"

"When she gets here." The security officer shrugged. "Good luck with customer service."

━━━━━

Tesla's key fob didn't work on the door to the Yacht Club's slice of the ring. The entrance lay behind the elevator bank that was closest to the R-Bar and was lined by ficus trees in planters in yet another attempt to create the feel of being on a planet. Gimlet snuffled the planter closest to the door as Tesla fruitlessly waved her fob in front of the reader again.

There were ways to hack one of these, but that seemed like an extraordinarily bad choice, given that they thought Shal had murdered someone.

Three tones chimed as the shipboard speakers introduced the painfully cheerful entertainment director. "Good morning, passengers! Who wants to get fit, *fit*, *FIT*?! Head to the Martian pool for an afternoon of water exercises with our fitness trainer, Mpenzi

Okeke! He was on the Gold medal aqua polo team at the Calisto Aquatics Championships, but he promises to be gentle!"

On a whim, Tesla tried connecting her subdermal with the ship's system again. The indicator in her HUD gave the same error message it had been giving since they'd gotten to their new cabin. It didn't seem as though the ship's intranet would really be down for six hours.

"And now, the person we all know, love, and trust, Captain Valdísardottir with an update about our cruise! Please give her your attentiooooon!"

Tesla knew, loved, and trusted exactly one person on this cruise. And one dog.

"Good morning, passengers. We are currently cruising at 298 kilometers per second en route to our destination of Mars."

Sighing, Tesla rang the Yacht Club's bell.

"That rate will increase until we hit our peak of 785 kilometers per second at the midpoint of our trip and do what we call the flippy-poo. That's a highly technical term."

As she waited, Tesla shifted from one foot to the other, wiggling her toes in the dense pile of the welcome mat outside the door. Passengers walked past, eying her. Or Gimlet. None of them recognized Tesla.

"But if we do our jobs, you shouldn't notice it as we maneuver to begin the slowdown. That constant thrust is what allows us to offer not only a twelve-day transfer to Mars but also is what maintains lunar gravity in our central core, supplemented by centrifugal rings for maximum comfort for all guests."

Maximum comfort, ha. Maximum comfort would involve not standing on the main promenade because they had locked her out of her cabin.

The small screen lit up with Auberi's concerned face. Their surfer's forelock seemed to droop with their mood. "Ah! Mx. Zuraw, I am so much disconsolate for the problem with your room."

"Not your fault." Although Tesla noted that the Yacht Club

door stayed closed. "I was hoping I could get my clothes and Gimlet's food and vest."

The captain's voice filled the gap caused by Auberi's hesitation. "If you're curious about how we operate, make sure to sign up for a bridge tour. Captain Valdísardottir, out."

On the screen, the concierge's face clouded and their Lunar French accent thickened into despondency. "I am profoundly sorry . . . I have the most unhappy of instructions and I cannot let you to access at your cabin. I am going to after all organize a credit for your account that you may to acquire the clothes in the interim. Do you have another matter in which I could help?"

"I understand." Tesla lifted Auberi's handheld. She hadn't been able to connect it to her account since they got Shal out of the brig. "Well, I needed to return this to you."

"Thank you." After a moment's hesitation, the concierge keyed the door open. "Please, come in."

Tesla let go of Gimlet's leash. "Gimlet. Release. Go say hi." The command gave the service dog her fondest wish and she bolted inside. Standing on her hind legs, she rested her paws on the knit red trousers of the concierge and wagged her tail in happy greeting.

"Hello! Hello, my sweet!" Auberi looked up from Gimlet. "Again, please accept my apologies for the uncomfortable situation about your cabin."

"I appreciate it." Since Gimlet was out of her vest anyway, Tesla may as well let the little dog do the softening up for her. As Auberi succumbed to the Westie's charms, Tesla eased into a question about the murder. "Have you managed to get any rest? Or did they keep you working since . . ."

A fleeting expression tightened the corners of Auberi's eyes before vanishing under a deliberate and well-rehearsed neutrality. "It is no trouble."

"Losing Mx. Saikawa must be so hard on Mx. Kuznetsova."

The concierge's lips tightened for a moment as they gave Gimlet belly rubs. "Well, we all miss you very much here."

"I can't believe that they were our neighbors and I never saw either before . . . that."

"Mm . . ."

A side effect of having an inordinate amount of power was that people would almost never tell Tesla "no," so she'd had to learn how to guess when an equivocation was actually a refusal. Kuznetsova was almost as rich, and right now she would place bets that Auberi was not fond of the man but could not say so.

"And now to be traveling alone in that massive suite . . ." Out of the corner of her eye, she scanned the Terran-level private lounge of the Yacht Club, hoping to see someone who had been in the hall last night.

"Is there another way that I could help?"

So much for subtly spying. Tesla placed the handheld she'd borrowed on the counter. "Actually . . . I was hoping you could help me get my subdermal system to connect. It just won't for some reason."

"Ah! Thank you and of course! I am happy to aid you." Auberi stood and took the handheld, sliding it back into their pocket. They made a note on a piece of paper, which was one of the ways high-end establishments signaled that they were taking you seriously. "It is probable that when you are at the new cabin, it simply has disengaged the card."

"Mm-hm . . ." The private bar here wasn't yet staffed and the only people in the lounge were a pair of kids hunched over an old-fashioned checkerboard. Their faces looked absolutely giddy each time they picked up a physical piece to move it.

Auberi's fingers hesitated over their screen. "Oh. Oh, I . . ."

Tesla leaned across the counter, standing on her toes to try to get a better view of the screen. "Something?"

"It is only that . . ." Auberi tapped a few keys, and their frown deepened. "It seems your account has been locked out by security."

"I see . . ." That weasel Wisor had the temerity to lock their account? No doubt to keep them from talking to Fantine. Tesla tapped her fingers on the counter. "Would you set up a bridge tour for me?"

That was the politest euphemism for "let me speak to the manager" that she'd ever used.

CORPSE REVIVER #2

.75 oz Lillet Blanc

.75 oz lemon juice

.75 oz gin

.75 oz Cointreau

Dash absinthe

Shake ingredients over ice for 15 seconds. Serve up.

The bridge of the spaceship *Lindgren* was a bland beige room, with bland beige carpet, and bland beige consoles punctuated by brilliant blue handrails. The screens on the consoles kept snagging Tesla's attention, itching a part of her brain that she'd kept dormant since the Accident.

It didn't matter. Tesla did not need to analyze any of the inputs coming into the bridge. This wasn't her ship, and even if it had been, she hadn't done anything hands-on since the Accident. Tesla kept her feet tucked under one rail, grateful for once for the season she'd spent on *Zero-G Dancing with the Stars*. Not that the central core of the ship lacked gravity, but it was a shade under lunar gravity, and it took very little effort to accidentally propel oneself into the air. She felt reasonably comfortable keeping her hands at her sides to control her skirt, which was decidedly not designed for this environment.

Captain Valdísardottir swayed in the middle of the room, supporting Gimlet with one hand while she nuzzled the little dog. She had been speaking Icelandic to the dog for the last five minutes and Tesla was aggravated because her HUD was clearly malfunctioning since it kept insisting that the captain was calling her dog an asshole.

"Þú ert svo mikið rassgat." She was short and space pale with a skullcap of fine gray hair over a broad face that had admirable cheekbones. The clean white ship's uniform had gold bands of rank rimming her sleeves. Finally looking up from Gimlet's cuteness field, the captain nodded to Tesla. "It must be difficult for you, expecting a honeymoon and then . . . this."

"Thank you." Tesla spread her hands in an entreaty. Her skirt eddied with the motion and she slapped the fabric back down.

"Wisor . . ." The captain rotated to the security chief, whose face was an alarming shade of red. "Make sure that Mx. Zuraw has access to her clothing, medication, and of course anything her small dog needs. *Elsku litla greyið mitt.*"

"Thank you. Shall I take her back?" Gimlet loose in low gravity was not a game that Tesla wanted to play without cause. Anytime they had to take a shuttle, the little dog was comedy in motion, but would be a disaster on the bridge.

The captain sighed and passed Gimlet to Tesla. "Thank you for bringing her up."

"Of course." Gimlet didn't weigh much more than a coffee cup, and it was easy to tuck her under Tesla's arm. Her skirt immediately floated up again. She slapped it back down with her free hand. "There is one other matter . . . With my shipboard account locked, we don't have access to the net, which means I can't contact our attorney."

The captain glanced back at Wisor, who shook his head. "Ah . . . yes. I'm afraid the complication there is that your spouse is being held on a murder charge."

"Which is why he needs his attorney."

"We aren't going to try him here." The captain laughed. "That would be in violation of the Titan Convention. We're simply ensuring that the ship is secure and that the information we present to Mars is as clean as possible. Given your spouse's profession—"

"He's retired." On one of the consoles, an amber warning light kept flashing, and Tesla pulled her attention away from the tech who was flipping through notification screens.

The security chief bulled his way forward, chest swelling visibly. "Your accounts are linked. Given your background, you can't pretend to not know that he'd be able to use your access."

"So unlink them."

He snorted and looked at the captain. "Their accounts were swarming with databots. I haven't figured out what half of th—"

"You went into our accounts? Our private accounts?" Tesla heard her voice flatten out. "Did you have a warrant?"

The captain shook her head. "It's part of securing the ship. We aren't presenting that in court; simply making certain that no bad agents can cause harm."

It took everything that Tesla had to not acknowledge Shal's sleuthing software, because he had, in fact, loaded it onto their accounts. But he did that to scan for people talking about her on social media or filing news reports about honeymoon activities. "The problem is I know for a fact that he was not near George Saikawa at that moment. Which means the murderer is still on the loose."

"Really? Because the concierge tells us that Mx. Husband left the counter and was out of sight before they heard the scream." The captain glanced at Wisor and then back at Tesla. Her lips compressed for a moment. "Mx. Zuraw . . . how well do you know your spouse?"

Tesla pulled her head back. "What are you implying?"

"Only that you are newlyweds. We have a witness who identified him. The murder weapon has his fingerprints on it—only his—and we found him with the victim's blood on his hands." Captain Valdísardottir shrugged. "This doesn't seem like much of a stretch."

Blood pounded in her ears and her mouth went dry. Gimlet booped her arm in warning. Years of boardroom negotiations and hours of therapy had given her practice at looking calm while she was not. Tesla tilted her head to the side. "I thought we weren't putting him on trial here. You were explaining why my account is locked and—"

"Captain?" The crew member at the console with the warning lights pushed off and stopped neatly next to the captain. "Sorry, but Be Clear needs an answer on this."

Captain Valdísardottir sighed and reached for the handheld. Above the console with the warning lights, the letters BECLR were emblazoned in a bland sans-serif font.

Tesla's mind unpacked a little further and the acronym expanded into Bioengineering Closed Loop Recycling. She cleared her throat. "What's going on?"

"You don't need to worry about it." The captain didn't even look at Tesla, just frowned at the handheld. "Seventy-three kilos? That can't be right."

"Is it high or low?" Tesla moved a little closer, not quite able to let it go, and got a glimpse of the screen. All of the numbers were over peak, which didn't make any sense. Interplanetary ships used closed-loop recycling. A decrease in mass would mean a leak. But a mass *increase*? All the mass on a ship like this was carefully logged. Seventy-three kilos didn't just appear from a vacuum. "I saw you check the purge tanks but didn't see if you'd looked at the Hinkley valves."

The captain wheeled on Security Chief Wisor. "Escort Mx. Zuraw back to her cabin—her original cabin—and let her collect her belongings."

"I strongly advise against that." Wisor settled his arms across his chest and tucked his chin in. "We haven't done a full inventory yet."

"Then let her take the clothes you have inventoried." Captain Valdísardottir barely looked up from the handheld, flicking through screens of data. "And for God's sake, let her have her dog food."

―――――

The rattle of ice against the walls of a cocktail shaker made their tiny cabin feel like home. Was one thirty too early for a cocktail? Not the day after a murder. Besides, it helped her to have something tangible to do. In Tesla's grip, the shaker's walls grew cold to the touch as she counted the seconds.

"How has Gimlet shed so much already?" Shal poked his head up from beside the bed holding a small wad of white dog fur. "Unrelated question: Is my embroidery stuff here?"

"Sorry." Wincing, she lowered the shaker and pulled the lid off. "I used the bag to try to stop the bleeding and . . ."

"And the rest is probably in evidence." He sighed and shrugged. "Well, I'm just glad you convinced them that the portable bar kit is medicinal."

"After the last day? Not a hard sell."

He laughed, the corners of his eyes crinkling. Still on his knees, he reached for the recycling chute and immediately got a faceful of Gimlet kisses. "Easy, girl! I'm a married man now."

Tesla poured a Negroni into a heavy bathroom tumbler. She lowered the shaker, struck by a random thought. Saikawa had been arguing with someone at karaoke. "Actually, maybe I should try to stop by the R-Bar tonight. To see if Josie can do room-service cocktails."

"And by that, you mean to question her. She probably has instructions not to talk about it." Shal leaned back against the wall by the bedroom window, grunting with the motion. He nodded toward one of the cameras and did a mock toast to whoever was watching. Gimlet snuggled into his lap and collapsed in complete exhaustion.

"Yes, but I tip well." Tesla picked up her Boulevardier and carried a bright-red Negroni to Shal.

"And you were chiding me about bribery!"

"It's not the same thing."

"It absolutely is. Mm." He sipped the Negroni. "Perfect."

"It absolutely is not. I mean tipping isn't. Bribery, I mean." She sat on the bed, fluffing pillows to support her back. "It's a thank-you for services rendered beyond the expected."

"That's a bri—"

Three chimes sounded, and then the chipper voice of the cruise director bounced into the cabin. "Good afternoon, passengers! I hope you're all having a splendid day aboard the *Lindgren*. In a few moments, you'll hear a series of tones, three short and one long, which are part of a routine drill. When you hear those, please go immediately to your muster station."

Shal frowned, looking at the ceiling, where the speaker was located. "Didn't we already do the muster drill?"

"There's no need to bring your emergency oxygen supply, since this is just a drill, but please do be prompt! Crew members are standing by to direct you and, before you ask, yes, this is mandatory! Have fun, everyone!"

"Fun . . . We did the muster drill when we boarded." Tesla turned the glass in her hand. "I could maybe see another one mid-voyage, but so soon?"

Sighing, Shal wiped his hand down his face and closed his eyes. Opening them again, he shook his head and took a healthy sip of his cocktail.

"What?" Tesla tilted her head as she watched him.

"That recycling system you told me about . . ." He grimaced and stared at the glass. "I'm placing mental bets about why the mass was high—"

The door to the cabin opened and Officer Piper leaned her head in.

"Hi, Officer!" Shal saluted her with his Negroni. "Want one? My spouse makes a mean cocktail."

"When the muster drill starts, stay put. I'll report that your location is known."

"Splendid! Gimlet, wait—" Shal reached for her too late.

The little dog bounded off his lap and sprang across the room like a wind-up toy, vibrating with delighted greetings. Tesla clambered off the bed trying to catch the Westie before she could escape into the hall, but Officer Piper stopped Gimlet with a leg. "Sorry, sweetness. You stay with your mama, okay?"

Gimlet whined.

"I know. I feel deprived too." Piper looked wistfully at Gimlet and backed into the hall, pulling the door shut. The lock was distressingly loud.

With a hand on her hip, Tesla stared at the locked door. "It would be easier to be mad at her if she didn't like Gimlet."

Behind her, Shal grunted noncommittally.

She turned and narrowed her eyes at her spouse. He was staring into his glass, rotating it slowly as if the dripping legs of alcohol on the side were the most important things in the universe. His mouth tensed and relaxed but he just kept rotating the glass.

"Are you going to tell me what's bothering you?" She took a sip of her sweetly bitter cocktail.

The sigh that escaped him made Shal wince and rest a hand against his side. He set the cocktail on the nightstand and used the small table to lever himself off the floor with a glance at the camera. "I'm probably wrong."

Something about the murder, then. Tesla squeezed past the end of the bed. "Poor thing, your ribs are still bothering you. *Lindgren*, play meditation music." As Titian flutes began playing under a soundscape of trickling water, she slid her arms around his waist and kissed his neck where the stubble had begun to roughen it. She murmured, "Tell me so I can tease you about being wrong later?"

He ran his hands down her back, leaving a path of warmth behind, and trailed a line of kisses from her forehead to her ear. His voice was barely audible under the double flutes. "I think the recycling tank had a body in it. I think the muster drill is because they don't know who it is."

Preakness

1.5 oz rye
.75 oz sweet vermouth
.25 oz Benedictine
2 dashes Angostura bitters
Cherry

Stir ingredients over ice for 40 seconds. Strain into coupe
and garnish with cherry.

The bathroom of the cabin had inadequate shelf space. Tesla balanced her eye cream atop her night cream and waggled the bottle of astringent mist in her hand while she tried to figure out a spot for it.

Outside the bathroom, Gimlet suddenly burst into a full barking volley of Delivery Will Eat Us. Tesla jumped and the bottle dropped to the counter, knocking toiletries in a clatter onto the floor.

The door to the cabin opened. "Shut up!"

That was not Shal. The hall-like passage formed by the closet and the bathroom was filled with Bob, the wall of security officer who apparently spent every spare moment in the ship's gym. The girth of his wrist as he blocked the door was accentuated by a polished teak watch whose leather band might have been a belt on someone else. All he needed was sunglasses and a cheap suit and you'd have a classic mob heavy, but instead this wall of muscle wore the basic blue jersey of a crew member.

She activated her subdermal system, and the Offline icon was still unhelpfully present. The system was designed to work with outboard storage, which meant she could record snippets, but nothing long-form.

From the cabin, Shal said, "Security Chief Wisor, you're just in time for cocktail hour. Negroni?"

"Sit down."

"Excuse me, Bob—" Tesla moved to the door, but the security officer in the hallway seemed to think his role in life was to be a wall. Gimlet wriggled between his legs, making him dance back for a moment before filling the door again. Tesla stood on her toes, trying to see past him. Some recording would be better than none. "Darling! Shall I call out for some canapés for our guests?"

"That'd be swell. Food for two, plus us, of course. Unless you plan on bringing some associ—" A dull thump broke Shal's voice and left a pained wheeze cutting through the room.

"Let me out!" Tesla advanced on the goon blocking the door, but it wasn't as if she were going to be able to budge him. She backed up and grabbed the astringent mist from the counter. "Move, now, or so help me, medical-grade witch hazel is going straight in your eyes."

"Babe. Just sit tight, okay?" Shal's voice was hoarse. Cloth rustled in the other room and then he said, in a low voice, "That wasn't necessary."

"I told you to sit." Wisor's voice was tight and brusque.

"Well . . . I'm sitting now."

"I have some questions."

"Sure. The classic martini is actually a two-to-one ratio, but I prefer a five-to-one ratio mys— All right. All right . . . What do you want to know?"

Tesla raised her voice. "Don't answer any questions. Shal? Do you hear me? Don't answer any questions unless they let you talk to Fantine first. And you should know that I'm recording this."

"Be my guest." The silver-haired chief of security walked up behind the human wall. "Ma'am, why don't you join us?"

Bob glanced at his boss and took a step back to press against the closet door. Even so, Tesla had to turn sideways to get out of the bathroom without touching him. Gimlet tucked into heel position as if she were using positioning data. Chief Wisor moved back into the main room and waved her to the tiny couch.

Shal was slumped against the far end, head down, squinting at the floor. He had both arms wrapped around his chest and tilted his head to look at her. "I'd offer you a drink but . . ."

Tesla sat on the couch next to her spouse. "What did he do to you?"

"Just pushed me down." Shal straightened as if his insides had to be peeled apart. "I hit the arm of the couch, that's all. Isn't that right, Chief Wisor?"

"Right." The chief smirked and Tesla wanted to drive a soldering iron into him. *Everyone has a secret, and everyone lies.* "Would you like me to ring for medical?"

"No." Shal sat back slowly. "Thank you."

The chief could make a nice show of concern, knowing that Shal had declined medical attention earlier. How involved, exactly, was Wisor? Gently resting her hand on Shal's back, she said, "I'm afraid I need to insist on a lawyer if you want us to cooperate."

He settled on the end of the bed as if this were a casual chat. "Whose body is in my composter?"

Tesla's back tightened, cold running through her nerves, but she wasn't going to be baited into answering. Gimlet put her paw on Tesla's foot. She took a slow breath and glanced at Shal, who studied the chief and then shook his head. "No clue."

Wisor pursed his lips, looking at both of them. "Neither of you is surprised. And she looked at you after I asked the question, so I think you know more than you're letting on."

Tesla rolled her eyes at him and discovered that she could, in fact, be baited into answering. "For crying out loud. I was on the bridge with you when the captain said there was a seventy-three-kilo increase in the recycling system."

"And you did a second muster drill three days out." Shal eased back against the couch. "I'd have been a piss-poor detective to not connect those two. And the third thing . . . You asked 'whose body,' which means that even after muster you still don't know who it is. So either you're missing multiple people or you're not missing anyone."

Wisor blinked rapidly. His mouth twitched.

Shal sat forward sharply enough that he winced. "Holy shit. No one is missing?"

"How do you know that no one is missing?" Wisor watched Shal narrowly.

"Because you didn't follow up by asking me where the other missing people were." He whistled. "So the body is slurry, huh? Sure you don't want a drink?"

Tesla rested her hands on her knees. "If someone else has been killed, that means it couldn't have been Shal. If you let him out, he can help you find the real murderer."

Wisor shook his head. "The body pre-dates last night's murder. So I have to ask, Mx. Steward, where were you on boarding day?"

Tesla put her hand up. "Stop. I want to be very clear that we won't answer questions without my lawyer present. If you'll unlock my account, I'll call her now and we can continue to cooperate. Otherwise, we have nothing else to say."

The chief nodded and stood. "That's all right. You've told me enough." With a gesture, he sent Bob out of the room ahead of him and then paused in the door. "One more thing—"

"Seriously?" Shal raised an eyebrow at him. "Look, no offense, but I collect detective novels and that is, quite possibly, one of the most annoying interrogation techniques."

With a smirk, the chief shrugged. "Be that as it may. One more thing . . . Your dining preferences list you both as vegetarians. Why order a steak?"

She almost answered him. Tesla's tongue was already shaping an answer when Shal lifted his Negroni and casually took a sip. He sighed. "Sure I can't offer you one? We've got Lunacy gin. Lovely stuff."

"I appreciate it, but I don't drink on the job. Enjoy your cocktails." The chief closed the door.

Gimlet stood up and barked at the closed door.

"Yes, you are the most ferocious." Shal let out a sigh and closed his eyes, letting his head drop back against the couch.

"So helpy." Tesla glared at the door and deeply empathized with Gimlet's urge to bark at it. "Of all the incompetent . . . mammering lobsters!"

"Mammering lobster? Is that a Fantine?"

She crossed her arms and flopped against the back of the couch. "Maybe. Probably. I don't even know what 'mammering' means. I hope it means inept."

"Whatever is going on, he's not incompetent. Old school, yes." Shal opened his eyes and stared at the door without lifting his head. "But not wrong about his line of questioning. Someone is working very hard to pin this on me."

═══════

Tesla slid onto one of the R-Bar's stools and waited for Josie to see her. She'd left Gimlet in the room with Shal and felt naked without the dog, but for this round of questions Tesla wanted to be as unnoticeable as possible. At the front of the room, on the stage, one of the activity leaders sat on a barstool, looking out at tables with people clustered around them.

"All right! Are we having fun?" The host's smile was legitimately blinding. "The next clue is 'What reality medical drama received a Sanhauser Award for what the Sanhauser board called an 'unorthodox lead host,' 'a slightly terrifying diagnostician,' and 'suspense fit for a medical Sherlock Holmes?'"

"Hospital Mod 50931," she muttered, having sat through every episode with Shal.

A table filled with blond perms turned and glared at her. "Don't say the answers out loud."

"Sorry." Tesla beamed at them.

Josie was behind the far end of the bar, slicing actual limes in half. For a flicker of time, a frown shaped her face, but it vanished into an almost-convincing smile of welcome. The air by her station was bright with tart resins. She walked over to Tesla, wiping her hands.

"Mx. Zuraw! Good evening." Josie placed a cocktail napkin in front of her. "How can I help you?"

"Mm . . . I think I'm in the mood for a Preakness." Tesla twisted the cocktail napkin, watching Josie gather the rye from the barback.

"The next clue is: 'What term for a group of people formally assembled for a special purpose can also refer to a group of eagles?'"

Josie concentrated on pouring a measure of the rye into a cocktail pitcher. "How's your spouse?"

"Annoyed at being cooped up, but otherwise mostly fine." Tesla tapped the napkin in thought and then released it to turn and study the room. As she turned, she felt the Coriolis effect a little, and she had to grab the stool to steady herself. The trivia players were clustered near the stage.

Mostly they were middle-aged cruisers and, oddly, a group of what appeared to be writers in one corner. She tried to imagine the room as it had been last night when George Saikawa had been arguing. It had been dark, with lights focused on the stage. With the lights up a little for trivia, it was easier to see the decor. The stage was a shallow affair, with three risers cascading down to the floor and a long ramp leading to it from the left side. A service door filled the gap between stage and bar, with a dock for room-service bots to pull into the end.

Overhead, a wrought-iron chandelier hung from the ceiling, giving the room an arcane feel. Behind the bar, wall shelves held bottles of bitters, fancy glasses, and a variety of ryes. An accent strip of mirrors above a bar rail ran around the room, breaking up the cozy darkness.

From here, she could see clearly into the booth Saikawa had been in, which was part of a line of booths ringing the back of the room. The magician would have had his back to the bar, as far as she could tell, but the bald passenger would have been facing it. Josie might have seen their face.

Tesla tried to swing the conversation that way. "Last night, I was so discombobulated when it was my turn. That tray that dropped just totally threw me off."

"You were a trooper though."

Tesla shrugged. "I should have expected it, I guess; they'd been fighting before I went up. Did you see them?"

Josie looked down and grabbed the bottle of Benedictine. "It was pretty busy. Sorry."

"Oh." Tesla tapped her toe against the foot rail. There was a limit to how hard she could push without being a privileged asshole. To Josie. She'd definitely been one to Wisor, but he deserved it. With Josie . . . It was so easy to forget how hard it was for someone to tell her "no," even when they didn't know who she really was. But maybe if she approached it from the side, she might be able to get answers without making Josie uncomfortable.

"The next clue is: 'What music genre that originated on New Jamaica Station in 2066 shares its name with a *Space Nine-Nine* villain?'"

She let Josie work for a moment longer, waiting until she had measured the Benedictine into the pitcher. "Oh, hey, can you tell me the name of our waiter? We forgot to tip last night. So stupid."

Josie grimaced in sympathy. Glass rattled as she swapped bottles for the sweet vermouth. She must have been feeling bad for Tesla, because she used the Carpano Antica instead of the well vermouth. "Yuki, he/him, was working with me last night."

"Splendid. Thanks." Tesla rested her elbow on the bar and

leaned her head against her palm. "How's the best way to get that to him?"

"He's—" Josie fumbled the bottle as she was setting it back down. "He's working now."

"The next clue is: 'What last name is shared by the actor who starred in a 2034 film adapted from a Sarah Pinsker novel and the inventor known for her giant robot?'"

"It wasn't a robot." Personal Assistive Mobility Unit. The prototype of the PAMU had looked like a giant robot and so that's how the media had reported it after the Accident. Tesla turned away from the room and ducked her head, using the bitter twinge of tight muscles to help focus on the here and now. Wood-grain bar. White cocktail napkins. Platinum-iridium wedding ring. Pebbled green rind. Blue trousers.

"That face didn't look like it went with a good thought." Josie paused with the bitters poised over the pitcher. "Are you okay?"

"Oh. Fine." Tesla shook her head to clear the cobwebs. Around her, people kept saying her name, but they weren't spotting her, just working on clues. "Just thinking that my lawyer must be spitting lawsuits by now, if she's trying to regain contact with us and being put off."

"Mm . . ." Josie stirred the cocktail with a long silver spoon, and they both watched the ice and ruddy liquid swirl in the glass.

"The next clue is: 'What orbital station are you visiting if you are eating a flatkaka while visiting Kolaportið Park?'"

Tesla shifted on her stool so she could watch the rest of the lounge as more of the before-dinner crowd wandered in. She did not recognize any of the people from last night.

But the magician was here. A couple sat at a table to her left, gazing with delighted bafflement as he made souvenir coins vanish for them. Could she just straight-up ask him what he'd been arguing with George about? It didn't seem like the ideal scenario.

"The next clue is: 'What actor in the Oscar-winning spy thriller

Ganymede Night was cast because of their previous career as a contortionist?'"

A young dark-haired waif, with silver piercings just visible along the curve of their ear, stood in front of the booth where George Saikawa had been sitting. From the back, they could have been anywhere from Lunar European to Terran Japanese.

She took a snap and attached it to a ping. *::Hey, Shal. Does this look like the person you chased?::*

::Connection unavailable::

Right. Because they still weren't letting her or Shal access the net. Sighing so heavily she could feel her nostrils flare, Tesla closed the messaging app on her HUD. She saved it locally to share when she was back online.

Until then, she would have to tell him about the possible suspect. Blue trousers. A snugly fitting top—wait. That was a crew member. The waif turned, holding a tray with a straw-pale pilsner on it. Tesla scanned the room. That was the *only* server in here, besides Josie. The person with blue locs wasn't anywhere. "Is that Yuki?"

"Hm? Oh. Yes." Josie set the finished drink in the middle of a fresh cocktail napkin. The russet liquid seemed to glow in the delicate coupe glass. A tiny bamboo skewer balanced on the edge, piercing a real candied cherry. "One Preakness."

"Your next clue is: 'What sport did the Calisto spaceracer pilot who won the Lunar Formula One system championships in three consecutive years go on to compete in after their final win?'"

"Thank you." Tesla waved her key fob over Josie's wrist register and the drink was subtracted from the credit Auberi put on her account. "I don't remember seeing him last night."

But the system wouldn't let her tip.

"It was pretty busy. He was definitely here."

Tesla tried again and could not transfer any of the funds to the tip field. "And the server with the blue locs?"

"Who?"

She paused, looking up at Josie. "Blue locs. Mid-back? Trim. Medium brown with freckles?"

"Yuki was the only one scheduled last night."

"Huh." *Everyone has a secret, and everyone lies.* Tesla looked back down at the reader, trying again to tip. It wouldn't let her make the transfer. She clenched her teeth so tightly that her jaw hurt. Terrific. She'd have Fantine argue about that, too, if her account was unlocked. "I'm so, so sorry. It's not letting me tip."

Josie whisked the wrist register away with a smile. "Don't worry about it. You were both more than generous earlier."

"I'll make up for it when we get our account unlocked."

"It's fine, really."

It might be fine, but not tipping made Tesla shockingly uncomfortable. She had an ungodly amount of money, and one of the ways she'd always mitigated that was by tipping high—in places where she didn't control the pay rate. In her own companies, people were paid living wages, which was just easier all around. Besides the general ethics of it, the problem with a tip-based system was that it made the server more loyal to the customer than to the nominal employer.

Maybe Shal was right and it was a bribe.

"Your final clue for this round is: 'Name the seven moons of Saturn that are large enough to be in hydrostatic equilibrium.'"

She turned her cocktail on the napkin and took a sip of the complex Manhattan variation with its layers of sweet bitterness. She granted herself a moment to just enjoy the flavors and sighed a little in appreciation. "You do such nice work."

"Thank you." Josie glanced past her, frowning a little.

Tesla looked over her shoulder, where the magician had paused next to Yuki. He was shuffling cards one-handed in what looked like the flashiest of fidgets. He had also, she was fairly certain, just looked away from her.

She turned back to Josie. "I heard an announcement for a magic show. The same person?"

"Yep. The Amazing Nile Silver, he/him. Do you want me to call Nile over?"

"No, I was just curious. Is he here every night?"

"Mm-hm. It's a teaser for his stage show." Josie pulled out a foil pouch labeled "OJ" and attached it to the rehydrator. She frowned at the pouch with more attention than rehydrating orange juice really required.

"That makes planning easier, I imagine. So . . . business as usual tonight?"

"Yep." Josie turned off the rehydrator tap and decoupled the foil pouch of OJ.

"You've got your clues! Bonus points for figuring out the theme of this category, so huddle together and see what you can come up with. Don't forget to visit the bar, where our talented Josie is ready to handcraft any beverage you desire."

"Listen, I hate to do this, but I'm about to be really busy." Josie nodded, still concentrating on the foil pouch.

"No problem. I was going to clear out anyway." But first she wanted a word with the Amazing Nile Silver. And also Yuki. She didn't remember seeing that particular person last night, but the lights had been low and she'd been somewhat distracted.

But they may have been the person Shal saw. About seventy kilos. Check. Lunar European or Terran Japanese. Check. Sleek bowl-cut black hair. Also, check. She swiveled back around on her stool, cocktail in hand. Yuki and the magician had disappeared.

Moonpool

1.25 oz Old Tom Gin
1 oz Bianco vermouth
.5 oz Ramazzotti
1 twist lemon peel

Stir ingredients over ice, strain into coupe. Squeeze lemon peel to release oils into drink and discard.

An installation of neon undulated overhead in the long transit corridor that girdled the Terran level, making a slow progression through the rainbow. Theoretically, it was supposed to help you know where on the ring you were. The nearest tubes were a sunny yellow, and to her right, over the clockwise moving sidewalk, they deepened to grass green. To Tesla's left, over the counterclockwise moving sidewalk, they progressed to orange and, farther along the sidewalk, to red, which was just visible as the ring curved up and out of sight.

More important, there was an information kiosk at the transfer point between sidewalks. She might not be able to get her HUD to connect to the network, but she still knew how to work a computer.

Tesla tapped the kiosk and opened the employee bios page. Ostensibly this existed to add charm to the voyage and to make it easy to give your favorite bartender a tip. But she was hoping that she could use it to identify the server with the blue locs.

Starting simple, she tried doing a search for "blue hair server," but it turned out that *all* the servers wore blue, which made it . . .

less than useful. Chewing on the inside of her lip, Tesla glared at the machine. Fine. Humans were good at pattern recognition, so she'd play to her strengths.

She reset the directory to show just photos and then set it to two hundred per screen. At that size, they were all tiny icons and impossible to see details on. But she didn't need details. Letting her eyes unfocus, Tesla favorited all those with blue in their hair and anyone around the right part of the skin-tone spectrum. Variants could be camera artifacts, so she gave herself fairly wide latitude there.

Of course, the mystery server might also change their hair color regularly, and then she'd just have go page by page. Maybe she'd make Shal do that. Speaking of whom, she should check in.

She'd seen her spouse yell at too many films when detectives wandered off on secret missions, followed by rants about how many missing persons cases would be solved while people were still alive if they would Just Tell People Where They Were Going. He would be . . . disappointed in her if she was stupid. Overly stupid.

Still, she could do two things at once.

As she navigated her way around the ship's directory, she used the kiosk to place a call to the room. The phone rang. Tesla pressed a thumb into the base of her spine, shifting her weight. The room phone rang again. She grimaced, used to an instant connection.

She narrowed the search down to five different servers. She resized them so she could see details of their faces.

"H-Hello?" Shal sounded drowsy.

"Did I wake you? Aha!" She opened the entry for Immanuel Rudawski, he/him.

"Mm . . . No." He cleared his throat, and she had definitely woken him up. "No. Aha?"

Tesla stared at the picture of Immanuel Rudawski, server. She now knew that Immanuel was assigned to the pool area. He was

Kenyan with a Polish father. He was twenty-three, a practicing Buddhist, and enjoyed rock-climbing in his spare time, and anything she told Shal would almost certainly be listened to by security.

"I'm going to print a swimsuit and head to the pool." She could explain why afterward and tell him about the magician and Yuki. "Do you need anything from the outside world?"

"No, thanks." He sighed, and cloth rustled as if he were lying on the bed. "I might order room service."

She hesitated and looked at the directory again. "If you get bored, try reading the *Lindgren*'s *Daily Bulletin*. Did you know that there's an art auction in the gallery and you can win a genuine reproduction by Windlass?"

"Is that so?"

"And there's a complete list of the crew and fascinating biographical detail. Josie? Our favorite bartender apparently hails from the Jamaican Refugee Orbiter around Earth and was a member of the Georgian Society of Jamaica, specializing in historic dance in college."

"Fascinating."

His answers were so short that he had to know they were being listened to. Or he was in worse shape than she thought. "Should I come back?"

He yawned audibly. "No, no. I think I'm going to nap."

She closed the kiosk, eyeing the moving sidewalks. The clockwise one would take her to the pool and counterclockwise would take her back to Shal. "Are you sure?"

"I'll live vicariously through you." His voice warmed a little with a smile. "Go on. Enjoy the pool."

═══

Overhead, the ceiling gave an approximation of an Earthside sky at sunset, all deep blues with warm orange wisps of simulated clouds. In the saltwater pool, passengers floated, some reading, some chatting. Beyond a vivid Mondrian-inspired art glass wall, a children's pool area swarmed with frolicking antics, but here, all was tranquil.

To look at all this relaxed leisure, you'd have no idea that someone had been murdered.

Two someones.

On the boardwalk that ran along the edge of the pool, Tesla spotted Immanuel carrying a cocktail tray. A young, warm-brown crewmember with blue locs, he had a tightness to his shoulders that did not match the smile he wore like a part of his uniform. Even without perusing the employee directory, Tesla would have recognized him.

She lowered herself into the pool and settled on one of the low loungers just under the surface. Water lapped around Tesla's shoulders, and for a moment, her back didn't hurt. She let out a long, slow sigh and didn't want to move.

But she had sleuthing to do. Tesla waited until Immanuel turned in her direction and raised her hand in a gentle "I'd like to place an order."

Unlike last night, this time he acknowledged her. With a nod, Immanuel walked over to her and crouched. "Good afternoon." His cheeks were round with a smattering of freckles that brushed his nose. This close, the concealer under his eyes made the dark circles more obvious rather than less. "How may I help you?"

Tesla sat up, skin chilling as the printed suit shed water instantly. She shifted on the lounger to make eye contact a little easier. "Tell me honestly . . . On a scale of 'order a beer' to 'mixology god,' how's the bartender on this level?"

The smile seemed to turn a fraction more genuine. Immanuel glanced toward the bar that bisected the glass wall. "I think I can safely suggest anything on the menu."

"Mm . . . competent but not inspired?"

Immanuel's mouth pursed a bit as if he were trying to hold in a laugh. "This is not, perhaps, the bar for inspiration. Relaxation, yes. You would, I think, find the margarita unobjectionable."

"I shall trust you on that." Tesla took a chance. "I'm afraid that Josie down in the R-Bar has me spoiled."

The tension came back into Immanuel's shoulders, and the smile set on his face like plaster. "Ah . . . Yes, she would be on the mixology god end of your scale."

"That she is." Tesla let the subject of the R-Bar drop for the moment. She wanted to know how much Immanuel had heard of the argument, but not scare him off. "May I upgrade to real lime juice and an actual lime?"

Immanuel inclined his head, fingers already dancing on the edge of his tray to key in the order. "It shall be my pleasure. A moment and I shall return."

"No hurry . . . I have a billion knots I need to soak away." Tesla settled back on the lounger as Immanuel headed to the bar.

If Tesla had been preparing for a corporate merger, or to meet with a bright young inventor eager to sell her start-up to Crane Industries, she would have done the research and have a deeper base of knowledge to work from. So what common ground did they have? Meditation. Both probably vegetarian, although honestly with printed food that could be almost anyone. Tesla had the means to have beef if she wanted it but consciously chose not to. A practicing Buddhist would also be making a conscious choice.

Tesla slowed her breathing and closed her eyes. She let her consciousness expand to the sounds around her. Water lapping at the edge of the pool. A man laughing with a staccato rhythm. Ice rattling against polyamide. In the distance, a child's squeal of delight. Closer, rubber-clad footsteps on the boardwalk.

"Here we are." Immanuel sank into an easy squat on the boardwalk by the head of Tesla's lounger. "One unobjectionable margarita with real lime juice and a real lime."

"Thanks." Tesla reached for the polyamide cup and smiled at the server. "Oh. Hey . . ."

Immanuel had that incredibly patient facade that service people got when they weren't actually interested in what you had to say but didn't want to blow a tip.

"Screw it." She couldn't tip anyway. Tesla set the polyamide cup on the boardwalk and shifted on the lounger to fully face Immanuel. "I was in the R-Bar last night when you dropped that tray."

Immanuel froze. His chest contracted as if he was struggling to breathe. "I'm not sup—"

"Not supposed to talk about it?" Tesla grimaced. "Look, I had this whole plan to try to sweet-talk you into a casual conversation and try to swing us around to gossip—"

Immanuel dropped his tray, standing up so fast that he knocked over the margarita.

"But the fact is that they're accusing my spouse of murder and I know he didn't do it, so I just want to know if you heard the argument that—"

"I can't talk to you."

"That's fine. I just need you to tell the security chief about the people that Mx. Saikawa was arguing with—"

"I can't." Immanuel looked at the comms badge on his chest and then said again, as if speaking directly to it. "I can't talk to you." Stumbling back, he turned and made a beeline for a service door.

That had gone splendidly. Sighing, Tesla righted the polyamide cup. A service drone had already trundled out of a wall and crawled toward the spill. Tesla climbed out of the pool, picking up the tray and the empty cup. She figured she may as well get a martini for Shal before she went back down. Granted, they had gin and dry vermouth in their travel bar, but no olives.

She carried Immanuel's abandoned tray to the bar, where a bartender with a crop top revealing broad shoulders and abs made of steel turned to her with a grin. A forelock of Venusian cloud-surfer hair fell forward. "What can I do you for?"

"A margarita. Real lime and juice? Also a martini." Tesla set the tray and the empty cup on the bar and glanced at the server's name tag. Steve. He/they.

"Do you want vodka or gin in your martini?"

"I said martini." It was snark, but she could tell a lot about a bartender by their response. The ones whose taste aligned with hers would perk up. The others, like this one, looked blank. "Fun fact: a martini made with vodka is called a kangaroo."

"No kidding?"

She needed to get off her very large, unnecessary, soapbox before she spent her time ranting instead of investigating a murder. Also, she couldn't tip this person to make up for having to put up with her—goddammit. Tips *were* bribes.

Fine. She'd use her other tools. A good trick in corporate trading was pretending you knew more than you did. "Oh, hey, Steve. Immanuel had to step out. You know, after last night."

"Nutballs." They flipped a cocktail shaker in the air. "Like, can you imagine? It's so off. Like. Seeing the person who, like, just totally soaked your grandparents and then someone else offs her before you can even tell her off?"

Tesla blinked. Immanuel knew Saikawa? She took a chance. "Right. And then to have had her in his section?"

"Soak me! Yeah! I mean, that sucks and all." As they spoke, they slung ingredients into the shaker from astonishing distances. "Like, Immanuel said his grandparents had gotten totally soaked. Investments or something. I dunno. Some soaking bank thing."

"A start-up?"

"That was it! Soak me, yeah."

Funny, the bartender didn't look like they were still in high school, and yet . . . "Very soaked," Tesla agreed, noting that they were going to shake the martini. "Could you—"

The shaking began.

"I already knew some of this 'cause, you know, you talk about why you're on the ship, right? Like, his family, they lost everything, he had to drop out of college, I mean, they were really, really soaked."

That martini was being shaken for far, far too long, although the motion did do nice things for the bartender's biceps. "He was, like, literally vibrational with the mads when I saw him and he is the gentlest person. Immanuel recognized her when she sat down. Had this whole rant in his head that he was going to give and then?"

They slammed the shaker down on the counter, staring at Tesla expectantly.

"Then . . . murder?"

"Boom! Yeah. Worst soak of all time." They popped the lid off the cocktail shaker and drained it into a polyamide martini glass. "Oh—we don't have real olives up here. Printed ones, okay?"

Of all of Tesla's concerns, that was the least of her worries. "No problem."

They slid the martini in front of her with a flourish. "Whaddya think?"

She picked up the martini and took a sip of the highly watered, monodimensional paint thinner. "Mm . . ." Wetting her lips, she raised it in a toast. "To Immanuel's grandp—"

The music cut off. "Would passenger Artesia Zuraw please report to sick bay? Passenger Artesia Zuraw, please report to sick bay."

It took Tesla longer than it should have to recognize her shipboard name. And then she was running before her martini had finished falling.

Blood and Sand

1.5 oz scotch

.75 oz sweet vermouth

.75 oz orange juice

.75 oz cherry Heering

1 orange peel

Shake ingredients over ice for 15 seconds and strain into coupe. Garnish with orange peel.

Sick bay was in the ring of the ship that had Mars gravity. Tesla sprang down the curving corridor, heart occupying a space in the back of her throat. She'd set her DBPS way, way past the safety margins so that she didn't have to think about pain while she ran. There were two possibilities that she was bracing herself for. In the first, the doctor had discovered something about George Saikawa's body and needed to ask her a question.

In the other, something had happened to Shal.

She had pinged him the moment they asked her to come to sick bay. Instinct had made her reach through that virtual space for him, even though she was cut off from the net. She was going to have Fantine crochet their souls into a dog toy for Gimlet if—

She rounded the last curve of the unadorned polyamide hall and misjudged the Coriolis effect, staggering into a wall. She didn't feel a damn thing but held still for a moment anyway as if she'd be able to tell if she'd jostled a screw loose in her spine with the DBPS set this high. And when she regained her footing, it stopped mattering because Officer Piper stood outside the door to sick bay. She had Gimlet on a leash.

Tesla put her hand against the wall as the floor seemed to lurch under her. The little dog saw Tesla first, and barked. Her ears were low and she dragged the leash to its full extension. Officer Piper saw Tesla and came to meet her.

"He's unconscious." She bent down and scooped up Gimlet, holding her out to Tesla. "They're examining him now."

Tesla clutched her dog with unfeeling hands. Gimlet pressed her face into the crook of Tesla's elbow, shivering.

Piper turned and led Tesla back to the entrance to sick bay. "Gimlet was barking and scratching at the door. It didn't sound right. Mx. Husband was on the floor. Dr. Fish is on call and she wants to ask you about his medical history."

"Of course." She followed Piper through a tiny reception area and into a small examining room.

Shal lay on a hospital bed, with an IV in his arm. Beneath the black eye, his skin was gray and his mouth hung open a little. Dermal patches dotted his body, at temple and chest, with the corresponding vital signs cutting jagged lines across the wall monitor. She had seen him without his shirt as often as feasibly possible, but there was a profound difference between asleep and unconscious. His limbs looked slack and waxen. The bruising around his torso seemed more livid than it had in their room.

The wall of Bob stood in a corner, arms crossed over his chest, watching Shal as if he were going to spring off the table at any moment.

A doctor with streaks of gray in faded brown hair held a medscan over Shal's chest and glanced up when Tesla entered. Then did a full-on double take, eyes widening. "You—"

Tesla welcomed the recognition. The tricks the cruise ship did to hide her identity only worked to redirect ID queries. If someone recognized her despite the wig, there wasn't anything she could do. And being a Crane would get her better medical service for Shal.

"You were the first on the scene last night."

She blinked, context shifting around her, removing the doctor's smock and adding in a robotic assistant. The medic from last night. All of her priorities changed in an instant. "Get away from him."

"Excuse me?" Dr. Fish blinked at Tesla and looked back down at the device in her hand. "He's stable, which I imagine is the first thing you want to know, and then I have a series of questions for you."

George Saikawa had been alive until Dr. Fish arrived and took her away. "Is there another doctor I could talk to?" There was the assistant . . . Candy, that had been the name. "Not Candy, either."

As if Tesla hadn't been perfectly clear, Dr. Fish continued, "He'll be fine. Vitals are very good, but at the moment, I'm suspecting OD on painkillers and booze. Why didn't anyone send for me sooner? The blow he took to the head alone is enough that he shouldn't have been drinking."

Tesla was shaking her head before the woman finished talking. "First of all, he doesn't take anything stronger than aspirin." Gimlet wiggled in her arms and she stroked the little white dog, using the contact to ground herself in the here and now. "Second, he has a head injury and broken ribs because your employees beat him up."

"He fell down the stairs." Bob spoke from the corner.

"Are you kidding me?" In her arms, Gimlet gave a sharp yip. "'Fell down the stairs.' That's the best you can do?"

Beside her, Officer Piper cleared her throat. "We found your oxyfeldone in the cabin."

Tesla's mouth dropped open. "I—I don't take. We don't have any oxyfeldone." At one point she had taken it, yes, and more than her doctor had prescribed, but the synthetic opioid was a safety net she hadn't needed to use in years. "I had spinal surgery several years ago and had a deep brain pain suppressor installed."

"Oh?" Dr. Fish repositioned one of the dermal patches. "Forgive my professional curiosity but—"

"The point is, we don't have any oxyfeldone."

Officer Piper was watching her closely. "Label says it's his."

"Then obviously it was planted." Tesla tried again to contact Fantine and got nothing. "Here's what needs to happen now. I want my lawyer and I want a different doctor."

Dr. Fish didn't even pause her work. "May I ask why?"

"No, you may not." Tesla bit down on the truth that Shal thought this doctor might have had something to do with the murder. The last thing she wanted was for the person treating him to think they suspected her. Which was probably a thought she should have had sooner. Tesla grimaced. "How long are you people going to keep me from talking to my lawyer?"

Dr. Fish lifted the scanner and looked up and to the left as if she were accessing a HUD. "Sorry, looks like my hunch was right. He has oxyfeldone in his system, along with a significant amount of alcohol."

Tesla stared at the doctor. "That's not possible. I have to fight to get him to take anything at all for pain."

"Are you certain?" The doctor looked at the medscan again, frowning. She wet her lips. "I mean, people with addictions are very good at hiding them."

"Why would he be addicted to painkillers? He's never been . . ." But Shal used to be a boxer. Gimlet whined in her arms and buried her nose in Tesla's armpit. Swallowing, Tesla looked down and scratched the dog's belly with the hand that supported her. "Look, I don't know where it came from, but that oxyfeldone is absolutely not ours. Now, get me my lawyer or so help me I will buy this entire ship just for the pleasure of watching it deorbit."

―――――

There was a special quality to hold music that, generally speaking, made Tesla want to murder people. Although, even in her own head, that metaphor sounded like a bad idea. She clutched the ship wallphone and paced in circles in the tiny room where Shal slept.

He was just sleeping. Now. His chest rose and fell with the regularity of an orbit. Gimlet followed Tesla as she paced, claws ticking on the hard floor, and the worry in her button-bright eyes seemed almost palpable. Biting her lip, Tesla leaned against the wall trying to steady her breathing, but she couldn't quite bring herself to close her eyes. The door to the room stood open, with the wall of Bob standing guard outside. It would have been too much to hope that Officer Piper would be the one assigned to them.

Tesla bent at the waist, trying to stretch the tight muscles of her back. The music cut off and the nice young person who had been helping her came back on the line. His pleasant tenor voice still made her tense. "I'm sorry, Mx. Zuraw, I've asked all through the legal department and we just don't know who you're trying to contact."

How many lawyers could they have on board the ship? Two? Three at the outside. This felt like she was being brushed off. Tesla spoke to the floor, staring at the old gray scuff marks on the tile. "I'm sorry, I don't know their name." All of the details she remembered Fantine saying about her lawyer friend who worked on the ship were not helpful in this context. "They play golf?"

"I wish I could help, I truly do."

"Security Chief Wisor had a message from them this morning." Tesla did not want to invoke Wisor, but she was more than a little desperate. She straightened, slowly and carefully. "Is there anyone who—"

Outside of Shal's room, Security Chief Wisor walked into the sick bay's cramped lobby, pausing to hold the door that led from the hallway. ". . . you to identify her."

Tesla lowered the phone and leaned into the lobby. "Chief Wisor! I hate to troub—"

Haldan Kuznetsova, head bowed as if he were carrying a literal weight on it, stopped just inside the lobby door. His head came up and he turned to stare at her, then past her to where Shal lay on the bed. "Is this some sort of joke?"

Well, shit. Tesla's fingers cramped on the phone. "Mx. Kuznetsova, I am so sorr—"

"Don't you dare. Don't you dare speak to me."

Tesla pulled her head back, nostrils flaring, and barely caught hold of her temper. He'd just lost someone. He thought she was involved.

Wisor turned to Bob. "Why is the door open?"

Before Bob could answer, Kuznetsova wheeled on Wisor. "The question is why isn't he in jail? How is anyone supposed to feel safe with a murderer on the loose? What if he comes after me next?"

Tesla's back tightened and she dialed the DBPS up until she could only feel the pressure of Gimlet's leash in her hand. "Mx. Kuznetsova. I understand you're upset, but my spouse was the first on the scene and has been misidentified. We are cooperat—"

"I told you not to speak to me."

Wisor stepped between Tesla and Kuznetsova. "I'm very sorry for the additional distress, sir. You won't see him again."

Tesla held her tongue, barely. Regardless of how wrong Kuznetsova was, she and Shal were the last people he wanted to see right now.

Shal was going to be fine. Even if Fantine let things get to a trial, there was no way that Shal would ever be convicted.

Oh, Tesla was under no illusions that being innocent would keep him out of prison.

Money would, though.

Money kept guilty men out, and it could certainly keep her spouse safe.

Wisor scowled and pointed at Bob. "Close that door!"

As Bob reached for the door of Shal's room, Dr. Fish burst out of another examining room. "What is all of this shouting? I have— Oh my God. Hal? What are you—"

The door snicked shut. Shaking with rage, Tesla pressed her forehead against the door. She wanted to yank it open, but that would not help anything. When she had contact with Fantine again—

A small, tinny voice said, "Mx. Zuraw? Mx. Zuraw? Is everything okay?"

Tesla still held the phone in one hand and lifted it back to her ear. She closed her eyes. "Let's try this again. Will you open my account, go to my emergency contact override, and enter the passcode 'Fettig Control Mechanism'?"

"Um . . ." The hapless thing had probably never been asked this before. "Give me a moment."

"Of course." She stood with eyes closed, one hand clutching the phone, the other clenched around the doorknob. Through the door, she could just hear voices, enough to tell that conversations were still heated in the little lobby. Behind her, Shal slept through the whole thing.

"There we go and—ohmygod! *You're Tesla Crane.* Sorry—sorry. I mean. How can I help you, Mx. Crane?"

———

Tesla had put Gimlet on Shal's bed as if she had magic healing energy that would suddenly make him better. She was curled up at his feet but watching Tesla. Her head rose suddenly, turning to the door. That was Tesla's first warning.

The rumble of Bob's voice was Tesla's second warning before the door opened. The wall of human stepped to the side to make way for a petite blue-black individual with an impeccable pencil-thin mustache.

"Mx. Crane, I'm so, so sorry—though of course not an admission of guilt on behalf of my company—simply an expression of my personal remorse for the distress you've endured." The embodiment of elegance swept into the room and offered her an immaculately manicured hand with a single gold accent nail on the ring finger. "Leigh Osbourne de Monchaux, he/him, at your service. Fantine, the darling, will have my hide for her collection if I don't take the very best care of you. Now, tell me, how is poor Mx. Steward? Dr. Fish? Dr. Fish, come here, please at once and tell me everything."

He had used Tesla's real name, and she welcomed that with all the social power and privilege it came with. She should have taken the mask off much, much sooner. Across the tiny lobby, Dr. Fish emerged from another room. Her eyes were red, as if she'd been crying, and she blinked several times, before answering. "Of course."

"Bob, I need you to— Oh my goodness! Who is this precious, precious creature? Hello, my darling, hello." Leigh Osbourne de Monchaux flowed past Tesla to offer his fingers for sniffing and then accepted tiny dog kisses. "Are you taking good care of your human? Yes, you are. Yes, I can see that you are. Such a good little doctor. Such a perfect chaperone. Now, Mx. Crane, what can I do for you, hm?"

The thing she wanted was for Shal to wake up. "I would like a different doctor for my spouse. On a ship of this size, you should have multiple on staff."

Dr. Fish stopped in the middle of the floor, a flush mounting to her cheeks. "On what grounds?"

"I am not required to justify any requests." She was aware of how obnoxious she sounded, but Saikawa should not be dead and her spouse should not be unconscious.

There was a fraction of a glance back to the room that Dr. Fish had emerged from before she seemed to catch herself. "I must insist otherwise. If you want to pull me off, that is all well and good, but knowing who to assign requires knowing why I am being removed."

On the surface, that was not an unreasonable statement, but in a world in which Dr. Fish was complicit in the death of Saikawa, letting her have any control at all seemed like a dubious proposition. Tesla lifted her chin. Sometimes you let people think you were an asshole because you were and that got things done. "I am accustomed to selecting my own doctors."

Dr. Fish drew in a deep breath, face reddening more. Her mouth opened and then Leigh Osbourne de Monchaux lifted his lovely hands as if to create a barrier between the two of them.

"Now, now, now . . . Shall we all take a moment to contemplate our choices?"

"I haven't exactly been given any choices. My spouse is unconscious. I've been cut off from my law—"

"'m awake." Shal's voice was rough.

Tesla whirled faster than she should, and she didn't care what damage she did. Gimlet stood up and yipped, stumpy tail wagging as if it were a new energy source for the universe. Shal's left eye was only a little open. The right was too swollen to be able to tell if he could see out of it.

"Shal—" Tesla grabbed his hand with her free one. "How do you feel?"

"Who hit me?"

"It sounds like the floor did." She pushed his hair back from his forehead, with her sense of touch reduced to pressure again. She dialed the DBPS back to a point where she could feel the warmth of his skin and the silky tangle of his hair curling between her fingers. Did the back spasms make her breath hitch? Yes. Was it worth it? Also yes. "Shal, they said that you took oxyfeldone."

His eyes were closed again and his breathing was slow and regular.

"Shal?"

"Mm?" He blinked, left eye opening too wide for a moment as he seemed to drag himself back awake. "Where's Gimlet?"

"She's on your—" Before Tesla could finish the sentence, Gimlet had wormed forward to lick Shal's chin, ears slicked down with worry. "Gimlet, be gentle."

Too late. Shal grunted as the little dog put a foot into his ribs.

Tesla snatched Gimlet off the bed, tightening her jaw with her spine, and tucked the Westie under one arm.

"I need the room clear, please." Dr. Fish had a medscan in one hand as Bob stepped to the side to let her into the room. "Mx. Crane, I'll need you to take the dog out so I can check Mx. Steward."

Not only did Tesla not get out of the way, she pivoted to find Leigh Osbourne de Monchaux. "How much clearer do I need to be?"

His slender mustache puckered with his frown. "Under the circumstances, might you let Dr. Fish examine your spouse until she can be relieved by one of her colleagues?"

"Is there a danger in waiting?"

"He has a head injury and overdosed. Yes, there's a danger!" Dr. Fish stepped too close to Tesla. "My question is why don't you want me to examine him? Is there something you don't want him to tell me?"

Tesla inhaled to shout, and a waft of bourbon filled her nostrils. She paused, tilting her head, and leaned in closer to the doctor. Bourbon clung to her skin. The woman's cheeks were too red. "Dr. Fish . . . have you been drinking?"

The woman looked briefly shocked and then furious. "Absolutely not."

Behind Tesla, Shal said, "Is anyone going to tell me what's going on? Why am I here?"

"Dr. Fish took care of George Saikawa last night." Tesla watched the doctor carefully. "So I've asked for someone else to tend to you."

Dr. Fish took a step back, lifting her chin. Her flush deepened. "What are you implying?"

When she'd shadowed her father at work, he'd once taken her aside before stepping into a meeting about a faulty spacecraft. He'd said there were three important things when someone else's lawyer was in the room. Never apologize for anything, or it could be used as an admission of guilt. Never lay all of your cards on the table. Never argue when your own lawyer can do the fighting.

"She smells of bourbon." She smiled thinly and put a hand on Shal's bed, facing Leigh Osbourne de Monchaux. "Would you like me to reiterate that I want a different doctor for my spouse, or would you like Fantine to do that?"

White Lady

1.5 oz gin
.75 oz triple sec
.75 oz lemon juice
Egg white
Lemon peel

Add egg white and lemon juice to shaker. Dry shake for 10 seconds. Add gin, triple sec, and ice. Shake for 12 seconds. Strain into martini glass. Garnish with lemon peel.

Leigh Osbourne de Monchaux had spoken with Fantine, who pulled up the passenger roster and found a doctor who was willing to suddenly be Tesla Crane's personal physician even at one o'clock in the morning. The new doctor was Terran-short and Anglo-Saxon-white, with absurd curls and a flamboyantly bright turquoise confection around his neck that was somewhere between a tie and a cravat.

Leigh Osbourne de Monchaux whirled back into the tiny room. "Mx. Crane! I've been talking to the concierge and have arranged for a Yacht Club Grand Royal Suite for you."

"Excuse me? They told me everything in the Yacht Club was full."

"In the Terran-gravity section, unfortunately, yes. But we have a spot for you in either the Martian or Lunar sections."

Tesla exchanged a look with Shal, which contained within it a conversation about how much bullshit was involved in this sudden about-face. Privately, Tesla was not looking forward to the

Martian level. The gravity was kinder to her back, but the smaller Mars ring had a more pronounced Coriolis effect than the Terran level. She did not enjoy being spin-sick, but extended time in Lunar gravity caused her back to elongate and that was . . . not great. She was also not ceding the ground that Fantine had gained.

"Martian would be acceptable." Tesla turned from her spouse to the lawyer. "I am assuming you understand that it will not reduce the magnitude of the lawsuit we're filing against the cruise line."

He wet his lips and looked down with a little bit of a sigh. "Fantine and I have known each other a long time. I only count my blessings that I am not a trial lawyer."

"She is my favorite."

"I can imagine."

The doctor that Fantine found for them adjusted a cat badge on his lapel. "Well, he's fit enough to leave the sick bay. No drinking for the next week, though. Clear?"

Shal grabbed the bed rail to hoist himself upright with a grimace. "Understood." His other arm wrapped around his chest as if he were trying to stabilize it.

"Is there anything to be done for his ribs?" Tesla lay a hand on Shal's back where his hospital gown sagged open.

"Aside from pain management, I'm afraid it's mostly time, and I can only control that so much." The doctor turned and took a step toward the medicine cabinet on the wall but hesitated, looking at Dr. Fish. "Sorry, have you any nanogen bandages?"

She crossed her arms and glared at him.

"It's just that the electricity generated by the bandages should speed the healing a—"

"I know what nanogen bandages do." She turned to look outside the room, where Leigh Osbourne de Monchaux was fluttering his luxuriously long lashes as if either he was the biggest flirt or he was consulting a hundred different virtual menus. Given the set of his jaw, probably the latter. "Leigh, do you want us to get sued for refusing to offer medical treatment or for failing to prevent further injury by releasing him too soon?"

The ship's lawyer blinked once and fixed a clear gaze on her. "Neither. My colleague has agreed to sign a waiver releasing Mx. Steward to the care of his personal physician."

"No." Dr. Fish snorted. "Even after treating the overdose, there's still oxyfeldone in his system. I will absolutely not consent to releasing him to his 'personal physician.'"

Tesla's lips thinned. "Your consent is not required." She lowered Gimlet to the floor, standing with a straight back, and smoothed the dog's leash as if it were a set of legal papers.

Dr. Fish tapped the communication badge on her chest. "Security, Fish."

"Security Chief Wisor here." His reply was so fast, it was as if he had been either waiting for her or listening to the entire conversation.

"Chief Wisor, I believe that Mx. Steward is a suicide risk and—"

"Oh, come on—"

"—should not be allowed to be unsupervised—"

"My spouse is not—"

"—and certainly not returned to a room with ready access to—"

Gimlet barked at Dr. Fish, voice raised in protest along with Tesla and Shal.

"There's no way that I—"

"Quiet!" Leigh Osbourne de Monchaux's voice cut through the din with shocking volume. The dazzling grace hid a layer of battle-hard iron. He shot Tesla a quelling look that made it clear why Fantine liked him. "Dr. Fish, do I understand you to suggest that Mx. Steward deliberately tried to take his own life?"

"That is correct." Her chin was high and her face flushed with triumph.

"Doctor—" Tesla turned to the physician whom Fantine had hired for them.

He looked pained. "I mean, in my opinion, he's perfectly healthy, but—"

"But you don't have authority on this ship." Dr. Fish's nostrils flared as she cut him off. "If I believe that a passenger is a risk to themselves or others, then that's something the cruise line takes very, very seriously. So yes, my consent *is* required."

From the tinny speaker on her chest, Wisor's voice dripped with arrogant satisfaction. "Suicide is not uncommon with murder suspects. Well, then. It seems that we have no choice but to restrain him in sick bay. For his own safety, of course."

———

Hours spent trying to sleep in a chair by Shal's bed had set Tesla's back into such a state that she'd bypassed the safeties again. He'd shooed her out, and that goddamned "personal physician" had supported him. Even Gimlet had seemed to be on his side, almost tugging Tesla out of the room. By the time they reached Tesla's new cabin, she had acquired a fluttering throng of ship personnel all trying to "make things right."

What would make things right was to be with Shal. Rage was still shaking her veins and rattling in her joints.

Behind her, Leigh Osbourne de Monchaux trailed with empty words. "I will, of course, speak to my supervisors back at the home company, but there is only so much I can do. Having identified a possible suicide risk, Chief Wisor is morally obligated to hold your spouse for evaluation."

With a bitter laugh, Tesla stopped outside the new cabin, nearly overbalancing between the reduced gravity of this centrifugal ring and the fact that she couldn't feel her feet. Gimlet looked up at her with doggy concern. Tesla accepted the hint and took in a breath, imagining golden sunlight flooding her. Facing the lawyer, she feigned calm. "What you are 'morally obligated' to do is many things, but confining my spouse against his will is not on that list. Why don't you ask Fantine about moral obligations?"

Leigh Osbourne de Monchaux's dark skin went ashen, and he fluttered his eyelashes. "I promise you that I have been keeping Fantine absolutely up to date on all of the new developments."

"And yet I am still without a connection to the net. I assume that Fantine spoke to you about that. So what's going to happen now is that I'm going into my cabin. I will make myself a cocktail. When I have finished drinking it, if I do not have access to the net, then when we reach Mars, I will instruct Fantine to add that to the list of grievances." The only concession Tesla had been able to wring out of them on her own was that Shal's personal physician attended him. But the ship still insisted on twenty-four hours of observation. "Good day."

Tesla turned her back on the fluttering horde, feeling the ship whirl about her, and went into her new suite. She almost shut the door out of habit, but caught herself before she did. Behind the curtain of rage, a tiny voice in the back of her skull made a muffled protest that she had no guarantee they wouldn't lock her into her cabin.

She turned the bolt to keep the door from shutting all the way and let it close gently, propped open by a half centimeter. Sighing, she knelt to release Gimlet from her lead. On this level, the floor had a slight but visible bow to it so that the centrifugal forces pulled you "down" wherever you were. On the Terran level, the ring was bigger and the architects could mask the curvature at doorways.

As soon as the Westie was free, she dashed in, bouncing off the floor in gazelle-like leaps to explore the room. The first room. The public sitting room, with the couches and chairs and bar and vaulted ceiling illuminated with a view of the Milky Way. Beyond that were other rooms and a sunken tub and genuine Egyptian cotton sheets, grown in irrigated fields and lifted out of a gravity well for her pleasure. Tesla let Gimlet snuffle all the things, and slipped her shoes off, sinking her toes into the dense cream carpet. Pressure, not texture. Closing her eyes, she sighed and looked at the settings on her DBPS.

She did not want to dial it down into standard performance range. Groaning with dread, Tesla clicked the DBPS down a notch. A dull ache, like a day-old bruise, seemed to tinge the room with purple and green. That matched her general state of being. It was six a.m. and her brain felt bruised with fatigue.

A message icon on the wall behind the bar lit, chiming softly. Simultaneously, the HUD in her visual field flashed.

::Connecting::

Snorting, Tesla grabbed the Lunacy Botanical Gin that they'd picked up on the Moon and poured two ounces into the cocktail pitcher. She still wouldn't be connected if her demands hadn't been attached to expensive threats. Goddammit all to hell. Truly, she should call Fantine before she finished making the cocktail but there was an argument to be made for listening to the messages first just in case they contained anything important. Fortunately, with a three-minute delay on calls—no, wait.

Traveling under constant thrust meant that in the nearly twenty-four hours since their last call, the round-trip delay was now about six minutes. Great. Well, that meant she could call Fantine, make a cocktail, *and* listen to messages. Wetting her lips, Tesla activated the speed dial for Fantine.

"*Lindgren,* play messages."

::New Message:: Fantine's face appeared on the wallscreen, peering over a length of vivid red crocheted fabric. "We got cut off. Call me back as soon as you reconnect and I'll finish replacing that buffoon's nether region with the contents of my recycler."

In the category of annoying and helpful, despite Shal's insistence that they wait until he could pack his own stuff, the crew had moved their belongings for them. Now the cruise line was being responsive when she didn't want them to be. That's what came from their sudden realization that they hadn't just whaled on a random passenger but Tesla Crane's brand-new spouse.

At least they appeared to have been delightfully careful about putting everything in exactly the same configuration as it had been downstairs. The Dolin Blanc vermouth was on ice, which they'd only had to do in the junior suite because the mini-fridge was too small for multiple bottles.

::New Message:: "It's been an hour. Still waiting. If this isn't sunspot activity or some technology trumpery like that, I am walloping someone with a haddock."

Tesla added an ounce of vermouth.

::New Message:: The crochet was abandoned, pushed to the side of the desk in a pool of spilled-blood yarn, and Fantine had a stack of actual paper and her reading glasses on. "Jesus, Mary, and Joseph! Fart-knocking mailbox agai—"

::New Message:: In the image on the wallscreen, the crocheted fabric was longer. "The hell— And now I have to add that to my list at confession. Are you trying to get me in trouble with my priest? I'm starting to worry, and that is never a good place for me to be. Three hours and no contact? According to the ship, the system is just fine, so why the h—*blazes,* can't I raise either of you? Switchboard says that you have messages set to go straight to voicemail. Seriously? Just call me when you finish having sex."

"If only . . ." Tesla added a dash of orange bitters to the shaker as the image changed again.

::New Message:: The crochet now occupied a swath of the table, as if Fantine had bathed it in blood. "If that beetle-headed walking bladder is keeping me from talking to you, he is already dead, stabbed, and run through the ear with a blunt butt shaft. And if you are just not calling me back, I am raising your father from the grave and he will be very, very disappointed in you. Call. Me."

She dropped ice into the pitcher.

::New Message:: The entire message had Fantine pacing and cursing for the forty seconds it took to stir the martini. It was impressive. Even to Tesla, who had known her for decades. And she was *definitely* going to be in trouble with her priest.

::New Message:: Fantine sat hunched forward at her desk. "Listen, if the situation is that you're getting these, but that milk-livered

dungbox of a security chief is keeping you from dialing out, go to Leigh Osbourne de Monchaux in Legal. Don't trust the vain coxcomb any further than the nearest airlock, but he at least knows what happens if you're kept away from your lawyer. Also, I'm running out of yarn, and there's a lot of yardage in a circulatory system." The shark teeth vanished for a moment and Fantine leaned toward the camera. "Seriously. I'm worried."

In her years of working with Fantine, Tesla had seen that expression of honest concern exactly three times: When she was nine and accidentally stabbed herself with a soldering iron. When Fantine had to read her father's will to her. And when she woke up in the hospital after the Accident and Fantine had been the only one willing to tell her that everyone else who had been in the PAMU lab with her was dead. Grabbing a coupe with one hand, Tesla half listened to the next message.

::New Message:: "Right. I just flat-out called Leigh and I'm billing it to you and we're including that in the expenses when we sue their festering nethers. Here's the deal—he says that my messages are all going to your stateroom and there's no block on your stateroom's access to the net. I've got you your fancy-pants doctor, and there's not even a thank-you? Leigh swears you aren't being held somewhere else, so . . . where does that leave us? I've got to—"

"TESLA MACKINSEY CRANE, DO YOU HAVE ANY IDEA HOW WORRIED I'VE BEEN?! And are you making a goddamned cocktail when I've been worrying my ass so far off I could sell it as a resurfacing technique for the stupidly wealthy?"

Tesla looked up at the screen. Fantine was on her feet, leaning over the desk, with a crochet hook clenched in her hand like a weapon. Lifting her glass, Tesla tried for jaunty ease. "Sorry, dearest, but these dreadful people did, in fact, keep us offline because of Shal's supposed involvement."

Six minutes behind, Fantine collapsed back into her chair. "Okay, you know the drill, so talk while I talk. I did some digging while I was waiting for you. Here are some interesting things I learned. First—Haldan Kuznetsova is not going to Mars for vacation. He's relocating—"

"It's good to see you too." Tesla saluted the screen with her glass. "There's a lot. They're holding Shal on a suicide watch, because they say that he tried to OD on oxyfeldone, which I'll point out neither of us have a prescription for. At least . . . I don't."

"Second. George Saikawa liquidated all of her assets before boarding the ship."

"Interesting about Saikawa. I found out that a server may have had a grudge against her." Tesla took a sip of her martini and spat it out, gasping. "Oh shit."

Gimlet came running. With one bare foot, Tesla warded her off from sniffing the spray.

"She reinvested in Martian companies, most of which I'm guessing are shell companies for Kuznetsova."

"Fantine, we have a problem." Tesla spun to grab the bottle of Lunacy Gin, and the combination of her back flaring and the Coriolis effect almost tipped her onto her ass. Lightning crackled along her spine, and she had to brace herself on the counter while the after flash faded. Slowly, she straightened and sniffed the bottle. The gin's nose was completely wrong. "Fantine. This isn't our gin."

Choke Artist

2 tsp (approximate) orange bitters

1 oz Tequila Anejo

1 oz Cynar

.5 oz dry sherry

1 orange peel

Rinse a coupe glass with orange bitters. Stir remaining ingredients over ice for 40 seconds, strain into glass, and garnish with orange peel.

Standing in front of the suite's matter printer, Tesla shifted from one foot to the next. The irony that the people least likely to eat printed food were also in the only cabin type with a printer did not escape her. But the cruise line couldn't trust the masses not to overdo it, of course. Tesla sighed. She held a multi-tool in one sweating palm. She'd had to lock Gimlet in the bedroom, because the small dog kept doing "incoming panic attack" alerts. But Tesla was fine.

She glanced at Fantine. "As soon as we're done, I'll send a message to Leigh Osbourne de Monchaux asking for a list of the people who had access to our cabin. Oh, speaking of—can you lean on them to unlock my account? I can't tip people, and it's rude."

The engineering part of her brain had woken up. The rest of her was more than a little sleep-deprived, which did not help the part of her brain that was sluggish and seven years out of date. She knew, in theory, that a matter printer had to also have a scanner in order to work. You could, again in theory, rig it to report about its detailed scan of an item placed into the scanner's bed even if it wasn't technically supposed to do that.

"Yes, I'll upload the full passenger manifest to you." Fantine looked like she was ready to come through the camera. "I would wonder why they haven't asked you to identify the passenger Saikawa was arguing with, but these eight-bit bozos are going to settle on Shal and not look any further. All right. What I need from you is a list of names of people who had access to your cabin as well as preserving that bottle. And you're sure it's not your gin?"

Tesla smirked at the out-of-sync conversation and twirled the multi-tool in her fingers. "I think it's been swapped to a well gin. But it might also taste wrong because of the drugs. Will you keep recording while I work on this? I'm pretty sure they're watching, and I want a counter record stored off the ship." She could do this modification. There was no danger here. No mistake that she could possibly make that would kill anyone. Besides her. But that didn't count. Her heart seemed to have wrapped around her lungs, squeezing the breath out with each beat. Swallowing, she pulled a chair up in front of the printer and sat.

"Now, let's talk about your physical safety, because I am not even remotely concerned about your legal safety. We are going to crush these lack-linen ash cans in a lawsuit that will compress the clodpolls into enough diamonds to make a complete set of crown jewels, and that's just where we're starting. I want you to stay in your cabin for the rest of the cruise—you and your 'It's my honeymoon I want to be alone'—did I or did I not tell you that this was a terrible idea?"

"You did . . . But my problem wasn't that someone recognized me. Also, did you just try to ground me?" Gritting her teeth, Tesla slapped the wireless power switch to disconnect the machine from its air-charge. None of this was complicated. "I want Shal with me. I do not trust them with him. Hey, since you got your hands on the manifest to get us that doctor, can you see if there are any roboticists? It's been occurring to me that it wouldn't necessarily have to be someone with direct access to the room."

"And there's your promise to ask Leigh . . ." Fantine made a note, frowning. "Actually, I'll also ask him about the people who had access. He'll probably give us the same copy-paste list, but I'm going to CC a Solar System Commerce Agency investigator that I know and see how that shifts his response. What do you mean you can't tip— Why in the name of Saint Jerome's dirty thongs is your account locked? I'll take care of it. Speaking of which . . . did you get far enough in listening to my messages to hear that I'd invoked power of attorney and filed a formal complaint on your behalf?"

"Missed that." She'd all but forgotten that Fantine could pull that trick if she wasn't able to reach Tesla for too long. "What'd they say?"

Gripping the multi-tool, she knew that she was stalling. Swallowing the bitter acid that rose in the back of her throat, Tesla pried the cover off the matter printer.

"Last on the agenda I had plenty of time to draw up while waiting for those rank idle-heads to stop obstructing our communication is that I do not, repeat, *do not* want you or Shal to investigate this on your own. And I know it's going to be a temptation for both of you, but you'll muddy things and I do not need that particular brand of carrion."

"Then you're going to love what I'm doing when it reaches you." She peered into the innards and grimaced. She used to be able to understand how something was built just by looking at it. Oh, sure, she still recognized parts, like that was a Serum 509v processor, which they also used at Crane Industries. But there was a difference between approving parts in a meeting and getting your hands dirty. "*Lindgren*, show me the schematics for a . . . MatterMaster series 630?"

"Keep recording while you work on what?" Fantine glared at the screen and then at her sanguine pool of crochet. "Look, I only brought enough yarn for the back of this dress to the office with me yesterday because I was not planning on spending the night, nor was I anticipating that bunch of mammering lobsters being quite this incompetent and my standards were not high to begin with."

"Ha! So, 'mammering' *is* one of yours. What does it mean?"

On a different wall, the schematics faded in with layers enabled and ready to be peeled virtually back. This made more sense and helped her map the physical components with her conceptual understanding. It had been seven years since she'd last designed something. She kept her knowledge active enough to be able to do final approvals, but . . . that wasn't the same.

"And four days of your fancy disguise working does not make traveling without bodyguards a good idea. It's a twelve-day transit. A ship that failed four days into a twelve-day transit would be a knicker-staining disaster. Catherine's wheel, a ninety-nine-percent success still means you crash on la—" She cut off, blanching. "Sorry. I wasn't thinking."

Tesla wouldn't have linked the Accident with that analogy, but technically, yes, a laboratory that deorbited was a crash landing.

Fantine cleared her throat. "Point being, you're right that getting Shal out and with you is top priority. Then I want the two of you to accept house arrest and yes, I know, but I think it's safer. Wait—roboticist? What part of 'do not try to solve this on your own' are you unclear about?"

Tesla grimaced, flicking through layers looking for the printing feedback scanner. She used to be good at this.

"What'd they say . . . Bartholomew's bloody skin, I've lost track of the conversation. Ask me again, but with more details this ti— And what the blazes are you working on?" Fantine leaned toward the screen, making a motion as if she were enlarging the image on her end. "I would tell you to try not to break anything, but trashing your stateroom is at least trouble that you can just buy your way out of and— Oh, flaming kidney stones. MatterMaster. Tesla, that's one of Kuznetsova's companies. Hang on . . ."

Flexing her fingers, Tesla stared at the MatterMaster. Did it make a difference if the company was owned by Kuznetsova? She owned a lot of companies but was involved with the daily workings of very few.

"Bash my pox-brained head in with tablets and stab me with blunt styluses . . ." Fantine leaned forward and rested her head on her hands. "The Kuznetsova shell companies that Saikawa invested in before leaving the Moon . . . I should have cross-referenced them. MatterMaster is part of Kuznetsova's Universal Mechanics, which also owns Imperial System Ships, which owns the *Lindgren*."

Ad Lib

2.5 oz sparkling water

1 oz simple syrup

1 oz lemon juice

4 sprigs cilantro

Muddle cilantro in shaker. Add lemon juice and simple syrup. Shake. Strain into coupe. Top with chilled sparkling water.

The matter printer's calibration mode was engaged to activate scanning functionality. Tesla had aligned the hemisoidal scanners. She'd made a makeshift cable to tap into the programming port with her handheld to update the firmware. She'd put her wedding ring in as the calibration object. She'd tweaked every sensor head she could find.

All she had to do was hit Start.

Sweat coated her palms and prickles clogged her throat. The muscles that ran along her spine to the base of her skull were tight and crackled as she turned her head.

Hit Start. That's all she had to do.

She'd had to keep the DBPS fairly low so she had good sensation in her hands while she worked. The hunched posture from wiring in less-than-perfect conditions had done her back no favors.

She just needed to hit Start.

Fantine was going to see all of this in about six minutes, and she'd have a damn good guess about why Tesla was delaying. Maybe she shouldn't have locked Gimlet in the other room. Scrubbing her hands on her thighs, Tesla looked at the ceiling. "*Lindgren*, release the hound."

The electronic lock on the bedroom door unlatched and Gimlet bounded out. She made an arcing series of leaps to Tesla and landed with a whine at her feet. Gimlet booped her calf with her snout. Bright eyes stared up, and the dog leaned forward to press her head against Tesla's leg.

Wetting her lips, Tesla raised her hand and put it back into her lap.

Gimlet put her foot on Tesla's and leaned against her harder. Her little head made a spot of grounding warmth against Tesla's shin. Tesla took a slow breath, trying for calm. On the screen, Fantine frowned at her crochet and occasionally looked up to watch Tesla.

She swallowed again, looking at Gimlet. "I think this is the first thing I've even modded since the Accident."

Whining, Gimlet snuggled closer, trying to do her job and keep Tesla centered.

"Right . . ." She put one hand on the little dog's head and with the other pushed the Start button.

The machine whirred. No sparks. No smoke. It just did what it was supposed to do, sending a pair of arms sweeping down and around the calibration object. When the arms stopped moving, her handheld pinged and lit up.

She read the output and nearly put her head down on the table to weep with relief. It had worked exactly as designed. Some part of her had fully expected it to explode, even though there was nothing in it that was explosive.

The room was too warm. Tesla wiped her palms on her legs and swapped her wedding ring for the gin. "Show me what you got . . ."

On the screen, Fantine spoke from the past. "Hey . . . you're all right. If you need me to yell at you, let me know, but you're all right."

"I know." She slid the ring on, feeling Shal's presence with its weight, and started the machine.

"Hacking a matter printer is about as far from the Accident—"

Tesla got off her chair too fast and the increased Coriolis effect of the smaller Martian level made her stagger for a moment. Wincing, she caught herself on the counter and pushed off to walk into the other room, leaving Fantine talking behind her. Gimlet followed at a trot. She stared up at Tesla as if watching her were the most important job in the universe. Tesla walked into the bathroom and got a glass of water. She washed her face. She leaned on the sink, waiting to vomit.

In the other room, her handheld pinged.

Tesla gripped the edge of the sink for a moment longer and then walked back into the main room. At her side, Gimlet hurried along with the quick, purposeful stride of a dog that was all business.

". . . probably bringing up a lot of triggers and I've got the manifest so I can find a shrink or something, if you need someone to talk to—Oh. Hey. Good job on getting that thing to work. Where—where are you going?"

"I was washing my face." Tesla looked down at the readout and had an absurd sense of triumph. "The profile matches Beefeater Gin, which is what the ship uses for basic well cocktails. Perfectly sound gin, but nothing like Lunacy. Shal is going to be so pissed."

═══════

Tesla lay on her side on the massive Martian king bed and let her acubot crawl over her. At her feet, Gimlet made a warm bundle, sighing with happy contentment as she slept. Tesla had the DBPS dialed all the way down so she could track what the acubot was doing. The cramping striations girdling her torso made her clench her teeth. She opened her mouth, wiggling her jaw to try to relax it. Envisioning golden sunlight flowing through her body, Tesla breathed slowly through the pain.

This was temporary. This would be worth it. The acubot was a compact octopoid marvel that used the resiliency of eight small minds to guide each needled limb independently while coordinating a treatment plan with a central core.

As the light prick of the needles found homes, Tesla flexed her fingers against the soft cotton sheet, breathing through the pain while she waited for the acupuncture effects to kick in. Most days, acubot time was a sanctioned opportunity for a nap.

This morning, the images from the hallway kept running through her head. Sighing, Tesla opened the passenger manifest that Fantine had liberated and splashed photos of people from Earth, LEO platforms, Mars, LMO platforms, and Venusian cloud cities across her HUD.

Shal should be doing this. He always said that most murder victims were killed by someone they knew. So who knew Saikawa? Haldan Kuznetsova, clearly. The magician, Nile Silver. The bald passenger.

Haldan had said that he didn't know anyone else on the cruise, but George appeared to have at least met other people. She tabbed through the manifest to George Saikawa's entry.

Apparently, Saikawa was staying in the Grand Royal Suites in the cabin next to her old one. And interestingly . . . George had a group code, which meant she was traveling with a larger group, but Haldan did not. Interesting, but Tesla didn't know what it meant.

"Data is only as good as the questions you ask . . ." She stared at the group code. "All right, Gimlet. Who else is in this group, because that's a group that knows George."

Tesla set up a search on the group code attached to George's account, which returned seven other passengers.

- Mahjabin Burke-Gafney (she/her)
- Annie Smith (she/her)
- Jalna Smith (she/her)
- Thersilochus Pilger (they/them)
- Barry Fagin (he/him)
- Michele Berdinis (she/her)
- Deston Koeben (ze/zir)

A total of eight people. The Grand Royal Suites on the Terran level had eight cabins, but she and Shal had one of those. She cross-referenced the group of individuals with the cabins, and of that list only George, Annie Smith, and Jalna Smith were staying in the Grand Royal Suites.

Their cabin number was on the other side of Kuznetsova's from Tesla's.

She opened Annie Smith's file and recognized her picture. She was the curvy older passenger with the low-rise chartreuse pants who had gone before Tesla at karaoke. She was an older white woman, and her face was overly smooth in the way of someone who indulged in excessive microaugma collegoidal skin treatments.

She'd also been in the hall later that night after George Saikawa had been murdered.

Tesla dismissed the acubot so she could get out of bed. As the needles withdrew from her skin, feeling like little taps, she read what information she could from the manifest.

Annie Smith's partner, Jalna, was thin and had a map of wrinkles lining dark skin beneath a cap of hair dyed a vivid sunset pink. Tesla would have remembered seeing her near Saikawa the night before last. She might have been in the karaoke bar but had definitely not been in the hall.

Had they been who was supposed to get the misdelivered steak dinner?

Tesla reactivated the DBPS and carefully pushed herself up. Gimlet raised her head, watching the acubot as it stowed itself back in its carrier. It was always tempting to spring up when she felt better, but that was a good way to make sure that feeling better didn't last. Hauling on a dark-green silk tank and a pair of flowing brown cotton trousers, she headed to the suite's writing desk with Gimlet trotting along beside her.

She settled in the office chair and pulled out a sheet of stupidly expensive stationery. The nib of her fountain pen glided across the paper as she wrote down Annie's and Jalna's names.

It was old school. Very old school. Archaically old school, which is why Tesla was writing on actual paper. Tesla's grandma had always said that the only thing that someone couldn't hack into was a piece of paper. Granted, they could steal it, but only if it was somewhere they could get to.

And then they had to be able to read it, which is why she was writing in cursive.

It didn't count as a murder investigation if she just made lists, right?

- Body in recycler
- George Saikawa in hall

She tapped her pen on the page. There was no telling who had dumped the body, but she had seen people in the hallway the night George Saikawa died.

- Dr. Fish
- Candy, medic
- Annie Smith, passenger

And then there were the people whom George seemed to know:

- Haldan Kuznetsova
- Nile Silver, magician
- bald passenger
- Immanuel Rudawski, server?

Other people of interest:

- Josie, bartender
- Yuki, server who also matched Shal's description

Of those, the two she hadn't talked to who seemed easiest to find were the Smiths. She tapped her nails against the desk and looked down at Gimlet. "Going to visit Annie and Jalna Smith on my own would be desperately stupid, wouldn't it?"

Gimlet cocked her head to the side.

"You're right. They aren't letting your daddy out anytime soon."

Gimlet's head cocked the other direction.

"Valid point. If I'm going to visit them, I should let someone know where I'm going. Any suggestions?"

The little dog stood, tail wagging, and opened her mouth to pant happily up at Tesla. She bounced off her front legs, her signal for wanting to go for a walk.

"Perfect! Cleverest dog." Tesla capped her fountain pen and picked up the ship phone that sat on the desk in Old Planet splendor. She called Shal's room in sick bay.

"This is Bob."

"Bob! What a delight." She folded the paper in half and stuck it in her pocket. "Are you guarding my spouse to keep him safe from the actual murderer who is still at large?"

"Chief Wisor asked me to stay here."

"Wooooooonderful." She pushed herself out of the chair and walked over to fetch Gimlet's gear. "May I speak to Shal?"

"No."

Tesla stopped in the middle of the floor. "No? Just, no? Come now, surely we can find a solution together."

"You can talk to Chief Wisor."

Even when he wasn't in person, Bob was a wall of annoying. Tesla wrinkled her nose and got the harness and vest. "All right . . . So, if he told you that I'm not supposed to talk to Shal at all, I'll take that up with him. But if he just said that Shal isn't supposed to have any unsupervised conversations, can you put me on speaker? That way you can hear everything and—"

In the background, she could just make out Shal's voice. The noise-suppression software muted him to an indistinguishable baritone, but she recognized the rise and fall of his voice. Bob sighed and the room tone on the line changed.

"—time when Fantine sued someone for wearing their own pants and—"

"Shal?"

"Hey, doll. Everything okay?"

"Yes." She knelt with the harness, pinning the phone between ear and shoulder. Presented with her walking accouterments, Gimlet stuck her head through the harness, tail wagging ferociously. "I'm taking Gimlet for a walk. I thought we'd go to the Terran-level Grand Royal Suites and then I'd bring her down to you."

"The Grand Royal, huh? Not the animal-relief area?" His tone almost visibly sharpened with interest.

"Well, Auberi is such a favorite of hers." She tapped her nails on the receiver of the phone, hoping he'd recognize the Morse code she was using to tell him Annie's cabin number. Not that he would know why she was telling him that, but she just kept repeating the numbers over and over.

"Okay . . . okay. Better get going. Bring her by when you're done, all right? I miss my two best girls."

"Sure thing." She stopped tapping and slipped Gimlet's red service vest on. The little dog settled, becoming all business. Tesla kept her voice light. "Send out the search parties if we're not there in time for dinner."

He laughed. "Dinner? I'll hope to see you by lunch."

"It's a deal." Tesla grabbed the back of a chair and used it to get herself up off the ground. "Thanks for your help, Bob!"

———

Being back on Terran level made Tesla's balance better, but she felt every footfall in her bones. Keeping her gaze on Gimlet, she walked past Auberi's desk at the Yacht Club, trying to look as if she were heading to places she was fully sanctioned to be. Gimlet helped by moving with the businesslike intention of a small dog on a walk. Her little legs trotted with swift purpose across the floor.

"Ah, good morning." Auberi beckoned her to the desk.

Darn it. "Hi, Auberi."

"I'm afraid your former cabin is still off-limits."

"It's fine. We're just going for a little walk as a sort of Gimlet release." Tesla dropped Gimlet's lead. The Westie heard the command 'Gimlet, release' and took off, tail wagging as she headed into the corridor that led to Tesla's old cabin, which was conveniently two doors down from Annie and Jalna's. "Oh, bother! I'd better get her."

Hurrying before Auberi could come up with another reason to stop her, Tesla followed Gimlet. The Golden Promenade with its sparkling floor jogged to obscure the curve of the ship and she walked past the giant painting of a woman wearing a crystal-blue ball gown in a bathtub filled with trees. Cruise ship art was so, so odd.

Glancing over her shoulder to make sure Auberi wasn't in sight, Tesla gave a formal command. "Gimlet, Gimlet, come."

She sniffed one more door frame and then trotted back, trailing her lead. Tesla steadied herself on the wall as she bent to pick it up. The Coriolis effect was so much more manageable on the Terran level. Right. Now to visit the Smiths' cabin.

Her old cabin had a Do Not Disturb sign on it, which must be the cruise-ship version of yellow caution tape. She braced herself for Haldan Kuznetsova to emerge from his cabin, but the door stayed mercifully shut. Next to it, the Smiths' cabin had a magnetic message board stuck to it with messages written in awkward print.

Happy Anniversary, Love Birds!
Don't forget the group meditation session tonight!

She looked up and down the corridor, taking note of things that hadn't seemed important before someone was murdered.

There were eight cabins in this section of the ship, and all of the doors were on the right-hand side of the corridor, except for a service door midway down. That meant the jog in the hallway was also intended to create more space for the cabins by allowing them to be twice the depth of the junior suites.

Annie and Jalna's door was directly across from the service entrance.

Wetting her lips, Tesla knocked. Gimlet sniffed the door frame. They waited. She knocked again.

Tesla considered leaving a message on the magnetic board, but what would she say? *Hey, want to talk about murder?!?!*

The service door opened and their old stateroom attendant pushed a room-service cart into the hall. Jenny was tiny and broad-shouldered, with enormous gray eyes, and she would absolutely recognize Tesla even if Auberi didn't report that she was here.

"Mx. Zuraw!" Jenny froze in the middle of the hall, shifting to keep the cart between her and Tesla. "I thought they'd moved you to a different part of the ship."

"They did. Gimlet just pulled on her lead and thought this was still home. It's good to see you." It did not look like the feeling was mutual. Was that because Jenny had been told that Shal was the murderer or because she was in cahoots with whoever was? Tesla needed to shift the mood. She glanced down at Gimlet, who was sitting calmly at her feet watching the conversation. Maybe she should let the little dog work her distracting magic. Tesla crouched and snapped the quick release on Gimlet's vest. "Gimlet, go say hi."

Melting a little, Jenny knelt at the end of the cart and hesitated. "Oh—oh, are you sure?"

"Absolutely. She likes you."

Jenny let Gimlet give her kisses all over her face. "Poor little girl. This must be so confusing for you."

"For all of us."

Shal had thought that the murderer might have been someone

on staff. Jenny had access to their room but didn't match Shal's description of the person he chased. She also wore a comm badge. Theoretically the ship would know where she was at all times, and any questions Tesla asked would potentially be heard by someone else on the ship.

How did you ask someone if they took a murder weapon out of your room? "I hope you haven't had any trouble because of"— Tesla waved her hand in the air to encompass—"everything."

Jenny scratched Gimlet's ears. "What—what do you mean?"

"Well. I mean, with the murder, there must be added security. That seems like it would make it harder for you."

"It's not—I should get back to work." Jenny stood, brushing the Gimlet fur off her dark-blue trousers.

"Of course." It sounded like there wasn't additional security, or at least nothing around these rooms. If she could give tips, she might try to bribe Jenny, although that would probably make it even more obvious that Tesla was snooping. "Well, I'd better let you get back to work."

Jenny smiled at her and went back to the cart.

Gritting her teeth, Tesla snapped the vest back on and walked Gimlet to the lounge.

The concierge was occupied with another passenger and merely nodded, smiling at Gimlet. The Smiths had to come back eventually. The lounge was a pleasant-enough place, and Tesla had more passenger manifests to review. She walked Gimlet over to one of the café tables tucked into a corner behind a ficus, just in case Kuznetsova came through, and settled in to wait.

Tesla checked her HUD. She had another two hours before "lunch" time could reasonably be said to have passed and Shal would worry. Officially worry.

Frisky Business

5 blackberries
3 slices jalapeño
3 wheels cucumber
1 oz lime juice
1 tbsp honey syrup
2 tsp Angostura bitters
4 oz soda water

Muddle blackberries, jalapeño, and 2 cucumber wheels in cocktail shaker. Add lime juice, honey syrup, bitters. Dry shake to combine and strain into rocks glass over a single large cube. Top with soda water. Garnish with remaining cucumber wheel.

She was nearly out of time and in danger of falling asleep at the table. Tesla had been trying to find the bald passenger in the manifest and had to keep backing up as her attention flagged. There were an astounding number of bald white people, and they honestly all looked alike.

The Yacht Club lobby doors opened and her targets finally arrived. The older couple made a study in contrasts. Jalna was thin and Lunar tall, but moved as if completely comfortable in the near one-g of this section. Annie was rounded and Earth short, wearing gold lamé pants around generous hips in a style from thirty years ago.

Tesla had had a long time to think about her approach. She had one sure weapon in her arsenal, and that weapon was now sans vest. Tesla stood as casually as she could. Quietly, she said, "Gimlet, release. Gimlet, go say hi."

Reliably, the little dog made a beeline for the new people who might, if the world were just and proper, have treats and be her new best friends. She was a dog, not a robot, and she was a dog who thought she was off-duty. Gimlet bounded up to them, tail wagging so hard her entire back end twisted from side to side. With her ears perked up and pointed toward the pair, she was so eagerly cute that she might as well have been a plush toy.

"*Oh! Oh! Tu es magnifique.*" Jalna dropped to kneel, and Gimlet responded by standing on her hind legs. The tall woman's voice was elegantly Lunar French with an unexpectedly low timbre. "*Ton parent était-æl un voleur? Parce qu'æl a volé les étoiles du ciel pour les mettre dans tes yeux.*"

"I hope she's not bothering you!" Tesla hurried after her dog, smiling at the other passengers. Her pulse was thrumming faster as she joined them. Annie, the smaller, curvy passenger, had definitely been standing in the group around George Saikawa in the hall that night.

"Not at all. She's just the cutest thing." Annie's voice had a decidedly Midwestern American accent. "Designer?"

"A Westie. It's an old breed." Tesla reached for Gimlet's lead, trying to act as if she had only just recognized the woman. "You were . . . you were at karaoke night before last? And then . . . after."

"Oh! Yes. Wasn't that just terrible? Poor Jalna missed all of the . . . well." She offered her companion a hand as the tall woman rose to her feet. "And how are you holding up? I don't mean to pry, but I couldn't help overhearing—well, I don't think any of us could the way Mx. Kuznetsova was shouting, poor thing. Are you all right?"

"Mm." It was as noncommittal a noise as Tesla could make. "You're in the suites too?"

"Yes." Jalna smiled down at her companion. "My spouse and

I . . . As it is our twenty-fifth wedding anniversary, we indulge a little."

"Just a little!" The curvy woman patted Jalna's arm. "The yoga is very spiritual!"

"As you say, Annie." Jalna planted a kiss on top of her head.

"Yoga, hm?" Tesla fell into step beside Jalna and Annie as they headed toward the godawful Golden Promenade, with Gimlet leading the way. "What style do you favor?"

"Anusara-revival." Annie winked at her. "Don't let this old body fool you; I can still put my feet behind my head."

Jalna tucked her hand into her spouse's arm. "Ask her what she used to do."

"Um . . ." Tesla followed them across the concierge reception area as if she were supposed to be going down the hall again, relying on her dog and her innate sense of privilege to handle the rest. "What did you used to do?"

"A contortionist!" Annie grinned. "I was a back-bender, don't you know. I couldn't fit into a box now, mind you, but—"

"Mx. Crane?" Auberi called from the desk. "Your spouse—"

She abandoned the two women and made a direct line for the desk. "Is he all right?"

"Yes, yes!" They slid a piece of paper across the desk. "I have a message that he was hoping you would join him for lunch."

"Wonderful. Yes. We had plans. Yes." Out of the corner of her eye, she watched the two women vanish down the corridor. Tesla had no reason to chase after them. Dammit. She had other questions she'd wanted to ask. She wet her lips. "Jalna and Annie were just telling me about a yoga class they're taking. Do you know when it is? I desperately need to center myself after everything."

"Ah, yes . . ." Auberi opened their screen and toggled through. "Here we are—A Yoga Tour of the Solar System with Mahjabin Burke-Gafney is holding sessions in the yoga studio on the Lunar level and—oh. I'm so sorry. My mistake. It is a private group and closed to the public."

"Understood." She swallowed. Shal had said that the person he chased was comfortable moving in lunar gravity. "Well . . . I guess I better not keep my spouse waiting."

━━━━━

Tesla carried a greasy vegetarian pizza into sick bay, smiling as she entered the tiny lobby. The wall of Bob sat outside Shal's door with it propped open. He was sitting forward with his elbows on his knees and almost smiling. "No kidding," he said.

From inside the room, Shal said, "I kid you not. They had been injecting heroin into the horse's knees."

"But why didn't—oh. Your spouse is here." Bob sat back and became a lump of leaden muscle again.

Tesla paused by him and offered the tray on which the pizza resided. If she couldn't bribe with money, she would bribe with food. "I brought pizza to share."

Looking down at it, Bob sighed. "I can't eat it."

"Oh, I'm sure the chief can't object to your eating pizza. That's why I got a whole one, from the pizzeria, so it was already made, and you can take first pick if you're worried about us poisoning you."

"I have celiac."

"Oh." She pulled the tray back and felt suddenly awkward, even though this guy had beaten her spouse. "I'm sorry. I would have . . . Darn it. They had gluten-free crusts."

He shrugged. "It's okay."

"Next time." Not that there would be a next time, if she had any say over it. At her feet, Gimlet whined as if she would be more than happy to eat Bob's pizza.

"Put the tray down." Bob stood, nearly filling the small space.

Exasperated, Tesla glared at him. "Oh, come on. I'm allowed to have lunch with my spouse. What am I going to do with a piece of pizza?"

"You could have a knife hidden under there. Or drugs. Or a garotte." He held his hands out for the tray.

"Now you have an imagination?"

"Tesla." Shal shaped her name into a plea to be a trifle less insulting. "He's doing his job."

"I know." That was what she objected to. She shoved the tray at Bob. "Fine. Go ahead. I'll just go in and—"

"I have to frisk you too." He took the tray gently and set it on the nearest chair.

Tesla's skin heated as frustrated fury sizzled along her nerve endings. She clenched her jaw and her fists, holding back all the shouting she wanted to do. This wasn't surprising. Using a fork, Bob gingerly lifted the edges of the pizza, peering under it, though whether that care was due to the gluten or out of consideration for their lunch was hard to say.

Shal called, "How's it looking, Bob?"

"Good." He sounded mournful, which was more emotional than anything else she'd heard from him. "It has roasted garlic on it."

"I am absolutely making a note that you like roasted garlic." Tesla smiled at him and held out her arms, dropping Gimlet's lead. "My turn?"

Gimlet sprang toward the door of Shal's room. Bob dropped the pizza-prodding fork and stomped on her leash. Gimlet jerked to a halt, looking back with an expression of such offended dignity that Bob actually apologized.

"Sorry." He crouched, patting the dog with hands as big as her head. "I have to frisk everyone."

"The dog. Seriously? Do you think she's packing a weap—"

"What's this?" He pulled a piece of absurdly expensive stationery out of Gimlet's vest.

Tesla's throat burned with tension. She reached for the list of suspects she'd written in the cabin. "That's private."

Slowly rising, Bob pulled it away and unfolded the note. He scowled at it. "What language is this?"

"Sanskrit." Thank God for cursive. Tesla held her hand out. "Give it to me."

"Can't." He took his foot off Gimlet's lead. "The chief wants to see anything I find."

The Westie huffed at him and trotted back to sit at Tesla's feet. She looked up at Tesla with deep concern in her big black eyes. Taking a slow breath, Tesla waited for her body to calm down a little for the sake of her dog. Gimlet leaned her head against Tesla's leg and let out an echoing sigh.

Bob gestured for Tesla to raise her arms. She was shaking with rage and embarrassment at getting caught trying to smuggle a note to Shal. She'd felt so clever, guessing that Bob would search her. She waited while he went through an impersonal and businesslike pat-down.

"I must say, your massage technique is splendid." Tesla lowered her arms when he finished. "They should transfer you to the spa."

"You can go in now." He stepped back, pushing the door open a little farther, which she tried to read as some form of courtesy instead of just making sure that he would have a clearer view of the room.

"Thank you." Tesla took a step toward the room.

"Wait." Bob turned and held out the tray. "Your pizza."

"Perfect." She took the tray, screaming inside her smile. This was fine. She and Shal would make out a little, and she'd tell him what she could. "You're a gem."

In the room, Shal was sitting up. He had stubble on his cheeks, but his color was better. He studied her for a moment before grinning as if he'd never been worried. "Tesla, baby." He gestured to the foot of the bed. "You remember the doctor, don't you?"

The damned passenger Fantine had found sat in a chair that had been hidden by the door. His ridiculous bow tie drooped a little when she turned to him, and she was fairly certain it was the least convincing smile she'd ever delivered. "Of course. Delighted."

And if she shooed him out of the room, would they let him back in? Probably not. So much for making out. "Pizza?"

========

After lunch, Tesla left Gimlet with Shal. Oh, she wanted the dog with her, but she kept thinking about the fact that Gimlet had called for help when Shal passed out. If her dog hadn't been in the room . . . Tesla sat at the desk in her cabin, resting her head in her hands. She was so tired that she was having trouble organizing her thoughts, and there were a half dozen different choices that she could make right now.

Talk to the captain again and show her that someone had swapped the gin in the bottle? Or should she try to find the magician and see what the argument was about? Or she could try to get more information about the body that they found. Or find the yoga studio. Or try again to find Immanuel. Or Yuki. Or see if she could find the bald passenger. Or . . .

Tesla took a slow, deep breath, trying to order her thoughts. A fresh bouquet of hothouse flowers stood on the side table, which was a lovely apology and also a sign that someone had been in her cabin. On the table, a cup of tea leaves from her own stash slowly unfurled in a mug of hot water, promising salvation in the form of caffeine. Had she run the tea leaves through the scanner? Yes, yes, she had indulged in that bit of paranoia.

The tea was fine. Tesla tapped the side of the porcelain cup. Fantine had the detailed scan of the gin bottle and was probably better suited to raising hell with the captain. Most of the other options involved going someplace without witnesses. "*Lindgren,* tell me about the close-up magician."

"The Amazing Nile Silver performs his captivating close-up magic in venues around the ship. Following a stint on Puerto Ochoa and—"

A discreet knock on the door interrupted the Lindgren's AI. Tesla sighed. Which complimentary apology gift would this be?

The chocolate-dipped strawberries? The bottle of sparkling wine? A cheese plate?

She pushed back from the desk and stood, turning to the door. Her back seized as if each separate screw in her spine had sprouted spikes into the surrounding muscles. Tesla grabbed the edge of the desk to brace herself.

Alone in the room, she let out a groan that she would have held in if Shal had been there.

The DBPS kicked in automatically, but the pain still left after-images of purple and white around the edges of her vision. Tesla closed her eyes, waiting it out.

"Are you all right?" A mid-range voice at the edge of the room made her eyes snap open. Haldan Kuznetsova stood in the foyer to her suite. "Sorry. The door was ajar. And then I heard . . . are you all right?"

She stared at him, trying to reconcile his look of apparent concern with the fact that he'd argued for locking up her spouse. "I . . . I am. Though I'll admit to being surprised to find you here."

He wet his lips and looked down. "Yes, well. I rather owe you an apology and an explanation."

"You do." As much as she wanted to tear into him, she also wanted to know why he was here. And then, of course, there was the partially disassembled matter printer on her counter. She could be polite for now.

Holding up his left hand, he showed her a spoofer. "For full disclosure . . . Is this all right? I used it all the way here and I want to make sure you know that I have it before we talk. Do you mind?"

"It depends on what we're talking about." Tesla led the way to the sitting area, offering him a chair that would put his back to the matter printer. "You'll understand, I hope, my discomfort."

"I do." His expression cracked into grief for a moment, and he covered his eyes, still staring at the floor. After a moment, he cleared his throat. "Sorry. It's . . . I keep thinking I'm okay and then—Listen. I know your spouse didn't kill George."

"And yet . . ."

"And yet, I'm pretending that I still think it was him." Haldan grimaced and rotated the spoofer in his hands. He leaned forward to set it on the coffee table. "I know. It's a shitty thing to do, but I was scared and when the security officer told me they'd seen Mx. Steward, I believed them at first. Later, it just seemed . . . safer."

She wasn't sure how to respond. Shouting seemed appropriate. So did asking questions. She went with hospitality to buy herself some time. "Do you want something to drink? Tea? Water? Something stronger?"

"God, yes." He bent his head, cradling the back of it between his fingers. Then he straightened abruptly. "Wait—they probably dosed your liquor too."

Tesla stopped in the process of rising and sank back into her chair. "'Too'? And 'they'?"

He dragged his hands through his hair, making a bedraggled mess of the carefully gelled style. Kuznetsova still stared at the floor, but it didn't hide the heavy lines creasing his brow. "George and Ruth."

"I'm going to need some context." She had no idea who Ruth was, which wasn't even the big question. "Forgive me but . . . George is dead."

"I know. I don't think she was supposed to die." Haldan scratched his nose and glanced back toward the counter. "Maybe if we print a drink . . . what happened there?"

Tesla cleared her throat and couldn't think of a plausible lie, so she threw the truth into the mix. "Modded the matter printer to be a scanner. Sorry."

"You can do that?"

"Once upon a time, I was a damn good engineer." It was hard not to bristle, but his surprise wasn't unwarranted. These days most people knew her from society reports or acquisitions and mergers. Tesla stood and crossed to the bar. "But if you trust me,

I can guarantee that the vermouth, bourbon, and Campari are clean. Boulevardier? Old-Fashioned? Manhattan?"

He stayed twisted in his seat, draping one lanky arm over the back. "Your call."

"Manhattans it is, then." She was going to test the rest of the liquor, but so far only the gin had been swapped and nothing else showed signs of additives. At the moment, it wasn't a priority. She picked up the Belle Meade Bourbon, imported from Earth. "So, if you didn't do my trick, how did you know your liquor was altered?"

"I draw a line on the bottle so—this is embarrassing . . . There was an incident with a cleaner several years ago, so now I draw a line on the bottle so that if someone is stealing some, I can tell. The volume went up on one. A sixty-year rum from before Grenada submerged." Sliding his hands under his thighs, he leaned forward as if he were pinning them down with his own weight. "When I checked it, there was a white residue on the bottom and part of it was still recognizably a capsule."

"To a sixty-year rum?" Tesla whistled. "That *is* a crime. Okay, and George and Ruth . . . ? Who's Ruth?"

"Ruth Fish. The doctor. She used to be my college roommate."

Tesla sloshed bourbon across the counter and nearly dropped the bottle. She set it down and grabbed a bar towel. "Lovely. I was already worried about fallout from pointing out that she'd been drinking. And she knows you."

"Yes." He nodded and his face was tight and grim. "I didn't know she was here until I went down to . . . They needed me to look at George's body. I had no idea Ruth was even on the ship."

Every instinct told Tesla to get out of this room and run to sick bay to get her spouse out. But more information was better, and she didn't know when she would have this opportunity again. If they were planning on hurting Shal, it was probably already too late. She swallowed and turned back to the bar. "But now you somehow think that she and George were responsible for . . . killing George? I need you to walk me through this."

"Right. Okay. Right. So . . . several months ago, George and I had a fight when I announced I was relocating to Mars. She was angry because I hadn't asked her before the announcement. I told her that I didn't require her to come with me and that she could work remotely, but she didn't see it that way."

Tesla weighed what Shal had told her against Haldan's account as she added the vermouth to the glass. "I . . . I can think of cheaper ways to break up."

"Ah . . . You know about—right." He fidgeted with the piping on the corner of the chair back. "Of course you do. She's been a good friend and I genuinely care about her, so I thought I was making the compassionate choice—all very Victorian romantic to go off to leave your ex-lover breathing space and instead . . . I just came off like an asshole. Anyway, two weeks ago, she said that she understood and that she wanted to come with me to help me settle in. Just as my assistant."

"I can hear the 'but' from here."

"But when we got on the ship, she was weird. I can't . . . I can't explain why. I mean, you know when you know someone and then something is just off, but it's all these little things that you can't articulate. And then the . . . the night she died, she said, 'You couldn't survive without me.'"

The ice clinked in the pitcher as Tesla added it and stirred, waiting for him to continue. She shifted her position at the bar so she could watch Haldan. He sat with his eyes closed, a hand over his mouth, as if he were stifling a sob.

Swallowing, he lowered his hand. "I'd thought she was one of my best friends, until this."

"What made you afraid?"

"The knife was from my suite. She'd ordered steak and kept playing with the knife, making 'jokes' about how much damage she could do with one." He swallowed and turned to look at Tesla. "And I have a demonstration model of an octobot. It's gone."

She wasn't sure where to start. With the fact that he thought the steak knife was his or that he had a missing octobot. She carried the cocktail to him, feeling pressure from the cut glass ridges and nothing else. "Am I understanding you to say that you think George programmed the octobot to stab her in an effort to make you worry about her or to frame you for attempted murder?"

"I'm . . . I'm not sure." He turned the glass in his hand, staring into the russet depths.

"And did I understand—earlier, you said that 'the security officer' told you that they'd seen Shal. Which security officer?"

He shrugged, grimacing. "I don't know. Chief Wisor told me that someone had seen him. That was before I realized that the octobot was missing. Or saw Ruth downstairs."

"Right. College roommate, who is part of a conspiracy to murder and poison?"

"College roommate with a drinking and debt problem. College roommate who hates me."

"Why does she hate you?"

He waved his hand through the air. "That's private, in the past, and was irrational to begin with. Did you know that she wasn't originally scheduled to be on this ship? She changed shifts with someone two weeks before we cruised. Right about the time that George decided she was going to come after all. And—*and* she focused on robotics in telemedicine before switching majors to become an MD."

Everyone has a secret, and everyone lies. What exactly was he hiding? "Mx. Kuznetsova—"

"Call me Haldan."

"Haldan. This is all fascinating, but I have to ask why you're telling me, instead of security or the captain."

"I did tell the captain." His shoulders hunched and he squeezed the glass hard enough that it looked like it might break. "She laughed at me."

"Rude." Tesla turned her drink in her hand. She frowned. "Hang on . . . You literally own this ship."

Haldan stared at her. "I'm so used to—" His hand was shaking as he set his glass down on the table and leaned forward to bury his face in his hands. He sat for a moment, his breath shuddering. "Sorry. You're right. I'm so used to George tracking things for me that I hadn't thought about the holding company that owns the *Lindgren*. I'm an idiot."

"So maybe talk to the captain again? She can check with Corporate."

His voice was quiet and husky. "Yes. That seems wise."

"And . . . there's the matter of my spouse being detained."

"I didn't know who you were."

"What does that have to do with anything?"

"If you wanted to harm me, it would be on the corporate battlefield or in a courtroom." He clenched his hands and dragged his gaze back up to meet hers. "And your spouse is a detective. I want to hire you."

Aviation

2 oz gin
.75 oz lemon juice
.5 oz maraschino liqueur
.25 oz crème de violette
Cherry

Shake ingredients over ice for 15 seconds. Strain into
coupe and garnish with cherry.

Overhead, the artificial sky was the bright blue of late-afternoon on Earth. The pool was filled with rows of people facing a grinning instructor, who was urging them to do jumping jacks. "Work those legs! Come on! Splash it up!" Water sprayed in shining arcs as rows of hands clapped in time with bouncy jazzfunk from the late double-twenties. Steve the bartender was at the ready, working their mixing magic. Or at least being serviceable.

Tesla stood on the little bridge that arced over the pool, surveying the area. Haldan walked back from the bar, shaking his head. "Immanuel requested another transfer apparently."

"Darn it." She rubbed her hand over her mouth, thinking. She could confirm that later by checking the directory to find out where Immanuel had transferred. "Okay, thank you for asking. I'd been hoping not to spook him, but . . ."

"Too late." He nodded and sighed.

They climbed down the bridge and wove between the lounge chairs to head out of the pool area. On the far side of the pool they passed into the long transit corridor. They stopped at the crossover point beneath the undulating neon. Haldan headed to the clockwise ring. "I'll see what I can do to get Mx. Steward released, and we'll meet you back in your cabin."

"Great. As soon as I'm finished with the magician, I'll head back there."

Stepping onto the counterclockwise sidewalk, heading toward green, she had a moment of lightheadedness as the sidewalk's motion ever so slightly counteracted the gravity produced by the spinning ring. She started walking as soon as she felt steady. Theoretically, if you ran fast enough opposite the spin, you could reduce your gravity load, but she was not in the mood for running.

On the moving sidewalk opposite her, a young Lunar ultra-femme pointed. "Hey! It's Tesla Crane!"

Behind her, another person swiveled. "Holy shit! I fly one of your ImmiPeer personal spacecraft!"

In front of Tesla, a person on the moving sidewalk turned around and looked back. They frowned for a moment and then looked up and to the left, as if reading an internal screen. When they looked back down, they waved. "Tesla Crane! Can I snap a pic with you?"

If they did, and tagged her, then everyone on the ship would know who she was and no number of disguises would help. She put on the broad New Tennessee accent that an acting coach had taught her for situations like this. "Shucks, you think I look like her? I feel so fancy now." She winked. "But I'm just Artesia Zuraw."

They looked back up and to the left again, and then laughed, shaking their head. "Hilarious! But the bot IDs you with ninety-seven percent certainty. So can I take a photo? I loved you on *Zero-G Dancing with the Stars*."

Well, shit. If their AI identified her, it meant that the bots that were supposed to be screening for queries about her identity were turned off.

"Oh, you're catching me all undone." She looked past them for the next off point. "And I'm on vacation."

"Aw, come on! It's just for my friends."

This was not the way things were supposed to roll.

"I LOVE YOU, TESLA CRANE!!!"

When she used the code to unlock her identity, that should have been temporary. And now the person she'd said "no" to about the pic was turning around to take a selfie with her in the background. Wonderful. Pasting a social smile on her face, she started to walk faster.

"Sellout."

It wasn't loud, but there was always someone. People who didn't understand that she could still believe in open source and run Crane Industries. Tesla's hands were sweating as she walked fast enough on the moving sidewalk to feel the gravity shift.

On the other sidewalk, people were doing double takes and using various forms of cameras, subdermal, paste-on, handheld . . . all of them pointing her way and snapping pic after pic after pic.

She was, as the kids these days said, utterly soaked.

═══════

The autograph that Tesla used was not the same as her legal signature. Another lesson from Daddy, reinforced by an impressive rant from Fantine. The crowd of people had pinned her against the wall outside the theater where Nile Silver was supposed to be performing. Most of these people didn't even care who she was, just that she was famous.

But if she reacted badly to being trapped then she would be the asshole, no matter the actual truth. This was why she usually had Gimlet with her as a distraction, and as a stabilizing anchor.

She smiled for another photo and used the motion to edge slightly closer to the door of the theater. If she could get through that, then the bottleneck would give her room to make a break for it.

Turning to the next person between her and the door, she stepped toward a waif with silver piercings curving up the line of one ear. Those cheekbones and full, pouting lips could have belonged to a Terran Japanese pop star.

Yuki. Josie said he'd been working with her the night of the murder and Tesla had seen him talking to the magician at the bar the next day.

Tesla nodded and smiled, as if she weren't facing someone who matched Shal's description of the person he chased through the halls. Mostly matched. People could take earrings out. She took a snap of him to share with her spouse when she was allowed to see him next. "Well, hello! Are we doing photo or autograph?"

"Actually, I need you to keep the walkway clear to the theater." He looked around at the group. "Honored guests! If you are here to watch the Magical World of the Amazing Nile Silver, then please proceed into the theater. If not, may I suggest one of our lounges, such as the R-Bar or Cap'n York's Piratical Lounge, which is more appropriate for a gathering spot than the walkway."

Tesla flushed, even though this was profoundly not her fault. "I'm so sorry. I didn't mean—"

"I'm sure you did not." He gestured toward the corridor leading to the main promenade. "But if you would not mind taking your followers elsewhere, it would ease things."

"Ah—actually, I was coming to see the show." She wrinkled her nose with a smile. "I do so love magic, and Mx. Silver has been amusing us with his clever way with cards."

Yuki glanced up and to the left, accessing the files that were linked to her cabin, no doubt, and his eyes widened a fraction. Had he just recognized her as Tesla Crane or seen a note that said she was married to a murderer? He nodded. "Is that so. Of course, our Yacht Club guests are always welcome. I have a private seat for you inside if you would just . . ."

"Clear the walkway. Gladly." Tesla offered him a little bow. "If you wouldn't mind leading the way?"

The sigh that escaped him was so small it might not have even existed. He glanced at the people who were drifting away with the speed of a rock, and probably did the calculation that they would go faster if the object of attraction were no longer present. "This way."

"Did I see you in the R-Bar the other day?"

"Possible." The young man waved her through the door into the blessedly quiet theater.

It was hung with heavy indigo drapes, spangled with silver stars that caught the dim light and gave a depth to the walls. The Martian-level balcony curved overhead in a long undulation of smooth silver. Rows of seats sloped down to the stage, filled with people. More than she had expected, honestly.

"Your earrings are so distinctive and lovely. I was just sure I'd seen you there."

Yuki paused by one of the box seats reserved for the Yacht Club members. "I hope you'll find these seats acceptable. One of our servers will be by to take your drink order in a moment."

"Thank you. That would be lovely. What would it take for me to meet the Amazing Nile Silver after the show?" She toyed with the key fob on her wrist, since she could tip/bribe again, trying to imply that a substantial tip awaited for helping her without being so gauche as to say it directly.

He followed the movement of her fingers and his lips pursed for a moment before he looked out at the theater and then back to her with a smile. "Let me see what I can—"

"*Oh, bonjour!* Where is your *si mignon petit* dog?" Jalna Smith, the elegantly tall French-Lunar woman on Tesla's list of possible suspects, paused at the entrance to the booth with a milky lavender cocktail, held in a delicate coupe, and a tumbler of smoky brown liquor.

Why was she here? "Oh. Hi."

"Annie? Come, here is Gimlet's parent— Pardon, my dear, I have now realized that I know the name of your precious dog but failed to note yours."

That could just be politeness. A mark of the extremely wealthy was that they often did not check the identity of someone else in their social class, granting privacy as a matter of courtesy. Tesla was marked by location and clothing and the attentiveness of Yuki. Hell, they might have seen the crowd outside.

Or, maybe Jenny, their room attendant, said that someone had been snooping outside their door. Or Annie was a murderer. In any event, there wasn't any point in trying to retain her fake identity now, not with snaps posted in scores of social accounts on the ship.

Dammit.

On top of everything else, how was she going to get back to her cabin? All of that was a later problem, so she bent her neck in a friendly bow of greeting and tried to pretend like she hadn't been stalking them. "I'm Tesla, she/her. Lovely to meet you. And Gimlet is with my spouse . . ." She gestured back to the door, as if Shal weren't being held against his will, and realized that Yuki had made his escape during her distraction.

"Are you sitting here?" Annie poked her head over the railing at the back of the box seat. "Oh—sweetie. Are you all right? You look—sorry. I'm being personal here—but you just look done in."

She had been all right. Not wonderful, not by a stretch, but functioning, which was a triumph on any day. And this woman—who really did not seem like a murderer—her kindness made pressure build at the back of Tesla's eyes with a burning that was going to turn into tears if she didn't manage it immediately. "What are you drinking?"

Jalna studied her for a moment too long before apparently deciding to accept the topic change. She raised the milky drink. "Annie is having an Aviation and I am having a Laphroaig Quarter-Cask." She nodded toward the bar situated at the back of the theater. "They will take your order, but I prefer to get to know the bartender at least somewhat."

"Not a bad idea." And it would give her a moment longer to collect herself. "I'll—"

The lights of the theater dimmed. A swell of symphonic music rolled though the room, with deep base notes thrumming in her sternum and the hint of binaural enhancements setting the hair on the back of her neck on end.

"Best sit, dear." Annie beckoned with plump, parental authority. "This is our second time seeing the show and I'm determined to be picked as a volunteer this time."

A resonant voice filled the air with the honeyed vowels of a broadcast neutral Orbital Singaporean accent. "Honored guests! Welcome, one and all, to the Magical World of the Amazing Nile Silver!"

Jalna smiled indulgently at her spouse and whispered to Tesla. "I did lie a little. I was not at the bar, I was—"

An explosion lit the stage.

The Obituary

2 oz gin
.25 oz dry vermouth
.25 oz absinthe
Lemon peel

Stir ingredients over ice for 40 seconds. Strain into chilled
coupe. Garnish with lemon peel.

Tesla's ears are ringing. The visor of the PAMU prototype she's
testing flashes as the laboratory and space spin past in nauseating succession. The suit should autostabilize but it's not and she's
having trouble thinking and something is crushing her spine so
all she can catch are short, gasping breaths that get cut off with
red-hot stabbing pain.

The hell, the hell—shit. She tries to activate the PAMU's manual controls and can't even get the HUD on the visor to show that
they're engaged, much less stop her spin.

She activates her comm. "Lab One? I have a problem. Controls
are nonresponsive."

It's not just her ears ringing. Alarms are pealing through the
comms of the PAMU as her power grid shuts down to nothing
but emergency auxiliary.

"Lab One? Do you copy?"

"Tesla, Lab One." Jonas's voice is breathless, but he's calm.
"We're showing that the PAMU's life support is stable, but I'm
concerned about your personal telemetry."

Something is very wrong and it's hard to think past the pain
and the spinning. Is that a mist venting into space from the lab?

"The suit is impinging on the torso compartment and—what's happening with the lab?"

"They're working on that right now. Let's concentrate on you." Behind his voice, she can hear more alarms. "Can you activate the escape system?"

"Try a remote reboot first. With the spin I'm as likely to hit the lab as I am to get clear of the PAMU." The media calls the PAMU a "giant robot," and they aren't kidding about the size. When her personal compartment separates from the PAMU, that'll make two possible things that can hit the lab. She keeps toggling through the menu, looking for any control that's enabled, but everything is gray and dead except comms, life support, and the escape system. How long before she loses one of those or blacks out from the spin?

"Already tried. I trust you to not hit the lab. Abort. Abort. Abort."

She thinks he's wrong. She thinks that she's too close to the lab. She's also having trouble thinking and the point of having a CAP-COM is that they can see the big picture and he's saying abort and the pain in her spine is getting worse and her vision is starting to tunnel and she's going to black out.

"Tesla. Do you copy? ABORT, ABORT, ABORT."

She can't draw breath to reply, but she sees the station flash into view, and as soon as the first edge of black shows past it, she triggers the escape system.

He is right. She doesn't hit the lab. Encased in an airtight fabric cocoon, she sails clear of the PAMU into the dark, star-laden sky.

But she is also right. For every action there is an equal and opposite reaction, and the PAMU really is too close to the lab to use the system safely.

Tesla is safe. The lab is not.

———

Tesla was not entirely certain if she had fainted or not. But she was definitely on the floor and someone had put a blanket or a shawl or a capelet or a something around her shoulders. She was shaking and her cheeks were damp, but her mouth didn't taste like she'd thrown up. So, that was something.

Slow breaths. In on a four count. Hold. Out on a four count. *In, two, three, four. Hold, two, three, four. Out, two, three, four. Hold, two, three, four.*

Flashback. *I am safe.* That had been a flashback, and she had mechanisms for coping with those. *I am safe.* Where was she? Right now. What were five things she could see that were here and now?

A patch of light falling on blue-and-gray carpet. A silver star catching the light. A bottle of water. Gold-spangled trousers. A plump woman kneeling across from her. Tesla had met her before and was trying to drag context back into her brain.

The theater. *I am safe.* She was in the theater, next to a box seat, waiting to see a show. There had been an explosion—a stage effect. Tesla's entire face heated with embarrassment. It had been a long, long time since she'd been triggered. But of course, she usually had people checking shows to see if there were any pyrotechnics or if there would be any depictions of spinning or vertigo.

Her heartbeat started to speed up. *Sparks flying across the blackness of space.*

In, two, three, four. Hold. Out, two, three, four. Hold. I am safe. She reached for four things she could hear.

"—and can you confirm for the audience that the box is completely empty?" A man's voice was projected around them in the darkened room.

"Yes. I don't see anything inside." A French-Lunar woman's voice . . . she knew that voice.

The hum of a service drone and the clink of ice in a glass.

Wetting her lips, Tesla swallowed. She forced herself to meet . . . Annie. Right, the woman from karaoke. And that was Jalna onstage. And both of them might be murderers.

Tesla met Annie's eyes. "Sorry," she whispered. "I'm all right now."

The compression of Annie's lips made it clear that she did not, for a moment, believe Tesla. She pushed the bottle of water closer. "I asked them to tell your spouse. Is there anyone else . . ."

"No." Tesla buried the heels of her hands in the sockets of her eyes, and only the flashes of light told her that she was pressing too hard. Among the many conversations that she did not want to have was explaining to this apparently nice woman that Tesla's spouse was not actually a murderer.

"You poor thing." She looked past her toward the stage. "There's more pyro in a few minutes. Do you . . . would it be best to step outside?"

Sparks and darkness. The room started to spin, and fresh sweat coated the back of her neck.

In, two, three, four. Out, two, three, four. Deep. Slow breaths. Name three things she could feel.

Pressure. Pressure against her back. Pressure of the water bottle. Pressure behind her eyes where she was going to burst into tears again. Tesla nodded and hated herself all over again.

Jonas Zuraw
Neomia Jakobsberg
Dalphon Karl
Vishal Tharman
Sarika James
Gerd Sýkora

She used to say their names every day until her therapist had convinced her that it was making her worse. The room started to spin again.

Slow breaths. Name two things she smelled. The deep, woodsy smoke of an Islay scotch. Cordite burning.

Tesla staggered to her feet, Annie's capelet dropping to the floor, and bolted for the lobby. Her limbs were shaky and uncoordinated and she almost blacked out again. It would be better if she could get outside.

There was no outside to get to. The lighting in the lobby was a twilight after the nighttime theater to create a transition to the walkway. Tinted glass doors fronted it, and through them she could see people waiting for her with cameras held in their hands or pasted to their foreheads. Most of them tried to look casual about it, as if they just happened to be waiting there for someone else or it was where they had paused to talk, but she'd seen this kind of grouping before.

Sweat still stuck her clothes to her body, and she knew that her eyes were dilated and her cheeks flushed because she'd seen photos of herself taken in this state by people who had no idea what was happening in her brain and just thought that she was on drugs, which, to be fair, there was a period when that had been the only thing that had quieted her mind and—

Tesla closed her eyes and took in a slow, deep breath. She was panicking. This was a standard response and she just had to wait it out. *What I'm feeling is panic. It is very uncomfortable but it is not dangerous.* She wanted Gimlet desperately but she could manage. Deep breaths. Slow breaths. *In, two, three, four. Out, two, three, four.*

Slow footsteps approached from behind, and Tesla flinched, eyes snapping open.

Annie stood at a distance, watching her. The woman looked out at the walkway and shook her head. "Vultures." She sighed. "Well, you can't go that way, can you?"

"I'll hide out in the bathroom." It wasn't the first time and wouldn't be the last.

"Let me see if I can get us backstage. You can get around them through the service corridors." She smiled sadly at Tesla. "I used to be famous, back in my day. Most of it, I don't miss at all."

Sophisticated Lady

2 oz cranberry juice
1 oz simple syrup
1 oz lime juice
Pinch salt
1-inch wheel of cucumber and 1 slice cucumber

Muddle cucumber wheel, salt, and simple syrup in shaker.
Add cranberry and lime juice. Shake for 15 seconds. Strain
into martini glass, and garnish with cucumber slice.

The backstage dressing room was bland with no effort to dress it
up for passengers. Everything was a serviceable gray-white and
battered. Tesla sat in a polyamide chair in front of a makeup mirror and tried very hard not to look at herself, so she wouldn't see
how incredibly obvious her panic still was.

Annie and Jalna sat opposite her, the mirrors repeating them in
a long reflective tunnel of kindness.

"You should come to yoga with us tonight. We were planning
to go right after the show for the end-of-day wind-down, and I
promise that no one will give you any trouble." Annie rested her
hand on Jalna's arm. "Sweetheart, tell her she should come."

*"Annie, si æl a besoin de calme, alors c'est mieux qu'æl soit dans sa
cabine."*

*"Le yoga est calme! Et æl ne devrait évidemment pas être seule dans
cet état."* Annie's Midwestern accent flattened even Lunar French.

"I'm sorry I made you miss the rest of the show." As soon as
a member of the staff appeared to escort her through the service
corridors to the Yacht Club, Tesla was going to hide in her room

and . . . what? Everything on her list of possible ways to find the actual murderer involved leaving the room. She had been trying to figure out where the yoga class was, and *they just invited her.*

"We've seen the show before." Annie brushed the concern out of the air. "Though I'll admit that I'm jealous of Jalna getting picked as the volunteer. Isn't that just the luck."

Jalna drew in a breath to speak and then exchanged it for a smile. "Well. Perhaps we shall try again and you will be the lucky one."

There was something that she hadn't said. Tesla was alert enough to be able to tell that, but couldn't pluck out what it might have been. She took a sip of her water and knew that she should carry on the conversation, but the amount of energy required seemed beyond her.

"But with everything you have going on, taking a little time to breathe and stretch will simply do wonders. I understand that you don't feel like it, Lord knows I understand, but I also feel so confident that yoga will—"

The door opened, thankfully, cutting off Annie's well-meaning monologue on the merits of yoga. In a long blue-and-silver cape, Nile Silver swirled into the room. "Good evening, dear friends, allow me to introduce myself, I am the Ama—" He stopped and dropped his arms, staring at Tesla. "Oh, shit. I'm so sorry—I'm so, so sorry. Are you all right?"

She was standing, pressed back into the corner. Her chair was on its side and the water bottle was rolling across the makeup table, spilling water as it went. Her body felt tight and sweat coated her. She closed her eyes against the too-bright makeup lights.

Stars and the lab are spinning past.

Gasping, Tesla opened her eyes and swallowed. "Sorry. I'm . . ." *Seriously messed up.* She dragged in a breath that shuddered as she did. *In, two, three, four.* It stuck in her throat and she forced it back out, *two, three, four.* "Sorry. This is your dressing room and I'm in the way."

"No, no." He shook his head and pointed at her leg. "You're bleeding."

She looked down and a stream of blood ran down her shin from a fresh gash that wrapped around the outside of her calf. It didn't hurt. She hadn't felt it at all. "Oh."

Annie jumped up. "First-aid kit?"

"Um . . ." Nile turned, looking around the dressing room.

Jalna shook her head, rolling her eyes, and went to the sink, where she grabbed a handful of recyclable towels. "Tesla, would you like to sit down, if you please?"

Nile fished in his pocket and pulled out a name badge. He slapped it. "Delta, delta, one, one, three. Repeat. Delta, delta, one, one, three."

The room had been too hot, and now it went as cold as orbiting into a planet's shadow. "You called security?"

Nile looked at her, mouth still open. "Um. No. I called a doctor. Delta-gamma is medical and security."

"Oh." She swallowed. "It's just a scrape."

Kneeling near her, Annie snorted and reached back for the towels that Jalna had pulled. "May I see?"

"It's fine, really. I do this all the time." When she had the DBPS turned up too high it was easy to hurt herself. That was a later problem. The now problem was that even without security attached, she did not want one of the ship's doctors. "You didn't need to call medical."

"I did. Actually. Ship's rules for a passenger injury." Nile swept a hand over his dark pomaded hair. "I'm so sorry. They told me that . . . *you* were back here and that someone had a bad reaction to the pyro—I didn't think it was the same person. Listen. I'm really sorry about that. There's supposed to be an announcement."

From the pause before he said "you" Tesla knew that he'd been about to say her name. That TESLA CRAAAAAAANE!!! was in his dressing room and that he'd come back here to impress her.

Would he have apologized about the pyro if she were just an average audience member?

She swallowed the rock in her throat. "It's very different than your close-up magic."

He winced. "Can I get you anything while we wait?"

"I'm fine, thank you." She pushed away from the wall, trying to ignore the trembling in her knees. *Stars and sparks and darkness.* "And I should be getting back to my cabin."

"Not while bleeding." Jalna bent down and righted the chair that Tesla had knocked over, and probably cut herself on. "Sit, if you please."

She sighed and sat down, because being a walking biohazard was a social faux pas under the best of circumstances. Here, they'd probably use it as an excuse to lock her in her cabin. Tesla held out her hand for the towels. "Thank you."

Frowning, Annie handed them to her while Jalna watched with an equally expressive frown. The tall woman rolled up her sleeves as if she wanted to help, revealing a faded tattoo of coiled pea shoots twisting down from beneath the fabric.

Jalna tsked. "There must be someone to accompany her through the service corridors. Is that possible?"

"Yes. Yes, of course. Yuki can take you through." The Amazing Nile Silver unbuttoned his cape and hung it on a hook near the door. "Or I can. Actually, yes, why don't I do it. You and your spouse were so nice to me earlier this week. Where is he?"

"Sick bay." Tesla picked up the water she'd knocked over as her brain slowly churned back into useful thought. She had come here specifically so she could ask the magician questions. Nile Silver had been arguing with a bald passenger and George before she was stabbed. Yuki looked like the person Shal had chased, and *someone* was lying *somewhere* about if he had or had not been in the R-Bar that night.

"Oh no!" Nile turned back from the cape. "And you came to the theater to relax and then my stupid pyro and now you're hurt.

I don't even like the effect. But the ship . . . I'm still so sorry about that."

"It's not your fault." The fault rested firmly in her. Tesla grabbed that train of thought before she could spiral down further. She needed to ask him questions. Keeping her attention on the bottle, she poured a little water on a towel and wiped away some of the blood. At another time she could be subtle, but being functional felt like a triumph. "You know about the murder?"

"Yes, it's terrible." He straightened his cuff links. "But let me reassure you that there's nothing to be afraid of. The security chief has told the staff that they've arrested the person who did it."

"My spouse." Tesla kept her gaze fixed on him. "They arrested my spouse. He didn't do it."

He stared at her like he'd never seen her before and then his eyes widened. "Oh—oh. That's . . . They didn't tell us who."

"I'm sure." She set the bottle on the table. "The thing is, we were in the booth next to George Saikawa at karaoke. You had an argument with a passenger in front of the booth. Bald. White. Gamer's belly. Sequined shirt and capelet? I'm trying to find them."

He pursed his lips for a moment, looking at the floor. "They've asked us not to talk about it."

All of the frustration and rage at the ship and herself boiled up and over, and Tesla had to hold perfectly still to keep from shouting at the man. There were many things she could do, but shouting at staff was never, ever one of them. He might be a magician, but he was still an employee and she was still a client.

The room was too hot, and energy made her joints crackle. She finished wiping off the scrape—which really wasn't that bad—and said, very carefully, "I see. Well, I wouldn't want to get you in trou—"

A dog barked.

Tesla sprinted to the door and yanked it open. Leash trailing across the floor, Gimlet charged into the room.

Her stumpy tail was wagging her whole back end as she barreled straight to Tesla and stood on her hind legs. Her eyes were bright and her ears pointed with full attention at Tesla. The tip of her little pink tongue flicked out to touch Tesla's hand in a tiny dog kiss.

A sob rose up her throat like a rocket launching. She kept her back to the room and scooped her dog up. Tesla let herself bury her face in doggy scent and focused on Gimlet's little snuffles and grunts. She skritched the ears and couldn't feel their silkiness or warmth, which meant she had to be careful not to accidentally hurt her dog.

Tesla leaned out into the hall, some part of her expecting Shal to be chasing Gimlet, that Haldan Kuznetsova had done as he'd promised and gotten them to release her spouse, while also knowing that he wouldn't be there.

Officer Piper jogged down the corridor toward her, annoyance clear on her face.

If Tesla started crying now, she wouldn't stop until they reached Mars. And then Shal sauntered around the corner, trailed by the wall of Bob.

Hanky Panky

1.5 oz sweet vermouth
1.5 oz gin
.5 oz Fernet-Branca
Lemon peel

Stir ingredients over ice for 40 seconds. Strain into coupe.
Garnish with lemon peel.

The dressing-room door clicked as Annie and Jalna followed Nile
out into the hall, leaving Tesla and Shal alone in the dressing
room. Gimlet huffed at the door, small tail wagging.

Mostly alone.

Shal ran a hand down Tesla's cheek and his brow furrowed with
concern. His lips parted with a question and she stepped into him
before he could ask if she was okay. That question turned into a kiss.

Her spouse's lips were full and warm and slightly chapped. His
arms went around her, pulling her against him with gentle pressure. She dialed back the DBPS so she could feel the warmth of
his hands playing along the length of her spine. He found the
tight spots and pressed against them as part of his caress.

There was a difference between the absence of pain and the
easing of pain. It was worth feeling the red knots of barbed wire to
also feel his gentle touch as he found each knot and rubbed circles
to break them apart.

::Hello, sweetheart::

At the ping from his system, she gasped and curled her fingers
in his hair. *::You're back online. Why didn't you tell me you were
coming?::*

His tongue just parted her lips, teasing her. ::*Local access only. So, you'll have to put up with lots of skin-to-skin contact if you want to ping me*::

::*Oh, yes. I would very, very much like to ping you. I'll try to survive the local network restriction.*:: She ran her hand down his front, carefully not putting pressure on his ribs, planning to circle back so she could grab his beautifully formed buttocks.

He squeezed her upper arms, rubbing his thumbs in circles on the balls of her shoulders. "Your new client came to see me. Fascinating story . . ."

"How much of it do you believe?"

"Mm . . ." His mouth quirked to the side and he ran his fingers down the side of her face. ::*Parts. But he's definitely leaving things out and highlighting only the things he wants us to focus on. I have a laundry list of things I want to follow up on.*::

::*Me too.*::

::*Speaking of which, good thinking to hide a note on Gimlet. What did it—*::

Someone knocked on the door. "Medic."

Sighing, Tesla stepped away from Shal, feeling his absence down the length of her body. She pulled the door open, and Ruth Fish was standing in the hall, bag slung over her shoulder. The medic looked up at Tesla and her eyes widened. "Well, shit."

"We're in agreement. What are you doing here?"

Dr. Fish's jaw tightened. "I was answering a delta-delta call since I was kicked out of my own infirmary because . . . *he's* here?" She turned to the side. "Bob. What is going on here?"

"Corporate said to release him. The chief told us to escort him back to their cabin."

"This isn't their cabin."

"Yeah . . . well, the little dog."

"My fault." Shal held his hands up in a gesture of surrender. "I said, 'Find Mama.'"

Gimlet huffed and shoved her face against Tesla's leg. She put a paw on Tesla's shoe, looking back at Shal as if he were an idiot for not knowing where Mama was. Tesla smiled at the little dog. "Good girl."

"He's not well!" Dr. Fish pointed into the dressing room, and her face was flushed. "Tell me that we're at least keeping him under observation. Confined to his cabin? Stop shrugging at me!"

Tesla shut the door and leaned against it.

Fish immediately hammered on it. Tesla raised her voice. "We decline treatment!"

She could make out a rumble of voices in the hall, but the knocking stopped. Sighing, she shook her head and looked at Shal. "Well, that was annoying."

"Tesla . . . what happened to your leg?"

"Oh. Bumped into a chair." She shrugged, moving away from the door, but the mirrors around them gave her nowhere to hide her face.

In the glass over the makeup table, Shal's gaze tracked her. "If I asked you how bad it was . . . ?"

Her face was still blotchy from sobbing earlier, and sweat had glued parts of her hair to her forehead, the rest frizzed in a wild, unsettled mass around her cheeks. Tesla resettled the synthetic setae adhesive that held the wig in place and tried to finger-comb the vivid hair back into something that at least looked intentional. "Will you let me lie right now with a promise to tell you later?"

He sighed, lips pressing together as if he were actively holding his tongue. But he nodded. "Catch me up on the things you can, now?"

"Got in touch with Fantine, finally." She went to the sink to run water over her hands. Gimlet followed, nails tapping against the floor, with worry in her furry face. As Tesla made an effort to repair her appearance with minimal tools, Shal stood behind her, running one hand down the length of her spine while the other worked the tight strands of muscle at the base of her skull. His skin was warm against hers, and she used the local connection to catch Shal up on her conversation with Fantine, the contents and reasoning behind her list of suspects, and send him the pictures of Yuki.

He sent back ::*Maybe. Take the earrings out . . . .*::

::*He'd certainly have access to the service stairs.*::

::*True . . . I'll see what I can find out about him, if we can talk them into letting me connect to a system.*::

::*If Fantine can talk them into letting . . . .*::

::*That's obviously what I meant to say.*:: In the mirror, Shal grinned at her and leaned forward to plant a kiss at the nape of her neck.

"If you keep that up, I'll lose my train of thought."

Over her shoulder, his grin flashed again before he gently nipped the side of her neck. ::*What else do you have to report?*::

::*I think that they put the oxyfeldone in the Lunacy gin and then dumped it after you were unconscious—*::

His head came up sharply. "They dumped the Lunacy gin? Monsters."

She snorted and turned to kiss him. "Naturally, that's what you're upset about."

"They don't export it! How are we supposed to replace it on Mars?" He kissed her back, following the line of her jaw to the tender point below her ear. "Scoundrels."

::*So! Someone tried to kill you. Why?*::

::*You mean besides the fact that I potentially saw the murderer? I'm more worried about the fact that they tried to frame me. Coincidence because we were next door or deliberate because I had a link to Saikawa?*::

::*And you're worried about the gin.*::

::*Gotta have priorities!*::

She sighed and glared at him, but his eyes were closed and half-hidden by his hair. ::*Haldan sounded like his liquor had also been dosed, so I want to sample it.*:: She nipped the rough stubble on his neck.

Shal pushed to back her a little away from him. "I . . . I said 'client' when I came in, but I don't think we should take this case. I think we should take Fantine's advice and hunker down in our cabin for the rest of the cruise."

"What are you talking about? Of course we have to. We can't just let the murderer get away. Ruth Fish—"

"Could have killed me."

Tesla shivered at the sudden chill in the air. "I know. That's my point. That's why I didn't want her treating you."

He shook his head. "No. I mean, while I was unconscious, before you were called. She had an easy opportunity to make sure that the overdose was permanent, and she didn't."

Tesla blinked at him. She blinked again as she remembered the doctor treating him when she first came in. "She didn't smell like bourbon."

He tilted his head to the side. "Unpack that for me?"

"When I came in, she didn't smell like bourbon, but she did later . . ." She replayed that memory, trying to figure out when that had shifted. Gimlet stood up on her hind legs and rested her paws on Tesla's thigh. Absentmindedly, she scratched her dog's ears. "After Haldan came in with Chief Wisor."

Shal rubbed his mouth, staring into the upper corner of the room as if he were putting pieces together in his mind. "So which one prompted her to start drinking, or was it both of them? Or something else?"

"See. You can't put this case down. And if Ruth Fish isn't the murderer—"

"I didn't say that she wasn't, I said that she'd had a chance to kill me and didn't." He sighed and ran his fingers through his hair.

"What about Annie and Jalna?" Even as she said it, Tesla had a hard time imagining either woman killing Saikawa. "They're staying in the Grand Royal Suites and in a yoga group with Saikawa."

"So . . . assassin wives?" Shal nodded. "Yes, that is definitely a possibility."

"Don't make fun of me!"

"Believe it or not, I wasn't."

"I am dubious about that claim. But if you're acknowledging that it's possible, then you'll be happy to know that they invited me to go with them to the class. I could scope out the other people."

"Look . . . If this thing about George and Ruth being in cahoots—"

"Cahoots? Really?"

"Mm-hm. It's a technical term. If they are *in cahoots* the way Haldan says, then he's probably the only one in danger, and more so if we start obviously pushing."

"So we hole up. And he . . . what? Holes up in a cabin that was already compromised once?"

Shal grimaced and cracked his neck. "There are other options. None of which involve you taking unnecessary risks."

"A yoga class."

"With people that you think might be murderers."

"Yoga. Class. I wouldn't be alone."

"You came to the theater alone. Did you tell anyone where you were going?"

"I told Haldan."

"Telling a potential suspect does not count!"

"Also there's a bajillion people in the theater. Not alone!"

"Hi. I don't know if you noticed this, but I found you backstage, in a room full of people that—"

"That I suspect of being murderers. Fine! You win. I was—" She bit off the explanation that she'd had a flashback. *That* would be a point in his favor. "They're accusing you of murder and you don't want to investigate? What is wrong with you?"

For a moment, anger made Shal's nostrils narrow as he forcefully inhaled. He held it. At her feet, Gimlet shifted, looking between them. Shal's voice was stiff and level when he spoke. "Are we having a fight?"

"I—yes." She blinked and some of the anger drained out of her. "First one of our marriage."

"Only a week in . . ." He widened his eyes. "Ooooh. This means we get to have make-up sex, right?"

She laughed and leaned forward to kiss him on the cheek. "I do recall that in the handbook."

"You got a handbook?" He snapped his fingers with faux chagrin and then sighed, looking down at the floor. "But seriously, doll . . . Please don't go places alone. It's— Do you understand how easy it is to abduct someone in broad daylight? Drug a drink. They say you're drunk. Please, please don't do things like going to the pool without telling anyone again."

She pulled her head back, almost irritated enough to start yelling again. "Without telling—? I told you."

Shal stopped. "What?"

"I told you where I was going. I called you and told you. And who I was going to talk to."

Seeing him go uncertain was startling. Shal was quiet about his cockiness, but her spouse was used to being smart and used to having answers or being able to find them. His tongue briefly grazed his lower lip and he swallowed. "Wh-When?"

"A little after six? I . . . I went to go talk to Josie. Do you remember that I was going there?"

He nodded and rubbed his forehead. "But not . . . Wow." His laugh was breathless and uneasy. "So . . . retrograde amnesia. Whee. I've seen it in drugging victims and it'll be useful to be able know what that experience is like. What . . . what else did we talk about?"

"Not much, because they were probably monitoring the call." She took his hand and ran her thumb over the back, smoothing the fine, dark hairs. The brevity of his answers when she'd called took on a new shape now. "You sounded tired. Said you were going to order room service."

"Holy . . . I remember none of that." He grimaced and tilted his head back to squint at the ceiling. "Maybe I should have let them keep me in sick bay—"

A light rap at the door stopped the rest of his sentence. Tesla stepped around him and yanked the door open. "For crying out loud, I said—Oh. Sorry."

Annie and Jalna stood in the door, while Nile Silver waited a little way down the hall, flipping a coin across the back of his knuckles. The security officers and Dr. Fish were gone.

With a wrinkle of her nose, Annie made a Midwestern smile-grimace. "So sorry, sweetheart, but Jalna and I are going on to yoga and just wanted to let you know we were leaving and make sure you were okay. Nile has offered to walk you back to your cabin through the service corridors."

Shal poked his head out of the room. "What happened to Bob and Maria?"

"Maria?"

"Officer Piper. I promised her a play date with Gimlet." He looked down at the little dog. "Who is the best bribe? Is it you? Yes, it is. Yes, it is. Good bribe. Such a good bribe."

Gimlet's tail wagged furiously and she looked up at Shal with adoring eyes.

Jalna waved her hand. "They were called away. But Nile will get you safely back to your cabin."

"Great." Shal slid an arm around Tesla's waist. "I am very much looking forward to seeing our cabin and plan to never leave it again."

She kissed him on the cheek as a pre-apology before turning back to Annie. "Is that invitation to come to yoga still open?"

Fourth Degree

.75 oz sweet vermouth

.75 oz gin

.75 oz dry vermouth

1 tsp absinthe

1 lemon peel

Stir ingredients over ice for 40 seconds. Strain into a
coupe. Garnish with lemon peel.

The service elevator was scuffed, unornamented, and smelled
faintly of bleach. Tesla had seen more service corridors than main
halls at almost every public event she attended. Nile's brow furrowed as he waved his employee key fob to transport the lot of
them up to the Lunar level.

"Sorry about the . . . state of this." He waved his hand vaguely
at the elevator. "I'm sure it's not what you're used to."

Tesla rolled her shoulders in a shrug and winked to set him at
ease the same way she'd done in a hundred other service elevators.
"Makes me feel clandestine."

Shal nodded at the corner of the elevator, where a camera resided. "Must be hard to do your close-up magic, with cameras
everywhere."

Nile shrugged. "You learn to compensate for cameras. And
there are blind spots, but if I told you where, I'd be giving away all
my secrets." The elevator doors opened. "Here we are."

Another service corridor with plain gray walls and scuffed gray
floors curved away from them in opposite directions. In lunar

gravity, Gimlet bounded with each step, legs windmilling until she touched down again.

Jalna turned to them and said, "Let me just run ahead to let Mahjabin know we have guests. How many want to join us?"

Beside her, Shal groaned under his breath and raised his hand. "I'm in."

On the list of Things Tesla Had Not Thought Through, number 47 was that Shal would want to join the class. "Oh, but your ribs—"

He glared at her. "I'm in."

In front of them, Nile said, "I have to prep for the next show, I'm afraid. But I can arrange for another escort after the class."

"Two then." Jalna nodded, hurrying ahead of them in the easy, shoulders-forward lope of a lunar dweller. Tesla had thought she was graceful in the Earth gravity section, but in lunar *g,* she was breathtakingly gorgeous. "See you there!"

As they passed a stairway, Shal slowed and then stopped. He walked back to it and poked his head in, frowning. "Are we directly over the Yacht Club now?"

Nile kept walking and glanced back. "I suppose." He reached for a door and dramatically drew it open onto a lobby area. "*Et voilà!* We emerge into the real world, returned like Orpheus rising from the underworld."

"Really? That's your metaphor?" Tesla laughed, tightening her hold on Gimlet's leash as she stepped through the door.

"Tasteless or on point, you decide." He leaned out into the main area of the ship, keeping one foot in the service corridor. "I'll leave you here, if that's okay. It looks like the coast is clear."

"Thanks. I appreciate it."

"Just ping me anytime you need an escort. I know that they're supposed to take care of you, but also"—he winked at her—"I'm a magician. I know all the secret shortcuts."

"How mysterious."

"I am the Amazing Nile Silver!" With a deliberately silly over-dramatic bow filled with flourishes of his arms and a deeply bent knee, he swept away as if he still had his cape. "Mwahahahaaaaa!"

Annie beamed after him. "You see why we like him so much?"

"He's charming." Tesla nodded as if she didn't have questions for him about the argument he'd had with George and the bald passenger. She had a brief moment of thinking that she might need to catch his show later, then remembered the pyro.

The room flashed hot and cold, and static crackled in her ears. She swallowed and looked down, waiting for the spinning to stop. Gimlet stood on her hind legs with her paws pressed against Tesla. She stared up with her white fur making a bright spot for focus. The carpet was magenta with large gold bumble-bees marching in rigid lines. A whiff of lavender and the sweet caramel of bourbon.

She frowned, looking around the lobby for a bar. No luck. It was a broad room, lined with artificial windows revealing a moonscape at Earthrise. On the far side, a glass elevator bank waited to carry passengers down the gravity well and, past that, a bridge extended over the promenade to the central core of the ship.

Annie led them across the bridge. "I just love this view!"

Below them, the ship opened up in a vaulted atrium, lined with balconies on each level that were subtly canted to provide the right angle of "down" for their level in the centrifuge. The Terran-gravity floor stretched across the base, filled with trees and shoppers. At intervals, bridges, living walls of greenery, and glass sculptures let light through but broke the space up just enough that they masked the curve of the ship.

She slowed on the bridge, looking back to wait for Shal. A moment later, he sauntered through the door from the hall, rubbing the lobe of one ear in deep thought. Sighing, he looked up to find her and smiled. "We could go back to the cabin if you just want to work on flexibility."

"And how will that help with my peace of mind?"

"I promise that I will do my level best to make sure that you are not thinking about anything past the bedroom."

"Hm." She arched her brows, suppressing a smile, and headed after Annie across the bridge. When necessary, she could still force her ass to roll in seductive circles with her stride.

Behind her, Shal cleared his throat and then followed. So that was one thing that was going right, at any rate.

On the far side of the bridge, a broad arch opened onto a large studio with floors that at least looked like hardwood and high ceilings to allow for lunar-gravity leaps. Flowing curtains, stirred by the ship's circulation system, gave the illusion of privacy. Inside, the lights were lowered to pools of warmth. Gentle Titian flutes were playing in the background in one of those innocuous melodies that was annoying because it worked. Tesla's shoulders relaxed, and she took a long, slow breath. Maybe yoga actually was a good idea.

Annie said, "I'll get some mats set up for us." She gestured to the corner. "The matter printer is just there, if you need clothes."

"Perfect. Is it all right if Gimlet comes in?"

"No one will object to that sweetheart!" Annie studied the room. "But you might be most comfortable in the back. Is that all right?"

"That sounds like a plan. Thank you." Tesla started to head to the matter printer, but Shal stopped her with a squeeze on her elbow. She raised her brows in question.

"Tesla . . ." He leaned into her, voice lowered. "Did you take the safeties off the DBPS?"

Yes. But she wrinkled her nose at him. "Now, why would you think that?"

::*Because my other hand is touching your arm.*::

"Oh my God! Tesla Crane?!" A reedy teenager's voice cracked on the last syllable of her name.

"Lo and verily, it is I." She smiled at the kid and stepped away from Shal, but she dialed the DBPS back down, inviting in crackles of yellow ground glass with each subtle shift of her posture.

"Sorry—oh, wow. Sorry." The teenager was as pale as salt and gawked at Tesla with enormous violet eyes that had to be enhanced with lenses. "I just didn't expect to see you here. Of all places! Sorry. I was a finalist in the Crane Robotics Competition? The Utah Team with the polydactyl octopoid? Three years ago? It was blue?"

With each question, the teen seemed to shrink a little.

"Of course! You had trouble with . . ."

"The navigation course." The teen nodded, eyes no smaller in their head. "Our octo broke a thumb and it messed with the sensors, so we just kept going in a circle around this one sign. It was epic. I'm amazed you remembered!"

She didn't. Three years ago, Tesla would still have been strung out on painkillers. But all of the teams had trouble with some part of the competition; that's the way it was designed. "Can you help me with your name?"

The teen hesitated, biting their lower lip, and glanced across the yoga studio to . . . the older bald passenger who had argued with the magician. The room went hot and cold.

"I'm, um, Ewen, they/them." The kid ran a hand over hair cropped so short as to be more aura than a discernible tint. "Yeah. Um. So . . . like. That was cool. And, um. Thanks and all. I— whoa! Is that a real dog?"

"She sure is." At her feet, Gimlet was panting happily up at Ewen and not in her vest. "You can pet her, if you'd like. Gimlet, go say hi."

"Soaking awesome!" They crouched, tentatively patting the little dog's white fur.

She kept smiling at the kid as Gimlet fell on her back to offer her belly for scratching. Over their shoulder, the bald passenger was frowning with their arms crossed over their chest.

Why were they here? Neither of them was on the list of passengers in the yoga group. Unless they, too, were traveling under false identities—except there were seven people besides George with the group code and nine people in the room. Maybe she could pull the kid aside to ask about robotics later and slip in some questions about other things too.

Beside her, Shal sucked in a short breath. He pursed his lips and murmured, "Oh, interesting . . ."

She followed his gaze. On the far side of the room, Jalna stood chatting with a Lunar European who was around 180 centimeters with a narrow, uncurved figure. Their straight black hair was in a bowl cut.

"Is that . . . ?" She took Shal's hand, leaning in as if just being affectionate. *::Is that the person you chased?::*

::Could be.::

She had other questions, but Ewen was still there and needed attention. "Ewen, may I introduce you to my spouse, Shalmaneser Steward."

"You're married?" The teen's eyes widened even further. "I mean. That's cool. Nice to meet you."

"Newlyweds. A whole week now." Shal's lips twitched and he smiled, offering the kid a shallow social bow. "Nice to meet you. So you're interested in robotics."

With a voice-breaking squeak, Ewen swallowed. "Um. Yes? I mean, yes, a lot."

"Well, you'll have to help me understand it sometime." Shal glanced at Tesla, a gentle smile curving his lips. "My spouse is a bit more advanced than me in that regard."

"She's like . . . I can't even." Ewen bounced on their toes, nearly launching off the floor in the light gravity, and leaned toward Tesla with excited glee. "And oh my God, you will get this and Pops totally doesn't, but did you see who's in here?" The last was hissed with delighted and not subtle urgency.

Tesla cocked her head, scanning the other people there for someone who would have excited a teenager's interest. A star? A musician? Another roboticist? Years of fan interactions had given her an edge on the art of appearing to know what someone was talking about. She winked at Ewen. "I see. Now what, specifically, makes you so excited about that?"

Their hands fluttered. "J. M. M. Tafani?!" A thumb jerked toward the corner where Jalna and the Lunar European woman were talking. "I mean, being in a class with her, even if it's not robotics is like acid dazzleflash. She's so nice. *So nice.* And it's the best because Pops totally surprised me with this yoga thing and like I wasn't too into it but then I found out that Jalna Marwe Mensah Tafani was in the class!"

The room seemed to rearrange itself again. Tesla had read robotics papers by J. M. M. Tafani, and she was *brilliant.* Jalna. Everyone in the industry had always called her Jem as a sort of pronunciation of J. M. M. And Smith? She'd guessed Annie and Jalna were traveling under a fake last name, but—"That's Jem Tafani? Holy shit."

"Yes! I knew you would get it!"

"Catch me up?" Shal's hand squeezed hers and she could just feel it as he played the baffled and genial spouse, smiling at the teen.

::*She wrote the literal book on octopoids*:: Sweat slicked her hand, and he had to feel it. There's no possible way that Jalna hadn't known who Tesla was when they met. The PAMU accident had been everywhere, and anyone in robotics would have been deeply familiar with the reasons a lab full of people had died.

"Oh wow," Ewen was saying. "Okay. Like. Wow. Like, her work on haptic feedback for non-anthropomorphic robotic interfaces is so jaw-droppingly transcendent that I almost went total blackout when I saw her. I mean J. M. M. Tafani and Tesla Crane in the same room?! My friends on the—" Ewen cut off and glanced back at their dad. "I mean. It's really cool is all."

The bald passenger pushed away from the wall, walking over to join them. "Hope everything is okay."

"Yes. Thank you." She turned toward the change in focus as a desperate lifeline. "We were just chatting about—"

"Yoga," Ewen cut in. "Pops, I was telling how you surprised me with the yoga trip."

Tesla concentrated on her breathing, trying to calm down. *In, two, three, four. Out, two, three, four.*

Running a hand over a skull-smooth pate, "Pops" gave a fond sideways smile at their child. "Well, gotta do something special for your sixteenth. After class maybe we can visit the burger-bot."

Ewen's entire face lit up. "Really?"

Grinning at the kid, Pops shrugged. "I mean, unless you'd rather visit the broccoli-bot."

"PAAHops. There's no broccoli-bot."

"Lettuce-bot? Brussels-sprout-bot? Spinach-bot?"

Ewen made the universal noise of a teenager faced with dad jokes.

"Pickle-bot."

Fidgeting, the kid hissed, "Pops, you know who this is, right? This is, like, *Tesla Crane.* I mean, it is so flash that she's on the ship."

"Hi!" She waved and offered a quick courtesy bow. "I'm Tesla, she/her. Did we meet in Utah?"

"Ory Slootmaekers, he/him." His brows came together in a confused frown. "I've never been to Utah, so I don't think that's possible."

Tesla had seen that exact look on more than one engineer's face when they were pretending that they hadn't gotten a memo. The studied confusion. The feigned surprise that one was being asked.

"Maybe it was a video call? Did you coach remotely?" Some of the poorer off-world teams did that and sent a proxy who could handle Earth gravity. The wealthy off-world teams were made up of kids whose parents could afford conditional training since infancy. She provided scholarships to offset what disparities she could, but gravity load wasn't something that money could compensate for in the short term. "Ewen's team had an eight-armed robot. I judged the contest?"

"We've never done robotics . . . Ewen?" He looked down at the kid.

"Oh—oh, she must have misunderstood." Ewen stood on one foot with the other pressed into their calf. "I just always wanted to, you know, so watched all the videos. I mean, like, all the videos. You remember that project I did? On robots for that one class?"

That was not at all what the kid had said before. She didn't push, because it was obvious that the kid didn't want Ory to know about the contest. Which was seriously weird. Parents had to sign a consent form and a waiver and . . . ah.

Someone had lied to their dad about a field trip. Well, she'd done that sort of thing herself. Smiling at Ewen, she said, "I'd love to hear about your robotics project sometime." Pivoting back to the dad, she tried to take some of the pressure off the kid. "This is my spouse, Shalmaneser Steward."

Ory's eyes widened. "The detective?"

She had her fans and he had his, albeit fewer. Shal bowed his head in acknowledgment. "Retired."

"From *Cold Cases*?!" Ewen blinked at him. "Oh yeah. Blond and younge—"

Ory cleared his throat. "So nice to meet you. I had no idea you'd be on the ship."

"We were traveling incognito, but . . ." Shal spread his hands with a self-deprecating smile. "Best-laid plans."

Jalna crossed the room to them, bringing the Lunar European with her. Nothing in her movement or expression said that she recognized Tesla, but she had to. It wasn't possible that she was in robotics and hadn't known exactly who Tesla was.

Jalna smiled easily. "May I introduce Mahjabin Burke-Gafney, she/her, our instructor for this excursion. She has been a rock for us. This is our new friend, Tesla, and her spouse, Shal."

"Namaste." Mahjabin bowed in greeting, with palms pressed together. Her voice was surprisingly deep and had the same Lunar

French accent as Jalna. "Our friend has told me that you were the first on the scene when we lost our dear George."

"I . . . I didn't know that George was in your yoga class." She *had* known that, but only because she'd been snooping. When she'd met Annie and Jalna, they hadn't mentioned it. Best-case scenario they hadn't wanted to make a scene.

"Yes. She had helped plan it and has been a great benefactor." Mahjabin inclined her head again. This time, her lips were compressed as if she were holding her expression to a firm, neutral calm. She lifted her head again and gestured to the back of the room, where an empty yoga mat lay on the floor with a black ribbon across it. "But of course, her spirit lives on in all of us."

CROW'S NEST

4 oz orange juice

1 oz cranberry juice

1 tsp grenadine

1 wheel lime

Ice

Shake juices and grenadine over ice for 15 seconds. Pour into rocks glass on ice and garnish with lime wheel.

Yoga was a terrible idea. There were times when Tesla said "yes" to something that she could have done Before and thought she might be able to fake her way through in the Now. Though, to be fair, this was not the first time she'd misjudged her abilities.

Stars and flames and darkness—

She focused on the fingers of her right hand pressed into the soft mat. At the front of the room Mahjabin's low voice said, "Feel your connection to the ground and the energy flowing up through the ends of your fingers." She walked through the room, pausing to gently correct posture. On one side of Tesla, Annie was balanced on one hand and one knee, with her other leg bent back to literally touch her skull. She had been unfairly flexible through the entire class, seeming to revel in extensions that ought to be impossible even in lunar gravity.

And for Tesla, most of them had been.

The cat/cow combination at the beginning was an exercise that she did often to loosen and strengthen her lower back. Nothing after that had been within Tesla's ability. There was a difference between pain and damage. With the DBPS, she wouldn't be in pain, but she could cause damage.

Beside her, Shal made a soft *mmph* and slapped his palm back down on the yoga mat, rebounding a little upward from the motion. He landed and froze, in table position, and then slowly sat back on his heels. His face was tight.

"Shal!" She broke her pose and reached to steady him. Gimlet slid into position against Tesla, as if her seven kilos of mass would be a help. It *was* a comfort, though.

Around them, several of the other yoga students broke their own poses. Mahjabin hurried between the yoga mats, moving with the easy grace of a lunar-dweller. "My dear. Are you all right?"

Shal's breathing was uneven and the muscle in his jaw so tight that Tesla worried for his teeth. He swallowed and bent his head to look at Gimlet. "I'm fine, but I think I need to sit this out."

They were disrupting the class. Tesla had questions, so many questions, and she wouldn't be able to really ask any of them. "Why don't we go back to the cabin?" She stood, carefully, but her back still forked lightning halfway down her leg. It stopped her rise like a robot binding on an electrical cable. Staggering a step to the side, she misjudged the amount of force needed to catch herself in lunar gravity and rebounded too high.

Jalna caught her and eased her upright. "There. Are you all right?"

"Fine. Thank you for the assist."

At her feet, Gimlet made a low *boof*, white whiskers blowing away from her mouth. Her tail wagged uncertainly. Tesla reached down for the leash. Her back seized again and with the DBPS's safeties back on, there were limits to how much it could suppress. She inhaled sharply, waiting for the crackles to fade.

Yoga. What had she been thinking?

When she straightened, Shal was standing across from her with a rueful smile and an arm still wrapped around his ribs. "Cabin?"

That had been the correct answer an hour ago. Tesla nodded. "Sorry for disrupting the class."

"Think nothing of it." Mahjabin pressed her palms together over her heart. "You are welcome at any time."

"Thank you." Wetting her lips, Tesla turned to Annie and Jalna. "Let me know if you'd like to grab drinks or a bite to eat?"

"Darlin', of course we will." Annie had a worried pinch to her brows. "Why don't we walk you back to your cabin? I don't want those vultures to spot you again."

"I can just call Nile Silver."

Jalna glanced up, checking ship time. "He is still in the late show, I am afraid. Come, we will accompany you, it is not a problem."

"I made you miss most of the magic show; I'm not going to make you miss yoga too."

"Then you shall make it up to me by letting me play with *le beau chien*. Yes?" She bent down and retrieved the leash that Tesla hadn't been able to pick up. Gimlet immediately sat at her feet, staring up with enormous dark and adoring eyes. "You see? It is settled between us."

She took the leash from Jalna. The longer Tesla fought, the longer she was going to disrupt yoga class. "Thank you."

Also, Gimlet took the leash in her mouth and pulled Tesla through the curtains into the hall as if she were about to have a panic attack. Which, to be honest, was probably not that far off. Jalna and Shal hurried after them, flanked by Annie. Ewen would either be flipping out that she and Jalna were hanging out or crushed that they were both leaving. She tried to glance back to wave, but her spine wouldn't let Tesla turn her neck to spot Ewen, so she settled for a general wave, hoping that they'd take it as meant for them.

"I . . . I don't know where we are in relation to our cabin." Hell. This was her third cabin on the ship, and the only reason she remembered what ring it was in was because she knew that it had been Martian gravity.

Shal shrugged. "I haven't been to the new one since they moved us. Again."

"Yacht Club still?" Jalna shrugged gracefully. "That is simple."

"Yes. The Martian level."

"One level above us, then. Perfect."

Annie beamed, heading through the lobby to the bridge that cut across the promenade area of the ship. "The Yacht Club elevator comes straight here, so the entire ship isn't trying to use it. Might be someone to notice you, but not as many as if you had to walk on one of the thoroughfares."

On the far side, the bank of glass elevators nestled against the open corridors of the promenade, which helped Tesla orient to where she was on the ship. Annie stopped in the middle of the bridge, patting her shoulder. "Dagnabbit. I left my capelet."

"We'll wait for you." Shal leaned against the high rail of the bridge with a flirty wink.

"She always is leaving something. And she will begin talking to someone when she goes in so will be quite some time. " Jalna shook her head. "It is best for you to not wait for her. If you take the elevator down, it will go straight to the Yacht Club suites."

"Thank you. Maybe you can finish the class? And we can do the playdate with Gimlet later."

"That would be much appreciated. I should like to have an opportunity to talk when there is not so much activity." She bent to fondle Gimlet's ears. *"Prends soin de ton parent, magnifique enfant."*

Jalna headed back across the bridge to the yoga studio. Tesla relaxed a little, leaning against the rail next to Shal. He had waved when Jalna left, but otherwise made no move to leave. He stared out into the large atrium, drumming his fingers on the bridge.

"Do you want to go back to our room?"

He nodded, but didn't move from the rail. Shal's mouth pursed and he rubbed his ear. "You can see the R-Bar entrance from here."

The Martian and Lunar levels had thoroughfares on either side of the atrium with broad plazas that doubled as stacked bridges spanning the gap between their promenades, each at a slight angle that the architects had contrived to blend with the design of the ship. On the Terran level, about midway down the length of the atrium, the facade to the R-Bar stood on the same side of the plaza as the elevators.

Further down, ficus trees marked the entrance to the Yacht Club.

"Interesting . . ." She twisted Gimlet's leash between her fingers, thinking. "The stairs we passed. Were those the ones you chased that person up?"

"Yup."

"And am I right that Mahjabin matches your description?"

"Yup."

"So, is she . . . ?"

"Dunno. We were moving fast and I never got a clear look. What about you? You looked at the group reservation."

Tesla nodded, thinking through the pieces, and pulled Mahjabin's entry from the manifest onto her HUD. "In the boarding photo, she's got her hair pulled back with a hair band. It wasn't obviously a bowl cut. And then there's Yuki. Maybe he and the magician are connected? Nile seemed pretty cozy with Annie and Jalna. Oh—and Ory and Ewen aren't on the yoga class list."

He sighed, tucking his chin into his chest. After a moment, he rubbed his ear again and shook his head. "Let's go back to the cabin."

"You aren't going to suggest that we hunker down again, are you?"

"Yup." He started walking toward the elevator.

"But you love this. And you're good at it."

Shal stopped and rested his hand on the railing. "Look . . . Tesla, I'm going to say this because it's relevant, but I want to ask you to respect that I made a choice to retire."

"I— Okay. May I—? It would be easier if I understood why."

He looked out into the promenade, sharp nose clear in silhouette. His mouth tightened, and he tapped a thumb on the rail. "You won't like the answer."

She came up behind him and rested her hand on his. "I don't like the nonanswer either."

He snorted and winced, still looking out at the promenade. "I don't like being bad at things. I retired because I couldn't do my job well and I hated that."

"What are you talking about? You're brilliant and—"

"And I got famous." He shrugged. "Not your levels, but enough that it interfered. So. I retired."

A cold pit knotted in Tesla's stomach, because he hadn't retired after being on *Cold Cases*. He'd retired after they'd gotten serious.

"So, I'll share our thoughts and observations with Marie and Bob, but otherwise . . . the best thing we can do is to—"

Someone shrieked behind them.

Tesla spun, her back spasming with the motion, and she had to grab the rail until she could move again. More screams came from below them. When her vision cleared, Shal clung to the rail and his face was tight.

Below them, on the floor of the Terran level, lay a body.

The overhanging balconies filled as people rushed to look at the scene below. On the plaza, some people were trying to help the person who had fallen. Others on the plaza looked up, pointing as if trying to figure out where they'd fallen from.

Except they were looking in the wrong place, planet-based instincts leading them astray. On a ship like this, the Coriolis effect would cause anything that dropped to appear to curve in midair as the ship turned around it.

The loudspeakers blared. "Delta, gamma, five-five-niner. Repeat. Delta, gamma, five-five-niner."

Most of the passengers were looking up. But some were following the direction of spin . . . Tesla traced a line in a long curve up and away from the body lying on the floor. If the person fell from the Martian level, then they would have come from just outside of an ice-cream shop.

From the Lunar level . . . the imaginary line intersected the yoga studio at the far end of the bridge she and Shal were standing on.

And they were alone on it.

Death in the Afternoon

5 oz sparkling wine

.75 oz absinthe

Pour absinthe into a Champagne flute, top glass with sparkling wine.

Shal backed away from the rail. "We have to move." He licked his lips, looking from the elevator back toward the yoga studio and then down the length of the promenade. "Shit. Goddammit. Maybe if we . . . Come on."

He started to walk back toward the studio, sliding his hand into his pocket as he went. Tesla had a hard time looking away from the scene below. Staff was pushing people back in an uneven circle as someone strung a yellow cleaning tape across the far end of the Terran level.

On the Martian and Lunar levels, people hung over the edge like gargoyles come to gawk at a tragedy.

Shal looked over his shoulder. "Doll, we can't stay here."

"Shouldn't we go down to help?" She followed him, still staring at the crowds more than the person on the floor.

"At the other scenes, they've been using a spoofer." His brow was knit tight with concentration. "We need to get back with witnesses so the gap when no one can vouch for us is as small as possible. Also, if they fell from the Lunar level, whoever pushed them didn't come this way, so would have had to pass by the entrance to the yoga studio."

Tesla's stomach went tight and queasy as the reality caught up with her. There were already two bodies on the ship, the chances of this being an accident were slim. There had been no accidents while Shal was in custody, and now . . . She looked again at the people crowded along the balcony rails on the Martian level, where the trajectory could have originated, and took a snap with her subdermal camera. "Do we pretend that we did or didn't see it?"

"We're honest but don't volunteer information. The more you say, the more apparent contradictions people can find—" He cut off as they approached the studio.

The class had spilled out past the curtains, most looking toward the railing. Jalna stood near the front, talking to Ewen, and seemed to be trying to keep them from approaching the rail. Other members of the studio gathered in the entrance, looking toward the atrium, but stayed packed in a protective cluster around the teen. Jalna glanced over her shoulder and saw Tesla and Shal.

"Ah—here! Our dear Tesla will have thoughts on this." She caught Tesla's eye and beckoned her closer with a smile that seemed more than a little strained. "She is a specialist in robotic enhancements of the human form."

"Was." Tesla's smile was definitely strained. The PAMU had been a robotic enhancement. This conversation with Jalna would have made her tense enough, but there was a body lying two floors below them. "But I keep up with the field."

The teen's face was flushed red, and they were shifting from foot to foot as if they wanted to go look at the railing but also didn't want to miss out on talking robots with Jem Tafani. "I was just acid-interested in octopoids and how their central brains make it easier to translate haptic feedback. So, such as, what do you think about ultrasound transducers versus air vortexes?"

"Well . . . those both still give analog sensations." Ewen's father wasn't with the group. Had she seen Ory Slootmaekers in the room when they'd left? "Gimlet, go say hi."

The little dog flopped down and rolled over on her back, legs sticking up at undignified angles. Her tail wagged as she gazed up at Ewen with an unabashed plea for belly rubs. Her trainer would complain that all of the people petting her was not good for Gimlet's training, but right now Tesla needed her as a distraction. Ewen succumbed to the inevitable and bent down to scratch Gimlet's belly.

"Yes. Direct brain stimulation is better at translation for non-anthropomorphic figures, although it also has its limitations." Over their head, Jalna's face tightened with concern again. She looked out the entrance of the yoga studio toward the bridge. In fact, all of the other members of the yoga class seemed tense except Mahjabin, whose placid expression was a perfect mask of tranquility.

And Annie, who wasn't there.

"Right. The analog options are usually the most accessible for those who cannot afford direct brain stimulation, which is where the octopoid's central brain comes in handy." Tesla scanned the room, which still had the same low, ambient Titian flutes playing, interspersed with the occasional chime. It would not have masked the scream.

Some of the yoga mats were askew, as if their occupants had risen quickly. A green running shoe lay on its side near a mat. The vivid magenta-and-gold capelet that Annie had loaned to Tesla was puddled on the floor by one of the columns.

Tesla used her subdermal camera to take a picture of it. She did a quick count and only Annie and Ory were missing.

From the way everyone was bunched around Ewen, she was guessing that they were trying to keep the kid from thinking the worst, so she went with the safer of the two questions. "Where's Annie?"

"I do not know." Jalna's voice trembled. "She was not here when I got back, and she is not . . ." She tapped her temple in the universal reference to a HUD. It wasn't unusual for families to share their locator information with each other even if it was only used for emergencies.

Shal's voice sounded more relaxed than it should. "Is it unusual for her to go offline?"

She nodded.

"It's probably just a system thing." Ewen spoke to Gimlet's belly. "My dad won't even let us run HUDs because they're acid-unreliable, and a ship like this is practically a Faraday cage."

"The ship has signal boosters for guest comfort." Jalna gave a strained smile. "But they are correct. The signal in the yoga studio is wildly unreliable. I am sure it is nothing."

Three possibilities. It was genuinely nothing. Or Annie was a murderer and had just killed again. Or the murderer had seen Annie at karaoke and eliminated a witness. And maybe the same three possibilities for Ory.

Tesla opened the pictures stored in her local drive, unspooling the selection across her HUD. Under any other circumstance, she would have avoided using it in polite company, so she didn't have the vapid eye twitches of a network addict, but right now she wanted to see if she could zoom in on the body.

A pixelated heat haze of spoofer distortion surrounded the figure on the floor. Two other spots in the image had the blurred fog of spoofer activity. One on the Terran level near a glass divider wall. Another on the Martian level at the ice-cream shop and . . . She blinked twice, enlarging the image.

"Annie is on the Martian level." In the image plastered across her HUD, Tesla could see Annie leaning over the rail on the edge of the spoofer distortion. She wasn't looking at the body though. She had been looking straight at Tesla.

"She is?" Jalna's brow was crinkling. "How do you know that?"

And this was why Shal told her not to volunteer anything. "Oh. Well . . ." Her mind emptied of possible lies that wouldn't create contradictions.

"The elevator hadn't come yet. So we . . ." Shal waved his hand out the door of the yoga studio and left a wealth of statement implied in his ellipses. "Do you want us to walk you down to her?"

Jalna's mouth compressed for a moment and she turned from them to walk over to Annie's capelet where it lay in a shock of color on the floor. The rough raw silk shushed against wood as she scooped it up. "That is not—"

"Hey, class over already?" Ory Slootmaekers sauntered into the yoga studio, grinning at them all. "And here I was, looking forward to corpse pose . . . what's wrong?"

Ewen looked up from petting Gimlet. "Someone fell off the balcony."

"Oh shit." Ory gaped and he turned to look out the entrance of the studio toward the balcony. "I was in the bathroom and . . ."

"And what, Mx. Slootmaekers?" There was a laziness to Shal's voice when he was questioning someone. It hid the sharp, acid bite of his wit.

"And I had—I didn't hear a thing."

"I hope you're feeling better."

Ory glanced over his shoulder at Shal, red blotches high on his visible cheek. "What do you mean?"

"Well, I mean . . . you were gone for a long time. I just hope nothing's wrong." Shal's shrug was a study in casual. His smile was gentle, as if he were sharing a secret with the other man.

"Yeah. Thanks. I have IBS. Always happy to have that pointed out." Ory ran a hand over his scalp, then turned to his child quickly. "Ewen. Let's go."

"Can we go down to look?"

"Absolutely not." Ory nodded to them all and walked over to bundle up their yoga mats. "Let's go. Now."

"But Pops—"

"Ewen." When he straightened, his face was red and sweat prickled on his scalp. "Hourglass."

Something changed in the kid's posture. Their face went still and they swallowed. "Copy." They clambered to their feet with the awkward gangliness of a teen. "Thanks for letting me pet your dog."

"Sure. Anytime." She smiled at Ewen. What the hell was going on? "Maybe you and your dad can come by and have a playdate with Gimlet."

The kid shrugged and moved to pick up their mat, then hurried out of the room with their father.

In the silence, Mahjabin cleared her throat. "I can lead anyone who needs it through some simple meditation exercises to clear our minds. In a time of loss and distress it is not uncommon for the mind to become unquiet."

That was an accurate statement and also the last thing that Tesla wanted to do in the moment. It felt like her brain was charged with liquid oxygen and steaming from overpressurization. She wanted to talk to Shal. Not just send pings, but actually talk. "Thank you. I think I need to head back to our room to lie down."

Shal nodded, and the relief in his features lay just below the skin. She tapped her left leg and Gimlet heeled into position with her gaze fixed on Tesla.

The leash was slick with sweat in her fingers. The threads bumped beneath her touch as they walked toward the bridge. A line of yellow tape stretched across it now, and there were uniformed crew standing at the entry to the bridge. People stood in clumps on the other side of the yellow tape and stared openly at the activity. And in the midst of the group, someone lifted what looked like a film camera and pointed it at them. Tesla turned her head away, heart rate ratcheting up.

A spoofer could mask things from digital cameras, but not from film. Almost every time Tesla saw one, it belonged to someone who was going to sell a picture of her. And now this entire secluded part of the ship was suddenly an area of focus and interest. She needed to get out of here as quietly and discreetly as possible.

And they were trapped on the wrong side of the bridge from the elevators.

"Seriously?" Officer Piper's voice stopped her. "Why am I not surprised to find you two here?"

"Maria!" Shal turned to face the security officer, who was crossing the bridge. "I'm not sure this is the best time for a playdate with Gimlet."

"Agreed. We're a little busy." Her face was hard and her mouth tight, as if she were holding in a torrent of anger.

"Of course. Do you have someone to spare that can get us back to our cabin so we can get out of your way?"

"Negative. I need you to stay put until I can ask you some questions."

"We're happy to help." Shal spread his hands in an easy gesture of openness.

That was all fine and good, but Tesla did not want to be here. "Absolutely. It's just . . . Gimlet needs to do her business."

"I thought you needed to go back to your cabin?"

"Potty pads." Tesla shrugged, and sweat beaded on her back. "I'd prefer the animal relief area, of course, but didn't want to put anyone out."

Officer Piper watched her for a long moment, then switched her measuring gaze to Shal. Her lips pursed quickly. She looked past them toward the crew members guarding the area at the end of the bridge and then down to the broad expanse of the promenade. Her shoulders shifted with a slow, measured breath, and for a moment Tesla thought she was about to let them go back to their cabin.

Then her gaze snapped back to Tesla. "Why didn't you want Dr. Fish to treat Shal?"

"Wha—I . . ." Tesla glanced at Shal, wishing she were holding his hand so they could confer. He gave a slight nod. *Answer direct questions honestly, but don't volunteer.* "She had been drinking and I didn't trust her."

With a flat stare, which seemed to be scanning her core components, Officer Piper waited. The urge to fill the void in conversation built in Tesla, but she'd heard Shal talk about leaving spaces for people to spill the beans. Tesla knew how to wait calmly. She imagined golden sunlight filling her from the top of her head. Soft warmth filled her toes, rolling up to her ankles. Around them crew members with safety vests over their uniforms directed people.

Nodding, Piper shot a look at Shal as if she knew exactly why Tesla didn't take that bait. She crossed her arms over her chest. "What else?" She held up her hand to stop Tesla. "I'm going to ask you not to pretend that your reaction to Dr. Fish was proportionate. You did not want her treating your spouse before you realized she'd been drinking."

"True." Tesla wet her lips, and by her side, Gimlet pushed her head against Tesla's leg. "George Saikawa was alive when Dr. Fish took her away. I had entertained the thought that she might have . . . been involved in Saikawa's death."

"Maybe she was." Officer Piper stared over the railing again. "We're going to hold you both for questioning."

"For crying out loud. We weren't—"

Beside her, Shal made a sudden inhalation, following Piper's gaze with his own. The officer turned to him, and her mouth quirked to the side. She nodded and walked away, catching the attention of a crew member. "Put these two with the others."

"Excuse me." Righteous indignation was never a good look, but it was hard to express anything except that. "What is your reason for holding us."

Over her shoulder, Piper said, "Ask Shal. He gets it." She kept walking, checking in with crew members and answering questions.

Tesla turned to Shal, whose mouth was turned down in a tight frown. She cleared her throat. Grimacing, he nodded at the scene around the body on the floor below them. "Pretty sure that's Ruth Fish."

Satan's Whiskers

1 oz gin

.5 oz Grand Marnier

1 oz dry vermouth

1 oz sweet vermouth

1 oz orange juice

2 dashes orange bitters

Shake ingredients over ice for 15 seconds. Strain into coupe.

"Hi. Did you want this personalized?" Tesla smiled at the eleventh person to approach her in the fifteen minutes since they'd been herded into the Olympus Mons Lounge on the Martian level with the other witnesses. She took the offered ship newsletter from a stylish passenger wearing a white asymmetric skirt with teal crocheted edging and a matching capelet.

"To Nora. And I just wanted to say that my parent has Parkinson's and uses a mini-PAMU, and having mobility again made all the difference in their life and thank you so much. I know how much developing it cost you personal—"

"Thanks." She jotted the name above her signature and kept her smile in place through long practice. The first person she'd tried to put off because she didn't have a pen, but a ship crew member had "helpfully" provided one. At least she could try to use the time wisely. "So . . . where did they collect you from?"

"Terran level. They passed just over my head. I thought it was part of the show at first and then . . ."

"I'm so sorry. That must have been horrible."

Tesla shifted in her chair, trying to ease the tension in the base of her spine. And by tension, she meant pain, and by pain she meant red webs of anger that spread out like a spider's revenge. These had to be the solar system's worst chairs, and she had to leave the safeties in place so she knew which positions would do the least damage. She hated everyone.

Tesla kneaded her fists into the tightest spot, trying not to grimace too visibly, since it felt like half the lounge was staring at her. The security team had rounded up anyone who was in the spoofer fields that Tesla had spotted. Or rather, they'd rounded up the people they could identify, but there was no telling who had slipped away before security got there.

Shal slid his arm behind her and took over. "You okay?"

"For God's sake, who designed these chairs?"

At her feet, Gimlet whined and bumped her head against Tesla's calf. She bent down to scratch the little dog's head, bracing herself with a hand on her other knee. It helped stretch her back out some, but not enough. Still, it meant that she could plausibly delay addressing the next person in her impromptu signing line.

The urge to ask for a manager was very, very strong, but would not actually do a lot of good. And she'd tried that already. The staff had set up blockers through the Olympus Mons Lounge so that no one had access to the network while they were investigating. "As a temporary measure," since they were clearly and obviously not preventing anyone from speaking to their legal counsel before answering questions. This was "just to keep communication lines clear."

The next passenger had a souvenir T-shirt in their hand and held it out. "Um . . . ?"

"Of course, I'm happy to sign your shirt." T-shirts were a total pain in the ass to sign. "What's your name?"

"Jakim Porter, ze/zir." The passenger had the remnants of a delivery tan, with pale skin around zir mouth and hands from wearing a courtesy mask and gloves outdoors, which meant that ze was from Earth.

"And where did they collect you from?"

"I was getting ice cream at the Snow Queen." Ze winced and shook zir head. "Heard the screaming and only caught a flash of color. I just found out that she jumped."

"She? Did you know her?" Shal stood by Tesla's chair, ready to bounce anyone who was a problem, broken ribs or no. When ze shook zir head, Shal said, "Who told you she jumped?"

"Um . . ." The passenger turned. "I don't see them now. They were Lunar though. White. Wearing a purple shirt? Or blue. Anyway, they pointed me to her social— You haven't heard it?"

Shal shrugged lazily. "Blockers . . . plus, our honeymoon." He made it sound like it was a choice. The hand he ran across the back of Tesla's neck seemed like simple affection. ::*See if ze has the video on a local drive.*::

She looked up at Jakim Porter. "What did she post to social?"

"I can . . ." Ze fished a handheld out of zir pocket and unscrolled the flexible screen to full size. "Here."

The page had Ruth Fish's icon in the upper right and the handle SpaceQuack. It was a handheld video filmed point-of-view walking up a set of stairs on the ship. The audio was hard to hear over the crowd, and ze frowned at it. "You can't hear it, but she sounds like she's crying. Do you want to borrow my—"

From the handheld, Ruth Fish's voice slurred, "This isn't my usual walking tour of the ship. In case you're wondering, in today's game of 'drunk or ship,' it's definitely drunk. I can't blame any of this on Coriolis effect, just on my own . . . Shit. I shouldn't have—" Her voice broke and she sobbed loudly enough that the echoes of it were audible. The camera showed the door to the stairs opening. "I'm drunk. And not drunk enough to forget what I've done. I swore to do no harm, and I killed George Saikawa. I just didn't know how to get out of this mess. Fuc—"

The video ended. Three more people had come up behind her current fan, leaning over Jakim's shoulder to watch the screen. Ze grimaced. "The way it ends, I don't think she meant to post it."

The time stamp said 11:13 p.m., which was maybe ten minutes before she died. It would have been right around when they were leaving the yoga studio.

"Thank you for showing me." Tesla handed Jakim's shirt back to zir. "That's horrifying, but . . . thank you."

The next fan took zir place, and Tesla tried to fall back into the rhythm of innocuous activity. Had Ruth Fish killed herself? But why? Why had she killed George Saikawa?

Tesla shifted in her chair. ::*So what about Haldan's theory that Ruth and George were planning to kill him? Was that the "mess" that Ruth was talking about?*::

::*We don't need to solve this.*::

::*So you think there's more to this too.*::

"Tesla . . ." His voice was as warm as his fingers on her neck, but she could still hear the plea to drop it.

::*Someone tried to kill you.*:: The pen slipped in the sweat on Tesla's palm and she nearly lost it.

Gimlet grabbed the loose coil of her leash and tugged. Why was she being such a brat? The little dog tugged again. Maybe she needed water; it was so hot in this room—

Oh. Tesla's palms were sweating. She was about to have a panic attack and Gimlet was trying to get her out of the room. The problem was that there wasn't anywhere she could go. Tesla took a slow breath. *In, two, three, four. Out, two, three, four.*

She couldn't leave. "Thanks so much for stopping by," she said to the fan.

Tesla put a hand on the chair to brace herself as she stood. Her left leg was sluggish and she thanked her lucky stars that they were on the Martian level or she might not have made it all the way up. For the moment, standing was kinder on her back than the horribly scoop-back butt-sprung chairs. The entire lounge reeked of too much effort and not enough thought.

Shal leaned in to kiss her, murmuring. "Are you okay?"

She nibbled the lobe of his ear. "I hate these chairs."

Even with Ruth committing suicide, there was still the other body. The vid talked about George Saikawa but nothing else. The security chief would probably see her death as confirmation of his totally unfounded theory that murderers often killed themselves.

Officer Piper strode up and shook her head at the scene. "Seriously? You can't wait until you get back to your room?"

"Maria." Shal grinned. "Here for your playdate with Gimlet?"

She rolled her eyes at him and turned to the people around them. "I'm sorry for the inconvenience, folks, but I'm going to have to ask you to return to your seats. We're trying to take your statements as quickly as possible, and it would help us do that if you remain in the seats we assigned to you."

Tesla sagged a little as people dispersed around them. "Thank you."

"I did not do it for you." Piper's face was hard as she turned back to Tesla. "And I need you to not ask people questions while there's an active investigation going on. Is that clear?"

"Yes." Tesla struggled for a moment, knowing that she should be quiet but also there was a murderer on the ship. "Did you see the person with the analog camera?"

Piper's sigh was an eloquent and scathing essay on people who asked unnecessary questions that implied that she was not doing her job. After pinning Tesla with a gaze that could be patented as a weapon, she turned it on Shal. "What?"

At Tesla's side, he shifted as if suddenly too warm, but took the opening. "Just wondering if anyone had eyes on Haldan Kuznetsova?"

Piper took too long to answer. "That is an odd and very specific question."

"I'm an odd and very specific guy." Shal inclined his head. "It occurred to me that his assistant and his college roommate are both dead. Either someone is targeting his friends and likely him, or he is."

"Mm-hm. Let me ask you a follow-up question: Can you think of a reason someone might make a list of people who were being bumped off?"

Sweat coated Tesla's body. The paper Bob took from her had a list of names that started with George Saikawa and Ruth Fish. A high-pitched squealing started in her left ear and she wanted to bolt from the room. She held very still, waiting for the surge to pass through her.

At her feet, Gimlet sat up and leaned her head against Tesla's leg. Officer Piper looked down at the little dog. "Huh . . . Never knew that a dog could be a tell before."

"There you are!" Annie's voice cut through the lounge as she wove between chairs. "I didn't see you earlier; there was a column between us and I was facing the wrong direction. Oh my goodness, isn't this just the worst thing in the worlds? And—oh. Jalna isn't with you."

Tesla shook her head, heart still shaking her extremities. "Sorry, no. They kept the yoga group up in the studio."

Shal gestured to Officer Piper. "We're just too attractive for Maria here to want to get rid of us."

With a sigh, Annie looked out the entrance of the lounge as if Jalna would be standing there. "They wouldn't let me go back to the yoga studio and I'm just sick with worry about her."

"She's fine. And just as worried about you." Not watching Piper, Tesla asked the same question she asked everyone, even though she'd seen Annie on the Martian level. "Where did they round you up from?"

"The gift shop." Annie fluttered her hands. "I'd gone to the restroom but it was out of order and so I went down a level and then— Oh, and I got you something."

"Something for me?" Tesla glanced at Shal, who was rubbing

his ear as he watched Annie rummage in a small shopping bag at her waist.

"Maybe it's silly, but ta-da!" She held out a courtesy mask and goggles. The courtesy mask was like something a station resident might wear for an evening out, in a muted purple with iridescent sequins scattered across it. "I thought it would help with people recog—"

"Excuse me." Officer Piper made a T with her hands. "Time out. Did you say the bathroom on the Lunar level?"

"The one next to the yoga studio, yes, why?"

All of Piper's attention left Shal and Tesla to focus entirely on Annie. "There was an out-of-order notice?"

"Y-Yes . . ." Annie fluttered her eyelids as if she were bringing up photos. "I thought it would be faster than walking to one at the next junction."

"What time?"

"I'm not certain. Oh!" She flashed her wrist key fob. "But we can check the receipt. It should only be a little before then."

"Did you record walking down there by any chance?"

Annie shook her head. "You're frightening me a little."

Piper chewed her lower lip for a moment, and Tesla leaned forward when the officer took a breath. "There was no scheduled maintenance for that bathroom."

Shal's body language shifted subtly next to Tesla, and if she hadn't been watching him she would have missed it. What had just caught his attention? Oh. Ory had also said he'd gone to the restroom and was gone a long time. If it was out of order, he would have noted that as his reason for being gone so long. But Annie wouldn't . . . why would she tell such an easy-to-check lie?

"So what I'm hoping is that you recorded the sign, or remember seeing or passing someone on the way past that bathroom who can confirm that there was a sign at the time you went past it."

"Maybe?" She looked to Tesla for support. "I wasn't honestly paying attention."

"Officer." Tesla couldn't believe that Annie would be mixed up in this in any way. She'd been nothing but kind. On the other hand, she had a long history of assholes being kind to her who were jerks to other people. But still. "If you have an accusation, make it. Otherwise, leave her alone."

"Oh, making accusations isn't my job." Officer Piper's voice turned bitter beneath her smile. "My job is keeping order and making notes for 'the proper authorities.'"

GIMLET

2 oz gin
1 oz lime juice
.75 oz simple syrup

Shake all over ice for 15 seconds. Strain into martini glass
or coupe.

The bed in their suite was so large that Gimlet had an entire side
to herself and had taken over two pillows. Tesla lay curled next to
Shal, with one leg thrown over his thigh, in a position that they'd
silently negotiated through the night to respect their various in-
juries. She had taken her DBPS off sleep mode so that she could
feel the fine hairs leading down Shal's torso and the warmth of his
skin against hers.

She nuzzled the side of his neck, preternaturally soft from shav-
ing, and redolent of Icelandic moss and volcanic ash mixed with
his own warm musk. He sighed, and the muscles of his leg flexed
under her thigh as he pointed his toes. Half opening his good
eye, he peered at her. Shifting in the giant Martian king bed, he
brought his hand down her back, gliding over her skin to draw
circles at the base of her spine, then trace around the curve of her
buttocks to—

The door chimed.

He eyed the door to their bedroom. "Please tell me you didn't
order breakfast in bed?"

"I did not." She brought her hand gently up his chest, dodging
the nanogen bandages that lay over his cracked rib, and into an
orbit around one nipple. "Did you?"

"Nope." He turned carefully toward her, sliding his knee between her legs. "And it's our honeymoon, so on the advice of our lawyer, I say we ignore th—"

The door chimed again. She kissed him, enjoying the rare delicacy of newly shorn skin. His lips were silken and warm. With one hand, he anchored her hips as he pressed closer to her. The other brushed over her hair, freed from its wig, and painted warm velvet across—

The door chimed again. Gimlet woke, snorting. She sprang off the bed, barking in a constant yodel of fury. As the irate ruffs transited across the living room, they changed into yips and whines of greeting. A message notification appeared on the ceiling from Security Officer Maria Piper.

Tesla's head dropped back against the pillow. "What time is it even?"

On the ceiling overhead, the time appeared—8:07 a.m.

Shal groaned and rolled to lie on his back. "I'll talk to her." Throwing the covers off, he started to get out of bed and stopped with a hiss.

"Shal?"

"I'm fine. I just forgot." He pushed himself the rest of the way upright. "*Lindgren,* lights."

The lights in the bedroom slowly brightened as if blue dawn were coming to Mars. Barefoot, Shal padded to the closet and the gentle light drew the most intriguing shadows across his buttocks. Tesla watched the play of muscles in his biceps as he pulled his bathrobe on. The light-blue cotton had a shawl collar that emphasized his shoulders.

Shal turned and saw her watching. "What?"

"I'm engaging in the traditional honeymoon activity of very, very much enjoying watching my spouse." She sat up, with more care than he had taken. "I'll come with you."

"You can stay in bed."

"Someone has to wrangle Gimlet," she called after him. Tesla dialed the DBPS up so she wouldn't have to fight to get out of bed. Even so, her left leg was still weak enough that she needed to balance for a moment before she got her pajamas. The matching silk tank and shorts were in muted heather with an aster that Shal had embroidered over her heart. The soft shush of the silk made her feel calm. It was an illusion, but one she needed. She followed Shal into the sitting room of the suite. Their Terran-level suite had been done in blues and greens, but this one was ruddy ochres and sands.

Piper was already kneeling on the deep pile of the gray-and-salmon carpet while Gimlet wiggled in frantic devotion against her knees, leaving a fine patina of white fur. "Are you the most neglected dog? I know. I know. It's terrible. I see your pain. Yes, I do. Yes, I do. Poor neglected girl."

"What brings you by this morning?"

"Sorry it's so early." Piper looked up from petting Gimlet. "Some questions came— Your hair is brown."

Tesla reached up and touched her natural hair, cut in a tight astrobuzz that left a longer forelock sticking up. "Wig. Previously, I mean."

"Couldn't tell. Damn good wig."

Given how often she had to wear them to avoid being recognized, there was no point in wearing uncomfortably cheap ones. Tesla hooked a thumb back at the room. "Wait'll you see the others."

"Noted. Anyway, some questions came up. If I may?"

Shal shoved his hands into the pockets of his bathrobe. "Sure, go ahead."

"Annie gave you as an alibi. Said you were with her until right before Ruth Fish fell. Tell me what your movements were?"

"Okay . . . We left the studio together and then she doubled back to get a capelet that she had left. And this isn't going to be your only question, so I'm going to order breakfast." Shal sauntered to the wall screen, calves bunching below the bottom of his bathrobe. "Anyone else want something?"

"Congee and some breakfast fries." Tesla slowly settled into the office chair by the curvilinear desk that was built into the wall as if it were a piece of Martian shale.

"Maria, what about you?"

"I wouldn't object to coffee." She masked it well, but she could not have gotten much more sleep than they had.

"I'll make that for you." Shal gestured to the espresso machine he traveled with, even before meeting Tesla.

"Spiffy, thanks. I'll join you in the fry order, but from experience they'll be soggy by the time they get to this part of the ship, so maybe use the . . ." Piper stopped, staring at the disassembled mess of the matter printer where it lay in a Frankensteinian jumble on the room's built-in wet bar. "What happened here?"

"Oh . . . I." Sure. There was a plausible lie for having gutted the cabin's matter printer and the array of liquor bottles surrounding it. "I was tinkering."

"Uh-huh." Piper fondled Gimlet's ear and looked over to Shal. "She do this often?"

"Nah—only after someone has drugged me." Shal tapped in the order on the wall display as if getting drugged was something that they regularly dealt with. "I'll order the fries and we'll deal with soggy. Tell Maria what you found."

"Shal—" What happened to "don't volunteer things"? This was going to be a longer conversation than she wanted to have over their local network. Tesla looked deeper into the suite past the billowing white curtains that almost masked the door to the bedroom. "Maybe we should put on real clothes."

Piper shrugged and shook her head. "I don't mind."

"But I do." It was hard to express hauteur with pajamas and bedhead, but not impossible. Tesla stared at Piper, relying on stillness to convey her unwillingness to do anything else until she was dressed.

Shal looked at her, and his sleuthing face appeared momentarily because he knew her well enough to know that under normal circumstances, she would not care. His mouth twitched. "Yeah . . . getting dressed is a good call. No telling when they'll haul me off somewhere again." He headed toward the bedroom. "But if we're not dressed and back when my cornbread arrives, I'm going to be crushed. It comes with real bu—"

Piper raised her eyebrows. "Let me get this straight. I arrive to ask you questions and you immediately want to talk privately?"

So much for being subtle.

"It's that or call my lawyer and we're at"—Tesla checked her HUD for the current delay—"eleven-minute lag for comms."

Sighing with such exasperation that she nearly ignited the entire room, Piper looked at the ceiling. "Fine. Leave the door open."

"Door yes. Curtain no. I really am getting dressed." Tesla pushed herself out of the desk chair, keeping her back perfectly straight, and could still feel Shal gauging the quality of her movement. "Gimlet, be a good girl."

In the bedroom, Shal drew the curtain and eyed the massive Martian king bed. "I swear that thing is so big it has its own gravitational pull."

"That's just your exhaustion." Tesla went to the dresser and pulled open a drawer.

"Speak for yourself. I spent most of my time in the sick bay sleeping." Shal grabbed a pair of gray linen trousers with artful grass stains on the knees. "Come back to bed."

She looked pointedly at the curtain, and Piper was right on the other side of it. "Is now really the time to have make-up sex?"

"I can think of worse times, but you're the one who got the manual."

"The manual says that if I lie down again, I'll never . . ."

Next to her, Shal had dropped his bathrobe and stood in the buff. He still had the trim build of a bantamweight boxer, with defined shoulders tapering into a narrow waist. The nanogen bandage wrapped around his ribs and the bruising seemed better.

"You'll never what?" He paused with the trousers in his hand.

Tesla shook her head and realized that she'd taken a step closer to him. "I'll never get up again." On the other hand, why not take a step closer to him. It was their honeymoon, despite . . . everything. Tesla ran her hand down his chest, feeling the dark tickles of the hair beneath her palm. *::What happened to "answer honestly but don't volunteer"?::*

His voice lowered into a husky purr. "Staying in bed seems like a feature, not a bug." He bent down to kiss her, dark curls falling across his face. *::Given that there's no way to hide the state of the matter printer and she asked a direct question, I don't think answering her counts as volunteering. We can't investigate this, and she can. Every case I've worked has gone smoother when I was able to cooperate with the law. Plus, Gimlet likes her.::*

::Gimlet likes everyone.:: She resisted temptation and stepped back to grab a dusky red cardigan that Fantine had crocheted for her. "We don't want to keep Officer Piper waiting, even if this is a flagrant violation of our rights." Her voice rose a bit at the end to carry into the other room.

"It's inconvenient." He pulled on the trousers, and she made a note for later that he was commando. "Look . . . I'm just going to take out a loan against possible make-up sex in the future and say something that'll piss you off."

"Fascinating . . ." She swapped the pajama bottoms for Lunar cargo pants, with snug ankles and plenty of pockets. "Go on."

"I know you make an effort to be conscious of your privilege, but . . . you're doing a lot of running roughshod over people right now."

"They arrested you. They beat you." Her cheeks were hot with embarrassment or anger, and she stalked away from him to the vanity. "That's what privilege is for. Fighting people who are abusing their power."

"Yeah . . . yeah, but servers don't exactly have power that they can abuse."

"Piper is not a server."

"No . . . but she's also trying to do her job and isn't an enemy. So could you just . . . just tone it back a little?"

"Sure." She swallowed, looking at the door to the outer room. "Sure, I'll be conscious of it."

"Thank you."

She ducked her head and opened the wig box, and the weight of needing to wear one made her shoulders slump. It was better than being trapped in the suite. In the mirror, Shal pulled on a nearly translucent cotton kurta with white work embroidered around the collar. He had to try two positions to get it over his head and even then he still winced.

Tesla smoothed her forelock back and pulled on a shoulder-length gold wig. Settling it, she triggered the wig's synthetic setae to cling to her skin, making a nearly invisible seal. The silence hung in the air between them, so she opted for a total change of subject. "So . . . Fish pretty much made a confession. Why try to poison you?"

"Yeah . . . I didn't chase Fish through the halls. So she'd have no reason to target me, unless she was working with someone and that's who I saw. Also, of course . . . that spare body in the composter." Shal rubbed the center of his forehead, pressing hard enough that his fingernails paled.

She pushed away from the wall, barely sinking into the dense pile of the carpet as she walked over to him. She put one hand at the base of his skull and ran the other through his hair to his forehead, taking over at the spot he was rubbing. He dropped his hand.

Shal let his eyes close, breathing slowly and easily under her touch. The only sounds were the quiet hum of the ship's ventilation system and the inarticulate cooing of a human playing with a small dog in the next room.

The sigh that he let out lowered his shoulders. "I should be offering to rub *your* back."

"I'll break out the acubot when Officer Piper is gone."

Shal shuddered and opened his eyes. "I'm not sure how I feel about the fact that you prefer that needled octopus over my— what?"

Tesla's hands had stopped without her say-so as a series of thoughts cascaded through her brain. "Haldan told me that he had a demonstration-model octobot that was missing from his cabin. Ruth Fish also had an octobot—a medical one—when she responded to George's stabbing. That type of machine tends to be a good climber."

Shal shifted so he could look back at her. "So are you guessing that it pushed Fish or stabbed Saikawa?"

"Why not both?" Tesla traced a circle below his shoulder blade. "But there are at least two other roboticists on board with us."

"Jalna and . . . you don't think the kid is involved?"

She shrugged. "I don't know, but what's very interesting is that Ewen used a polydactyl octopoid in a competition I judged."

Shal raised a finger. "Are octopoids and octobots the same thing?"

"Oh, you are so adorable . . ." She leaned over and kissed him. "An octopoid is based on an octopus and has eight semiautonomous drivers, one for each leg. An octobot has a central processor and can be any eight-legged creation. And before you ask, my acubot is an octopoid."

"I'm going to smile and nod because I recognize all of those words."

Tesla laughed and headed for the closet, stepping just wrong enough on the curved floor that her back seized. It made her stride falter but didn't stop her. "Hang on, I can show you how to spot the difference."

Behind her, cotton rustled as Shal followed her to the walk-in closet. "What I'd like to know is if there's a significance to Ewen using an octopoid versus an octobot."

"Two things . . . First, the octopoid is a more complex machine. Second. They didn't want me to talk about it with their dad." Tesla pushed the activation button on the acubot's all-in-one sterilization and carrying case. The case played a gentle chime and whirred open on a glowing deep lavender and thoroughly empty chamber.

"Aw, hell . . . Seriously?" Shal looked at the ceiling. "I mean, it's not as if you specialize in robotics and could modify that and drive it remotely without even thinking about it."

"Specialized. Past tense. I'd have to think about it these days." Tesla stared at the interior of the case where her acubot should be. "Dammit. Also . . . now that I think about it. Why was Haldan taking an octobot to Mars as a demo model? They aren't exactly cutting-edge technology unless it does something super-interesting."

"I love your brain so much. Do we know what Ory does?"

"Nope."

Shal backed out of the walk-in closet. "Let's go talk to Maria. And yes, I hear your indrawn breath of protest, but we don't have time for make-up sex right now."

Tesla laughed, following him. "You know that's not what I was going to say."

"Hey, I didn't get the manual." He leaned in and kissed her, lips parting. She dialed the DBPS back down so she could feel the fine lines his fingers traced across her back.

It made the fact that her left leg was tingling with pins and needles more obvious and the clamor in her lower back louder, as if—*and something is crushing her spine so all she can catch are short, gasping breaths that get cut off with red-hot stabbing pain*—Cabin. The walls were gray. The comforter was a deep rose. Shal's eyes were creased with worry. One curl hung on his forehead separated from the others. Tesla clenched Shal's upper arms and held still, trying to wait out the surge of sensations.

He watched her carefully. "You sure I can't talk you into lying down again?"

It was the smart thing to do. She'd had this particular pinched nerve before, and it was deeply aggravating until she could get it straightened out. Tesla bit her lower lip and let her breath out, nodding. "Maybe just until—"

Piper called from the other room. "Food's here."

"Maybe after I eat." She smiled at him, knowing there was a brittleness under it that she couldn't quite hide, and leaned up to kiss her spouse. "Let's not let the fries get soggier."

He snorted but stopped arguing with her. He hovered a little as they left the bedroom, but he didn't try to stop her again. The restriction in her stride wasn't a new thing, but it meant she was going to have to break the cane out if they left the cabin. Yoga had been painful, but those chairs. Who had designed them?

Shal held the curtain aside for her and she limped through, tempted to dial the DBPS back up again. Her focus shifted as she crossed the threshold into the suite's lounge. The savory scent of deep-fried starch and salt filled the room. Piper was talking to the server that had brought the food, who was crouching to pet Gimlet.

"—treating you that way. You want me to talk to anyone?"

Immanuel Rudawski, the server who had been at the R-Bar, looked up from Gimlet. His dark-blue locs were twisted into a pair of low buns at the back of his head. "Thanks, I'm—" He saw Tesla and did a double take. Immanuel jumped to his feet so quickly that, in Martian gravity, he bounded back a meter. "I have to go."

Gimlet shied away from the sudden movement and bolted for Tesla. The little dog stood on her hind legs, paws rested against Tesla's thigh so that she didn't have to bend down to scratch her ears. "I'm sorry that I startled you."

"Immanuel?" Piper looked from him to Tesla and Shal. "You wanna—"

"I have to go. I have other orders to deliver." He backed away, then turned and practically ran out of the cabin.

Piper stared after him. "What the hell was that?"

Probably he was afraid that Tesla was going to ask him questions again, this time in front of someone who could report on him. Shal ran his hand through his hair. "I have no idea. Unless it's my devastating charm and good looks. It's often a problem in casual social interactions. Why, I once derailed an entire Titian diplomatic contingent's deliberations on which sherry to purchase as a commemorative gift by raising my left eyebrow." He raised the right eyebrow. "Like so, I'll spare you the full force of using my good side. You may thank me later."

"It's obvious when you're trying to change the topic, you know." Piper turned from him to Tesla. "What about you? You know why he ran?"

That was a direct question, so Tesla nodded. "Partially. He was working the R-Bar the night that George Saikawa was murdered."

Piper froze. She stared at Tesla long enough for it to be uncomfortable. "No. He wasn't."

"Um . . . yes. I saw him there."

"Are you certain it was him?"

"Blue locs, freckles. Yes. It's possible I misremembered, but the bartender on the pool deck also said that Immanuel was there."

"Got multiple reactions to that . . ." Piper looked up and to the left as if she were accessing something on an HUD. "First of them is that he's not on the employee roster for the R-Bar that night. Second, why the hell were you talking to the bartender on the pool deck about the murder?"

"Because you were holding my spouse."

Piper pinched the bridge of her nose, staring at the floor. She snorted and dropped her hand. "These fries are getting cold."

Shal followed her to the tray of food and lifted a silver dome to reveal a small cast-iron skillet filled with golden cornbread. Steam still rose from it, carrying sweet and savory heaven into the room. "Look at that!" He snapped his fingers and turned to the espresso machine. "Oh, Maria. You wanted coffee? Cappuccino? Loonie pressure steep? Flat white? We have real cow milk."

"You know you could have just ordered coffee, right?" Piper picked up the plate of fries and looked at the couches and the bar stools by Tesla's reconfigured matter printer. "Cappuccino, if we're being all flash. Where do y'all want to sit? On comfy chairs or next to your science project?"

Tesla snagged her congee, relishing the warm bowl's promise of savory goodness. "Comfy chairs. And ordering coffee from a known, good restaurant is delightful. From a random barista, it's a roulette of possible failures."

"Besides, I enjoy the rituals of beverages." Shal opened a canister of beans and poured some into the compact machine's built-in grinder. He eyed the bottles of liquor on the counter between the espresso machine and the reworked matter printer. "I'm still pissed about the Lunacy gin. Doll, which tea did you want?"

Piper picked up a fry and gestured at Tesla with it. "All right, I'm trying to understand why you let him call you 'doll.'"

"Oh . . . it's a joke." Tesla shrugged as she lowered herself into the firmest of the chairs. "He has this collection of antique detective novels—"

"First editions, where I can find them. But which tea?"

"The Zhu Lu." She pushed back out of the chair and it took both hands for her to stand. "Hey, Shal . . . I've been out of the room, so it's probably best to run the milk. In answer to your earlier question, Officer Piper, I made a scanner so I can tell what's in each of the bottles. I wanted to see if there was any oxyfeldone in them."

Shal paused with his hand on the grinder. "Shit . . . the Lunacy gin was bad enough. If they've taken my cappuccinos from me too . . ."

Piper dipped her fry in garlic aioli and watched Tesla cross the room. "And was there? Oxyfeldone?"

"Not yet. But the Lunacy gin, which is our favorite, had been swapped out for a different gin."

"They don't export it!" Shal pulled the foil pack of milk out of their minifridge and studied the contraption that Tesla had made. "How does . . . Oh. Thank you."

She transferred the foil bag to the open chamber of her make-shift scanning unit. "Do you want to tell us who would have had access to our things that could have swapped the gin?"

Behind her, Piper sighed. "Is Gimlet allowed people food?"

"No, but she'll lie to you."

"That's what I thought. Nice try, girl. No fries for you." Her chair creaked as she leaned back in it. "All right . . . I've had some serious misgivings about how this investigation is going—I said no fries, seriously."

On her handheld, Tesla opened the app for the scanner she'd cobbled together and tapped Start. "Can't we just get everyone together and have Shal deduce in front of them to scare the killer into confessing?"

Shal leaned against the counter. "It doesn't work that way. Careful interviews and lots of footwork. It's part of why I don't want to spend my honeymoon investigating." He snapped his fingers. "Oh! Maria. Someone stole Tesla's acubot."

"Her what now?"

"Acubot. It's a needled monster for—"

Someone knocked on the door.

Tesla froze as the matter printer whirred into life beside her. "Did we order anything else?"

"Nope." Shal glanced at Piper. "Immanuel having second thoughts?"

"Not the way he lit out of here." She transferred the fries out of the reach of Gimlet, the ever-hopeful, and stood. She pulled her handy out of her pocket and swiped across it, then frowned. "They're using a spoofer."

"Swell." Shal pushed up the sleeves of his kurta and cracked his knuckles. "I'll take it. If they're friendly, so am I. If they aren't, you're better situated to call for help than I am."

The suite felt unnaturally quiet as he walked to the door. The long, sheer curtains stirred in the breeze from the fans. Gimlet started to follow him, but Piper blocked her with a foot. "Stay put, little girl."

Tesla cued Fantine up on speed dial. There were legitimate reasons to use a spoofer, but the timing on this did not make her feel good. Shal leaned against the door and looked out the manual peephole. You could lie to a spoofer, but lying to the human eye was harder. He grunted. "Well, that's a surprise."

And he opened the door. "Mx. Kuznetsova. What can I do for you?"

Suffering Bastard

4 oz ginger beer

1 oz lime juice

1 oz gin

1 oz bourbon

1 dash Angostura bitters

1 orange wedge

Add all ingredients to a collins glass over ice. Stir. Garnish with orange wedge.

From the hallway, Haldan said, "I, um, I told your spouse I would meet her here after getting you out of sick bay, but she wasn't here and then . . . May I—may I come in?"

"Sure thing." Shal stepped back. "I hope you don't mind that Officer Piper is here from security. Just for playtime with our adorable rogue—you remember Gimlet?"

"I . . . Yes. I do." Haldan paused inside the doorway and hesitated, looking at the little dog, and then found Tesla. "You okay?"

"Fine, thanks." It was a question she should ask him. His cheeks were pinched with exhaustion and the cuff of his blouse had a coffee stain, and not in an artful, expensive, my-clothes-need-special-care status sort of way. "And yourself?"

"I'm—" His voice broke and he stopped, staring at the Martian-tan walls with his fists clenched by his sides. He swallowed and looked back to them. For a moment his gaze flicked to Piper and then he nodded at Tesla. "I'm fine. You've got company and I don't want to disturb you. I just wanted to make certain that you were both safe."

Piper stepped forward. "I'm sorry for your loss."

"Thank you. I'm still in—" He stopped again and the lines of tension in his shoulders could have been scaffolding for a ship. Bending his head, Haldan appeared to stop breathing for a moment. He took a careful breath. "I'm still in shock. About George. And then Ruth. Dear God. I knew the drinking was a problem, I just didn't think . . ."

"Come sit down." Shal gestured deeper into the suite, guiding Haldan, who seemed to cave in on himself with each step.

He sank into the office chair, which was the seat that was easiest on Tesla's back. But she couldn't begrudge it, looking at him, with his elbows on his knees and his hands buried in his teal hair. "In college she was always . . . moody, let's say. But who isn't?"

The man seemed just wrecked. Tesla patted her dog on the shoulder. "Gimlet, go say hi."

Gimlet trotted over to him and lay down with her head on his foot.

Piper sat in the chair opposite Haldan, pushing the home fries closer to him. "When was the last time you ate?"

He raised his head, pulling his foot out from under the little dog. "I . . . I don't. Last night?" He sniffled, fishing a cloth handkerchief out of his pocket. "I figure I'll go to the buffet at some point."

"That should be fine, as long as you avoid the reconstituted veal." Piper made a face. "Not even Gimlet would eat that for dinner."

Gimlet's head came up. Her tail wagged ferociously.

"Uh-oh. You've said the magic word." Tesla limped to the cabinets to grab Gimlet's food. "And someone hasn't been fed breakfast."

A double bark punctuated that remark, and Gimlet trotted after her.

Piper nudged the fries again. "They're soggy, but the aioli is good."

He nodded, still staring at the floor.

"Don't make me Mom you without a license." Piper watched until he picked up a fry and mechanically put it in his mouth. "Is there anyone else on board who would know both Ruth and George?"

He blew his nose, trying for discretion. "Maybe? But I didn't even know Ruth was on board until I went down to sick bay."

Tesla paused in front of the scanner. "How about Ory Slootmaekers, he/him?"

"Who?"

"Bald. White. Early fifties. He's in George's yoga class."

"I don't know—" His voice broke and he lowered his head, twisting the handkerchief between his fists. "Ruth and I didn't really stay in touch after college."

Shal stood with his head lowered, looking out from beneath his brows, just behind Haldan, but he was watching Piper. Her mouth was pursed as she picked up another fry.

Tesla cleared her throat. "I mean, we don't . . . we don't think Dr. Fish really killed herself, do we? If it was an isolated case, sure, but not with two other bodies."

"What?" Haldan's head came up sharply. "What do you mean two?"

Piper sighed. "Not common knowledge."

"Oh." Tesla removed the foil milk pack from the scanning bed and checked the results. Clean. Sighing with relief, she stuck the bag of dog food in its place. "I just thought . . . I mean, *we* figured it out. And then Wisor told us, so . . ."

"Doll, you were on the bridge. And he thought I'd done it."

Gimlet scratched at the counter, whining that her food was Right There and she didn't have it yet. Tesla started the scanner app. "Right. I forgot. Great."

"Who else did you tell?" Piper asked.

The matter printer whirred as the scanning mechanism moved down and around the bag of dog food. "I don't think—"

"Excuse me." Haldan's voice was shaking and he had gone completely ashen. "Who else is dead?"

The layers of Piper's sigh contained information about Tesla's upbringing, her inconsiderate nature, and deep concern about the amount of paperwork facing the security officer. "We don't know."

"You don't know?" Haldan stared at her with abject horror. "How the hell can you not know who they are? I mean, the ship has a roster. We have to sign God knows how much paperwork to board and you don't know?"

"Nope. Let me assure you, I am pretending to be calm about this." Leaning forward, Piper swiped a fry through the aioli. "I am not."

"But Ruth— She left a suicide note."

Tesla shook her head. "That was a confession . . . She didn't actually say anything about killing herself, did she?"

"Blood." Shal closed his eyes, brows coming together as he tilted his head. "Tesla— You took a picture. Is there blood on the floor?"

Shaking, she pulled up the snap she'd taken. Yellow caution tape. Blurred spoofer zones. "I can't tell. It's in the spoofer zone."

"Dammit." Shal turned to Piper, expression tense with the weight of memory. "I'm remembering right, though. There was no blood. She was dead before she hit the floor."

Her expression was flat and cold. "You know I can't share any information about the cases."

"That's—that's a yes. Why would someone—?" Haldan covered his mouth, looking like he was barely holding down panic. He turned in his chair to find Shal. "You saw someone, didn't you? When George was . . . You chased someone."

"Yeah . . . narrow, straight build. Pale. Seventy-three kilosish. Black bowl cut. Sound like anyone you know?"

Haldan frowned, looking up and to the left as if he were accessing his memory or a HUD database. "Not personally . . . but George's yoga coach? At least the bowl cut."

Tesla said, "There's also a ship employee, Yuki Something, who was with Nile Silver in the R-Bar looking at the stage."

"Pierced ears," Shal said.

"What?" Haldan frowned.

"Yuki has multiple piercings in one ear. No piercings on the person I chased." Shal wheeled around and headed for the bar. "On the other hand, from below and behind, a bowl cut hides a multitude of ears."

"And you can take earrings out." Gimlet rested her paw on Tesla's foot and made a sigh that was halfway to being a whine. Dragging herself away from the conversation, Tesla checked the scanner and the results were clean. She poured food in Gimlet's bowl. "Sit." Gimlet sat. "Down." Gimlet was the most downward dog ever. "Stay."

Piper watched Tesla carry the bowl a little away from Gimlet. "I did not think she obeyed commands."

"When breakfast is on the line, she is the most obedient." And when Gimlet was on-duty, but Tesla didn't feel the need to advertise her PTSD to Haldan. She gripped the counter with one hand, bracing, as she set the bowl down.

"I asked Fantine to get a list of names of people who had access to our cabin and gin. If we ask for the same thing for your cabin and compare, then that ought to narrow the field. Gimlet, release."

Before Tesla finished the "R," Gimlet shot forward and began to inhale her food with ferocious snarfing snorts.

"I was actually wondering if we could take this contraption to Haldan's cabin and test his booze . . ." Shal scowled at it. "Can this be moved?"

"Y-Yesss . . . ? Yes. But it would be easier to bring the rum here."

"Better, as evidence, if we don't move it."

"Ah . . ." She studied the collection of parts loosely connected by wires. "With a cart? Yes."

"I'll order it and you can make that coffee you promised while we wait." Piper slid off her chair to kneel on the floor and patted her thigh. "Gimlet? There's my sweet girl. Let me know who your lawyer comes up with, and I can compare them to my list."

So Piper wouldn't share anything with them, but was perfectly willing to take their work and—and it was different for her. She might lose her job. Fantine would get Shal out of any trouble.

"Would your list come from the same source that said Immanuel wasn't working in the R-Bar?"

"Swapping shifts doesn't change security access levels—no, the fries are still not for you—and yes. Comparing my lists to your lists gives an additional data set."

Shal said, "Now that I've bribed you successfully with Gimlet playtime, and we're trading names . . . Can you tell me who ID'd me?"

"Can't. You know that."

He shrugged. "Fair. Can't blame me for trying."

Tesla should not push, but there were so many things the cruise ship wasn't doing. "Have you interviewed Ory or Nile Silver? They were arguing with George before she was killed."

Gimlet snuffle-snorted with delight while Piper concentrated on petting her as if that would give her plausible deniability about being in the room as the conversation continued.

Piper's hand slowed on Gimlet, pausing on the little dog's ear. She fondled it, her mouth tight. "There was an active spoofer in the R-Bar. None of our interviewees have given accounts that match yours. No one remembers seeing George at karaoke at all."

"Oh, come on. Immanuel definitely saw George, because he dropped an entire tray of glassware on her. Ask him."

"Thank you for that hot tip." Piper's voice was level, but there was an edge under it. "I need you to understand that just because you don't see me working doesn't mean I'm not doing my job when I'm out of your direct line of sight."

Tesla bit down hard on a retort. She was mad because she

wanted to win, not because she was right. She took in a slow breath, felt the air expand her lungs, and breathed out, letting it carry away some of her disproportionate anger. Piper was doing the best that she could in difficult circumstances. "I know. I'm sorry. And thank you for keeping us in the loop as much as you have."

"Sorry." Haldan raised his hand. "But who's Immanuel?"

"A server." Tesla pinched her nose, trying to keep from just yelling at everyone. Everyone in the room was trying to cooperate, and Piper, at least, seemed willing to consider that Shal was not the only suspect. So they needed to work together and play to their strengths. Hers was money. Shal's was detectivey stuff. Piper's was . . . also detectivey stuff, combined with access to the ship's information. And Haldan's was . . . "Oh, hang on. Haldan, it just occurred to me that you can probably get the list of passengers with access easier than Fantine can."

He stared at her for a moment, mouth a little open, and squeezed his eyes shut. A single tear escaped before he lowered his head to rest it in his palms. "Right. I own the goddamned ship." He half laughed, blowing his nose again. "George said I couldn't survive without her, and I think she was probably right."

Remember the Maine

2 oz rye
.75 oz sweet vermouth
.25 oz cherry Heering
1 dash absinthe
1 cherry

Stir all ingredients over ice for 40 seconds. Strain into
coupe. Garnish with cherry.

The elevator music tried to be upbeat and calming at the same
time and was doomed to failure. Tesla leaned against the glass
elevator, gripping her cane with one hand and Gimlet's leash in
the other. Cradling a cup of coffee, Piper nudged the service drone
back further into the elevator so it wouldn't block the door as Haldan and Shal got on.

They'd thrown a tablecloth over the modified matter printer,
and a corner of the cloth trailed on the floor. Shal had said that
they needed Piper with them so they had an official cruise line
representative to record the process. It was so annoying when he
was right. Tesla hooked the end of her cane under the tablecloth
and tucked it back onto the drone.

Shal stood at the glass wall, looking out. "Pretty good view of
the Yacht Club entrance from here."

The floor of the Terran level was clear of caution tape. Pedestrians walked down the terrace without any sign that someone had
died there the day before. Tesla chewed the inside of her cheek,
thinking. "Do we know where Dr. Fish was scheduled to be before here? I mean, the ship."

Piper pressed the button for the Terran level. "What do you mean?"

"She changed ship rotations . . ." Tesla turned to Haldan. "Two weeks before? Can you find out?"

He nodded. "I only know because she told me, but I can get the—"

"Hold the door!" A teenager slid into the elevator and pressed their hand against the door.

Five more giggling kids, damp from a pool, crowded into the elevator. "Soak me, that was awesome!"

The kid who'd held the door let it close, turning to their friends. "I told you the Martian pool was flash. That surface tension is— Hey! A dog!"

"Oh my land! She is so cute!"

Even on-duty, Gimlet was fully aware that she was, indeed, the most adorable and worthy creature ever assembled by nature or laboratory. Her tail was generating its own electrical current of delight.

"Can I pet your—shiiiiit. You're Tesla Crane."

"That's right." She'd been so focused on making sure her jerry-rigged scanner hadn't come apart that not only had she left the courtesy mask in their suite but now she was stuck on a slow elevator as it transitioned between gravity levels with a bunch of kids. It was time to deploy her secret weapon. "And this is Gimlet, who would be happy to be petted. Gimlet, go say hi."

Gimlet's tail wagged faster.

The one who recognized Tesla grinned. "I dressed up like your dad for Halloween when I was a kid. That suit! So cool. Pew! Pew!" They mimed firing bolts from their hands. "Why didn't you use it on *Zero-G Dancing with the Stars*? It would have been flash. Like, epic, acid flash."

"Also outdated and unsafe." Not that her version had been better. *Stars and black.* Elevator. Dog. Teenagers. Shal. Tablecloth. "Did you have an interest in robotics?"

"He thinks he do." One of the other teens draped their arm over the boy's shoulders. "Boy Wonder here can't change a light."

"Hey." Boy Wonder blushed. "It was one lightbulb."

"Well, you'll be happy to know that Gimlet is not a lightbulb." In fact, her dog would already be belly-up if there were space in the elevator. For that matter, as Earth gravity asserted itself, Tesla would also not mind going belly-up. "Go ahead. Really. You can pet her."

The kids crowded down, pressing Tesla farther back into the elevator. Her spine settled and compressed under the slowly increasing gravity load. One of the kids leaned on the cart, trying to squeeze in and something under the tablecloth made a quiet snap. Great.

The doors to the elevator opened on the Terran level, and the kids tumbled out. "Thanks for letting us pet your dog!"

Haldan held the door as Piper guided the luggage cart out. Tesla followed, leaning on her cane more heavily here than she had on the Martian level. With each step, it felt like a butter knife extended from her spine into the muscles on the right side. A dull pain but not terrible. The dragging weakness of her left leg was more annoying. She couldn't mask that.

Shal was trying to look like he wasn't watching her, but she could tell by the way he was oriented toward her with one hand slightly away from his body as if he were ready to catch her. Gimlet didn't pull on her lead, even though she clearly wanted to follow the kids, and stayed in perfect heel position. Even Haldan was watching Tesla with a line of concern between his brows.

On the other hand, she wasn't sure she'd seen him *not* concerned, so that was either his natural expression or the situation. He leaned down. "How often does that happen?"

"Often enough." She waved at the kids as they left. "And now you know why I take Gimlet with me everywhere."

"Smart." He led the way past the ficus trees toward the entrance to the Terran-level Yacht Club.

The doors whooshed open and they entered the calm oasis of the lobby. Auberi looked up from behind their concierge desk. Their face brightened as they rose. "Mx. Kuznetsova! Mx. Crane, and Mx. Steward! And the petite Gimlet! I am so pleased to see you all. So happy. Ah! And Officer Piper, you are well, no?"

No, but that wasn't the answer they wanted. Shal grinned at the concierge and took Tesla's hand, raising it to his lips to kiss. "Now that I've got my best gal, nothing could be finer."

On his other side, Piper snorted, shaking her head. She gave a nod to Auberi, who hesitated before responding with a renewed smile for Haldan. "Ah! Mx. Kuznetsova. Your friend was looking for you about the tea time."

"Tea time?" He stopped in the lobby and looked baffled. "I don't have any plans for tea."

"My apologies. They were speaking of golf. Tee time." They looked back at the ostentatious paper notepad where they had written the message. "Mx. Smith."

Haldan still looked baffled and then frightened. "Smith?" He turned to Piper. "Smith . . . ?"

Tesla said, "Annie or Jalna?"

Auberi shook their head. "No, no. No one from the Yacht Club."

Piper stepped forward and set her cup of coffee on Auberi's desk. "When was this?"

"About a half hour ago." They consulted what looked like a paper planner, but it had smart ink controls at the edges. "Specifically, 8:53 a.m."

Piper nodded and scrolled through a couple of screens on her handheld. One she tapped three or four times, and then sighed. "Okay . . . Old-fashioned way then. What did Mx. Smith look like?"

"They wore a courtesy mask but were European, I believe, with hair that was quite curly. Red. A natural red, to my eye. But at the shoulders with layers. Mm . . . freckles. About Mx. Crane's height, perhaps?" They looked at the ceiling as if trying to picture them more clearly. "If I were supplying them with a complimentary T-shirt, I would guess that they wore an XXL."

"Pronouns?"

"They did not say, I am so sorry."

Piper nodded, tapping her screen again. That could be Annie, if she wore a wig and heels. Although her skin was more olive than natural redhead. Definitely not Jalna. From where Tesla was standing, she could see Piper pulling faces together on the page, and it included Annie and Jalna.

After a moment, she turned it to face Auberi. "Do you see Mx. Smith here?"

Auberi studied the screen, frowning, and then shook their head. "I am sorry. I do not."

"You're sure."

"*Oui.* If I were . . . if I were to guess gender based on stereotypes, then I would have said that this passenger was a man."

"Thanks." Piper picked up her coffee mug and took a sip. Turning, she rejoined their group, looking at Haldan. "Ring any bells?"

"No. I don't know anyone who looks like that." He swallowed, looking at Auberi and then back at Piper. "What is going on?"

"Smith. Not Doe?" Shal muttered and rubbed his ear for a moment before exchanging a glance with Piper. "Let's head to his room."

She nodded, guiding the drone forward. Tesla leaned on her cane as they followed Haldan down the Golden Promenade to his room. They didn't talk about the mysterious note, but you didn't need to be a detective to tell that someone had just wanted to know if Haldan were present.

As they passed Tesla and Shal's old cabin, it was weirdly hard not to notice the absence of blood. George Saikawa had died here, and her death was scrubbed from the ship as thoroughly as if it had never occurred.

At the door next to their old cabin, Piper stopped Haldan in the corridor. "Why don't you let me go in first?"

"You don't think . . ."

"I don't know, and I don't like what I don't know. If I go in first, then we'll know."

Shal grunted and stepped up to the side of Haldan's cabin door. "After my own heart. You want . . . ?"

She hesitated and shook her head. "Best not. Unless I call for you."

"Understood." The flatness of his expression said that he wasn't happy about it.

Piper handed Shal her coffee. "Don't spill that. It's the best goddamned coffee I've had, and I'm mad about it."

"I'm delighted to piss you off."

"Don't be sure about that." She used her key fob to unlock the door and pushed it open. Gimlet stood up, ready to go inside. Tesla tightened her grip on the dog and cane while they waited for Piper. Shal had his head tilted forward and down, eyes half closed as he listened.

Tesla could really only hear the hum of the ship's environmental controls and the faint sound of laughter from the lounge. At the end of the hall, a laundry cart rested against one wall. The other direction turned before the curvature became clear and had nothing more threatening than a service drone and the art on the wall. Granted, it was the "zombie squirrel" painting, but there were no people or footprints or anything else that gave a sign of what they were waiting for.

Piper reappeared in the doorway. "So you really like towel animals, huh?"

Haldan blushed. "They're clever."

They followed him into a suite with a floor plan that was the mirror of theirs, but done in blues and greens for Earth. Towel animals sat perched on chairs and counters. A bat hung from a coat hanger. There were more animals than days of voyage.

Tesla paused next to a literal octopus of towels. "Why do you have so many of them?"

"I . . . um . . . complimented Jenny, my steward, and now she leaves two or three every time in little dioramas." He gestured to a set that had been crafted to look like a dinosaur surfing. "I mean . . . look at that. It's art."

"It's a towel animal." Piper parked the service drone next to the room's wet bar. "You want this here?"

"Yes, thank you." Tesla sat down so that she could reach Gimlet's leash to unclip it.

"Don't be distracted by the medium. Just because it's untraditional doesn't make it less of an artistic expression." Haldan tapped one of the bottles of rum. "This is the one I saw the capsules in."

"Right." Tesla pulled the tablecloth off the contraption. "Let's get . . . dammit. I was afraid of that."

The connection to the reader had an obvious break where the body weight of an exuberant teen had been just enough to separate a cross-scanner from its socket. Tesla sighed as if the entire gravity well of Earth were funneled through her shoulders.

"Problems?" Shal turned from where he was examining cabin walls.

"Snapped connection." Her palms were sweating at the thought of fixing something. "Ironically, I left the tools I printed in our cabin."

"I have some you can use." Haldan headed for his bedroom. "Save you a trip."

"Thanks." She used to travel with a custom set, instead of needing to print them. Not since the Accident. This would be fine. She had assembled the contraption, and the functioning of the scanner wasn't a life-or-death matter. Worst case, if it didn't work, they would turn the bottle over to an analyst on Mars.

Shal tapped a full-length mirror and leaned against the wall to look behind it. "Mm-hm. Hey, Maria. Is this a suite door?"

She glanced across the room, muttering under her breath. "Ye-Yessss."

"You sound surprised."

"A lot of cabin classes on this ship—" She held up her hand to stop his next words. "I didn't clear this room. If I had, you can be damn sure I would have looked at the schematic."

"Who did?"

"Why do you ask me questions you know I won't answer?"

He grinned at her. "You might slip." Fidgeting with the edge of the mirror, he asked, "Any chance you'd open it—I mean, since it leads to our old cabin, it does seem mildly relevant."

"Mm."

Haldan's eyes widened as he stared at the mirror. "Wait. So anyone can just come into my cabin from yours?"

Shal turned and looked across the room to another mirror. "Or from Annie and Jalna's, but I'm not going to ask for access to their room. C'mon, please, Maria? I just want to look around while my cleverer spouse does science things."

"'Science things'? You always this technical?" Piper bent to study the bottle that Haldan had indicated, without touching it. She took pictures with her handheld, which would be higher resolution than a subdermal camera.

"Only when I'm feeling adventurous." Shal sighed. "C'mon. I can't go in there unsupervised."

"I want to be here when she scans the bottle."

"I still have to do the repair." Tesla braced herself on the edge of the cart and bent to look at the break. "It'll take me a while, because I'll have to recalibrate the hemisoidal cross-scan."

Shal took a step toward the door. "See. The hemorrhoidal cross-scan is all uncalibrational, and she'll have to reverse the polarity and shit."

"You have got to get better at bs-ing science." Piper sighed and crossed to the mirror. She put her key fob against the frame, and it slid out and to the side, revealing a security door. "Ten minutes. And only because I have questions too."

"I'll make you all the coffee you want."

"I'm still mad about how good that is." Another touch of her fob opened the door, which opened onto a matching security door, and then beyond that, the back of the other room's mirror.

"So this isn't a fast, discreet passage, then. Hm . . ." Shal headed through the door. As the two of them left the room, Tesla pulled her chair up to the service drone. Leaving the scanner on the cart meant that she could position it anywhere she wanted and get better lighting. She'd need to make sure that the visible break was the only one and also print a calibration test. None of this was a big deal; it had just been a while. Having an audience did not make her happier, but at least she'd handled tools already.

From the bedroom, Haldan made a low, startled sound.

"You okay?" She stood quickly enough that her back seized and she let herself grimace as she gripped the cane to steady herself.

"There's . . . there's a note. On my dressing mirror."'

Tesla limped into the bedroom, stabbing the ground with her cane with each step. Her heartbeat felt like something knocking against her rib cage. Haldan stood in the middle of the floor, holding a slim anodized tool case. The bright-teal metal caught Tesla's eye for a moment. Haldan was facing the wall to her right, opposite his closet.

Scrawled in bright-red lipstick, the note was in large block letters.

REMEMBER THE MAIN

It was easy to see why he hadn't noticed it until he was coming out of the closet. His face was tight around the mouth and he was breathing too fast. Beads of sweat stood out on his brow.

Tesla came to stand beside him, with Gimlet fast on her heels. "Do you know what it means?"

He stared at the mirror, then abruptly shut his eyes. Grimacing as he opened them, he paced in a tiny, tight circle on the floor. "Shit, shit, shit."

"Tell me?"

"It's misspelled." He walked out of the bedroom, as if that

explained anything. "I thought Ruth and George were trying to kill me, but I was—dear God. I think they were . . . But why wouldn't she have told me? Did they not know?"

"I need help connecting the dots here."

"It's a cocktail. It's named after a battleship that sank in the 1800s. Started the Spanish-American War. 'Remember the Maine! To hell with Spain!'" Setting the tools on a side table as he came into the living room, Haldan turned to face her. "You've had experiments go wrong. What's the worst thing that's ever happened?"

Her throat went dry. "You mean, besides killing six people?"

He winced and looked away. "Sorry. I knew that. The point is . . . I mentioned that Ruth was my college roommate. That's also where I met George. We were all in a group of—"

Someone knocked on the door.

Tesla and Haldan both jumped. Gimlet barked, stomping her feet, but stayed by Tesla. A moment later, the housekeeping chime sounded gently through the suite. Haldan grimaced. "It's Jenny. I'm usually out of the room at the gym now."

"So, more towel animals?"

"There are worse things in the world." He headed for the door. "I'll ask her to come back."

"I don't think you should answer the door." Tesla followed, letting her limp be more visible for the sake of speed.

"She'll just come in, if—" The door unlatched with a soft click.

The room went dark and Haldan screamed.

Too Close for Comfort

1.5 oz vodka

1 oz Southern Comfort

1 oz lemon juice

.75 oz simple syrup

1 lemon peel

Shake over ice and strain into martini glass. Garnish with
lemon peel.

Gimlet barked twice in the hall. Without windows, the suite was
as black as space, lit only by a constellation of tiny indicator
lights from the service drone. Tesla dragged in a breath. Four
things she heard. Gimlet growling. Scuffling. Footsteps running.
A door slamming.

She shouted, "*Lindgren,* call security and medical!"

She turned the DBPS down so that she could feel her way
across the room, leading with her right leg. As her eyes adjusted,
dimmer blue nightlights made pools on the floor and the yellow
glow of emergency lights from the hallway defined the door to the
suite. She hit the speed dial for Fantine.

Over the loudspeakers, a calm voice said "Delta, gamma, one
five five three. Delta, gamma, one five five three."

Along the wall next to the door to Haldan's suite, a great smear
of blood was nearly black in the yellow emergency lights and arced
down to point at Haldan, who was slumped on the floor. Tesla
grabbed a towel animal from the side table, shaking out the hip-
popotamus as she went.

She dropped to her knees next to Haldan and her DBPS dialed

up so that she hit the floor with numb ease. Blood soaked his shirt from two wounds. One across his left forearm and another deep in the meat of his trapezius, where a pair of scissors was still sticking out of him.

As stomach-turning as that was, the wound on his arm was more immediately worrying, because it was spurting blood. Tesla set her cane on the floor and clamped the towel on Haldan's arm, squeezing for all she was worth.

Piper burst back into the room from the hallway. "What? Shit. Did you see—"

"It was dark. Haldan? Hal? Look at me." Not again. His eyes were rolled back in his head and he was sliding farther down the wall.

Above her, Shal said, "Split up? You take that direction and I—"

Tesla spared him a glance. "Don't you dare go chasing after whoever did this. I'm not going to have them blame you again."

In the hall, other voices were starting to fill the air with questions about the blackout. None of them were aware that a man had been stabbed. Blood was soaking through the towel as if all she were doing was containing it.

Piper stepped back into the hall, frustration clear on her face. "Folks! The power will be back on in a moment. I'm going to ask you to stay in your cabins—"

"It's dark in there!"

"Yes, I apologize for that and recommend that you leave your cabin door open for the emergency lights, but—"

"What's happened?" That was Annie's voice.

"Our engineers will be able to tell us that later. Right now, what we need is for everyone to remain calm and—"

Someone else grumbled, "This is unacceptable! I want to speak to a manager."

The fury visibly gathered under Piper's skin and she took a breath as if she were going to shout at them, but the wave passed over her and she spoke calmly. "Certainly. I'll call one now." She tapped her badge. "Security. Piper. Requesting backup."

"I—I didn't ask for security."

Piper's smile was grim. "If you want to talk to my manager, that's security." She turned and knelt inside the door, fishing a flashlight out of her pocket. "Let me see?"

The white circle of light burned Tesla's eyes for a moment and painted the towel bright arterial red. Under her hands, Haldan didn't flinch, with his head canted at an awkward angle. In the tight skin of his throat, she could see his pulse beating fast.

The scissors flashed silver in the light. Shal's sewing scissors. She'd had them forged, by hand, as a wedding gift and recognized the pattern of badgers on the handles. Tesla opened her mouth to say something but could hear Shal telling her not to volunteer information. And right now, keeping Haldan alive was the priority.

Piper tapped the badge on her chest. "Wisor. Piper. I'm first on the scene. We need a medic fast."

"What the hell happened?" His tinny voice sounded out of breath as if he were running.

"Haldan Kuznetsova has been stabbed. He's alive but losing blood." She glanced out into the hall. "The power is out here, and there are passengers all over the scene. We need the lights on and to lock this hall down."

"Copy. I show Bob and Candy heading your way and they should beat me there. I'll talk to engineering—coming through—We'll get you lights."

Tesla looked up at Shal. "Grab Gimlet's leash from the chair. We can use that to tourniquet his arm until the medics get here."

"Not ideal . . ." But he moved into the suite, looking for the leash.

"Dead is less ideal."

Annie's voice cut through the murmurs in the hall. "For pity's sake, people. Have sense and keep the hall clear for these folks."

Shal brought the leash back to her and wrapped it below the elbow. As he was doing that, a voice echoed down the hall. "Medic, coming through!"

For a moment, Tesla thought that Ruth Fish was somehow still alive and that she was going to be the one on the scene. A moment later, light and shadow sliced through the dark as a person carrying a flashlight, a full megamover, and a med kit ran down the hall.

Piper waved. "Candy! Bob! Over here."

The medic had been with Ruth Fish when George Saikawa had been stabbed. Candy was older and built like a Russian weightlifter, wearing her gray-and-purple hair in a high side ponytail with a silver lamé bow clipped to the front of it. She skidded to a stop at the door.

Stepping into the room, she pulled bright-blue nitrile gloves out of her pocket. "What happened?"

"I didn't see it—" It felt like déjà vu or a flashback but was happening here and now. This was the second person who had been stabbed in front of her. "He answered the door. The lights went out and he screamed. I can't get his arm to stop bleeding."

"That's my job." The orange med kit unpacked at her command and extended an octopus worth of probes. Tesla's brain quietly noted the movement and sensors and confirmed that the robot was an octopoid. "I need room. You've done well."

Tesla reached for her cane, but her hands were covered in blood. Again. What was she supposed to do? Put her hands on the wall? On the floor?

Shal snatched a towel palm tree off a table and handed it to her. While she wiped the wettest of the blood off, he slid his hand under her bare elbow and braced to steady her as she stood. *::Are you hurt?::*

::No.:: She nearly didn't make it to her feet anyway. Thank heavens the room was dark enough that no one would really be able to see her face. *::Those are your scissors in his shoulder.::*

::*How?*:: His hand tightened on her elbow.

::*I dumped your embroidery bag the night Saikawa was killed.*::

::*Who* is *this person?*:: His hand stayed under her elbow as if he were afraid she was going to topple over. "Let's get you a chair."

Behind them, Bob said, "What are you doing in Kuznetsova's room?"

"They're with me," Piper cut in before Tesla or Shal had to say anything.

"And you had eyes on him the whole time?"

"I was always in the room with him."

"What about her? The bastard had another spoofer. Those goddamned things ought to be outlawed."

Piper sighed in response, and it contained a monograph on comparative work ethics and training as well as a rundown of the various faults that belonged to Bob's most basic abilities. In the clearing of her throat was a brief telegram that simply said Not. Worth. My. Time. "Candy, is there anything you need?"

"What's up with the lights?"

Piper turned and looked deeper into the room. "It was a full power outage, because the emergency doors tripped. Bob?"

He snorted. "No idea. Diagnostic is slow."

And lights would take away the last tiny fraction of privacy Tesla had. She clenched her fists and even after wiping them on the towel, her fingers were sticky with blood. "I need to wash . . . Oh shit. Piper? I need to show you something in the bedroom."

"I do not need anything el—" She came up beside Tesla with a flashlight and handed her the cane. "What is it?"

"Writing on the mirror. Haldan said it was related to something he, Ruth, and George did in college, but then . . ." She waved her hand to encompass the darkness. The carpet caught and dragged the sole of her left foot as she walked to the bedroom.

Who had access to Haldan's room? His towel artist? Would a server like Immanuel have been able to open the door?

"It's on the mirror to the right." At the door to the bedroom, Tesla paused to let Piper go first. "Gimlet, heel."

Piper walked in and turned. The halation of the flashlight uplit her face just enough that Tesla could see her lips purse for a low whistle. "'Remember the Main'?"

"It sounded like they had an experiment go wrong." She turned back, looking for a patch of white in the dark. "Gimlet? Gimlet, come."

Shal stood in the middle of the room and patted his thigh. "Gimlet. Come to Papa." He turned in a circle. "Gimlet?"

On the other side of the room, Candy had transferred Haldan to the megamover and was prepping to haul him out of the room. The scissors still protruded from his shoulder but his eyes were a little open in the medic's flashlight.

Piper came out of the room, shining the flashlight low on the walls. "Gimlet! Where are you, girl?"

Clutching her cane, Tesla stared into the dark corners, willing her dog to be hiding under a chair. And yet . . . "Gimlet?"

Her subdermal chimed, and in her pocket her handheld buzzed. Tesla jumped and flinched and fumbled to get the handy out of her pocket. Fantine glared out from the screen. "Most people would just send me a text message or, heck, I think at this point writing a paper letter and inventing a drone ship to run it back to me would be cheaper than all of these calls. What in the name of Agatha of Sicily makes you think you should—Is that blood? Holy fartweasels on a flying carpet, did you—why does Haldan Kuznetsova have scissors sticking out of him?"

"Someone, who was not me or Shal, stabbed him." This was why Tesla had called Fantine, so that she would be there when they were inevitably brought in for questioning. Her eyes burned trying to see into the darkness. "I'll tell you all about it, but not right now. We can't find Gimlet."

Last Word

.75 oz maraschino liqueur

.75 oz lime juice

.75 oz Green Chartreuse

.75 oz gin

Shake ingredients over ice for 15 seconds. Serve up in a coupe.

Outside the "window" in the Yacht Club's lounge, the projected starfield appeared to drift past as the ship journeyed through space. Tesla sat with her back to it, hands clutching her cane so that she wouldn't throw it at Wisor while they waited for Fantine to hear the list of questions he'd given her. The lights were back on, but it had been over an hour since they'd taken Haldan down to sick bay. She had no idea how he was, and Gimlet still hadn't turned up.

The coffee that the staff had given to the Yacht Club members had long since grown cold. She pulled up her HUD, checking for Gimlet's tracker again.

Offline. Last location shown.

It still showed Haldan's cabin. They'd checked it, looking under and in everywhere a little dog could hide before Wisor had sent all the guests to the lobby for questioning.

Tesla shifted in her chair, which was less uncomfortable than the ones in the Olympus Mons Lounge, but clearly made by the same designer. "Couldn't we just give you a statement? Officer Piper was with one of us the entire time."

"She wasn't with *you*." Wisor was scrolling through things on his handheld, swiping with more vigor than strictly necessary. "You could just answer my questions though."

What was the point of having a very expensive lawyer if you didn't let them do their job? "It's just that our dog is missing and I'm worried about her."

"I am not concerned about your dog. I'm concerned about the man who was stabbed." Wisor continued to stare at the handheld. "I'm concerned because you made a list and the top two people on your list are dead and the third has been attacked. I'm concerned about the fact that you've been in proximity to all of the deaths on the ship."

"Oh? I didn't know we'd been near the body in the composting recycler. Do we know who that is yet?" Shal stretched and casually put his arm behind Tesla's back. *::Don't let him—::*

Wisor glanced at him over the edge of the screen. "Move away from each other. I don't want private conversations."

"Aw, but it's our honeymoon." Pouting, Shal withdrew his arm.

Lips tight, Wisor bent back to his work. One did not need to be a retired detective to be able to tell that he still didn't know who the body in the recycling system was. On the screen of Tesla's handheld, Fantine counted carmine stitches and scowled. Tesla could tell when his words reached Fantine, because she set her crochet aside and started jotting notes on a pad.

"All right. I'm sending a memo to Leigh in your legal department, because someone at your pribbling, Earth-vexing company has to be competent. My clients can answer questions two and seven. Everything else we'll cover in a written statement, and before you object to that, let me make it clear that they are cooperating out of a courtesy that you have not earned and that if you try to fight me on this, I will file so many formal complaints against you that they'll have to terraform Jupiter to plant enough trees for the paper required." She picked up her crochet again, stabbing the hook through the red yarn as if it were Wisor's liver. "As soon as we're done here, which is going to be very soon, because my clients need to eat lunch, you're going to have your staff make another announcement about Gimlet. And you'll keep doing so until my client has her dog back."

Wisor looked as if the act of holding his tongue was going to strangle him and add to the body count. "Questions two and seven?"

Tesla had no idea why the others were off limits, but it would get her away to look for Gimlet faster. "Question two: I did not see the note in the bedroom until Haldan called me in to look at it. Question seven: My recollection is that the lights went out before he screamed."

Wisor looked at Shal, who shrugged. "Two: I did not see the note until Maria and I went into the room after the incident. Seven: The lights went out and we heard the scream through the closed door."

"Can we go now?" Tesla settled the tip of her cane on the floor as if she were about to stand and go without waiting for permission.

"No, of course you—" Wisor flinched and looked up and to the left at something on his HUD. "Goddammit. Fine. You can go. Give your statement to Leigh in Legal."

"Thank you!" Tesla powered herself to her feet and wanted to charge away, but waited for her body to settle.

Shal stood slowly with a hand to his side and nodded to Wisor. "A pleasure speaking to you, as always."

Wisor scowled and pushed his own chair back. "Get me that statement by end of day, I need to file it with the home off—"

Three cheerful tones sounded over the ship's loudspeakers. "Good morning, passengers! We're still looking for that little white dog we mentioned earlier. She answers to Gimlet, and if you spot her, don't chase her! Just call security so they can get her back to her parents. Meanwhile, Martian Hoop Ball is open in Module 14."

Without waiting for an answer, Wisor stomped off to the next interviewees, a couple whose wardrobes were so stylish that the clothes were wearing the people.

Tesla headed across the lounge to the concierge desk, stabbing the floor with her cane. At her side, Shal leaned into his stride, hands in his pockets as if he were in a hurry and totally casual about it at the same time. She could feel the worry crackling off of him.

At the desk, Tesla stopped and tried to give the concierge the option to say no even while knowing that the young person really had no choice. "Auberi, could I trouble you for a moment?"

"Mx. Crane. Mx. Steward. Of course. How can I help?" The concierge smiled at Tesla, but the pleasant mask didn't quite cover their expression and let frazzled worry seep around the edges.

"Did you see Gimlet earlier?"

Auberi stood, looking around the lounge as if Gimlet would suddenly materialize. "I have not seen sweet Gimlet since you have come with Mx. Kuznetsova earlier."

Shal squeezed Tesla's hand and made the new wedding ring shift around on her finger. "With the blackout, how dark was it in here?"

They shook their head. "The rescue lights lit almost immediately. Even so, the little dog is impossible to miss. I would have seen her, I am certain." They hesitated and gestured to the doors to the Yacht Club. "In addition, the automatic doors are deactivated during a power breakdown for the reasons of security. Have no worry! They can always be opened manually, but this gives me the certainty that Gimlet is not escaped; she must therefore be here."

Tesla tapped her forefinger on the head of her cane, thinking. "Suite doors were open up and down the corridor. It wouldn't be the first time she decided to make a new friend."

Nodding slowly, Shal tilted his head and squinted toward the Golden Promenade. It jogged to the right, which would take them past the bathtub tree woman picture. "My recollection is that guests have to pass through the lobby to exit . . . Could we check the service corridor?"

Auberi hesitated. Dammit. They were going to need to get permission, and Wisor wouldn't give it, just because he was pissed about Fantine. Auberi made a small snort with a quick nod. "If you please? This way."

Two keystrokes later, they had locked the concierge station and risen. Moving at a pace calibrated to feel hurried but not beyond Tesla's ability, Auberi led them down the Golden Promenade. Past the bathtub lady and the zombie squirrels, the hall was empty of passengers again, and aside from yellow caution tape across Haldan's door, the only other sign that anything was off was the laundry cart, which had been bumped at some point and towels were still scattered on the floor. One was half-formed into a swan.

"Was Jenny working this shift?" Tesla asked.

Auberi raised their eyebrows. "Yes, to be sure. The room stewards are not . . . they do not have shifts per se; even on their breaks still they are always on call. If she has seen your little dog, she will, of course, let me know immediately."

Past the laundry cart, they paused at a plain white service door and waved their wrist over the reader. The door unlatched with a whir and a click. Auberi pushed it open. Tesla wanted Gimlet to be waiting on the other side of the door.

She was not.

The scuffed floor of the service corridor stretched to the curvature of the ship, intersecting at intervals with other service corridors, but there was no sign of their dog.

Tesla should have brought treats with her. But Gimlet had never been gone this long before. "Do we split—"

Her HUD lit up with an incoming call from—"Haldan?" Tesla's knees sagged with relief and she put a hand against the wall to steady herself. A part of her brain had been waiting to hear that he hadn't survived. She transferred the call to her handheld so Shal could hear it. "Hi, how are you?"

"I was stabbed." He winced and the camera wobbled. "How do you think I'm doing?"

"Not great, I imagine." Also clearly dopey from pain medication. But if the medic Candy were involved and wanted him dead, he already would be.

"Why aren't you here?" His voice sounded thick and slurred. "I hired you to keep me safe and I was stabbed and why aren't you here?"

Past Shal, Auberi turned their back to give an illusion of privacy. Shal walked up to Tesla and she raised the handheld to frame him with her. Haldan's image showed just his eye, with a blown-out black pupil, and a corner of his teal hair.

"You asked us to look into things. I'm not a bodyguard. Neither is Shal."

"Why aren't you here?"

"Gimlet is missing." Tesla's stomach was twisted into prickling coils of anxiety for Gimlet. The fact that Gimlet might be with the murderer right now or . . . she had never wanted to receive a ransom note so badly.

He lifted his head and pulled his handheld away from his body. His mouth hung a little open. Then he laughed. "Of course. Of course, that's what you're worried about. I was stabbed. While you were supposed to be helping me."

"I did tell you not to open the door."

"So this is my fault now?"

"That's not what I meant."

"I think that's exactly what you meant." He clenched his jaw and stared away from them as if he could bore a hole in the wall. "I'm only as valuable to you as your needs. Get your spouse out of jail. Help you find your dog. My actual life doesn't have any value to anyone unless there's some kind of payoff."

"Haldan, I know how that feels, and I promise you that I don't care about your money."

"No, but you care about the fact that I own this ship." He laughed again with a wild, frantic edge. "Hell. Maybe Shal stabbed me. I mean, after all, he's done surveillance on me before."

Beside her, Shal took in a sudden startled breath. "Your ex-spouse. You and Leo met in college."

"I'm well aware."

"My point is—Leo would have known Ruth and George. Would he have known about 'Remember the Main'?"

A look of horror swept over Haldan's features and he shook his head, pressing back into the pillows with his eyes squeezed shut. "No. No. He is not on this ship. No."

"He wouldn't have to be." Tesla felt cold. If you had enough money, you could pay for anything.

The image on the screen flashed and bounced as if he'd dropped his handheld. It did nothing to mask Haldan's horrible racking sobs. Tesla glanced down the hall to Auberi, who had actually stuck their fingers in their ears and stood with their shoulders hunched.

On the handy, the image shook as Haldan brought his handheld close to his face again. Tears were brimming in his eyes and his voice was hoarse. "Please come here?"

"Sure." She bit the inside of her cheek and glanced at Shal. "Sure. See you in a bit."

When she hung up, Shal rubbed his earlobe, staring down the hall, but his eyes moved as if he were looking at another place altogether. "'Remember the Main' . . . what the hell happened?"

"I have no idea." Her hand was sweating as she slid the handheld back into her pocket. "Should we split up? One of us keeps looking and the other goes to see Haldan?"

"No . . ." Sighing, he turned back to face the concierge. "Sorry about that, Aube—hang on."

One of the troubles with a real dog is that they shed, and the only thing that saved Tesla's home from being covered in poofs of white fur was a robot vacuum cleaner named Wilbur. A puff of white fur lay in the corner behind the door that Auberi had opened for them.

Shal was already halfway to the door before Tesla started

moving. When she got there, he was kneeling, head bent to study without touching anything. Gimlet's fur clung to a torn scrap of dark-blue fabric.

"Oh, good girl . . ." Shal muttered. "Server blue."

"What?" Tesla scrolled through her memory of the other ship staff and realized that every server wore the same blue trousers. Trust her spouse to notice textiles. "Oh."

"Yes, oh." He looked up at Auberi. "Could you please call Officer Piper? I think we may have found our murderer's second mistake."

"Second?"

"The first is that Haldan Kuznetsova is still alive."

Which was all good, except for the part where Gimlet had chased someone who wasn't shy about killing people. What would they do to a small dog?

Brainstorm

1.5 oz bourbon
1 oz dry vermouth
.75 oz Benedictine
Orange peel

Stir ingredients over ice, strain into coupe. Garnish with
twist of orange peel.

After they'd turned the scrap over to Piper, there'd been nothing
for them to do, and yet the entire way up to sick bay to check
on Haldan, Tesla had a dragging sensation like she was going to
the wrong place. The cramped beige corridors did not help with
her sense of being trapped. Or maybe it was just that the butter
knife that had been emerging from her spine was developing
serrations.

Tesla plucked at the fabric of her new courtesy mask as they
walked. Her scalp itched under the cheap souvenir captain's hat
she'd jammed over her hair, but between that and the cane no one
had yet noticed her. She hadn't wanted to take time to do either
thing, but it was that or be trapped again.

Shal held the door to sick bay for her as they entered the
cramped beige "lobby" with its three cramped beige chairs. Bob
occupied the same chair as before, camped outside the same door,
which was now clearly Haldan's. He looked up from his handheld
and grunted.

"Bob!" Shal grinned at the man. "It's been ages. I'm surprised
you aren't still upstairs investigating with the rest. Don't tell me—I

know you can't anyway—but you had the same thought we did, right?"

"You have to ask Chief Wisor about any thoughts."

Shal snapped his fingers and pointed at Bob. "See. I knew you'd have to say that. Blink twice if you had the same thought."

"I don't have any thoughts."

Well, that was clear. And as much as she wanted to make a snarky comment, Tesla tried to stay on course. She took the courtesy mask off. "May we talk to Haldan and see how he's doing?"

"I'm supposed to guard him."

"Sure. I get that." Shal looked around the tiny room, fully half of which was filled with the wall of Bob, even seated, as if checking for spies. "The thing is . . . Haldan asked us to come."

Bob looked at them for longer than strictly necessary to make a decision and then unfolded out of his chair, filling the tiny room with a new wall. He opened the door, blocking the entrance with his body and leaned his head in. "Crane and Steward are here. You want to see them?"

Raising a brow, Tesla looked at Shal. "Crane and Steward could be a nice name for a detective agency."

He snorted. "Retired. No." With a finger raised, he shook his head. "No. None of this counts."

"You never let your license lapse . . ."

He leaned over and kissed her on the cheek. "Clearly I need to do a better job of distracting you from—"

Bob stepped to the side of the door and pushed it the rest of the way open. Stuffing himself back into the beige chair, he picked up his handheld again. "Keep the door open."

"Sure. Sure." Shal's curls fell across his forehead as he beckoned to Tesla and went through the open door.

She followed Shal into the tiny room, where Haldan lay propped in the hospital bed. He was pale and gray under the harsh lights and struggled to sit up as they came in.

Haldan grabbed the remote and powered the back of his bed

higher for support. "Thank you for coming." Waving at his hand-held, which lay on the bed, he grimaced. "Sorry I was . . . forceful earlier."

As much as she wanted to agree with him, she was talking to a man who had been stabbed and nearly died. If anyone on the ship had the right to be "forceful," it was him. Tesla laid her hand on the rail of his bed. "You sound better."

He winced and rested a hand on the bandage peeking out from beneath his hospital gown. The other arm was swathed in nanogen tape and lay across his lap. "I am making a note not to make calls while coming out of anesthesia."

"From experience, I can confirm that it's best avoided. Don't buy or sell anything this week, either, FYI." She hesitated, not wanting to ask him to exert himself at all, but . . . Gimlet. And he had asked them to come here. "Did you . . . did you want to tell us what you saw when you were attacked?"

"I already told Wisor everything I could, which wasn't a lot. At least they're finally taking me seriously." Haldan thumped his head back against the pillow and glared at the ceiling. "No one laughed this time."

Shal nodded. "Good. I'm glad. The trouble is that they won't share information with us. I hate to ask you to repeat yourself, but . . ."

"It was dark. There wasn't a lot to see." He sighed, grimacing. "The lights went out as the door opened, so all I really saw was a hand, moving. They were wearing a blue glove, so I don't even have skin tone for you."

Tesla drummed her fingers on the bed rail. "There's . . . there's a technique I use sometimes to focus. Five things I see, four things I hear, three things I touch, two things I smell, one thing I taste."

Teal hair limp across his forehead, Haldan turned to her, frowning. "I . . . I see. So, you're thinking if I focus on the glove, is that right? Like a—a hypnosis regression thing?"

Waggling her hand, Tesla shrugged. "If it helps to think of it that way. Like, the hand was attached to something. It was moving in a direction. It was holding the scissors in a grip."

"Got it." He swallowed and closed his eyes, brows coming together in concentration. Wetting his lips, he swallowed again. "Blue nitrile glove. Black cuff? Coming straight at me—no, up a little. They. They were shorter than I am. Sounds . . . dog barks."

Tesla's heart clenched. Gimlet.

With his eyes still closed, Haldan cocked his head to the side as if he were listening. "A grunt or pant kind of a *mmph*." He raised the pitch of his voice when he made the sound as if he were remembering an alto or soprano. "Metal clicking, like a door latch? Or maybe an instrument case? Footsteps running to . . . to my right."

Toward the service door. Or to the service cart that had been parked partway down the hall. Tesla glanced at Shal, who listened, balanced forward over his toes.

"Touch." His face twisted, grimacing as if he were remembering being stabbed, and his hand grazed the bandage on his arm. "I tried to block. Oh. Oh, they had a solid bosom. When I put my hand up to block, their chest didn't give much. And . . . ropes? Fringe? I'm not sure."

Shal's head came up, head cocking to the side as he watched Haldan. Tesla tried to figure out what had caught her spouse's attention by imagining the scene based on what Haldan was saying. The assailant trying to stab him but Haldan blocking. Then stabbing again. Why the rope though? Were they going to tie him up? Or was it fringe from . . . from a costume or clothing?

"Smell. Dog and . . ." His eyes pinched more tightly closed. "Bourbon? I—I didn't taste anything."

"Unless you were licking the walls, I would have been surprised if there had been anything with the last."

Haldan's eyes opened with something like triumph in them. "That was more than I thought I remembered. Thank you."

"Hey! Trauma therapy can have unexpected side benefits."

Tesla looked at Shal before Haldan could ask her any questions about the specifics of the trauma. "How about you? Do you have any questions?"

"If he has the energy, yeah." Shal had settled into himself, watching Haldan with an easy calm. "I want to know about 'Remember the Main.'"

The triumph wiped away and Haldan's face went dead. "I don't want to talk about it."

Shal shrugged and took a step back from the bed. "All right. I'm sure the ship security will keep you safe for the rest of the cruise."

"Wait—" He reached for them, stopping with a hiss. "Wait. Bob?"

The wall of Bob filled the door. "Yeah?"

"Close the door and give me some private time with these two."

The wall shrugged. "Okay."

He shut the door and Shal whistled. "How'd you get him trained so quickly?"

"Technically, I own the ship and he's been very cooperative since I pointed that out."

"I imagine he has." Shal raised his right eyebrow and was dangerously handsome as he leaned against the wall, facing Haldan. Crossing his arms over his chest, he nodded to the man in the hospital bed. "'Remember the Main.'"

Haldan grimaced and wiped his hands down his face, then stayed for a moment with his face covered and tension in his shoulders. "I don't want to talk about it, but I will." Swallowing, he sighed and lowered his hands. "With you. Not with Wisor. He's an idiot."

Tesla would not argue with him there. Shal nodded slowly and waited.

After a moment, staring across the small room, Haldan said, "Please remember that college kids are stupid. I would not do any of these things now but . . . but I did. The misspelling was intentional . . . The 'main' refers to a power main."

Tesla had a sudden chilling sensation that she knew where this story was going. She had tapped into more than one main in her life and had yet to screw it up, because she was slow and careful. If you screwed up, your best-case scenario was getting blown across the room.

"Speaking in hypotheticals . . . if a group of college kids were running an experiment using university equipment and kept blowing the fuse in the lab, they might decide to tap into the main." He swallowed and looked down, face grayer than it had been. "That might go . . . badly."

"How badly might that go? Hypothetically?"

"A fire."

In the silence, Tesla flicked open her HUD and did a fast search on fires at Haldan's alma mater focused on the years he was attending. There were multiple fires, because college kids will college, but no mention of Haldan, Ruth, Leo, or George. Kuznetsova was from an extremely wealthy family. Property damage would have just been paid for. He would have gotten a slap on the wrist.

She looked at Haldan. "Who died?"

Haldan flinched. "I didn't— Why do you think someone died?"

"Because when I was in college, Daddy would have paid off property damage." She narrowed the search again, looking for deaths. "Willem Munroe? Freshman?"

He froze and she could see panic beating at his temples. Haldan closed his eyes, pressing a hand over his mouth as if he were about to vomit. Lifting his hand to cover his eyes, Haldan cleared his throat. "Where—where did you get that name?"

"A search on your alma mater and fires, looking for ones on campus with a fatality." She softened her voice. "Who was he?"

He was silent long enough that she thought he might not answer. Shal shifted his weight by the door, eyes darting across the man as if he were measuring his reaction. When Haldan lowered his hand, his eyes were red and damp with brimming tears.

He looked at Tesla. "You know what this is like. I was going to step into a decision-making role at massive corporation and people were already trying to impress me. I was too stupid to tell him no. And he died."

Shal pursed his lips. "Who knew you were there?"

"I didn't think anyone did." Haldan picked at the bandage on his shoulder. "It was me, Ruth, George, and Leo. And Willem."

"Okay." Shal tapped a finger against his arm, then nodded and pushed away from the wall. "I'll recommend that they keep you here with a guard for safety."

"Where—aren't you going to stay here?" Haldan sat up, wincing as the movement pulled at the bandage on his shoulder.

"Bob'll take care of you. Just tell him not to let anyone in." Shal pulled the door open. "Bob! Sweetheart! Don't let anyone in to talk to Haldan, okay?"

Tesla paused before leaving Haldan's bed. She couldn't tell him that everything would be okay, because that was obviously not the case. "We'll be in touch."

He nodded, sinking back into the pillows. She had a moment of thinking that she should leave Gimlet with him before the memory that her dog was missing stabbed her sideways through the gut. Steadying herself with her cane, Tesla followed Shal out of the hospital room.

He looked back at her and smiled fondly, reaching for her hand. ::*You are brilliant. I'm keeping the five senses trick.*::

::*I thought you were retired.*:: She leaned in to kiss the dimple that appeared when he laughed. Running her thumb down the side of his hand, she asked, ::*I saw you perk up during the Touch memories but didn't know why.*::

::*Rope or fringe.*:: Shal made a gesture toward his shoulders. ::*Like maybe an officer's epaulets.*::

The weight of two memories bore down on Tesla and stopped her in the hall. Her grip on Shal's hand half turned him toward her. "The captain doesn't have epaulets." No one on the bridge crew did. In low gravity, fringe didn't make sense. "It's not rope or fringe. It's hair. Locs. Immanuel Rudawski, the waiter who was in the karaoke lounge, has long blue locs."

She could see Shal turning through his own memories. He slowly nodded and pulled her forward. Wrapping an arm around her back, Shal pressed in for a deep, long, extremely detailed kiss. *::I love your brain so very, very much.::*

She ran her tongue across his lips and twined her fingers in his hair. *::So what's our next move?::*

::Honestly, I was just kissing you.::

Laughing, she broke apart from him to look at his face, black eye and all. "I love you so much."

He grinned, going completely goofy around the edges. "I love you too."

"But seriously." She raised her courtesy mask. "Do we call Piper?"

"But seriously . . . I'm not sure." He took her hand and bent his head in thought as they walked through the corridors leading out of sick bay.

She let him think, steering them as his sleuthing face sharpened while he worked through scenarios. The ship got progressively more polished until they were back on the main promenade. They walked past one of the potted ficus trees, and Tesla's heart wrenched a little, remembering how much Gimlet loved sniffing them.

She stopped. Shal went a step past her and turned. "Something?"

The tree was in a white clapboard box that was broader at the top than the base, with a lip around the top that kept it from being pushed all the way up against the wall. "Could Gimlet fit behind there?"

"Maybe?" He tilted his head. "You're thinking about the way she hides under things when she's scared?"

Tesla nodded and walked over to the planter. Grabbing the

edge of it, she started to lower herself to her knees so she could look behind it. Shal caught her arm. "Hey—let me do that."

"Getting off the floor isn't any easier for you right now."

He opened his mouth and then grimaced. "No. But—"

"But it won't add to my damage and it might yours." She tightened her grip and sank to the ground. "Besides, I have the DBPS. And practice."

He grumbled, shoving his hands in his pockets.

"I didn't hear that." Tesla put one hand on the wall and carefully braced herself to look behind the planter.

"I said that I love you very much."

"Uh-huh." Gimlet could fit back there, but a discarded piece of cookie made it clear she hadn't been here. Tesla squinted down the hall, trying to look under others, but the curve of the floor got in the way.

Getting back to her feet, even with the DBPS, was not fast. Shal's hands were visibly clenched into fists, but he waited while she steadied herself with the planter and her cane. He sighed. "Do you know how hard it is to not help?"

"I'm very proud of you."

"Are you going to check all of the planters?"

"Not all . . ." She took his arm, walking with him into the transit corridor. Gimlet would be fine. They would find her.

"Can I borrow your handheld?" Shal stepped nimbly onto the moving sidewalk.

"Calling your BFF?" She followed a step behind, leaning against the handrail.

"Yep."

Tesla pulled the handheld out of her pocket and waggled it at him. "You don't think she's been lying to us?"

"Oh, sure. That's my default assumption for everyone." Shrugging, he took the handheld and didn't bother to unroll it to place the call. "But she's very clear about where the boundaries are, which makes her lies more reliable than other people's."

"And yet you—"

"Mariiiiiiia . . . Tell me how much you love me—no, wait. You'll need to revise your opinion upward in a moment. We have new information about Immanuel Rudawski." Leaning next to Tesla, he put his arm around her and winked. "Talked to Haldan— What? No, I'm not questioning your witness, he asked us to come. Ask Bob, he'll back me up."

Whatever she said made Shal tilt his head back and laugh, then hiss, and pinch his eyes shut. Tesla put her hand on his arm.

::*I'm fine*:: "No, no. I'm fine." But his voice was a little strained. "Anyway, Haldan mentioned that when he was attacked he felt two things about his attacker. A solid chest and locs. Who does that make you think of?"

Grinning, he turned and planted a kiss on Tesla's cheek.

"Us too! Uh-uh. What? What's that? You're breaking up. Listen I can't hear you so we'll just meet you at the kitchen." Shal hung up and turned the handheld off.

Tesla raised her eyebrows. "Speaking of everyone lies . . ."

"Immanuel is still on room-service duty. He's moving about the ship but will have to return to the Terran-level main kitchen." His grin broadened. "It's really too bad that I couldn't hear Maria clearly. She said, 'Something-something go there.'"

Orbital Decay

1 oz Laphroaig
1 oz red vermouth
1 oz Aperol
Orange peel

Stir ingredients over ice for 40 seconds. Strain into coupe.
Garnish with flamed orange peel.

The door to the kitchen area was closed and they didn't have an access badge to get through it. While Shal peered through the round window in the door, looking for Piper, Tesla turned to scan the hall for a service drone. They'd passed a handful on the way here, along with live servers hurrying under the weight of trays.

She pulled off her courtesy mask. "Let me know when you see a drone coming this way."

"Um . . ." He glanced back at her, brows together with curiosity. "Yes. I mean, one is coming now, but the doors are only going to open wide enough for it."

"True, but . . ." She stood to the side of the hall with the cane in one hand, mask dangling from the end like a flag. "There's a trick."

When the doors slid apart to let the drone out, Tesla lowered her cane in front of one of its forward sensors so the courtesy mask blinded it. The drone turned to avoid the apparent obstacle.

And like magic, the doors opened wider to accommodate the angle of the machine. She slid the improvised blocker to the other eye and the drone turned the other direction, making a gap between itself and one door. Shal slipped through and she was right on his heels into a steaming bath of sound and heat. The sliding door clipped her elbow as she released the service drone, but it wasn't a hard hit. Probably.

She checked the settings on her DBPS and decided that they were fine. For now.

Shal had stepped to the side of the door, pressing against the wall of the large service area, trying to stay out of the way of drones and live servers. They moved with hurried efficiency, plating food and carrying it away. Two other doors led out to different corridors, and on the wall directly opposite them a large window opened onto the kitchen proper. Blazing lights lit a large room full of stainless steel, induction stoves, and chefs in white hats.

A mélange of aromas melded everything from the spiced cuisines of New Jamaica Station to briny Lunar aquaculture with stops on Friggjarhöfn for rye and caraway and Estación de Ganimedes for heat from Mexicanx residents. She sidestepped to avoid a server with a tray who was heading to the door on her left. The server did a double take but didn't stop moving.

Shal grinned at her and back at the door they'd come through. "Pretty slick."

She shook her head. "It's pretty kludgy, but it worked to get me out of boarding school, so I'm happy it's still a useful exploit."

"Is that a known thing? I've been thinking we were looking for a service person, because—" He stopped, still looking at the door. "Hang on. Why could I get through the service door from the hall? It just opened the first time. When we went with Auberi, they had to use their fob to open it."

"A timed relocking? Disabled? Maybe—"

A tray clattered to the ground, plates shattering in a cacophony that silenced the rest of the room. To their right, Immanuel stood, eyes wide and staring at Shal. He backed two steps away from them, shaking his head, then turned and bolted down the hall.

Shal pushed away from the wall, springing after him before Tesla could move. The courtesy mask ear straps tangled around her foot as she tried to follow and she had to pause to rip it free from her cane. Around her, service people, all wearing blue trousers, were staring down the hall or at the food that was scattered across the floor.

"Excuse me—" Tesla pushed her way past someone, using her cane to navigate over a blood-bright streak of borscht.

Down the corridor, Immanuel was nearly behind the curve of the ship. Shal was chasing, but with one arm hugging his ribs. He ran in fits and starts, bracing himself with his other hand on the wall of the corridor.

Behind Tesla, someone yelped, "Watch it!"

A moment later, Piper dashed past, leaning into a run with hands knifing through the air. She dodged past Shal, who staggered to a stop. With the curve of the ship, it looked as if Piper ran uphill without slowing and tackled Immanuel. The two went down in a tangle, rolling across the floor.

Piper rolled on top of Immanuel, pinning him. She pulled Immanuel's wrists behind him and slapped cuffs around them. "What the hell were you thinking?"

The young server lay on the floor, not fighting, and his sobs echoed down the corridor. Piper got off of him, and propped him into a sitting position. It looked like she was moving a sack of potatoes for all the response Immanuel gave.

"Where did you think you were going to run?" She stayed crouching and scowled at him. "Huh? I'm wanting to be sympathetic here, but you're making it hard."

"I told her I couldn't talk to her." Immanuel gestured to Shal and Tesla with his chin. His voice broke and he stared at the floor again, tears rolling down his cheeks. "I didn't know you were—please. Please help me."

Piper spared a glare for Tesla. "So you tell your shift supervisor that you have a problem customer and let them handle it. You don't run. You've got to know better than that."

Immanuel's face folded, crumpling around more tears. "I was scared."

"Of what?" Piper fished in her pocket and pulled out a packet of tissues. She leaned forward and wiped his cheeks. "Come on, I can't help you if you don't talk to me."

"We just want to—" Tesla stopped as Piper used a scowl worthy of Fantine.

"What part of 'go to your cabin and don't investigate' was unclear?"

"Lousy connection." Shal sauntered closer. "But since we're here, mind if I . . . ?"

"Yes, actually." Piper turned her attention back to Immanuel, ignoring Shal and Tesla as they inched closer. But she didn't tell them to leave. "All right . . . Tell me about the night that George Saikawa was murdered."

With a gasp, Immanuel's head came up. "No—no, I didn't have anything to do with the murder."

"Running doesn't look good." Piper reached for her comm badge and paused. "You want to tell me how things went down before Wisor gets here? I can explain things to him."

Immanuel nodded, eyes huge. "I don't know what to tell you. It was a pretty normal shift—"

"You weren't scheduled."

Immanuel's head came up. "I . . . I always work the R-Bar. I mean, I did. Before . . ."

Brows coming together, Piper pursed her lips. "All right. I'll check that later. So . . . you turn up for your normal shift."

"Yes. And everything was normal until . . . Saikawa got out of the booth." For a moment, his eyes cut to Shal and then he stared back down at his knees again. Swallowing, Immanuel grimaced. "I'd been trying to avoid that table all night because I was so . . ."

"Angry?" Piper's voice had gentled.

"Disgusted. I was afraid I would do or say something and lose my job." Immanuel laughed bitterly. "That would have been ironic, given that I had to take this godawful job because of what those bastards did to my grandpa—sorry."

"Hey . . . I was a server, too, once upon a time. It *is* a godawful job. So you dumped a tray of drinks on her?"

Immanuel bit his lip, glancing from Piper to Shal. Tears and snot streaked his face as his breathing went hiccuppy and panicked. Piper grabbed his ankles and spun him so his back was to Shal and Tesla. "Shal . . . Back down the hall, but stay where I can see you."

Tesla said, "You can't still—"

Shal grabbed her hand, sending, *::Quiet::* at the same time that Piper said, "Back. Down. The. Hall."

::She can't still think that you had anything to do with the murders.:: Tesla followed him, limping backward.

::I would, if I were her.:: He stopped at a nod from Piper, still within earshot of the conversation. *::But even if she doesn't, Immanuel is terrified of us, and that's complicating things.::*

"All right . . ." Piper settled on her heels and rested her arms on her knees in a position that Tesla would never be able to attempt now. "Did someone hurt you? Or threaten you?"

Immanuel shook his head. His hands, cuffed behind his back, clenched and unclenched. "I . . . I took a tip and I was afraid that—" His shoulders shook as he bowed his head. In front of him, Piper waited, until Immanuel's breathing slowed and steadied. "It was huge and I was afraid that Chief Wisor would think I'd been paid to do more than I had."

"What did you do?"

Immanuel's mumbled answer vanished in the hum of the ship fans and the distant rattle of the kitchen.

"Okay . . ." Piper nodded. "Can you describe the passenger who gave you the spoofer?"

"He was wearing a courtesy mask. Dark, curly hair. About 180 centimeters. Nice shoulders."

"Was it the passenger behind you?"

Shal tightened his grip on Tesla's hand before she'd realized that she had opened her mouth. *::Let her do her job.::*

::But you didn't—::

::Interfering will make me look guilty.:: His thumb ran down the side of her hand. ::Just wait it out.::

Immanuel sniffled. "I thought it was."

"But you don't now?"

"He seemed taller?"

Piper pulled her handheld out of her pocket and unrolled the device, snapping it into an open and locked position. The flat rectangle glowed as her fingers danced above it, entering hand-gesture commands. She turned the screen to Immanuel. "Is he on this screen?"

Over his shoulder, the screen glowed with images of passengers and crew who bore a passing resemblance to Shal. All of them had ancestry that might have begun in the Middle East on Earth or under the sunlamps of Estación de Ganimedes. Shal's picture had his half smile smoldering directly at the camera.

"I'm . . . Maybe the third from the right? Top row?"

That was not Shal, and Tesla sagged against him. He kissed her temple. ::Don't get too excited. They'll pull me in for a real lineup when we dock and by that point he'll have seen me enough that—::

"Or the second from the left on the bottom?"

That was Shal. That was definitely Shal.

Piper turned the handy back to scroll through some additional screens. "We can look at the tip."

"It was cash." Immanuel hung his head, hands in tight fists.

"I see." Piper glanced up at Shal as if, despite herself, she wanted to know what he thought.

Tesla tried not to feel left out of the silent conversation that they had. She saw Shal mouth something, but he was turned too much toward Piper for her to be able to tell what it was. Whatever he'd said made Piper grimace.

Piper turned back to Immanuel. "Who was working Saikawa's table if you weren't?"

"No one." He hunched more miserably into the wall. "She was in my section, I just . . . didn't go near her."

"Did you see anyone who did? Was she there with anyone?"

He nodded. "I mean, she didn't arrive with anyone, but Nile—the magician—he stopped by Saikawa's table. And then another time I went past, there was another passenger and they were arguing."

Tesla wanted to cheer. She'd been right.

"What did they look like?"

"White passenger. Early forties? Bald. Carried weight in the belly." He shrugged, which could not have been easy with his arms pinned behind him. "Wearing . . . I think they had on a sequined shirt and a capelet that night?"

::I told her! That's Ory Slootmaekers.:: Tesla took a step forward.

Piper saw her and raised her eyebrows while somehow also conveying that Tesla needed to stop where she was. At the same time, Shal pinged, *::Don't.::*

::We have to tell her.:: Sweating, Tesla pulled her hand free from Shal's and concentrated on Piper. "Can I . . . can I talk to you for a moment?"

Sighing, Piper got to her feet. "If I don't, I'm sure your lawyer will find something to sue me for." She glared at Shal. "Back up."

He held up his hands and backed farther down the hall. Tesla met Piper a few steps away from Immanuel and lowered her voice. "He's describing Ory Slootmaekers."

"I hate to break it to you, but there are a lot of bald white passengers on this ship."

"And apparently a lot of hot Persian masc passengers too. Sure. Right. I get that—"

"Immanuel said the passenger told him that it was their honeymoon. Asked Immanuel to help protect their spouse from photographers."

"Come on . . . Do you really think that if Shal had nefarious plans he would have given details to make it easier to identify him?" She grabbed hold of the rising whine in her voice and buried it under a corporate boardroom calm. "His description of events matches mine. And Ory Slootmaekers is the one that went to the bathroom right before Ruth Fish died."

"The bathroom that Annie Smith reported as being out of order?" Rubbing her forehead, Piper chewed on her lower lip. She glanced over Tesla's shoulder to look at Shal, eyes narrowing in thought. "All right . . . all right. I'll set up a digital lineup of passengers and crew that match those descriptions and I'll include him. We'll get Immanuel to look at them. Will that make you happy?"

"Thank you."

Piper's sigh said that she would rather not be thanked and would honestly prefer it if everyone on the ship would lock themselves in their cabins for the duration, but especially Tesla and Shal. She tabbed open a screen and started dragging faces around.

Piper paused and looked back at Tesla. "What did you say his name was again?"

"Ory Slootmaekers, he/him."

"You're sure."

Shal took a half step closer and stopped himself, balancing forward on his toes. "What do you have?"

"It's what I don't have." Her fingers flicked through pages in agitation. "There's no one on the passenger list named any variant of Ory Slootmaekers. Not on crew either."

"Maybe he's using a cover, like I did? And Jalna and Annie. Smith isn't their last name either." Tesla wet her lips. It couldn't be that big of a deal that his name wasn't in there. "Can you do a visua—"

"Already am." She offered the handheld and beckoned Tesla closer. "Flip through these and tell me if you spot your person."

As Piper said, there was no shortage of bald white people on the passenger and crew list. But after going through all the pages of bald white people, Tesla shook her head. "I don't see him . . . Shal?"

He looked to Piper for permission before joining them. He flipped through the same pages, scowl deepening as he went. "No . . ."

"I didn't make him up." The edges of a panic attack made her skin feel too tight. Ory wasn't on the list of the group yoga class. "Other people have seen him."

"I didn't say you had." But the flatness of Piper's tone said that she'd clearly thought it.

Tesla gnawed on the inside of her cheek. She wanted to call Fantine, but the comm lag was twelve minutes by now, so she sent a ping asking her to look for an Ory Slootmaekers. Meanwhile, there had to be other ways to find him. "Officer Piper, what about footage from the yoga studio? I know some times when he was definitely there."

"Worth a try. When?"

"Last night. Ten-ish." She paused, considering. "Also, there's Ewen. His child. Maybe you can spot them? Sixteen? Also white. Shaved head. Violet eyes."

"Got it." Piper flipped to a secure page on her handheld, frowning at the device as she worked.

While they waited. Tesla had plenty of time to become aware of the servers standing at the far curve of the hall gawking up at them. She didn't have her mask on and wasn't even sure where it was. Tesla turned so her back was to them, taking refuge in the captain's hat. It put her facing Immanuel, who had sunk into himself again.

"Goddammit." Piper swiped furiously at her handheld. "There too?"

"What?" Shal leaned over her shoulder to look at the handheld. "Oh . . . everywhere?"

"Yep."

Tesla raised her hand. "Everywhere, what?"

Piper lowered the handheld to glare at Tesla. "Everywhere you tell me he's been, there's been an active high-grade spoofer. I can't find a single image of this guy or the kid."

BLACKTHORNE

2 oz Irish whiskey
1 oz sweet vermouth
2 tsp absinthe
2 dashes Angostura bitters
Lemon peel

Stir ingredients over ice for 40 seconds. Strain into martini glass and garnish with lemon peel.

Tesla shifted, trying to ease the high, thin whine of discomfort from her back. It was like a tinnitus of the spine, very present and annoying unless she kept the DBPS dialed up past its safety margins. Piper tapped a finger on the edge of the handheld, face creased in thought.

"Right." She minimized the search and brought a different one to the front. This one had dozens of people with black bowl cuts and builds similar to the one that Shal had chased. She spun around and walked over to Immanuel. "Do you recognize any of these people?"

Immanuel sniffed and leaned closer to the handheld. "Um . . ."

Lower lip between her teeth, Tesla waited, half certain that Immanuel was about to point to Mahjabin. The yoga instructor had matched Shal's description and would have had a reason to make a run for the yoga studio. Ory had to have registered for her class and yet wasn't on the list, so she had to be involved in some way.

"I mean . . . I know Yuki. But that's not surprising, is it?"

Piper pulled the handheld back. "Was he there that night?"

"Sure." He shifted on the floor. "But that's not unusual. He helps Nile Silver with his magic stuff."

Shal leaned toward Piper and whispered in her ear. Her face stayed blank, but she gave a small nod before turning back to Immanuel. "Which end of the bar was he at?"

"The far end. By the prep station. I kept having to ask him to move when I came to pick up orders."

The prep station had been right next to the service door, so it would have been very easy for him to slip out and walk down the corridor to the Yacht Club.

"And was he there all night?"

"Um . . ." Immanuel looked at the ceiling, squinting as if he were drawing the bar in his mind. "Yes. Well, I mean, until . . . the delta-gamma went out. He would have gone to the doors to make sure they were secured."

"And you saw him there?"

He shook his head. "I was . . . in a corner puking."

"Hm . . ." Shal slid his hands into his pockets and shrugged his way into a question. "Oh—there's a thing I'm curious about. You said that the bald man and Silver were arguing. With each other or with Saikawa?"

"Shal." Piper sliced her hand in front of him. Then sighed and faced Immanuel again. "All right . . . how much of the argument did you hear?"

At this, he hesitated, mouth pursed in thought. "I don't know? Something about Nile's show, maybe? I was only catching snippets as I went past."

Piper studied the young server, one finger tapping on the edge of her handheld as her only sign of unrest. Blowing out a sigh, she turned to Shal and Tesla, shooing them back down the hall. "Right . . . I need to confine him."

"Seems sensible."

"Then I'm going to the theater to talk to Nile and Yuki. I'm going to ask you not to go to the theater without me." She put her hands on her hips with a glower that could have served as the fuel source for a Pluto-bound rocket. "What I want is for you to go back to your cabin. You cannot pretend that the signal is poor. I'm right here in front of you. Go to your cabin."

If they did, Piper would go to the theater without them and she wouldn't share anything she learned without having her hand forced. Tesla hadn't even gotten to see the show because the pyro—

Sparks fill the void. Tesla's ears are ringing. The visor of the PAMU she's testing flashes as the laboratory and space spin past in nauseating succession. The suit should autostabilize, and it's not and she's having trouble thinking and something is crushing her spine so all she can catch are short, gasping breaths that get cut off with red-hot stabbing pain.

"Tesla? You're safe." Shal was crouching in front of her, hands out but not touching her. "You're on the *Lindgren*. We're in a hall-way and we're on the way to Mars. You're safe."

She was bending over, hands on her knees, and her cane was on the floor and the thrumming of her pulse in her ears sounded like the whoosh of recycled oxygen in a spacesuit. Her heart was going too fast and there wasn't enough air in the corridor and she needed her cane and she needed to get away from here. No, wait. She knew what this was.

Her next breath in was ragged but slow and she held it. *I'm safe.* The bruise around Shal's eye. Immanuel's blue trousers. The handheld in Piper's right hand. A scuff on the floor shaped like a dragon. She let her breath out.

"I'm all right." Her voice shook. She inhaled slowly again.

The hum of life support. Clatter of dishes. A service-drone whine. Footsteps in the distance. Exhale.

Shal shook his head. "I'm going to be bossy now, and we're going back to the cabin."

Tesla straightened and could feel the sweat beading on the

backs of her knees and prickling in her armpits. "Can you hand me my cane?"

Shal scooped the cane off the floor and gave it to her. When she took it, he rested his hand on hers. ::*C'mon . . . let's go lie down and watch* The Great Mars Baking Show.::

"Gimlet is still missing." She pulled her hand away and wiped her palm on the leg of her trousers.

From behind Shal, Piper was watching her, hand half-raised to her comm badge. Slowly she lowered it. "I'm going to side with Mr. Cockypants here."

Tesla's hands were shaking still. She swallowed the cotton that seemed to fill her mouth. "There's a murderer on the loose. I'm an adult and can set my own goddamn boundaries."

Wetting his lips, Shal glanced at Piper and then back to Tesla. "She's got to take Immanuel in. Maria can check in with us after she does and we'll see how you're feeling then."

That was a reasonable suggestion and she wanted to push back anyway. She was not okay and would be feeling this for hours. *In, two, three, four. Hold. Out, two, three, four. Hold.* She'd put too many hours into therapy to not recognize that what he was saying was true and sensible.

And she also hated being treated like she was fragile. "Why don't you and I find a place to review my pics from earlier?"

"A place like our cabin?"

"If you get me back there, you'll pull every trick in the book to get me to stay."

He winked, and even with a black eye, it was devastatingly attractive. "I mean, it is our honeymoon. I wouldn't mind a trick or two."

"Thank you for demonstrating my point." Tesla busied herself with brushing imaginary lint off her shirt. "Officer Piper, do you have a suggestion that isn't our cabin? Quiet and with no flashing lights, if possible."

"You can call me Maria, you know. C'mon, Immanuel. Time for us to go." Maria Piper walked back to Immanuel and slipped her hand under the server's arm. "The Irish pub should be quiet in the afternoon. If you don't mind servers with truly terrible fake accents and an abundance of green."

=====

As promised, the Irish pub—O'Shenanigan's—had an overabundance of green, from the cushions to the menus to the random green bowlers the servers wore cocked back on their heads. Everything else looked like dark wood or brass that had been here for three hundred years and was a testament to the matter printers they'd used to fabricate it.

Tesla slid into a booth, which was the least offensive of the available seating options.

A server with a green vest and bowler cap tipped back on artificially bright-red hair jogged up to their table. "Failte ter de O'Shenanigan's! 'Oy can oi 'elp yer the-day?"

"Wow. She was not kidding." It wasn't an Irish accent so much as the accent of a cereal-box cartoon character. It reminded her of the time she and Shal had gone to her cousin's performance of *Dancing at Lughnasa,* which the director had accidentally turned into a comedy by insisting on Irish accents at a Southern community theater. Tesla scanned the menu as she cleared an inappropriately hysterical laugh out of her throat. "Um . . . mulligatawny soup, soda bread, and a cider?"

"It wud be me pleasure! An' for yer?"

Shal was literally biting his lips as if he were struggling not to laugh. "The same. Thanks."

"Pure gran'! I'll be roi back wi' dohs." The server actually skipped away, whistling.

The moment their back was turned, Shal's grin broke out and he turned to her. "Didn't we see him in *Dancing at Lughnasa?*"

"I was just thinking that."

He mimicked the weird falsetto quaver of the terrible Irish accent: "When I cast me mind back to that summer of 1936 . . ."

"This is what happens when you let the director star in a production. And to be fair, Marilyn did try to warn us off."

"Yes, and then she also trapped us by asking what we thought of the show in front of everyone. I think she secretly enjoyed seeing our pain."

Tesla laughed and it felt like something in her chest unlocked a little. "'It was everything you promised it would be and more.'"

"And the set!" Matching her, Shal laughed. Then he tensed and was silent, with his arms around his ribs and his face sealed tight.

"Shal?"

"Fine." He shook his head and breathed in slowly. "Worst thing about this is that most of the time it really is fine. Sore, but fine. And then . . . laughing is not ideal."

"You need to let it heal."

"I'll go back to the cabin if you will." One corner of his mouth twisted in a wry half smile. "But we can assume that we've gone through our respective arguments and rebuttals on that particular discussion, come to an impasse, and skip ahead. Show me the pics you took after Ruth Fish died?"

The raft of arguments that she had queued up came apart and crashed into one another. It took a moment for Tesla to be able to nod. "Sure." She pulled her handheld out and set it between them. "Besides the spoofers, I don't even know what to look for."

The image had three blurred spots. Shal pointed to the one by the body. "That is probably an official one, to keep passengers from taking pictures and posting them to social . . . The one by the glass wall might also be. We can ask Maria."

Tesla placed her finger on the one at the Martian ice-cream shop. "And this one?"

"More likely to be a passenger." He grimaced. "If I had access to all my systems, I could look for the spoofer's signature, but I have to trust that Maria is doing that."

Mixed in with the other passengers, Annie leaned over the rail not far from the ice-cream shop. "Annie." Tesla closed her eyes and pulled up the image on the larger apparent screen of her HUD. "She doesn't have the shopping bag yet."

"Interesting—"

"'Ere yer go. Yer soup, bread, an two av de finest ciders in dis part av de galaxy! An' 'oweya both enjoyin' dis gran' day?"

Shal said, "It is everything we were promised, and more."

The laugh jumped out of her before she could stop it. Opening her eyes, she tried to ignore Shal's too-innocent smile and focused on the poor server. "Thanks so much. We'll call you if we need anything but for the moment . . . Our honeymoon." She wrinkled her nose in a smile. "You understand."

"That's gran'!" They winked over-broadly at her in a move that involved the entire side of their face. "I'll leave yer be den. Jist gie me a call if yer nade anytin' at al'." They skipped away, whistling, and she really expected a rainbow to sprout from beneath their feet.

Shaking his head, Shal said, "On the list of ways to make a terrible job more humiliating, requiring a fake accent is one of the worst things I've heard of. It's hard to maintain under the best of circumstances . . . huh."

"What?"

"Random thought. The line between a fake accent slipping and a real accent code-switching. Like the way Jalna's accent shifts to match Annie sometimes."

"Does it?" Tesla selected a piece of the dense bread and thought back through conversations. "I hadn't noticed."

"Maybe I'm wrong." Shal picked up his spoon and tried the soup. "Ahh . . . at least the soup is good. Now, where were we?"

"Annie doesn't have the shopping bag yet." Tesla sipped her cider, which was clean and refreshing.

He hunched forward, studying the image. "Right . . . so she goes to the gift shop after Ruth dies."

"Because that's a normal impulse." Although, maybe for some

people it was. Retail therapy was a way to exert control and a sem-blance of normalcy. "She and Ory were both gone from the yoga class and Annie reported the bathroom being out of service but Ory said he used it."

"So one of them is lying."

"Just one? To quote a great detective, 'Everyone has a secret, and everyone lies.'"

"A mediocre retired detective would argue the point by asking which secrets were relevant to the crime." He traced patterns on the table with the condensation from his glass. "I wish I knew who had been dumped in the recycler."

Tesla very carefully did not point out that he was still trying to solve the crime, even while protesting that they shouldn't get involved. If she pointed it out, he'd stop, so she dunked her bread in the soup and waited while he continued to ruminate.

Shal leaned back in his seat and stared up at the faux pressed-tin ceiling. "The service stairs come out near the yoga studio . . ."

"And that covers a shocking number of people who were in the yoga class as being potentially involved."

"Not really shocking, no." He tipped his head back down and reached for his cider. "Most murders are committed by someone who knows the person. So who knew all three of the deceased and Haldan? Also, why did our culprit go up instead of out to mix into the crowd? They had a spoofer, so they could have gone anywhere on the ship, but they went up. Why . . ."

"After we finish eating, why don't we go up the service stairs?" It would give her more ground to search for Gimlet, among other things. "Time the run up, maybe? Look at the bathroom and the studio?"

He shook his head and took another sip of his cider. "You saw us trying to run on a level surface. Run the stairs? As likely as that server being from Dublin."

Her insides clenched with an urge to shout, and she held it in, because he was right. "We have to do something."

Shal set his cider down and reached across to take her hand. "Hey . . . we'll find her."

Eyes burning, Tesla covered them with her free hand and held her breath. God, she hated the aftermath of a flashback when every emotion could tip into its most extreme variant. On the back of her hand, Shal traced circles with his thumb and gave her time to catch her breath.

She squeezed his hand back and lowered her other to grab a cocktail napkin to wipe her tears away. "What if we take the elevator up?"

"Sure." He lifted her hand and kissed the back of her fingers. Studying her, his gaze went a little roguish. "Tough question: Which of us is going to endure more *Dancing at Lughnasa* to get the check?"

Tailspin

.75 oz sweet vermouth

.75 oz. Green Chartreuse

.75 oz gin

.5 tsp Campari

Cherry

Lemon slice

Stir ingredients over ice for 40 seconds and strain into coupe. Garnish with cherry and lemon twist.

Shal had been right about taking the elevator up to the Lunar level. Tesla's left leg moved as if it were made of lead and attached to her body with thistles. Tenuous and prickly, punctuated with occasional bright pops. The stairs hadn't even vaguely been an option.

She stopped outside the elevator on the Lunar level and cupped her hands to her mouth. "Gimlet?"

The hum of conversation and the cheerful background music of the ship continued uninterrupted.

"Gimlet?" Shal's voice vanished into the scrum of other sounds.

Tesla sighed, limping over to look behind the closest ficus, not because she actually thought Gimlet would be there but because she needed to know for sure that she wasn't. She was not.

They crossed the bridge, heading to the stairs on the far side. As they came down the slope, Tesla saw a spot of white behind the ficus at the other side, curling like a tiny dog's tail. "Gimlet!"

It didn't move.

Shal's hand tightened on hers. "Shit."

Tesla tried to move into a run, but her cane and the lunar gravity tangled her feet. She stumbled, grabbing the railing, and didn't take her gaze off that unmoving white tail. Shal stopped, reaching for her, and she shook her head. "Go!"

Nodding, he took off at a hunched jog, one arm around his ribs. He slowed as he reached the ficus. His shoulders slumped. Shal reached into his pocket and pulled out a pair of blue nitrile gloves.

Heart choking her, Tesla staggered after him. Getting down on one knee, he peered into the dark space behind the ficus.

As she reached him, he turned to face her with a gloved hand out to stop her from getting too close. "It's not Gimlet."

Tesla bent forward, catching her weight on her cane with her head bowed. "Oh God. I thought—"

"I know." He sucked air in through his teeth. "Can I borrow your handheld? I need to take photos and call Maria."

Slowly, she straightened. "Why . . . ?"

"It's an Out of Order sign. For the bathroom." He pointed to the white tail, which was now more clearly the end of a decorative tassel that matched the decor of the ship. "I'm thinking this is not an official storage area."

"So . . . so Annie was telling the truth."

He waggled his hand. "Hard to say. It doesn't make sense for someone to have blocked the bathroom and then forgotten this here."

"You think she was framing Ory?" Tesla pulled out her handheld for him.

"I don't know anything at this point." Shal reached up and took the rolled cylinder she offered. Shuffling on his knees, he took shots from a few angles.

Tesla stood behind him feeling useless and shaky. She clenched her hands on her cane, using it to create a tripod of stability as Shal worked. When he was finished, he sat back on his heels and tapped the screen a couple of times.

"Want to place bets on how long it takes Maria to call?" Pushing up carefully, he rose with relative grace in the lunar gravity.

"Thirty seconds?"

He shrugged. "She's bus—" The handheld buzzed and he lifted the rolled cylinder to his ear for a voice-only call, grinning. "Maria. Hey. Yeah. We just spotted it on the Lunar level. Uh-huh. Yeah. Yeah, that's not going to happen and you should be ashamed of asking. Promise we'll wear gloves until you— What? Whoops! You're breaking up. Byeeeeeeeee!"

Shal disconnected the call and handed the device to Tesla.

It rang again immediately. She raised her brows as she silenced it and tucked it into her pocket. "So . . . what are we doing now?"

"I want to look at the bathroom." He dug in his pocket and produced another pair of blue nitrile gloves, which almost floated in the light gravity, and held the pair out to her. "In case we find anything?"

"Where did you get those?" Tesla leaned her cane against her hip as she worked the gloves on.

"Liberated them from sick bay. If you see anything, take a picture before you move it."

"Noted." Even with the constant undercurrent of worry for Gimlet, Tesla had a surge of adrenaline at the thought of doing something potentially useful. "What counts as 'anything' in this context?"

"Things that . . . Wow, that's hard to articulate." He stopped and held up his hand. "Wait. Okay. Picture a generic bathroom. When we go in, we're looking for things that don't fit. Some stuff will just be a product of the design. Some will be accidental damage. Some might be evidence. Part of why we take photos is so we know what something looked like in situ and also because it's often not the thing itself but the context in which it is found. Am I making any sense or am I just rambling?"

"You're making sense." She snapped the second glove into place. "Let's see what we find."

Shal pushed the door open and held it until she was through. Inside the door, he stopped. Without moving anything except his head, he studied the room. Tesla stood beside him, trying to see what he saw.

A long, narrow room, with gray faux-marble walls on the left and a Lunar urinal vacuum, also done in faux gray marble. On the right, a bank of three sinks and a mirror. In it, she was briefly startled by the captain before she remembered she was wearing a hat. Her eyes were red-rimmed and her pupils were too big.

Tesla pulled her gaze away to the bank of stalls on the right side for people who wanted to sit. Beyond that, the larger accessibility stall—why they were always at the far end was beyond her understanding. The air was scented with lemongrass and mint, and low, soothing music played a popgrass rendition of the theme to *Miracle Man*.

Beside her, Shal bent, bracing on the sink, and peered under the nearest stall. "They're all empty." He stood, looking up at the corners of the room. "No cameras. Which is as it should be, given privacy laws, but sometimes . . ."

Tesla checked out the hand sanitizer and the sinks, as if she had any clue what she was looking for. To her, it looked like a bathroom.

"I'm going to start at the far end and work my way back."

"Okay. I'll meet you in the middle." Tesla went into the nearest stall, and the lid of the Lunar-style toilet slid back with a cheerful melody that masked the sound of its suction fan and paired with the room music. Blue sterilizing lights flashed across the surface of the seat in an unnecessarily complicated dance.

Behind the toilet, the wall had a recessed shelf to put necessary items on. It was empty.

Bracing on the cane, she bent down to look behind the toilet. Even in the reduced gravity, she could feel the muscles in her back refer their tension down her leg to a hot spot behind her knee. Nothing behind the toilet. Nothing in the trash recycler. Nothing in the corners.

She went into the next stall and was treated to the same singing light show from the toilet. A wadded-up bit of tissue was stuck to the floor in one corner. Gross, but not out of place.

From the far end of the bathroom, Shal hissed.

"Find something?"

He was silent for a moment and when he spoke, his voice was strained. "Twisted the wrong way."

Probably, that's all that it was. Or a murderer was holed up in here and had pulled a steak knife on him. Her heart was beating too quickly as she left the stall and walked down the row to where he was.

In the second to last booth, Shal had one hand against the wall and the other pressed to his side as he looked behind the toilet. He glanced up at her. "Afraid I was being held at knifepoint?"

"Mm . . . I have a question." Also true, or true enough now. "Things like wadded-up toilet paper? Normal refuse or something to note?"

"If this were the first day, and we had a forensics team in here, they'd catalog it, run labs on it and tell us definitively." He shrugged. "Here, it's probably refuse. A cleaning crew has been through since."

"How can you tell?"

"Toilet paper rolls are all full." He nodded to the front of the room. "Also there's a sign-off checklist by the door. They come through every four hours."

"Oh . . . So this is pointless."

Shal rubbed the back of his neck. "Not pointless. It's good to be familiar with the lay of the land. And if something kept whoever it was from coming back for the out-of-order sign, then maybe they missed something here too."

She sighed and went back to looking at toilets. It was pointless, and he was humoring her and she still didn't know what else to do. The longer it went without Gimlet turning up, the more she was sure that someone had killed her dog. That tassel had looked so much like—Tesla stopped where she was, clenching her cane with both hands.

Gimlet would be fine. Everyone loved her. Even if they intended something nefarious, one look at those big dark eyes would melt them.

She reached for the familiar comfort of ritual. Toilet. Walls. Blue lights. Blue nubbin—

"Hello." It was stuck to the wall nearly at the ceiling. Tesla took a snap with her handheld. "Shal?"

"Yeah?" He poked his head out of the stall.

"That's a suckerfoot." She pointed to the spot of blue. This happened with octopoids sometimes, when they got really good suction on a surface and a suckerfoot pulled free of the limb. It was stuck high up on the wall next to a brass accent that ran along the top. "And that's a cable run. And *that* is an access hatch for a junction box."

He stared up at it. "A suckerfoot as in an octobot?"

"Or an octopoid; they use the same general movement vector but one is running—" She caught herself before she could get into the weeds talking about processors and latencies. "The point is that neither my acubot nor the medical octopoid are blue. But . . . when I met Ewen, they said the robot they used in competition was a blue polydactyl octopoid."

"I have to lean on you for this . . . Is that a rare enough combination that it's likely to be the same one?"

She sucked air through her teeth, thinking. "Well . . . most of the commercial ones are a neutral gray or off-white. My design teams work with the fashion industry colors, and this season those were purple, teal, and metallic gold, so blue isn't a 'this year' model. I could compare it to photos of the one Ewen used back in competition?"

Shal nodded and wandered over to stand under the suckerfoot. He reached up to grab the top of the nearest stall and stopped abruptly with a hiss of pain. For a moment, he held still before slowly lowering his arms. "Nope. Not a chance." He stayed with his back to her, head bent. "Goddammit. Give me a sec to document it. And will you send some shots to Maria and Fantine for safety, since I'm still offline?"

"I can ask Fantine again to deal with that."

"As if she's stopped trying. She'll keep hounding them to reconnect me to the net until she gets the answer she wants." Shal took another look around the bathroom. "Not a lot of people use this, do they?"

"There's not much cause to go past it, unless you're here for yoga, I guess."

"All right . . . Let's leave it there until Maria gets up here." He had an energy in his voice that ran shivers down her spine. "Want to take a look at the yoga studio now?"

"You always invite me to the nicest places."

He winked at her, then kissed her on the cheek. His breath was warm and feathered against her ear. ::*Have I told you how deeply sexy your brain is?*::

Tesla went warm all over as heat radiated out from her core. ::*I love you too.*::

He took her hand, still clad in nitrile gloves, as they headed out of the bathroom. Tesla grabbed a new courtesy mask from the wall dispenser so that she didn't have to deal with being recognized. Rather than heading straight into the yoga studio, Shal veered over to the rail of the bridge that spanned the plaza below. "Cable run is out here too. The same one?"

Tesla leaned over the bridge to look at it. "I'd have to see a schematic, but if it's inline the junction box would let it—"

"Shit." Shal tensed and moved farther across the bridge, looking down to the Martian level. "I see Ory and Ewen."

"Where?"

He pointed, and it still took her a minute to spot them walking in the crowd. Ewen was talking animatedly, gesturing with their hands as Ory listened. He slowed them and pointed to the ice-cream shop. Ewen nodded and the pair turned in.

Shal headed across the bridge, keeping an eye on the Snow Queen's open storefront. Tesla followed him, with one hand on the rail. "That's where the spoofer was."

"Take a picture, then review it. Is there a blur?"

She snapped the Martian level and it seemed largely innocuous, with a mix of pedestrians moving along a promenade with open storefronts that were designed to seem like quaint shops in a real town. What broke that casual appearance was a ring of haze where Ory and Ewen were. It wasn't staticky but had a slight halo around a group of folks where an AI had sent out a false signal to replace the scene. "A very, very high-grade spoofer where Ory and Ewen are."

"Surprised face." Shal glanced at Tesla. "I need you to hang back far enough that Maria can spot you on the security cameras. Your job is to keep an eye on me, and my job is to keep an eye on them. Okay?"

She nodded, pulling the courtesy mask on. "You aren't going to engage with him, are you?"

He shook his head as they arrived at the elevator. "Not by choice." He pushed the button and leaned back around the corner to stare down at the Snow Queen. "Call me when it comes?"

"Will do." Her palms were sweating inside her gloves. She stripped them off so she could wipe her hands on her trousers. Everything felt sticky and too tight. *I'm safe.* The elevator doors were glass and she could see through them and the glass wall beyond to a slightly distorted view of the ice-cream shop. It looked like Ory and Ewen were still in there, but she didn't have a great view.

The elevator finally crawled up into place, completely filled with a wedding party. "Shal! It's here." She stepped to the side to let them off.

The bridal dress filled most of the elevator, with members of the wedding party in an assortment of purples and teals taking up the rest of the space. They were laughing and passing around a bottle of Champagne to top off glasses. None of them moved to get off the elevator.

One of them spotted her and wrinkled their nose. "Sorry! Meant to go down."

"Overheard at an orgy!" Another one laughed and jabbed the Door Closed button.

At her side, Shal growled under his breath. He blew a gust out through his nose and glared at the descending elevator. "All right. Look. I'm going to take the stairs. I need you to stay here and keep an eye on them. I won't be able to spot movement from the stairwell. If they start to go before I'm down, trail them on this level and call m—dammit. Point to direct me."

"Got it." She pushed the call button for the elevator as he hurried to the stairs. Since it would take forever to arrive, she went back to the bridge, where she'd be able to see the elevator coming up through the glass walls and have enough warning to get back to it.

Ory and Ewen were leaning on the ice-cream display, pointing to different flavors. She sent out a silent prayer that the kid would want to try one of everything before deciding. Around her, the rest of the passengers moved along the various promenade levels as if nothing bad had ever happened to them or to anyone.

She took a pic of the Snow Queen and played it back. The shop was blurred and out of focus. Dismissing the photo, she clung to the rail and hated being a spectator.

Tesla went back to the elevator and pushed the button rapidly, as if that had ever made one come faster. She split her attention between the ice-cream shop and the promenade, waiting for the moment when— There he was. Shal was threading his way through the people on the far side of the promenade.

The elevator started to rise. Tesla opened and closed her hand on her cane. Slow breaths. *In, two, three, four. Out, two, three, four.*

It arrived and she got in, pressing the button for the Martian level. She turned back to the glass wall to look for Shal. As the doors closed behind her, a dog barked.

"Gimlet!" Tesla spun and her back seized.

The doors closed. She dragged herself to the control panel and frantically pressed the Door Open button. The elevator started to descend. "No. Goddammit. No!"

Shaking, she turned back to the glass to wait for the elevator to get down to the Martian level so she could go back up again. She brought up Gimlet's tracker on her HUD, hoping something had changed, but her dog's beacon was still situated in Haldan's cabin with the same damn note.

Offline. Last known location.

She wanted to scream. Staring out the glass side, she watched Shal approach the ice-cream shop. Inside, Ewen finally had a cone. Ory was laughing at something they said and turned.

He saw Shal. He took a step back. Turning, he took Ewen by the arm and moved the kid around the counter. Shal moved forward and she couldn't hear him, but she could see that he was talking. The ice-cream shop staff was as well, but Ory ignored them and took Ewen straight to a service door.

It opened for him.

Shal sprang forward and just caught it with his foot. Then he chased them through.

Tesla pressed her forehead against the glass as she continued to descend the gravity well to Mars.

Reckless Generosity

2 oz sweet vermouth
1 oz rum
Dash orange bitters
Pinch cayenne salt
Orange peel

Stir vermouth, rum, and bitters over ice for 40 seconds.
Drain into coupe. Add dash of cayenne salt. Garnish with
flamed orange peel.

The elevator doors opened on the Martian level. If Shal hadn't
gone through that goddamned door, she would go back up to look
for Gimlet, but he was an idiot and she was going to kill him herself. Gritting her teeth as she left part of her soul in the elevator,
Tesla dialed the DBPS past all the safeties.

She went as fast as she could to the ice-cream shop but it was
still little more than a fast walk. Even though she didn't hurt, the
nerve in her back was still pinched and her left leg moved like she
was pushing it through an ice field. She dialed Fantine, knowing
that the lag would now be thirteen minutes for the round trip
and that there was nothing Fantine could actually do. Mostly,
she wanted to have a recording stored off the ship of whatever was
about to happen.

"Fantine, when you get this, I'm calling because Shal just chased
Ory Slootmaekers and Ewen into the service corridors on the Martian level. Also, I heard Gimlet bark." Her voice was breathy as she
threaded through the passengers meandering across the bridge.
"I'm following Shal, which I know you'll tell me not to do, but

I'm doing it anyway. I'm also calling Officer Piper to ask for help so I'm not being totally stupid."

As Tesla rounded the corner at the end of the bridge, she opened another line and called Piper.

"Hello, this is Bob."

"Bob." Tesla's heart kicked sideways. "I was calling Officer Piper."

"She's occupied. Her calls are being routed to me."

"Aren't you supposed to be guarding Haldan?"

"Yep." His shrug was almost audible through the handheld. "I can do both."

The archway to the Snow Queen shop, in all its pink confectioner's glory, loomed on the left side of the walkway. "When will she be available?"

"You'll have to ask Chief Wisor."

A scream lay under her skin, clawing to get out. She did not want to talk to Wisor. "Can you transfer me?"

"He's occupied. His calls are being routed to me."

"Oh my God." Tesla stopped outside the Snow Queen and a passenger carrying a baby glared at her for the random outburst. "Fine. Look. Tell Piper that Ory Slootmaekers and his kid went through the service door of the Snow Queen and that Shal is chasing them. Also, I heard Gimlet bark near the elevator on the Lunar level. I'm following Shal."

"Wait—" For the first time she heard some urgency in Bob's voice. "You can't do that."

"Then come and stop me." She hung up and stalked into the ice-cream shop. It smelled of sugar and cinnamon.

The blue-trousered servers behind the counter smiled at her as she aimed straight for the service door next to the counter. "Welcome to the Snow Queen! Would you like to try— Um. Excuse me. That's not a door for customers."

"My spouse went through this a bit ago." Tesla pulled on the knob and the door didn't budge. Shal was behind this and Gimlet was upstairs. "Could you?"

"Oh, no. I'm sorry. I can't."

"But I just saw my spouse and two other people go through." Her voice was completely reasonable and only a little brittle. "I would like to join them."

The servers exchanged looks with each other and the one closest to her said, "I'm really sorry, but I can't. Would you . . . would you like some ice cream?"

"I would not." Tesla wet her lips and tried to calm down. Nothing that was happening was this young person's fault. "May I speak to the manager?"

"I am the manager."

Tesla took a controlled breath and stretched a smile across her stiff cheeks, even though they wouldn't be able to see it through her courtesy mask. The act of smiling made her voice less harsh. "I'll make other arrangements."

A little less harsh. Climbing the management chain was possible, but she didn't need to, she had Haldan. She stepped back from the counter and dialed Maria Piper's number again.

"This is Bob."

"Bob. May I speak to Haldan?"

"No."

"Look, you mammering lobster, I need to talk to Haldan, right now."

He hung up on her. Fury painted everything bright red. She almost called back. But winning would take too long under these circumstances. She looked at the lock and the door and the window into the service corridor beyond. Shal was somewhere back there. Gimlet was upstairs. Maybe. But she knew for certain her spouse had gone this way.

Stabbing the floor with her cane, she stalked out of the ice-cream shop and turned to her left, to the gift shop that Annie had gone to. Bright vacation wear filled it, with artful faux stains in hot beet pink and grass green. Tesla browsed as quickly as she could, grabbing a battery recharger and looking for anything else useful and why the hell hadn't Fantine picked up yet and why was Gimlet on the Lunar level? Or had she been somewhere else and her bark had just sounded like it was on the Lunar level because Tesla was in an elevator and . . .

Glasses-repair kit. That was useful. She snatched it and headed to the checkout, grabbing a pack of chewing gum on her way. Her hands were shaking as she waved her wrist fob over the scanner and accepted the charges. She ripped the battery pack out of its packaging and smiled at the attendant. "You don't mind throwing that away for me, do you?"

She tucked the battery pack under her arm, opened the gum, and pulled her courtesy mask away so she could put a stick in her mouth. Rolling the foil wrapper between her fingers, she stalked back to the Snow Queen. The servers were helping a bevy of teenagers, and Tesla blessed them for their tumult. She went around the end of the counter and carefully lowered herself to kneel in front of the lock.

Sweat poured down her back. Her chest was tight. For safety, she propped her handheld so that it could work as a sort of rearview mirror and record the scene behind her. She fished out the screwdriver from the glasses-repair kit and began to dismantle the key-fob reader.

When she had been a teenager, she'd been—charitably—a handful, and her father had sent her to boarding school. During the course of her year and a half there, she had learned to hack every system that the school had for containing troublesome youth. They thought they could keep her out with a key-fob lock? Ha. She was a Crane.

She had the housing off the lock and had the first gum wrapper installed before any of the servers noticed her.

"Hey! Excuse me. Hey. You have to stop."

Tesla kept working. "Feel free to call security." One way or another, she'd get backup. "But my lawyer is on the phone, so think twice before anyone touches me."

The second gum wrapper rolled between her fingers to become a makeshift wire and her breath smelled amazing. She tied the wrapper in and reached for the battery pack as if she had never stopped being an engineer. The right kind of panic could be a useful focusing tool.

"Oh, for the love of Saint Lawrence's gridiron—" Fantine stopped talking and in the HUD, her brows came together as she listened to Tesla's summary. She closed her eyes for a moment and then looked straight at the camera as if she could stare directly into Tesla's soul. "Tesla. I know you and I'm going to tell you right now that neither Shal nor Gimlet are going to be served by you trying to chase a murderer down on your own. I need you to stop. Don't go into the ice-cream . . . Frozen farts on a stick. Do you have any idea how frustrating it is to give you advice thirteen minutes too . . ."

"Hey. Good to hear from you." As Tesla worked, she kept one eye on the handheld. In its view of the shop behind her, Chief Wisor jogged into view. "So listen, Fantine, you're authorized to draw on my accounts as necessary to handle whatever damages I'm incurring."

Her lawyer didn't hear her and kept talking. ". . . is like watching a horror film. Don't go through the door. DON'T GO THROUGH THE— Oh, thank the Virgin's left tit, it's locked. Listen. I need you to stand down and not try to get through the door."

Wisor's face was blotchy red as he loomed in the handheld's field of view. He reached for her, slowing to a stop when he saw himself on the screen and realized that she was recording.

"Hi, Chief Wisor. Did Bob give you my message?"

"I need you to stand up and move away from the door."

Tesla took the gum out of her mouth and stuck it over the ends of the wrappers to help it stay in place. It wouldn't last long, but she only needed it to work for a literal second. "Will you let me through the door?"

"Negative. But I'm more than happy to assist you in not going into a restricted area and will, in fact, escort you back to the safety of your cabin."

"Great. The safest way for me to move about the ship is through the service corridors, so . . ."

"Your adoring fans." He looked around with exaggerated interest. "Yeah. They're really swarming you."

"Hat. Courtesy mask. I had an assumed identity until your system—you know what? It doesn't matter. What matters is that Shal is on the other side of this door with someone that your own staff thinks might be involved in the murders."

"What matters is that you're trying to dismantle my ship."

"I find it fascinating that you are more interested in stopping me than you are in stopping the actual murderer." She picked up the battery pack.

"My job is to maintain order on this ship. I need you to step away."

On her HUD, Fantine said, "Oh, good. You're leaving the ice-cream shop. Thank God you are showing some sense. Now listen, I've got people working on finding out more about Ory Sloot-maekers. Surprising no one, that's a fake identity. He must have paid as much as you did for privacy."

"Step away from the door." Chief Wisor loomed closer, casting a shadow across her workspace.

"Open it, and I will." She toggled the battery pack to wired charging, exposing a port on its side. With the screwdriver she worked the end of one of the gum wrappers into the port. Sub-vocalizing, she replied to Fantine. ::*Fantine, understood about Ory.*::

Wisor snatched the charger out of her hand. "Oh no—not on my ship."

"Murders are fine though, right?" Tesla grabbed her handheld in one hand and her cane in the other. "Tell me what you're doing besides stalling? How many more people are you willing to have die on your watch, hm?"

"That's enough." He reached for her.

She tapped her temple, reminding him that she had a subdermal. "Don't you dare touch me. You've already beaten my spouse and if you think that Corporate is going to protect you, you are sorely mistaken. I'm not asking for anything complicated. I just want you to open the door, because Shal is on the other side with someone that your own—"

"I'm not interested in the fictions you've spun."

She had to get him to let her through this door. Fantine could argue for her, but waiting the thirteen minutes for each round of argument would take too long.

"Tesla . . . I don't like the collection of things you're buying."

Tesla took off her courtesy mask. Swallowing bile, she pulled the hat off and did her best to fluff her hair. She had damn few tools, and Daddy had always said that sometimes your weaknesses were your best tools. She raised her handheld and took a selfie. It took five shots to get one where her dishevelment looked intentional.

Wisor stood with his arms crossed over his chest. "Just like a—"

"If you finish that with 'woman,' I will end you." She glared at him over the handheld. "Last chance to let me through."

"No way."

Tesla shrugged. "All right . . ." She ostentatiously narrated each word as she keyed it in. "Getting ice cream at the Snow Queen on the Martian level. Mislaid my battery charger. Anyone got a spare?"

He smirked in disbelief. "And this is supposed to fright—"

"Soak it. Tesla Crane was just—wait." One of the teenagers spun from the ice-cream display. "Holy shit. You're still here!"

"I sure am! How are you doing?"

As a group, they abandoned the ice-cream display. Wisor stepped back involuntarily as the teens swarmed toward her. They stopped in a slight arc as if there were a protective bubble sur-rounding her.

On her HUD, Fantine covered her eyes with her hands. "Tell me you are not trying to hack the lock. Why am I asking? Why am I not just drafting letters about the unnecessary emotional distress the ship is putting you in?"

One of the teens was clearly messaging a friend. "My buddy has a charger. I'm telling her to come right now."

"Soak that! I've got one." The smallest of them swung their bag around to the front and dug inside it. "Here you go!"

Wisor snatched it out of the kid's hand. "Nice try."

"You'll need to do paperwork about anything you confiscate, right?" Tesla stepped over to stand in front of the kid whose battery charger Wisor had taken. "Sorry about him. Want to selfie?"

The kid's eyes got huge. "Seriously?"

"Sure!" She smiled at Chief Wisor. "You want to get in on this? Because there's going to be a line later."

He rolled his eyes at her. But behind him, she saw someone do an about-face. Farther down the promenade, another passenger was jogging toward them, staring at their handheld. Tesla had once accidentally broadcast her location and the crowd had mate-rialized with alarming rapidity. These days, her social media was set to post a day later unless she did an active override.

There were distinct problems to growing up in the public eye as the literal poster child for Crane Industries. There were problems with unwillingly saturating the public consciousness when you were the sole survivor of a dramatic disaster. And when you tried to rede-fine yourself by appearing on a dancing contest? Tesla had damn few places she could go and not be recognized, which usually sucked.

"Excuse me, is—" One of the bajillion generic bald, white passengers on the ship poked their head into the ice-cream shop. They saw her. "Oh, hi! I have a charger for you."

"You are the sweetest—"

"I'll take that . . ." Wisor pivoted toward the bald passenger and held out his hand but faltered a little as he finally saw the growing crowd.

It was still a small crowd, but just the fact that a crowd existed was causing other people to slow down and drift their way. Tesla had her back to the door and raised her handheld. "Chief Wisor!" When he looked at her reflexively, she snapped a picture of him holding three different chargers. "Smile!"

Gimlet barked.

Any fun that Tesla was having evaporated. That was somewhere outside the shop, and it was the "delivery arrival" bark, which meant that Gimlet felt threatened. She looked at Wisor. "Tell me you heard my dog."

He hadn't, and even if he had, the line of his brows said that he didn't care. Incandescent rage filled Tesla and she pushed away from the door. Then stopped.

The crowd had her utterly trapped.

A person in stiletto sandals tottered around the corner. "Oh— you're still here. I have a battery charger!"

Wisor tucked one of the chargers under his arm and held out his hand. "Absolutely not."

Tesla forced a smile at the newcomer. "Sorry. This is the security chief and we're having a little disagreement." She gestured to the door. "I want to go through here and—"

Someone ran into the store with a charger held aloft in each hand. "Is Tesla—"

"I have a charger!"

"Me too!" From behind the counter, a server handed one across to Tesla. "Sorry! I didn't recognize you before."

"Hey, is Tesla Crane still here?"

Wisor's hands were full, and there was a gaggle of teens between them. Bitter victory made her teeth hurt as she took the charger from the server and waved it at the security chief. "Well? Which of us is going to open this door?"

SCOFFLAW

2 oz rye

.75 oz dry vermouth

.5 oz lemon juice

.25 oz grenadine

1 dash orange bitters

Shake all ingredients over ice for 15 seconds. Strain into coupe.

Wisor's teeth were grinding so loudly as they walked through the service corridor that Tesla was fairly certain he was going to break a molar. If Fantine had been audible on the handheld, her assessment of Wisor's actions would not have improved his mood.

". . . through a lawsuit so long and dry that the desiccation will dehydrate the overgrown toadstool you reason with." She glanced to the side. "Tesla. If you haven't already, move me to your HUD. I have an update."

"Already did . . ." Tesla's cane made a *pock* sound with each step on the unadorned service floor. Wisor was walking faster than Tesla could comfortably go, and as much as she wanted to hurry, she also didn't want to face-plant. "And thank you for—"

"If I'm not on your HUD by now, you have no one to blame but yourself." Fantine's face loomed closer to the camera. "WHAT IN THE NAME OF SAINT JOAN'S FLAMING DILDO ARE YOU THINKING? If you had actually used that battery charger, he would have been completely justified in locking you up as a fire hazard—"

Tesla huffed. "I'm not an amateur."

"—and honestly, I should probably have let him because you'd be safer than roaming around after murderers." Fantine settled back in her chair. "The only reason I'm not is because of Gimlet. If one hair is harmed on the most perfect of dogs, I am training an apprentice who can continue the lawsuits after my death of old, bitter age."

Ahead of Tesla, Wisor turned to the right.

The stairs to the yoga studio were to the left. She shook her head at his back and turned left.

Behind her, Wisor said, "Hey—where are you going?"

"It seems to me that Ory and Ewen would be trying to get back to their cabin, which is probably on the Terran level, and the closest stairs are the other way."

"I'm escorting you to your cabin."

"And I'm looking for my spouse." Tesla turned her back on him and walked to the stairs. "It won't take a minute for me to look."

In the HUD, Fantine cracked her knuckles. "Moving on. I have reports on the various things that you've asked me to research for you, as if you didn't have an office of assistants."

"My assistants are clever, but none of them have the clout you do."

"You requested a list of people who have access to your cabin as well as a list of people who had access to Haldan's. That's coming your way via encrypted quad-lock with your eighth passcode to decrypt. I won't detail what I had to do to come up with these lists, but I will tell you that your next bill will not be cheap—Wow. Nice fan club you're gathering there."

Behind her, Wisor's sigh was deeply dramatic, but his footsteps joined hers and he caught up as they got to the entrance to the stairwell. "We'll step into the stairwell and if there are no signs of them, then we're going to turn around and go back to your cabin."

::You're never cheap and always worth it,:: she subvocalized to Fantine.

Wisor raised his brows. "Do we understand each other?"

"Absolutely." Tesla nodded to the door to the stairs. "After you."

In her HUD, Fantine said, "Back to business. Even though you didn't ask me to cross-reference them, I did so for my own amusement. They divide the ship into zones and in each zone there are a ton of potentials. But there are eleven people with cross-zone access permissions."

Wisor pulled the door open. Voices echoed up the stairs.

"—down. Only want to understand—" Shal. He sounded calm and reasonable.

"Move. I don't want to hurt you." Ory. His voice sounded agitated.

Wisor held out his arm to block Tesla. His face had suddenly gone serious and he caught the door with his foot before it could swing back closed again. With his other hand, he raised a finger to his lips to urge silence.

Competing for Tesla's attention, Fantine continued to talk about things thirteen minutes in the past. "Clever to ask them to bring chargers, but again, I tell you that if you actually use one . . . People with potential access to your cabins, which is not the same as verifiably accessing it. One: Captain Valdísardottir, she/her."

"There's no need for anything like that. C'mon . . . there's just some things I'm curious about and thought you might know the answer. Questions can't—whoa. Hey now."

"Two: the copilot, Chris DiBono, he/him."

"Hey." Bob's voice joined Shal's. "You're scaring the kid."

"Three: the chief operations officer, Shyamasri Caruana, they/them."

Rising on his toes, Wisor moved into the stairwell with more grace than she expected and hesitated. He turned back and beckoned her through, then eased the door closed.

"I'm scaring them? What about the person who chased us in

here? Why are you focused on me instead of the fact that this person is harassing us?"

"Four: our friend Chief Wisor."

Leaning down, their friend Chief Wisor whispered, "I have a body cam, but if he's using a spoofer, I want a witness. Follow me down, but for the love of God, stay a flight behind because I don't want your lawyer suing me for endangerment."

"Five: Maria Piper, security."

Wisor started down the stairs without waiting for her.

"Six: Bob Cook, security."

Bob—who was supposed to be guarding Haldan—said, "I don't make judgments."

"You're making a judgment now, when you're stopping us from going to our cabin."

Tesla stood at the top of the stairs and transferred her cane so she could grab the banister with her other hand. Under normal gravity conditions, stairs would have been difficult. On a ship like this, stairs were the unholy love child of Dalí and Escher. Each stair tilted by a degree so that as you descended the centrifugal gravity well "down" was always at the right point.

"Seven and eight: the senior medical staff, which includes our deceased Ruth Fish and her able assistant, Candy Star, she/her—and really, a missed opportunity for a career in porn or a role in a Christmas pageant. So close, sometimes." Fantine squinted at the camera. "Looks like he's letting you through, so no need for me to yell at that open-dunghole canker-blossom. This time."

Wisor was out of sight already. Below them, Bob said, "You aren't supposed to be in the stairwell."

"But neat trick with the door." Shal's voice was affable and breezy. "How'd you do that? I mean, I thought you had to be staff to go through the staff doors."

Tesla tried to pick up the pace, tensing with every motion. She had the DBPS turned so high she could barely feel her feet touch the stairs, and had to watch every step.

"Nine: Melissa Meade, she/her. Head of maintenance."

"Hey, hey . . . if you don't want to talk to me, why don't you go with Bob?"

On the landing, she peered over the edge of the stairs, trying to catch a glimpse of Shal. The twisting nature of the stairs meant that one level below her was shifted just enough to the side that she had a clear view. Halfway between her and Shal, Wisor was hanging back on the landing below her, peering down the next flight of stairs.

"Ten: Larry Holden, he/him. Head of housekeeping."

Below Wisor, Shal was standing in a boxing stance, favoring his side but blocking the pathway up the stairs. Ory stood, with Ewen behind him, in a corner of the landing, while Bob was blocking them from below.

"Eleven: and for no reason that makes any sense to me . . . Nile Silver, he/him, magician."

Tesla's left knee buckled.

No warning. It just went out from under her. Flailing, she clutched the rail and managed to control the fall. Mostly control it. She swung into the rail, and wound up half kneeling on the landing.

And somehow, she'd managed to set her handy to project. Fantine's voice filled the stairwell. Her face splashed on the wall and the underside of the stairs above. "That's it for who could have gotten into the cabins. Now—"

Below her, Fantine's voice broke the impasse, and the sound of tussling broke out on the stairs. Grunting and flesh striking flesh and the heavy sound of a body hitting something solid.

Any attempt at stealth botched, Wisor bulled down the stairs. "Stand down! All of you."

"—having said that, a sufficiently motivated person could bribe servers in each zone, which could give them access to any cabin. So, get your hotshot detective spouse to look at the full list and see what he comes up with."

Shaking, Tesla dragged in a breath. Nothing hurt. The DBPS settings were so high that nothing could hurt. So she had no way of knowing if she'd done more damage.

Shal charged up the stairs to her. "Tesla, are you—?"

"I slipped." She held out her hand. "A little help?"

"Next on the list of things you asked about, are the passengers in the yoga class—"

"Leave my dad alone!"

"Kid, step back." Wisor's voice was harsh.

"Your mystery man does, in fact, have a passenger account, which is locked down the way yours was with an added 'religious exclusions' clause relating to photos of him and his kid. I have not yet cracked it, so that's going to have to come from the tickle-brained ship authorities. I've put in a request to Leigh." Overhead, Fantine sneered with all the teeth of the shark she was.

Tesla watched Ory relax with apparent relief that Fantine hadn't found a photo, even as Wisor held him against the wall with his arm twisted up behind him. Ory had made it impossible to find photos of himself, but she knew where there was a picture of Ewen. Aloud, so they could hear her, she said, "Fantine—go through the archives for the Crane Robotics Competition from three years ago. Ewen was on the Utah team that entered with a blue polydactyl octopoid robot."

With internal apologies, she ended the call with Fantine so that it wasn't a distraction and watched to see what would happen next.

Ory cranked his head around to look at Ewen. Under the weight of that glare, they shifted from one leg to the other. "Pops, I can explain—"

"Don't." Ory's voice was low and patient. "Ewen, I need you to be quiet."

"But Pops—"

"Hourglass." His voice broke on the word. "Please, kid . . ."

Ewen hesitated and then nodded, brows together and serious.

Their face closed up and they stood with arms wrapped tightly around their chest, shoulders hunched.

It was weird and very uncomfortable to watch. Tesla glanced at Shal, who was rubbing his thumb against the side of his finger and concentrating on the two of them. Right, the fact that they'd gone to the robotics competition, clearly without permission, was a weakness she could exploit.

But she was on the landing above them and even if there wasn't a potential spoofer, there was no way she was going to make it down to the small group. She carefully lowered herself to sit on the steps and sent the pic of the blue suckerfoot, which she'd taken while in the bathroom, to the projector. She pointed at it. "That's a suckerfoot from an octobot or octopoid."

Bob asked, "What's the difference between an octobot and an octopoid?"

Sitting down next to Tesla, Shal said, "They're both based on octopuses—octopi?"

"Octopods." Ewen clapped their hand over their mouth.

"Thanks. Anyway, an octopoid has eight autonomous drivers—"

"Semi—" The kid stopped and stared at the floor.

"Semiautonomous. Right . . ." Shal nodded and winked at the kid. "And an octobot has a central processor, right?"

Ory was glaring at his child, but it wasn't quite enough to keep Ewen's small nod constrained. This was a child who loved robots. Tesla couldn't believe that Ewen would be involved in any of the deaths, but she wouldn't put it past Ory at this point to use his kid's robot. She watched Ewen but directed her words to Wisor. "The robot that Ewen entered in the competition was also blue."

"That's not mine."

"Ewen."

"Yeah, but Pops, like, I don't have a robot and—"

"I'm not mad about the robot." Ory breathed in slowly as if he were, in fact, very upset about the robot and trying not to yell. "We've talked about this, and both of us need to stay quiet. Okay?

When the government comes for you, they'll lie and cheat and use everything we say. I shouldn't be talking now, but I need you to remember the drill. Please. For me."

Ewen's eyes were huge, but they nodded and looked at the floor.

Still pressed against the wall by Wisor, Ory scraped his head back around. "I'd like to contact my lawyer."

"Sure. I've never wanted to get between a customer and their legal counsel. Go right ahead." Wisor cranked Ory's arm a little higher. "We'll walk to the brig now and on the way there, you can think about letting me know who you were working with."

On the arm that Wisor had pinned, Ory wore a standard key-fob band. Tesla frowned, remembering him going through the door in the ice-cream shop. "Shal? When Ory went through the door, did he use his key fob?"

Her spouse slowly nodded, eyes narrowing as he thought. "He did. What security clearance do you need to do that?"

Bob grumbled from where he blocked the stairs with his wall of body. "Anyone on staff could go through. But he's not on staff."

"So . . . why was he able to open the door?"

"Good question." Shal kissed her on the cheek. "Let me add a follow-up. Whose identity is he using?"

Wisor sighed and tightened his mouth as if he really did not want to admit that they'd asked a good question. "Let's find out."

"Lawyer." Ory pressed his forehead against the wall.

"Bob. Logs."

The wall of Bob opened his handheld and scrolled through a series of screens. "Um . . . says here that Nile Silver accessed the door."

Kir Royale

5 oz sparkling wine
.5 oz crème de cassis
1 twist lemon

Pour crème de cassis into a Champagne flute. Top with sparkling wine. Garnish with twist of lemon.

The closer they got to the theater, the more Tesla was sweating. It wasn't just because they had hurried to beat Wisor there. He and Bob had needed to take Ory and Ewen to the brig, and that bought them time to get to the theater before the chief messed up the scene for Shal. For the discomfort that came from walking faster than she comfortably could, she just gritted her teeth and bore down on her cane, letting the limp be more obvious than she liked. For the sights and sounds that might serve as a trigger again . . . She breathed with conscious deliberation. She imagined golden sunlight as a liquid filling her from above.

What was here in reality? Five things she saw. Dim lobby. Velvet curtains. Tiered stairs leading down and up to different gravity wells. Annie, beaming with delight, spotlit on a dark stage. Stars.

Nile Silver's warm voice filled the theater. "Now I'll ask my charming volunteer to look inside the box and tell the audience if you see anything out of the ordinary."

The smell of cordite in the air. Tesla swallowed. She was on the *Lindgren* in a theater and they were waiting to talk to Nile Silver. At the entrance to the box seats, Shal slipped his hand into hers. ::*Maria said she was going to talk to Nile after dropping off Immanuel, so I'm guessing she'll be backstage if she's here. Do you want to wait outside while I look for her?::*

Tesla shook her head and dialed the DBPS down so the bright cords in her back could serve as a focus. The pain was familiar and came with the slight relief that she hadn't done any new damage. Shal's hand was soft and warm in hers. She pressed her other hand against the cool silver rail surrounding the box seats, and sweat slicked the surface.

Tesla's chest was tight. Gimlet would have had Tesla outside by now. She wet her lips. *::Neither of us is going anywhere solo, and I'm embarrassed for you that you suggested it.::*

Teasing him was better than admitting that she was afraid they'd shoot off pyro again. Annie and Jalna had said it was at the beginning of the show and then . . . when? Intermission? They were coming up on that soon, according to the ship's timetable.

Sounding thrilled, Annie's amplified voice answered Nile: "I don't see a darn thing except a box."

"Oh really?" The magician chuckled as if he had a secret that he could not wait to share. "Watch."

With a grin as forced as her own, Shal ran his hand down her back as if trying to ground her. *::Dammit. I can't argue with you when you're being sensible.::*

She kissed him on the cheek in thanks. Sensible or not, she didn't trust herself to not . . . react badly if the pyro went off again. Head down, she walked the narrow blue carpeted aisle to the backstage entrance that Annie had taken her through when she'd panicked the first time.

As she reached the door, Shal stepped ahead of her to open it, which he did only on cane days. Tesla grimaced, pausing to wait. And wait. Pursing his lips, he shook his head. They were close to the stage now and he mouthed, *Locked.*

How had Annie gotten her through it before? She had been fairly out of it, but it seemed like they had simply walked backstage. Tesla turned so she wasn't facing the show. It was fine. Pyro was a contained effect and not related to what had happened to her. It was a set of tubes containing a pyrotechnic compound, probably nitrocellulose, and was highly controlled.

The stage door opened and Shal jumped to catch it. Tesla looked up as she made room for the person to exit and her sidestep stuttered as Jalna emerged from the backstage door. The roboticist's eyes widened at the sight of them. For a moment, Jalna opened her mouth, as if to speak, but her gaze went past Tesla to the stage.

The theater was silent, as if everyone were holding their breath watching the show. With a nod, Jalna hurried up the aisle toward the Yacht Club box seats. Shal watched her go, brows raised. He took a step in that direction and then stopped, shaking his head. He beckoned for Tesla to step through the door.

The plain, unadorned walls of the service corridor backstage wrapped around Tesla like a shield. She wiped her hand over her face as Shal eased the door shut behind them. She swallowed, trying to work moisture back into her mouth. "So, does everyone have some sort of security clearance but us?"

"I was wondering the same thing . . . She was friendly with Nile Silver, wasn't she?" He stared at the door as if it would have some answers. "Let's see if we can find Maria."

———

There was no sign of Gimlet. Maria Piper, on the other hand, was watching Nile Silver from the wings. Shal squeezed Tesla's hand. ::Be right back.::

Quietly, he approached Piper, swinging as wide as he could between the heavy black curtains. She turned, face silhouetted against the lights of the stage as Shal held out his hand. The security officer looked down at it for a moment, before placing her own in what might be a businesslike handshake. Tesla waited, fiddling with the handle on her cane as Shal used the skin-to-skin contact to have a silent conversation with the officer.

Onstage, Nile guided Annie into a bow. "Thank you, again, to my charming volunteer. Please give it up for Annie!"

As the music rose, Tesla heard the same crescendo that had preceded the pyro from the opening. She bolted for the hall. Pressing her back against the wall, with her eyes closed. Her cane clattered to the ground as she pressed her fingers into her ears. *I'm safe.* She was holding her breath.

In, two, three, four. Hold. Out, two, three, four.

I'm on the Lindgren. Beyond the muffling of her fingers, a distant *whoomph. In, two, three, four.* The smell of cordite curled around her nostrils. *Hold.*

"Tesla?" Shal's voice was low and directly in front of her. "You're on the *Lindgren.* You're—"

"I'm fine." She snapped her eyes open. Swallowing, she wet her lips and gestured to the stage. "I knew that was coming and . . . I'm fine."

He held her cane in one hand and held the other out as if he might need to catch her. Maria Piper stood a little down the hall, studying Tesla with a knowing wariness. She waved to the door to Nile's dressing room. "When you're ready."

"Now." Tesla took the cane from Shal, brushing his skin as she did. ::*Thank you. I really am okay.*::

::*Okay.*:: He nodded, still watching her more closely than strictly necessary, but didn't argue or push even though he had to know that she was lying. She was very much not okay. He let her have that secret and lie and just walked with her to the dressing room. "Great. I've briefed Maria on our findings at the bathroom."

"Y'all have been busy." In the dressing room, Piper settled on a chair across from the door. She had pulled out two others from the mirrored tables lining the dingy room.

"Well, I'd hate to waste any of our vacation." Tesla sat, but Shal leaned next to her against one of the tables. She wanted to tell him that she didn't need a nursemaid, but that would involve having a longer conversation that she did not want to have with Piper in the room.

Snorting, Piper leaned back in the chair and glared at the ceiling as if it had personally offended her. "So the chief thinks Slootmaekers did it now?"

Shal spread his hands. "I will not presume to guess."

The door to the dressing room opened. ". . . Mx. Flopsy needs his nails trimmed. He almost tore my—oh." Nile Silver stopped in the door to the dressing room. "Well, hello. We meet again."

Shal pushed away from the dressing table he'd been leaning against. "I don't want to take up a lot of your time but just had a couple of questions for you."

Nile's eyes stayed pointed at Shal as he turned to face Maria Piper. "What's going on?"

She answered, "You can wait for Chief Wisor to come, if you want."

"Or you can talk to us." Tesla sat with her hands resting on the handle of her cane. "We're nicer and not official."

"Maria is." Nile walked to the dressing table and sat down.

"Sure, sure . . ." Shal nodded, crossing his arms over his chest as he watched Nile in the mirror. "I just wanted to know how you knew Ory Slootmaekers."

He paused with a small sponge in his hand. "Who?"

"Bald white guy. About Shal's height. Carrying a little padding around the waist. He was in the yoga class you took us up to."

"Oh yes." Nile nodded and dabbed the sponge against his forehead, reapplying a layer of makeup. "Right . . . has a cute kid. He wanted me to teach them magic, so I taught them Wilson's Picnic—it's a card trick—and they weren't very good at it. Because it takes practice, for crying out—"

The door opened and Wisor walked into the room. "Hey, Nile. I've got a—" He saw Piper and did a double take, his glower deepening as he spotted Tesla and Shal. "Piper. You want to tell me what these passengers are doing in a restricted area?"

"You and I have the same question." Piper kept her arms folded across her chest and shrugged. "I was just here to talk to Nile, when they showed up."

The chief put his hands on his hips, looking at them, then pulled his handheld from his belt and unscrolled it. "Fascinating . . . The logs show that Nile used his security code to come backstage here while he was onstage. So maybe it wasn't Slootmaekers using his code at the Snow Queen."

Nile flinched, dropping the sponge on the ground. "Excuse me, what?"

"You heard me."

Nile glanced at Shal. "Is that why you were asking me about Ory Slootmaekers?"

"You know him?" Wisor stalked into the room, rolling the handheld back up.

"Yes, because they just asked me about him." Nile bent down and snatched the sponge from the floor. "We talked about magic for his kid. That's it. I don't know anything about the—" Again, the door opened. "Oh, for crying out loud. What?"

Yuki hesitated in the door, eyes widening at the number of people in the dressing room. "Your five-minute call."

"Thank you, five minutes." Nile sighed and set the sponge very carefully back on the table. "Do you want to cancel the second act so we can establish that I barely know the guy you're asking me about, or do you want to wait to ask me questions until afterward?"

Wisor stepped clear of the door and waved Nile to it. "Go on. I'm sorry that these people interrupted your break."

"You're letting him go?" Tesla tightened her grip on her cane. "We know he's involved."

"We know his ID is involved." Wisor hitched his thumbs in his belt. "But Silver's worked for the company for multiple cruises and no one has ever died before on them."

"There was that one . . ." Piper crossed her ankles and leaned back in her chair. "If we're being technical."

"That was death by stupid and doesn't count." Wisor gestured to the magician. "Nile's fine. But to save you from getting your lawyer to insult and harass me, I'll threaten Nile and that'll solve everything. Nile. You know there's nowhere to run, right?"

"No kidding?! Really. Wow. Stunned. Stunned I am that there's nowhere to hide on a spaceship between Earth and Mars and—" Nile snapped his jaw shut, grimacing. He forced a smile. "So if you aren't canceling the second act, then I need to preset Mx. Flopsy."

"The show must go on." Wisor smiled and shrugged. "I'll have them out of your room by the time you're back."

"Wonderful. If there's nothing else, this has been a very restful break."

Tesla raised her hand. "Sorry—just a question for Yuki. Why were you and Nile in the R-Bar together?"

Yuki hesitated, looking to Nile. Dropping his head, Nile sighed and then turned to her. "We're considering doing a scaled-down version of my show in the R-Bar and were talking about sightlines. Anyone else have 'just one more question'?"

Wisor shook his head and waved him off. "Break a leg."

"Probably will." Silver checked his hair in the mirror and gave them a bow. "Charmed."

Wisor stood back to let him and Yuki exit the dressing room. It was as if he didn't care that these two people were almost certainly involved in the deaths on the ship and if not that, then at least some highly shady security breaches.

As soon as the door was shut, Wisor wheeled on Tesla, towering over her. "Do *not* interfere with my investigation. I don't care who your family is or who your lawyer is; do not get in my way."

She tightened her grip on her cane. "Then do your job. You just let people we know are involved walk away."

"That's right, I did. Piper, escort these two back to their cabin. Through the service corridors, for their own safety."

Tesla stamped her cane on the ground. "Oh, come on. You're

totally ignoring Yuki and the fact that he checked with Nile before answering and then didn't answer. They're clearly collaborating."

"You aren't part of my staff, and placating you every five minutes is really getting old."

Shal held out his hand to Tesla. "Come on."

"No! Yuki also matches the description of the person you chased." The effort it took to not scream got greater with each passing moment. Her skin crawled with the frustration trapped inside. "Chief Wisor, you've got to see by now that Shal can't be a suspect, so why aren't you taking his report or mine seriously? Why are you brushing off the fact that Nile gave his security codes to Ory? And—"

Shal rested his hand on her upper arm. ::*Tesla. Let's go.*::

She sidestepped so he couldn't ping her with reasons to calm down. "You're just pretending like he's not involved because he works here." She was using her outside voice and did not care. "It would look like shit for the company if an employee turned out to be a serial killer. I mean, Nile knows all the blind spots for the cameras on the ship."

"I'm sure Chief Wisor is aware of all of this." Shal's voice was soothing. Why was he soothing her?

"Does he also know about the Out of Order sign? Does he know that Immanuel confirmed that Nile and Ory were arguing with George?" She turned to Maria for support, but the security officer's face was set and blank. "You were there. If it was just about Ewen learning magic, why was George Saikawa involved in the argument?"

Belatedly, her brain raised a flag. Nile knew all the blind spots on the ship, but figuring out the parameters of those would require someone watching the monitors while he tested the range. So who helped him? Who had access to all of the cabins? Who had control of the investigation?

Wisor shook his head and looked at Shal. "As one professional to another, I'll tell you why I let Nile walk away and hope you can get it through your wife's head that sometimes other people actually know how to do their jobs. There are things I need to check and I can't do that if Nile or Yuki are spooked."

From her chair, Piper chimed in. "Plus she's right that he knows all of the blind spots for cameras on the ship. 'There's nowhere to hide' applies to everyone except him."

"So he could be hiding my dog." Tesla's chest hurt and her eyes burned. "Why aren't you doing anything? Besides announcements."

Maria Piper stood up, folding her handheld. "I promise you that I've got people looking for Gimlet."

But she didn't promise that they would find her. Tesla let Piper herd them into the hall, but stopped and faced the theater. She was stressed and sweating, but also the fact that Jalna had been backstage was nagging at her. Especially knowing that Nile's security code had been used. Wetting her lips, she turned to Shal. "Do you want to watch the show before we go back?"

He studied her, eyes drawing paths across her face as if he were counting neurons. "You sure?"

She nodded. If necessary, she'd keep her eyes closed, but she wanted to talk to Annie and Jalna. And it would be easier if they just happened to be in the audience at the end of the show.

Shal and Maria exchanged a glance over her shoulder as if her thought process had been a cartoon bubble over her head. Slowly, her spouse nodded. "Sure . . . let's watch the rest of the show. If that's okay with you, Maria?"

"Barely. But I'm pretty sure that if I don't stay with you, you'll wander off and get into a different mischief."

They headed out to the audience, taking care to let the door shut gently behind them so it wouldn't bother the rest of the spectators. Even with the carpeting, Tesla had the urge to tiptoe as they headed back to the Yacht Club box seats.

Onstage, Nile had a slender pedestal with a small shopping bag on it. "Honestly, you can get anything from the convenience store on the promenade level—and they aren't just making me say that as veiled marketing." He paused while the audience chuckled. "But seriously, if you need to make things even more romantic, they've got flowers."

In the box seats, Annie leaned forward, smiling like a child. Beside her, Jalna had her arm across the back of her partner's chair, rubbing her shoulder gently.

From the bag, Nile pulled a large cloisonné vase with a giant collection of broken green stems. "Oh . . . oh. Um. That's—that's not . . . um." He set them down onstage. "Sorry! Right. Well, if you don't like the flowers, maybe a cake? Their carrot cake is to die for . . ."

At the edge of the box, Maria stopped, looking it over as if for danger. At the motion, Jalna looked around and saw Tesla and Shal. She smiled and waved to the empty seats beside her. Perfect. The invitation made it look a lot less like Tesla was stalking them.

On the stage, the magician was peering into the bag. "Huh." From it, he pulled out an enormous cake that looked as if someone had swiped great handfuls out of it. Nile wiped his finger through some of the remaining icing. "Well . . . it's delicious?"

Tesla slid into the seat beside Jalna, while Maria lurked at the back of the booth. Annie leaned forward across her spouse, offering Tesla her hand. Tesla accepted it and the handshake ping that came with the skin-to-skin contact. *Annie Barnes, she/her.* Tesla hesitated and then sent her own to establish the intimate connection. *Tesla Crane, she/her.* On her HUD, Annie pinged *::There won't be any pyro until the end of the show. I'll give you plenty of warning.::*

::Thank you, that's very kind.:: A knot eased between Tesla's shoulder blades. That was one thing, at least, that wouldn't ambush her.

"Champagne? That's always—" Liquid sprayed up and out of Nile's shopping bag as the audience laughed in a collective guffaw. Nile scrambled to extract the Champagne bottle as it continued to gush. Slipping on some of the icing from the cake, he knocked the stand over and it hit the stage, facing directly toward the front row.

An absolutely adorable brown-and-white rabbit hopped out. Their little nose twitched. They had a long, red rose hanging out of their mouth and munched happily.

Nile scooped the bunny up. "Mx. Flopsy, everyone!"

As the audience applauded, Shal kissed Tesla on the cheek. In a low voice, he asked the row, "Champagne sounds like a good idea. Can I fetch drinks for folks?"

"How about a French 75?" She glanced over at Jalna and Annie and withdrew her hand. "Anything for you?"

"For the Champagne theme, a Kir Royale for Annie, and since I doubt they have true Champagne on this ship, a Tranquility Royale for me." Jalna's gaze turned back to the stage, where dancers in spangles and little else cleared the performance area in a flamboyant display of musculature and reset it for the next trick.

Shal gave something akin to a scout's salute and sauntered out of the box. He paused to murmur to Maria. Tesla bit her lips, wanting to go with him, but staying here made more sense. She had questions for Jalna and Annie, and sharing an experience would make an easier segue. She turned back to the stage, where spotlights picked out two deep blue boxes silvered with an Art Deco–inspired solar system.

Annie was leaning forward in her seat again, hands clasped together with rapt attention on the stage. Jalna was looking at Tesla.

"The laws of time and space are mysterious. They can be bent by a small rabbit at whim, but what about a person?" Nile opened one of the boxes, and Yuki stood inside, dressed in silver fringe that contrasted with the dark interior of the box.

Jalna leaned in to Tesla. "I wonder if we might speak later? Privately?"

Every adrenaline-producing cell in Tesla's body doubled its output simultaneously. She wasn't sure which was more alarming, that Jalna might be related to the murders or that she would want to talk about robots. "Of course."

"It is possible for Yuki to get from here to there, by ordinary transit." Nile opened the second box on a dark, empty interior as his assistant stepped gracefully out of the first box and walked over to the second. "Just as we are transiting to Mars."

"Thank you. I have wanted to find the time, but with . . ." She gestured as if trying to include the entire ship. "Everything, there has been no opportunity."

Dry cotton filled Tesla's mouth. "I've wanted to talk to you too. I wonder if it is the same topic?"

"But what if we could go instantly? If they produced the transporter that they have been promising since the middle of last century?" Nile closed the door, with Yuki inside. He pressed his hand against it. "Is it a matter of technology, or will? I believe that it is will. Watch." The other hand went on the case. Nile breathed out and strained as if pushing the box, although it did not move.

The other box shuddered.

Jalna tapped a finger on the arm of her chair, watching the stage. "Perhaps. I suspect so, yes."

As Nile sagged, the door to the far box opened and Yuki stepped out. He looked at his hands and then out to the audience with astonished triumph.

Annie leaned across Jalna and whispered. "He always looks amazed! And I believe him every time, even though we've seen this show . . . How many times?"

"This is our fourth." Jalna's hand caressed the nape of Annie's neck as she smiled indulgently at her partner. "Tesla and I are going to have a tête-à-tête after, is that all right, my love?"

Nile looked at the audience and winked. Then stepped into the dark box.

"Oh. About your robot?"

"Among other—"

Metal ground on metal mixed with a scream. The scream cut off abruptly. For a moment, the theater was dead still and silent. And then Yuki ran to the box as blood began to drip onto the stage.

Magician's Nibling

1 oz rum
1 oz Lillet Blanc
1 oz Aperol
Dash absinthe
Orange peel

Coat coupe with absinthe. Stir other ingredients over ice
for 40 seconds. Garnish with flamed orange peel.

The lights in the theater had been turned up to full and cast deep shadows under the eyes of everyone Wisor had dragged in. Tesla sat in her chair, focusing on her HUD, and tried not to look at the curtained stage where Nile Silver had died. Been killed. She swallowed heavily, remembering the abrupt edge of his unfinished scream.

Shal held her hand and was patched into her HUD, since he still only had local access, so he could hear Fantine while she ranted. ". . . per your request, I was able to pull the photo of the Crane Robotics Competition and—as an interesting and unsurprising side note—one of the kids in that competition had a forged ID."

She flashed the group shot of the competitors, including a version of Tesla that was emaciated, wearing sunglasses, and standing with the help of a pair of crutches. The image zoomed in on one kid with long blond hair in a pair of braids. "This child doesn't exist anywhere but here—Oh, Methuselah's swim trunks! Is he taking you back into the theater? Hey! Flaming lard brain, what in the name of Saint Ives are you doing taking my clients back to a murder scene, and don't you dare pretend that the death of Nile Silver was anything except murder."

Buzz the kid's head, age them to sixteen, and Tesla was staring at Ewen.

On the screen, Fantine ostentatiously punched buttons on a physical calculator. "Calculating Lard brain's net worth so I know how long I have to let him live to pay off the lawsuits I'm bringing against—"

His hand on Tesla's, Shal did a double take, leaning forward to stare at the screen. ::*I know this kid. Why do I know this kid? When did you take this?*::

::*Three years ago.*::

Shal smacked his knee. "Hey, Fantine— She's frozen."

Tesla looked back down at the screen, where her lawyer sat in a freeze-frame, with one eye half-closed and her mouth smooshed to the side. She tapped the screen, then checked her HUD. "I'm offline."

"Hell baskets." Shal nudged her and pointed to the far end of the row. "And devils spoken of . . ."

A security officer pressed Ory down into a chair at the end of their row. Ewen slipped past their dad to sit hunched in the chair next to him. Tesla looked from the picture to the kid and back again. Same child. She saved the photo locally and consulted the metadata on it. ::*In the photo, Ewen is named Eve Smith.*::

::*Eve Smith . . . Eve . . . If they were—*:: "Oh-ho!" Shal suddenly grabbed her knee and gestured with his chin to the entrance of the theater.

Bob was escorting in Yuki, except Yuki was sitting in the row in front of them with Annie and Jalna. Mahjabin was in the same row, and from behind the two could be twins, but not as much as the man Bob brought in. He was dressed in the same outfit as Yuki, and his hair was disheveled.

She was not the only one doing a double take. Ewen was openly gawking at him. "He's an identical twin? Pops—"

Ory put his finger across his lips. His hands were cuffed in front of him, and his fingers had gnawed, raw cuticles. His eyes were red and swollen as if he'd been crying.

Tesla leaned into Shal. ::*Twins makes it very handy to be in two places at once, eh?*::

He slid his arm around her back and kissed her ear. ::*What I want to know is why no one on the security staff has seemed interested in this shockingly relevant detail.*::

::*You think Maria knew?*::

::*The ship has a problem if she didn't.*:: He scanned the room. ::*Also, she's not—never mind.*::

Maria Piper walked in, her face set like carbonite, escorting Josie and Immanuel. She led them down the stairs to the small grouping and, at a gesture from Wisor, put them in the row with Candy the medic, behind Tesla and Shal.

Wisor strode back and forth in the aisle in front of the small group, counting them. "All right . . . Everyone shift so that there's an empty chair between you and your neighbor. I don't want any local network sharing during this."

Tesla was not the only one who grumbled. Before she moved a seat farther into their row, Shal squeezed her hand, getting in one last ping. ::*It'll be okay.*::

Wisor waited until they were all settled. He looked up into a corner of the room and nodded, then turned back to face the group. "There have been deaths on my ship. I don't like that. I don't like that when it's an accident, and what we have here is a series of deliberate murders committed by one of you."

"Oh boy . . ." Shal's eyes rolled so loudly, Tesla could hear them.

"Something to say, Mr. Steward?" Wisor stalked down the aisle so he could loom over them.

Shal slouched back in his seat and grinned up at the man. "Just wondering what your favorite detective movie is. I'd ask about books, but I'm guessing that's not your medium of choice. Or maybe the telly? Shorter . . . Sherlock or Columbo or Metta?"

"You just have to be the smartest guy in the room, don't you?"

"Ah . . . Dragnet." He waved his hand toward the stage as if he were the one in control, not Wisor. "Carry on. I'm curious to see your process."

Tesla raised her hand. "And I'm curious to know why I can't contact my lawyer."

Wisor grinned at her. "Not my doing. Your row mates each have an embedded spoofer."

Ewen's head came up and they stared at Wisor and then at their father. From the front row, Mahjabin had turned to watch Wisor, frowning. "I beg to differ. Mx. Slootmaekers can track Ewen, which surely he could not with a built-in spoofer."

Things were beginning to click into place, Tesla shook her head. "If you create the spoofer, you can track its signature."

"Oh." Shal pressed his hand to his forehead. "Oh . . ."

Ewen's eyes widened and they looked as if some things were coming together in their own head. Like, maybe how a spoofer would explain why they'd had navigation trouble with their robot in competition. They were biting their lips as if it were taking all of their willpower not to start asking questions.

Crossing his arms over his chest, Wisor glowered down the row at Ory. "According to Ms. Crane here, you were seen fighting with both Ms. Saikawa and the late Mr. Silver."

"Except that still leaves two bodies and another attempt with no connection . . ." Shal stared at the ceiling. "Also, Ory wouldn't have taken a risk of being involved in murder."

"You sound very certain of yourself, Mr. Steward. Why is that?"

Shal sighed and leaned forward to look around Tesla, trying to make eye contact with Ory. "Look . . . you know it's going to come out. You know what's about to happen, because you've been afraid of it for years. Silence isn't going to help Ewen."

"What—" The word burst out of Ewen, and they clamped their mouth shut again, shifting in their seat with anxious energy.

"You watched me on *Cold Cases*, right?" Shal tilted his head so he was talking to Ewen, and his mouth twisted in a sad smile. "We scanned trade magazines for cases and picked the ones that we were pretty sure I could solve, which made me look brilliant. There was one with this toddler who'd been kidnapped a couple of years before. Never found. They'd tried all the tricks, including aging a toddler photo to see what the kid would look like as an eleven-year-old. But the best AI software couldn't find a match anywhere. But if we'd done the show three years later, I would have found this . . ." Shal raised the handheld and showed it to Ewen.

The kid's eyes widened even further.

Shal looked like his heart was going to break. His voice was low and quiet. "You move a lot, don't you?"

"Pops—Pops said we were going to start over on Mars."

Tears were streaming down Ory's face. "Ewen, please. Hourglass. Don't talk to them. Don't—"

"I don't understand what's happening. You said my mother was a surrogate and that she died."

"Hourglass, hourglass." Ory's voice was hoarse. "Please. They're going to lie to you. I'm your father and I will keep you safe."

As Shal turned the handheld so Wisor could see it, the security chief's forehead creased into lines of confusion. "So he was killing people to keep them from revealing his secret."

"No." The eye roll was not quite audible this time. "No. The point is that Ory wasn't intentionally involved, because he's going to do everything he can to avoid attracting attention."

Wisor asked, "What about the 'not what we agreed' conversation?"

Yuki—or his twin—had turned, hooking his arm over the back of the chair to watch, and said, "Nile sometimes smuggled things in his magic chests. Perhaps they had an agreement about that?"

"It could have been the blue octopoid." Tesla glanced briefly at the stage and then away from the curtains that masked the box that had mangled Nile.

Wisor narrowed his gaze at her and tapped his finger on his chin in contemplation. "Officer Piper has told me that you also raised questions about the medical robot, as well as Haldan Kuznetsova's missing robot. And when did that go missing? Your original cabin was right next to his. What other robotics expert do we have on this ship?"

It was Tesla's turn to roll her eyes. "First, you don't need to be an expert if the thing is well programmed to begin with. Second, there are at least three of us in this room. Why aren't you asking Jalna your fascinatingly insightful questions? I mean, she was backstage—"

Shal cleared his throat. Dammit. He'd warned her not to volunteer information, but at this point cutting off was going to seem more suspicious than—

"Backstage?" Wisor shot a quick glance up, as if he were checking something on his HUD. He focused his attention on Jalna. "What were you doing backstage?"

Annie turned in her seat. "You were backstage?"

She shook her head. "It is nothing."

"Bribing me." The other Yuki raised his hand. "She was bribing me to pick her partner as volunteer."

"Jalna! You didn't."

The tall woman switched to low and rapid Lunar French. Listening, Annie shook her head and then sighed.

Nodding as if he'd pieced things together, Wisor stalked down to the couple. "Ah . . . yes. One or both of you have been present at each of the deaths. Annie Smith, aka Annie Barnes, who was in the hallway when George Saikawa was killed. Who just happened to be onstage, with access to the apparatus that killed Nile Silver."

Annie lifted her chin. "I was in full view of the audience the entire time."

He smirked. "I've seen *Ganymede Night*. I know what you're capable of."

Mouth dropping open, Annie sputtered before getting out,

"Thirty years ago, forty pounds lighter, and with editing to hide my position switches *in a film* that was *fiction*."

"So you were onstage while your partner was backstage, according to her." He jerked a thumb at Tesla as if he had never had any doubt about any of Tesla's statements before this.

As Jalna settled back in her seat, she met Wisor's gaze with calm. "While I am willing to cooperate, I would prefer to consult with my lawyer first."

"You can't possibly think Jalna had anything to do with any of this!" Annie ignored her partner's attempt to stop her and surged to her feet. "Why would she?"

"Getting rid of business rivals is a popular motive." Wisor ticked things off on his fingers. "She and Kuznetsova both make octobots."

"Octopoids," Ewen muttered, nearly in time with Tesla and Jalna.

"Then there's Crane back there. Discrediting her and her husband would leave the playing field wide open for Ms. Tafani to be the leading robotics exp—"

Annie scoffed. "As if anyone takes Crane seriously as a developer after that PAMU disaster. Do you know how many systems failed on that—"

Stars and darkness spin past the edges of her vision. Tesla's ears are ringing. The suit should autostabilize, and it's not and she's having trouble thinking and something is crushing her spine so all she can catch are short—

Gasping, Tesla looked up, trying to find something to catch hold of. *I am safe.*

Lighting grid. The smooth silver curve of the Mars balcony. Wisor was talking to her beyond the ringing in her ears. She was on the *Lindgren*. Above the Martian level lay the Lunar balcony. Scuffs on the polyamide laminate. Blue velvet seats.

Four things she heard. Her own breath whistling in her ears. Wisor talking. Servos whirring. Shal's voice, "Tesla, you're on the *Lindgren*."

"I know." Servos whirring. Tesla's mind skipped back to the Rorschach of dents and scuffs on the Martian level balcony. Some of them looked like an engraver had drawn long lines down the side of the curve. Others were like a pointillist drawing an eight-note scale and—

Actually. That was the standard grip pattern for an octobot.

"Let's reconstruct that first murder, shall we? We have—"

"Second." Shal tilted his head back, following her gaze up to the Lunar balcony.

Wisor said, "Excuse me?"

"Second murder. There's the body in the recycler." Shal waggled his fingers at Wisor, drawing attention away from her. "Go on. I'm very interested in how we all gained access to a restricted area with a dead body. Also how we got someone aboard without clearing the manifest—oh. Dammit. *That's* why Nile Silver was killed . . ."

Something moved in the darkness. She didn't have to be able to see it clearly to recognize the quality of the movement. There was an octopoid on the Lunar balcony.

Shal leaned forward in his seat. "Yuki, do you know which containers Nile Silver used for smuggling?"

"No . . . but I know which crates we weren't allowed to handle."

"Any of them big enough to hold a person?"

"Or a dog?" Afraid to lose track of the octopoid, she didn't turn to see their response. But someone who could smuggle a person on could also smuggle things off. A dog would be exotic anywhere that wasn't Earth, and she could imagine a purebred Westie would be . . . tempting.

She felt Shal begin to rise. "With Chief Wisor's permission, of course . . ."

"Why . . . why would he be smuggling dead bodies?"

The octopoid was moving down the stairs, coming in and out of shadows. This seemed very wrong. "Excuse me." It was a fashionable muted purple, exactly the same shade as her acubot. Tesla grabbed the chair in front of her, using it to brace as she leaned and carefully twisted for a better view.

Shal continued, "Interesting thing . . . the interesting thing about that kidnapping case was that the police thought the kid was dead. They'd gotten close once and there was a fire. Everything burned except a couple of teeth that were verifiably the child's. But kids lose baby teeth—"

That was her acubot. "Shal? There's a—"

It flung something toward the stage. Tesla grabbed Shal and yanked him down.

The theater went black. Something hissed past. In the row behind them, someone grunted and then was silent.

Dangerous Words

.75 oz Green Chartreuse

.75 oz amaretto

.75 oz lime juice

.75 oz rye

Shake ingredients over ice for 15 seconds. Strain into coupe.

Shal's weight knocked Tesla to the floor between the seats. The pressure of his body intersected with hers in ways that locked them both in place for a moment. The safeties on her DBPS muffled the incoming bruises and the yellow-green knots of pain where her back had wrenched in the fall.

Wisor shouted. "Lights! Get me lights!"

Beams of waving light cut through the gaps between chairs as people turned their handhelds on.

"Oh God!" Immanuel shouted. "Candy! Help me!"

"Where did it—?"

"The stage!"

Shal scrambled back, trying to get off of Tesla, and still made the pain spike past what the safeties could muffle.

"Coriolis." Tesla grabbed his arm blindly, overriding the safeties so the pain vanished under a dull blanket. *::Lunar balcony. My acubot.::*

"Shit." He hesitated, half over her. *::Will you be—?::*

::Yes. Go.::

He grimaced, using the arm of a chair to push the rest of the way up. "Maria!" He pointed up. "Coriolis effect."

And he was gone, running up the aisle with one arm wrapped around his ribs. Tesla dragged herself out of the valley between rows one joint at a time.

"Ewen! Get back here."

The kid appeared over her, hands flexing as if they needed to do something. "Do you need help?"

The spoofer zone meant the octopoid could not have been remote-controlled by the kid. Or Ory for that matter. Tesla stretched her hand out to Ewen. "Thank you. Yes."

They tried to pull her to her feet but were too teenage lanky to do much more than steady her. Tesla needed that. They bent down, digging under the chairs, and came up with her cane. She took it and leaned heavily on the handle.

Behind her, Candy was bending over Josie, who was slumped back in her chair. Immanuel held a light over them, which made the blood spattered across the bartender vividly red. Hundreds of silver nails glittered among the red, making a pincushion of her face, neck, and chest. Even though Tesla knew what they had to be, it still took too long for her brain to recognize the piercings as hundreds of acupuncture needles, driven deeper into Josie's body than they were designed to go. The needles were incredibly fine, but puncture an artery or the lungs and it was possible to kill someone. It wouldn't be fast, but slow death was still death.

Down the aisle, a cluster of people were running for the stage. The stage didn't matter. The Coriolis effect meant that any object thrown in a straight line would continue its path while the ship rotated around it, making it appear to turn in the air.

On this ship, if someone had actually thrown the needles from the stage, the Coriolis effect would have twisted their path to hit the wall to the left of the theater. Instead, they'd hit Josie.

No—wait. Josie had been seated behind them. Those needles passed through the air where Shal had been. They tried to kill Shal. Tesla's pulse thundered in her ears and adrenaline shook every joint in her body.

They'd tried to kill Shal. And she'd just sent him running up to the balcony.

She swallowed the sour terror rising in the back of her throat and looked up. She was never going to be able to catch up with him. And she didn't have to. The octopoid didn't matter.

What mattered was the person running it.

The way the ship was built, it was a Faraday cage, which the cruise line masked by installing signal boosters everywhere. But boosters introduced lag, and for the kind of precision throw the octopoid had just done, the operator would need to be close.

Only two people sat in the front row now. In the darkness, it was hard to tell who they were. With their heads bowed, it looked like they were praying, but no telling what conversation they were having on their own local network.

"Ewen . . . Will you go back to sit with your dad?"

They looked to the end of the aisle, where Ory was backlit by the emergency lights. "Is he?"

"I . . ." She grimaced. "I'm so sorry. But I need to see if someone was in the range of your spoofer fields. So I need—"

"The conditions to be the same as when the lights went out." The teen nodded, shoulders slumping, and turned to walk back to the person who had raised them, and apparently stolen them.

Leaning on her cane, she limped down the aisle toward the people in the front row, throwing out a constant string of network requests to see when she was outside the spoofer field.

Connection unavailable.

She fumbled for her handheld, but her fingers were too numb to find the edge of her pocket.

Connection unavailable.

At the end of the row, her left foot caught on the carpet, and Tesla stumbled, knocking into a chair. She caught herself and dialed the DBPS back down a notch. The edge of her vision seemed to go a dull greenish purple that matched the queasy ache in her spine. She gripped the edge of the chair, breathing in golden sunlight until she could see again.

The auditorium was in chaos, and in the uneven emergency lights it was hard to tell where anyone was. A calm voice echoed through the theater.

"Delta, gamma, seven seven four. Delta, gamma, seven seven four."

For all the good that would do with Wisor and most of his team already here. The security chief had run onto the stage with Bob, leaving a couple of junior staff members to try to corral the remaining passengers. One had gone to assist Candy. The other was blocking the end of the aisle to keep Ory from standing. Ewen was slumped in their seat.

Connection unavailable.

She had a better view of the people in the front row now. The twins were gone. Tesla turned in place, looking for them in the echoing shadows. Nothing. And it was too dim to tell who was still seated. She limped across the front row.

Connection unavailable.

Tesla stopped in front of the pair, who were little more than shadows in the dark. In silhouette, Jalna raised her head and her eyes caught the yellow beam of an emergency light. Mahjabin held her hand. Annie was not with her.

Connection unavailable.

The spoofer field apparently reached far enough to surround them. Tesla swallowed. "Where's Annie?"

Jalna looked at the seat next to her and her eyes widened. "I—I do not know. She was just here."

"What did Annie do after she stopped acting?"

"What?"

"Did she just retire or change fields?" Tesla glanced up to the lunar balconies, catching sight of Maria Piper running under an emergency lamp. Where was Shal?

"She—she came to work for me." Jalna frowned. "Why?"

The operator had to be—they had to be close. Where could someone be reasonably assured of not being interrupted and still be close? Backstage.

Except that if you wanted to misdirect people, you wouldn't make the needles appear to come from your actual hiding place. "Do you know where the bathroom is?"

Mahjabin twisted in her chair, pointing with her free hand to a door at the back right of the theater. "Just off the lobby."

"Thank you." Tesla rode the DBPS, letting enough sensation through that she wouldn't trip over her own feet as every fiber of her back lit up with alternating distress signals. As she walked back up the aisle, she braced herself with cane and chairbacks.

Her route took her past the bar, and in line of sight to the door to backstage. Most of the main theater was obscured by a sidewall that curved around the back row of seats, so she didn't have a clear view of what was happening in the audience. Back here the emergency lights cast harsh yellow puddles that created a path to the exits.

Connecting . . .

From the auditorium, she could hear the occasional shout. Once she heard Shal yell, "Clear."

Connected.

Without chairs, Tesla pressed her hand against the sidewall to steady herself. She got to the lobby door and the bathroom door stood just to the side.

It had an Out of Order sign across it.

She rotated the cane in her hand and made a call to Fantine. "Hi. I'm about to do something very stupid. I know you're surprised."

She took a breath and put her free hand on the knob. Twisted. The door was locked.

Grimacing, she looked down the aisles for anyone on staff who might have a key. The curtain billowed onstage and she thought she heard Bob shout, but no one useful was in view. Not even

Wisor. Fine, then. Kneeling with a straight back, she pulled the eyeglass-repair kit out of her pocket.

She didn't have the battery charger, but she had her handy. She didn't have chewing gum, but she had her anklet. Gold was a damn good conductor. Bending to reach the anklet sent lightning shooting down her leg in ways that screamed of new damage. Fine. She set the DBPS so she felt nothing. She had to watch her hands to unhook the anklet, but she got it off. Breathing through her teeth, she lowered the DBPS again so she could feel her hands and set to work. This would fry her handheld, but it was fast. She transferred the call to her HUD. "Sorry to cause problems. Just . . . keep Shal safe and out of trouble, please?"

She set the handheld on the floor and shoved the screwdriver into the edge of the case, popping the lid off with a quick twist. Another twist popped the cover off the lock.

As soon as the anklet was in place, her finger hovered over the Power button. With a grimace, Tesla used the doorknob and cane to drag herself back up to her feet. She was stupid, but not quite stupid enough to open the door while she was kneeling. She gripped her cane with one hand and the handheld in the other.

Power.

Sparks flew. She closed her eyes, darkness spinning around her.

She was in the theater. The person who had tried to kill Shal was on the other side of this door. Tesla pushed the door open with a quiet pop.

Light from a portable lamp bled under the accessibility stall at the far end. She stepped into the bathroom, left leg stuttering and dragging like an engine out of oil. Being stealthy wasn't an option. The person at the end had to have heard her.

"Come out." She tried to infuse her voice with the faintly annoyed sound she used during corporate takeovers. "You're caught and the game is up."

From the stall, a leather shoe squeaked against the tile floor. A man sighed. "Tesla, baby . . ."

Her heart stopped. "Shal?"

He sighed again. "Yeah . . ."

"But you were . . . but you were beside me." Sweat poured down her back. She had assumed that the needles came from the octopoid, but how much simpler they would be to throw from one row away.

"I can explain."

"You can explain?" The room spun around her as her collar seemed to tighten around her throat. Everybody has secrets. Everybody lies. "Explain what?"

"I need you to know that I love you." He sighed again. "But I also had a job to finish."

"Oh my God!" Tesla shoved the door to the stall open.

His hand, in a bright-blue nitrile glove, grabbed her and shoved her against the wall of the bathroom, with her face pressed against the tile. The DBPS fought to keep the pain at bay, but her vision still went red and white.

Something cold pressed against her temple and Shal whispered, "I loved you so much. I'm so sorry."

Click.

The DBPS turned off. Jagged purple blue bolts twisted through her spine and ribs. Bruises and torn muscles and layers and layers of pain lit up long-deadened pathways. Tesla convulsed. Her knees gave out.

Connection lost.

She dropped to the floor and felt every piece of her knees and forearms slam against the cold tile. Keening, she tried to push back up, but pitched over on her side.

Haldan Kuznetsova stood over her.

"Well, damn." He sounded like Shal. "I did not expect turning off your subdermal systems to drop you like that."

"What—" Why did he sound like Shal?

He kicked the cane away from where she'd dropped it. "Still, your lawyer—who I'm assuming you had on speed dial, since you always do—should have heard my little confession, so that's something. What to do with you now . . ."

She pressed her hand against the floor, and a piece of rebar seemed to wedge into her vertebrae. Tesla gasped, blinking aside tears. Goddammit. She was not going to just lie here while, while Haldan Kuznet—

Now. When she couldn't use it, her brain pointed out that this man hadn't remembered that he owned the *Lindgren*. He hadn't known that you could convert a matter printer to be a scanner. He owned an octopoid. And all of that gave her the useless answer to who the dead body in the recycler was. "You aren't Haldan Kuznetsova. Who are you?"

He grinned and offered a little bow. His voice shifted and he sounded like Chief Wisor. "A very good actor with an uncanny resemblance. And while it's nice to briefly have the recognition of my skills, that's all the monologue I'm going to do now." He opened his coat and pulled out a steak knife. "Best to be consistent."

Apparent Cocktail

1.5 oz gin
1.5 oz Dubonnet
Dash absinthe

Stir ingredients over ice for 40 seconds. Strain into coupe.

Haldan, or whoever he was, switched his grip on the wood handle of the steak knife. "Whoops—your spouse is right-handed, isn't he? Gotta get that right for character consistency."

Her back spasms were sending familiar bolts down her left leg. This was just pain. She'd lived with pain for years before getting the DBPS. She knew how to do this. Tesla took short breaths, tightening her core to try to keep things stable.

Work with the body parts that are functioning. Compensate for the rest. Tesla pulled her right leg solidly under her. Teeth gritted, she grabbed the stall's accessibility bar and hauled up.

"Oh no, you don't." Haldan swung the knife at her throat.

Letting go of the bar, Tesla dropped to the floor. She was very, very good at falling. The knife slammed into the tile, skidding along the wall. Haldan raised it over his head, pivoting to follow her.

Tesla thrashed with her good leg and connected with his ankle. It didn't drop him, but he staggered, catching himself against the tile with an elbow.

Shoving off, she rolled to the side, passing under the bottom of the partition into the next stall.

"Dammit!" His shoes darted into the main bathroom.

Lurching up, Tesla slapped the lock on the stall door. Behind her, the toilet played its jaunty tune, lights dancing as the lid slid open. Haldan slammed against the outside of the stall.

The metal door rattled in its lock. On her knees, Tesla leaned against it. *Golden sunlight. Breathe through the pain.* The door wouldn't hold. He could get under it. She had to get out of here.

She dropped back to the floor and rolled into the next stall. As she rose to her knees, the toilet chimed. Lights splayed across the stall. She slapped the lock closed as Haldan slid to the next door.

In the distance, Gimlet barked.

Tesla gasped, almost sobbing. She dropped to the floor again. Under the edge of the stall, Haldan took a giant step and slammed the door to the next stall open. The toilet played a happy greeting.

He knelt, bending to look under the partition at her.

Tesla kicked him in the face. The knife hit the floor. Snatching it, she rolled back under the partition to get a stall away from him, and then again, to get back into the last one on the end. The toilet sang its announcement of joy at her arrival as she pushed up on her right knee and shoved the door closed, locking it.

There was no gap between one burning ache and the next. *Golden sunlight.* She grabbed the accessibility bar and pulled. Tight core. Pushing with her right leg, she dragged the left under her. *In through the nose, out through the mouth.* Standing, she held her left leg straight and tried to lock her knee.

Gimlet barked again, closer, sounding as if she were chasing a delivery person.

Haldan slammed against the outside of the door. "You bitch." His voice was unfamiliar. Droplets of blood hit the floor.

"Are we really going to add gendered insults? I thought you were a great actor." Hopefully the fact that she could kick him would keep him from trying to come under the door, but this sort of lock was dead simple to pick. She stepped to the side of the door, ready with the knife. "So you were planning on taking over Haldan's identity with the move to Mars, where fewer people knew you. When did the plan start to go wrong? When George came on the cruise or when you met Ruth?"

He laughed and his voice shifted again, becoming Ruth Fish's. "Sloppy research." It shifted again into Haldan's voice. "I didn't spot her name on the manifest, or I would have picked a different ship."

"So did you stab yourself or—"

He grabbed her ankles and yanked. Tesla fell, cracking her shoulder against the toilet. It sang as Haldan dragged her under the bottom of the stall door. Writhing, Tesla tried to kick him off. He stomped on her knee, sending red-and-white sparks across her vision. She screamed, sobbing.

In one nitrile-gloved hand, he held the controller for her acubot and lifted it, taking aim at her head. "Lover's spat. That'll work."

Outside the bathroom door, Gimlet barked as if the delivery person were Right There. *Golden sunlight.* She still had the knife. Tesla lurched, half-rolling, and sank the knife into his thigh.

Haldan shrieked. She wrenched the knife out as he dropped to the floor. Falling back, Haldan dropped the controller and grabbed the wound on his thigh.

The outer bathroom door rattled with soft thumps, punctuated by frantic barking. Tesla pushed up to her knees, holding the knife with one hand. With the other, she grabbed the controller, yanking it away before he could reach it.

Sobbing, Haldan let go of the wound in his leg and crawled into the nearest stall. The toilet sang happily.

Tesla shook her head, pressing against the wall for support as she forced herself to stay upright. "That's not going to work. Do you think you can get away?"

The bathroom door opened and a white streak burst into the room. A wiggling, barking, tiny Fury ran straight to Tesla. She dropped the controller and pulled Gimlet close. "Baby, little girl. I've been so worried."

Wiggles and kisses and whines whirled around her as Gimlet

spun, trying to press herself against every part of Tesla. Nothing hurt less, but with Gimlet safe and there, the pain didn't matter.

In the doorway, Annie and the Yuki twins stared at her. Annie took a step into the bathroom. "Oh my lands. Are you all right?"

"She has a knife!" In the stall, the man's sobs were ragged and sounded genuine. His voice was back to being Haldan's. "Be careful! She tried—"

At the sound of his voice, Gimlet pointed at the stall and went into full Delivery bark. A long rolling wave of furious, unending yaps of hatred.

"Good girl." Tesla scratched Gimlet's rump and turned to Annie, who was staring at the knife in her hand.

The bloody knife. That she had, in fact, just stabbed Haldan with.

Tesla swallowed and set the knife on top of the controller. "It's not what it looks like."

"It's exactly what it looks like. If you hadn't come in, she would have killed me." Haldan cracked the door and peeked out. Blood dripped from a split lip. His eyes were red and swollen and sobs shook his chest. He staggered out, trousers gashed and bloodstained. His hands were bare and the palms were wet with blood from his leg.

"Oh my—" Annie looked from Tesla to Haldan and back, her expression dropping into horrified disbelief. "But . . . but you seemed so nice."

He was a damn good actor. She had to give him that. Gimlet did not care.

"Arrooooorororooooo! Arrooooo! Arooooooooooorooorooorooroo!"

"Don't let it bite me!" Haldan gasped, and stumbled back into the stall.

The toilet sang a happy song and flushed. Goddammit. He'd just flushed the nitrile gloves.

Tesla tried to stand, but the adrenaline that had let her power through the pain had left shaky weakness in its wake. "I found him in here with the controller for an octopoid robot, which he used to throw acupuncture needles in the theater. It clearly could not have been me, because there was a spoofer field."

"Gimlet!" Shal caught himself on the door frame right behind the Yuki twins. Sweat coated his face and the dim light made his skin look even grayer. "Tesla? Oh shit."

Annie backed away from him. One of the twins turned to the theater and cupped his hands. "I need some help here!"

Arm wrapped around his ribs, Shal stepped into the room, heading straight for Tesla. She held up a hand to stop him. "Crime scene! Don't come in."

Shal stopped, on his toes, as if his momentum were going to pitch him forward into the room. His jaw tensed. "First. Do you need medical attention?"

She shook her head.

Inside the stall, Haldan gave a breathless, horrified laugh. "She stabbed me, but I'm not taking any help from you."

Shal did a double take, gaze going from Tesla to the stall, to the knife, to the controller, and back to Tesla. "Haldan?"

"He's an actor. It's an identity-theft scheme. I think he's been killing everyone who could give it away and trying to make himself look like the victim."

"I was stabbed. Twice!" Haldan gasped. "Oh my God. In the cabin. When the lights were out. Those were your scissors! You were the one who stabbed me then, too."

Shal's breathing was tight and rapid. He wet his lips and looked at Tesla. "Did he just try to kill you?"

"Just a little."

"Screw the crime scene." He strode into the room, slammed the bathroom stall open, and dropped into a boxing stance.

Haldan yelped, and Tesla did not think he was acting.

Shal's fist slammed into Haldan's jaw. The other caught him in the midriff. Haldan crumpled like a ragdoll.

Wheezing, Shal bent double, both arms wrapped around his

ribs. Tesla found her feet, somehow, and rested her hands on his back to steady him while he breathed through the pain. Gimlet slid past him and grabbed Haldan's trouser leg, yanking at it with short, furious growls.

"What the hell is going on?" Wisor strode into the room, followed by the wall of Bob. He looked at the blood and the knife, and the man crumpled on the floor and straightened. "Shalmaneser Steward and Tesla Crane, you're under arrest for murder."

COGNAC STINGER

2 oz cognac
.75 oz crème de menthe
Fresh mint

Shake cognac and crème de menthe over ice for 15
seconds. Strain into coupe. Garnish with mint leaves.

The cushion that Fantine had argued for barely softened the hard
metal chair. Tesla kept her hands in her lap, running them over
Gimlet's warm fur to try to distract herself from the shape of her
spine. She couldn't actually feel the screws holding her back together, but she could imagine each rigid piece of titanium burrow-
ing into bone.

Slow breath. Golden sunshine. Gimlet's silky ears.

Thank God—or just Fantine, that she'd argued them into allowing Gimlet to stay with Tesla on medical grounds. She knew
that Shal could take care of himself, but having Gimlet out of her
sight again would have broken her. Broken her more.

On the handheld that Leigh Osbourne de Monchaux had
propped on the table beside his immaculate cuff, Fantine fumed.
"—don't care if he owns the entire solar system. The man im-
personating Haldan Kuznetsova has endangered the lives of my
clients multiple times. By treating my client as if she were a guilty
party, it's as if the cruise line wants to be complicit in his attempts
to add them both to his list of murder victims."

Leigh Osbourne de Monchaux's mouth twitched. He steadied
his gaze on Tesla again. "Regardless of who owns the ship, we have
witnesses who are making very serious claims against your cli-

ents. Mx. Crane's fingerprints were on the knife that stabbed Mx. Kuznetsova. They were on the octopoid controller. We have her story for how that took place and we also have Mx. Kuznetsova's."

"My client will only answer the following questions . . ."

From his spot next to the lawyer's, Wisor leaned back in his chair. "One of those stories has physical evidence to back it up."

Tesla's willpower gave out and she responded, hearing her voice rise with each sentence, "Yuki pulled my dog out of Nile Silver's trunks! One of which was big enough for a person and had a breathing apparatus in it." Apparently the twins had decided to be as cooperative as possible and had opened the trunks that Nile had forbidden them to touch.

"That only tells us that Nile Silver was smuggling."

She held in a groan. He was right, only so far as they had no idea how Silver had gotten Gimlet from their room to the theater. Or why. The only person who would know some of those answers was the actor, and he was still pretending to be Haldan Kuznetsova.

"She will answer question three: The state of the bathroom when she first entered it."

Maria Piper came back into the room. She set a bottle of water on the table and a small bag with a single pill in it. "Oxyfeldone, per your lawyer. Neither of these have been out of my hands since the matter printer."

"Happy, Counsel?" Wisor rolled his eyes. "As if she could fend off her 'attacker' as she claimed if she's got the medical conditions you say she does."

"And also question seven: Her best recollection of the timing of events between the theater lights going out and the arrival of Annie Barnes, aka Annie Smith. Note: this focus is on the timing solely to allow your investigation to connect it with activities of other parties."

She was tired. She hurt. And while she shouldn't talk without Fantine in the room, it was hard to think about anything except the muscles knotting themselves into tighter and tighter balls.

Tesla scraped the pill off the table and held it up. "Tell me why I would have turned off my own DBPS if I had any goddamned choice in the matter?"

"Sympathy ploy." Wisor's mouth turned down sourly. "I see this all the time. People who pretend to be handicapped to get a better room or skip a line."

"Wow. Pretending. Handicapped?" She turned to Leigh Osbourne de Monchaux. "Someday, I'd love to talk about licensing the time travel technology that has allowed you to be able to hire someone from 1980."

He twisted his neck in a strained acknowledgment. "Imperial System Ships believes in accessible travel and recognizes that not all disabilities are visible. I believe Chief Wisor meant to merely offer speculation of possible motive rather than an expression of the corporation's views on individual abilities."

"Right. Yeah, that's exactly what I meant."

"But somehow it's more believable that I have been running around killing people all over the ship?"

Wisor shrugged. "Well, not alone."

"He wasn't working alone either." She opened the bottle of water. "He had all of you working for him. That voice trick of his—"

Oh. That was why Shal didn't remember that she had called him. She hadn't called *him*. The fake Haldan had answered the phone. Had he been in the room, or just rerouted the call using an owner override?

Wisor snorted, looking at Leigh Osbourne de Monchaux. "Do we really have to do this? We caught her, literally red-handed."

"There's a recording of him talking to me as if he were Shal, on my lawyer's phone, and it happened while Shal was with Maria." She rolled the old familiar capsule between her fingers. It would dull the pain, as long as she didn't mind all the side effects. Getting the DBPS, on the other hand, had been like having a switch flipped in her brain—which, in fact, was literally what it was—and allowed her to go whole hours without pain. It let her sleep through the night. It let her function without having to measure every single goddamned step she would have to take in a day.

"According to Maria, she was *not* with your husband at that time, because he suggested that they separate to do a 'better search pattern' for the alleged octobot."

"Octopoid." Tesla tossed the pill into her mouth and took a sip of water.

"Answer the questions, like your lawyer says. Why did you take a knife into the bathroom in the theater?"

It wasn't exactly the question that Fantine had told her to answer, but Tesla just didn't care. "The spoofer zone around Ory and Ewen meant that no one in that section of seating could have been using the octopoid—"

"I'm not asking about the octopoid."

She glared at him and did not make any attempt to hide her disdain. "I'm answering one of the two questions my lawyer approved and explaining the timing of events. But if you want me to shut up, I will, but I'll tell you what happens as a result. What happens is that we get to Mars and 'Haldan' gets off the ship. While the real investigation happens, with actual detectives who know their jobs, the actor cleans out Kuznetsova's accounts, and vanis—"

"And your lawyer gets you out of jail, scot-free. Right." Wisor leaned forward, face mottling red. "Let me tell you, then, that I'm sick and tired of rich people like you coming on and thinking they can get away with anything they want. You—"

Leigh Osbourne de Monchaux cleared his throat. "I would suggest that we keep our comments to ones in line with corporate policy. Just as anything Mx. Crane says can be used against her, the same is true for us." With a single long, gold nail, he indicated the handheld on which Fantine crocheted while she waited out the twenty-minute lag.

"All right, all right." Wisor shrugged, then leaned back in his seat. He stretched his legs out in front of him in a show of ease. "Go ahead. Tell me about the octobot."

In her lap, Gimlet raised her head and huffed. Tesla ran a soothing hand down the little dog's back. "The *octopoid* operator needed to be close to avoid lag. I remembered that Annie had said that the restroom by the yoga studio had been out of order. We'd also found a blue suckerfoot there." She looked at Maria. "Was one there when you checked?"

Wisor sliced his hand through the air. "Don't answer her."

Behind his back, Maria met Tesla's gaze and gave a tiny nod that might almost have been nothing more than a blink.

"Annie was missing from the theater, so I thought I would check the bathroom, mistakenly believing that she was the octopoid operator."

"If you were so sure the murderer was in there, why didn't you ask someone to help you?" Wisor looked at the screen. "If I'm allowed follow-up questions."

What Tesla should do was to wait the twenty minutes for Fantine to give her the go-ahead, but she was tired and angry and the longer this took, the longer she had to sit in this goddamned chair. It hurt to lean back. It hurt to sit forward. "Besides the fact that I hadn't been given reason to trust the security on the ship? Hm . . . I wonder. I did contact my lawyer so that there would be a record of my entry, which will show that events line up with my account until my systems were disabled."

"Yeah. Your husband was in the bathroom. I heard."

She stretched one shoulder, trying to ease a knot. "And now I'm covering for him allegedly attacking me, because . . . ?"

Wisor waved a hand. "We see this all the time. A couple has a fight, it comes to blows, but the moment we go to restrain the aggressor, the victim has a change of heart. They looooove them."

"Or." She bared her teeth in a boardroom smile. "Or. The explanation that fits all of the facts, instead of the gaping holes that your theory leaves, is that an actor is engaged in identity theft."

"There are easier ways to steal someone's money."

"Not if you want the lifestyle to go with the wealth." Tesla rocked her feet up on their toes to try to shift her relationship with the chair. "There are connections and people and access that you don't get with just money. I could lose my entire fortune and people would still just give me things because of the connections I have. I could—"

"You could murder someone and people would still love you." Wisor snorted. "But you've done that already, haven't you? How many people were on that lab? Fewer than you've killed here."

Leigh Osbourne de Monchaux flattened his hand on the table. "I will object on behalf of my colleague."

"Who do you work for?" Wisor swiveled in the chair to stare at him.

"The company. Not for you." His perfect pencil mustache twitched in annoyance. "I would prefer to limit the opportunities for lawsuits."

Tesla leaned forward so Gimlet's warm body pressed into her belly. "Come on . . . why was Haldan in the bathroom? I didn't have time to go to his room and drag him there. Even if I did, why would I have brought him so close to all the security people— Hang on." She looked at the wall of Bob, standing in the corner. "You were guarding Haldan in the infirmary. And then you were in the stairwell. Why did you leave him alone?"

"Maria—" He stopped and shook his head. "I'm not supposed to answer your questions."

Maria pushed away from the wall. "Wait a minute. I what?"

Bob looked to Wisor for permission to speak and the security chief shook his head. "Uh-uh. Crane is not running the show here."

Tesla's mouth rounded into an *O*. "Did Maria call you?"

Maria said, "I did not."

Bob's brows came together. "Yes, you did. You said that the chief needed backup."

"I absolutely did not." Her nostrils flared and she turned to look at Tesla. "I'll be goddamned. He wrote that message himself. It's why I didn't see it on the mirror when we cleared his room."

Wisor slapped his hand on the table. "That's enough!" He turned to the lawyer. "Piper's been cozying up to Steward and Crane since they got on the ship. For all I know she could have been collaborating with them."

"Oh for—" Tesla straightened in her chair, spine popping as she did. For a brief moment, her vision went white as she gasped.

In the room, Maria was objecting and Leigh Osbourne de Monchaux was trying to restore order and Tesla focused on visualizing golden sunlight pouring down from above. Gimlet licked her hand as she slowly breathed. *In, two, three, four. Hold. Out, two, three, four. Hold.*

A spot of tension in her back eased as if whatever it was had slid back into alignment. It got a tiny bit easier to think. She swallowed as a thought slid into the place where the pain had been.

"Hey." She looked at Wisor. "Did Haldan Kuznetsova tell you to help Nile map blind spots? Before he got on the ship?"

The lawyer's eyebrow went up and he turned to the chief.

Scowling, Wisor grabbed the handy, wiping Fantine's window into an upper corner. He jabbed at it. "I am so tired of this bullshit theory about Kuznetsova being an actor. Look." He turned it to a shipboard picture of Haldan sitting in the arboretum, surrounded by trees and laughing as he held a glass of Champagne.

"And this is the same man from two years ago." The other half of the screen showed him on the cover of *Time Solar Man of the Year,* posing in a forest somewhere on Earth, with an ancient German shepherd. The dog's white muzzle was pointed toward Haldan, and the photographer had caught him laughing as the dog licked his chin. "You're telling me he's been an actor this whole time?"

The chief was right. It absolutely looked like the same man. With one critical difference.

"He loved dogs."

"What—"

"Test him for a dog allergy." Tesla tightened her hands in Gimlet's white fur. "I thought he was crying. His eyes started watering and his nose ran when he came to our suite. He was standoffish with Gimlet the entire time. There's no way a dog person wouldn't have fallen in love with her or at least petted her. He never, ever touched her. He was *mad* when she was missing and we wanted to look for her. A real dog lover would have understood. An actor might be able to fake a lot of things, but if he was allergic to dogs . . . before he gets off the ship and disappears, test him for a dog allergy."

Across the room, Maria pursed her lips and looked at Gimlet, then at the image on the handy. "I mean, she's kind of got a point . . ."

"Seriously? You're going to exonerate her because you like that do—"

"It's about goddamned time you got her that pillow!" Fantine's voice boomed out of the handy, and Wisor nearly dropped it. "And no, I am *not* happy. I am about as close to happy as Saint Margaret the day she died, only being pressed to death over a stone is faster."

Wisor threw his stylus on the table. "God, I hate her."

Maria sucked in a breath and looked up from her handheld.

Clearing his throat, Leigh Osbourne de Monchaux made a note on his handheld with a sidelong glance at the security chief. "You do remember that my esteemed colleague will be able to hear you in—"

"Princess? *Princess?!*" Fantine's voice carried escalating legal bills into the room. "Excellent. Hey, Leigh! I'm adding discrimination to the lawsuits that we're piling on you, in addition to the wrongful imprisonment and emotional distress suits that I was already drafting. Sorry, the actions of that galumphing sack of cheese curds means we won't be able to play golf until this is over."

Leigh Osbourne de Monchaux folded his personal handheld and pushed his chair back from the table. "Fantine, I will trounce you in golf at the first opportunity." He stood, tucking the handheld into his pocket. "Maria, would you escort Mx.—"

"Your security chief wouldn't recognize evidence if it was piped directly into his cranium. I demand that you cease this farce and escort my clients back to their suite at once. If you want to let the actual murderer wander around your ship, that's on you. My only concern is making sure— Mother of God! Accommodation for medical needs is not 'pampering.' As if your clear prejudice against my client weren't already obvious."

Leigh Osbourne de Monchaux took the handheld from Wisor and swiped it back to Fantine's screen. She was gripping her crochet hook like a dagger and pressing the tip into the desk blotter. "Fantine, by the time you hear this, your clients will be back in their suite. You have my personal apologies as well as the apologies of the entire cruise line."

Wisor stood to gape at him. "You can't be serious. Because of her dog?"

"Yes. Essentially." He tilted his chin as he continued to work on the tablet, using his gold nail as a stylus. "It did make me pause to think, because she is correct that anyone who is not charmed by that absurdly cute wee doglet is somewhat suspect. That and, of course, I've just confirmed the message that Officer Piper sent. You . . . you did send it?"

Maria nodded, taking a step away from Wisor to stand closer to Bob. "I was right?"

Bob looked from her to Wisor, whose face was mottling with red. The chief asked, "Right about what?"

"Payroll. There was a . . . significant raise."

Piper pulled her cuffs from her belt and turned to Bob. "Give me your hands."

Bob's eyes widened. "You're . . . you're talking about me?"

Wisor's face paled and then turned bright red. "What?!"

"I thought it was legit." Bob looked down at the floor, crossing his arms over his massive chest. "Jeez . . . I'm real sorry."

Watching the wall of Bob, Tesla replayed things in her mind.

"I get how he could have fooled you into thinking that Maria was going to take over your shift . . ."

"But why leave before I showed up?" Maria reached for his arm. "Bob, don't make me ask you twice."

"Oh, come on." Wisor took a step toward them. "It's *Bob*. Of course he didn't know."

Bob looked at the chief and then looked at Maria. He sighed and then spun, swinging at Wisor. His huge, meaty fist caught the security chief square in the eye. The chief staggered back, fetching up against the table. Maria reached for Bob and he shoved her back with one flat palm to the chest. He spun, advancing on the chief, and hit him again in the nose with the crack of breaking bone.

Gimlet leapt off Tesla's lap, barking at everyone. Bob's fists were sledgehammers, driving into the chief's ribs. Wisor dropped to his knees with a groan. Bob took a step toward him, and Gimlet tangled in his ankles.

Bob danced, trying not to step on the little dog. In that gap, Maria unholstered her taser and fired it at Bob. The big man spasmed and the wall of Bob came tumbling down. Maria was on him, pinning his hands behind his back. Gimlet licked his face.

Bob started to laugh.

Wiping blood from his face, Chief Wisor wheezed on the floor. "What the hell is funny? You broke my nose."

"You thought I was stupid because I'm big." Bob's face was pressed into the floor, but he peered up at the chief with one eye. "I always figured that if I got caught the one thing I wanted was to break your nose. Thanks for that. Nicest thing you've done for me."

Leigh Osbourne de Monchaux sniffed, straightening his sleeves with a nod to Maria. "Thank you for your quick thinking."

"Not quick enough."

Tesla stared at Bob, who was still laughing into the floor with his hands pinned behind him. "You know he would have eventually killed you."

"Nah." His chuckles were deeply unnerving. "He was only offing people who could out him. All I had to do was pretend to be too thick to know that he wasn't really Haldan. Loyal bodyguard who one hundred percent believes you? It would've been a good gig."

"Nonetheless." The lawyer's mustache was flattened with disgust looking at Bob, a look that lingered until he turned to Tesla. "Would you allow me to escort you and Mx. Steward back to your suite?"

Wisor wiped his nose on his shirtsleeve, leaving a streak as vivid as Fantine's yarn. "I'm not finished with them."

"Yes, you very much are." Leigh Osbourne de Monchaux straightened his spine. "I've put in a request to Corporate to relieve you from duty."

His mouth dropped open, blood from his nose staining his teeth. "Wha— I was doing my job."

"Incompetently. You may take any concerns up with Corporate."

Tesla raised her hand and smiled at the ex-security chief. "I would offer to recommend a lawyer, but I can't imagine a universe in which you could afford her."

Extra-Dry Martini

2 oz gin

Stir over ice. Say the word "vermouth." Strain into martini glass.

Tesla reclined on the couch with a pile of pillows supporting her back. Opposite her, Shal sat propped against the other end of the couch, his legs intertwined with hers. She ran her thumb down the arch of Shal's foot and watched his toes curl a little. For a moment, his eyes fluttered shut.

Gimlet lay on the floor, gnawing on a bone that the ship had sent by way of apology. The grinding of her teeth on the bone was both deeply annoying and strangely comforting.

Running his hands up her calf under her pajama bottoms, Shal dug his fingers into the tight muscles there. Her DBPS was back online, but there was a substantial difference between muted pain and lack of pain. Shal knew exactly where to find her trouble spots. "So you didn't actually think that was me, did you?"

"No, of course not."

"Because on the recording you kinda sounded like you did." He reached over to the coffee table and pumped some more of the massage oil into his palm. "I mean, I wouldn't blame you if you had."

"You would completely blame me." She tugged on his little toe. "I'll say that I was confu—"

Gimlet jumped to her feet, barking, and ran to the door. A moment later, the chime rang.

Looking at the hothouse flowers that stood in the corner and the remnants of the chocolate-covered strawberries, Shal sighed. "What do you think? Champagne as the latest apology gift?"

"Mm . . . They haven't offered us a choice of Fine Art Available Now in the Promenaaaaaade!"

Gimlet continued to bark, but it had shifted to mingle with her happy whines.

Laughing, Shal swung his feet off the couch. "I'll get it. Bet you it's room service with truffle fries."

"Oh good, that'll pair well with my whisky." She picked up the glass of twenty-one-year Kadenokoji she'd been nursing and straightened on the couch. She slid her other hand between the cushions of the sofa to touch the bespoke taser she'd made and hidden there. Just in case.

She didn't need to follow Shal to the door. She could stay put on the couch and enjoy the whisky.

From the hall, Shal's voice warmed. "Maria! Come in."

"Gimlet! Who's the best girl? Is that you? Is that you? Yes, it is, and I know you are the saddest, most neglected creature in all the worlds."

From the couch, Tesla could hear Gimlet's excited whines and snorts of delight.

"Oh, hey, Shal, sorry I—"

"No, no! I'm very clear where I stand in the hierarchy. Come in and join us when you finish your reunion."

"Let me just give Gimlet her present." Paper rustled and then Gimlet ran back into the main room holding a cloth weasel. She stopped in the middle of the room and shook it ferociously.

Shal led Maria into the main room. She carried a paper bag in one hand and had a shiny new Security Chief badge on her shirt. "I'm not interrupting, am I?"

"Not at all." He moved a stack of apology gift certificates from a chair to make room for her. "Just relaxing a little. Sit down, sit down."

Maria looked at the massage oil on the table and then at Tesla's mountain of pillows. The corner of her mouth turned up in a smile. "No thank you. Y'all are canoodling and I'm not going to get in the way of that."

"It's fine." Tesla pried herself out of the sofa, pausing when she was on her feet to make sure everything was lined up. She stretched, enjoying moving with acceptable amounts of pain. "And as you noted, Gimlet is perishing for lack of attention."

Her dog was on her back, stumpy tail wagging against the floor as she stared adoringly up at Maria.

"Yes, I see that." She knelt by the little dog again, setting the paper bag on the floor. Gimlet rolled over to snuffle it, and Maria pushed her gently away. "You got yours already."

Tesla headed to the bar. "What can I get you to drink?"

"Seriously, nothing." She levered herself to her feet. "I just stopped by to let you know that, yes, our friend is allergic to dogs."

"Ha! I knew it." Tesla peered at the selection of alcohol on their bar. "This calls for a drink. Let me pour you something."

"What's his real name?" Shal asked.

"Max Astaire. Before you pour a drink you should open your own present." She handed the paper bag to Shal. "Compliments of the cruise line as a 'please only sue us a little' apology."

"Do we know where he came from?" He dug into the bag.

"Cincinnati, on Earth. Mostly a stage actor known for 'disappearing into his roles.' Like, a *lot* of reviews said that. He met Nile on the theatre circuit. Astaire actually thought he was a good enough actor to fool George Saikawa."

"Wow . . . That's some chutzpah."

"Indeed it is. And wait, you'll love this next part. Turns out, Astaire is a cousin of Haldan's whose grandfather was disinherited by their mutual great-grandmother. He had a little bit of work done to fine-tune the resemblance for biometrics but . . ." She shrugged. "He's allergic to dogs."

"What happened to the dog on the magazine cover?" Tesla had a sudden fear that the fake Haldan had had him put to sleep.

"Died of old age at fifteen last year." Shal looked up from the bag. "Also, Maria, you are officially my favorite."

"Hey! What about me?" Tesla crossed the room to join them.

Maria shook her finger at Shal. "I see someone is enjoying snooping with their network access again."

Shal almost blushed. "I mean . . . I still had all the tags cued up from when I'd investigated him a decade ago. It was just a matter of activating the searches again. His dog's death is what prompted Haldan's move. He didn't want to subject Rocky to launch so was waiting for him to pass before relocating."

There were so many things Tesla still didn't understand. "So . . . all of that 'Remember the Main'? Total BS?"

Nodding, Maria grabbed the weasel and offered it to Gimlet again. "Oh yeah. He and Nile expected the body to completely dissolve in the recycler so that no one would even know it was there. When we started talking about it, he panicked and had to come up with a whole different story."

"Hold on. What about the kid that died in the fire?"

"Improv is a hell of a drug, apparently. He had no idea that someone had died and just spun a story when you came up with a name." Gimlet grabbed the weasel's head and tugged on it, growling viciously as Maria held its tail. "Get him, Gimlet. So vicious."

Shal kissed Tesla on the forehead and glanced at Maria. "Tell me if I have this right? Nile smuggled Astaire aboard in his magic equipment with the plan that they would replace Kuznetsova en route and then use the cruise to establish Haldan as the real deal. Any changes in manner would be chalked up to the death of his beloved assistant."

"Pretty much."

"The man who bribed Immanuel and who ran up the stairs were . . . both Astaire? Trying to frame Immanuel and me?"

Maria nodded, "It was a toss-up between framing you or Jalna and Annie. He decided on you because, get this, Annie was famous and you were just regular people. He's telling us everything now, which Leigh thinks is because—now that he's caught—he wants to sell the rights to his story. Kill it, Gimlet! Kill the weasel. So in this version, he's an actor who was duped into helping a very dangerous magician who was having an affair with the famous Tesla Crane, which is, of course, why you assaulted him."

"Wow."

"I know. I'm just letting him sing all he wants." She let go of the weasel so that Gimlet could shake it.

"Any idea why he went up the stairs instead of back into his room?" Shal asked.

"He didn't say this, but I've got a bet." Maria grabbed the other end of Gimlet's weasel and tugged. "Grr. So fierce. The Terran ring is huge, and it can take half an hour to get from one side to the other, but if you go up to the Lunar level and back down it's good shortcut. Ooh! Who has the weasel?"

Gimlet ran in a tight circle, shaking the weasel with satisfied growls.

"An alibi!" Tesla nodded as pieces clicked together. "He mentioned that he was coming back from the casino, which is on the far side of the Terran ring."

"Yep. Hey, Shal? Since you've got that network up and running again . . . Any chance you can shed light on Ewen Slootmaekers? I've got them and Ory separated, but I feel terrible for the kid."

Sighing, Shal nodded. "Yeah, I don't even have to look it up. I already found the article that I remembered reading. Ory Slootmaekers's real name is Philippe Olson. He was in a two-year relationship with Ewen's mother that started about three months before Ewen was born. He sought visitation rights when they split, but without legal standing . . . He was always the top suspect and very, very careful. He worked in cybersecurity, so when he decided to vanish, he had all the tools to create a new identity."

"Ah . . ." Maria nodded as if that unlocked something for her. "So the 'not what we agreed' conversation was either about Nile giving them security access or him providing a fake identity for Astaire."

"Not a fake ID, or Astaire would have killed him . . . probably before George, if I were to guess." Shal sighed and ran a hand through his curls. "I've got contact info for Ewen's mom. If they want it."

Tesla cleared her throat. "I may have offered them an internship."

Maria raised her brows. "Swimming in opportunity. Jalna did too."

"I would have too." Shal carried the paper bag over to the bar. "But that would involve me not being retired."

Maria's brows went higher and wrote a treatise questioning what he meant by "retired."

"So . . . that smuggling that Nile was doing." Shal pulled a bottle of Lunacy Gin out of the bag. "Is that where you got this?"

"No, because that would be interfering with a criminal investigation." Maria clambered back to her feet. "However, Captain Valdísardottir opened her personal stash and adds to the cruise line's apologies with her own apologies."

Tesla smiled. "Well, tell her thank—"

The chime rang and Gimlet sprang to her feet, running to the door to fend off whoever was outside. "Gimlet!" Tesla sighed and raised her voice to be heard over her dog. "Sorry about this. She's never been fond of delivery people, and this has all made her more protective than ever."

Maria nodded and walked to the door, fishing in her pocket. "Gimlet, treat?"

The little dog abandoned her efforts and came to sit in devoted adoration at Maria's feet with her silky ears in perfect triangles of attention.

Handing her the treat, Maria looked through the peephole, and then opened the door. "No. They don't want balloons." She looked back into the room. "Unless I'm wrong?"

"Not even a little." Shal raised the bottle. "This is plenty."

"And none of it is going to stop Fantine from suing." Tesla shrugged apologetically. "She would crochet my soul into a garrote and use it to strangle my body if I tried to keep her from having fun. If they are trying to butter someone up, she likes yarn . . ."

"Noted." Maria came back into the main room, tapping on her handheld. "Do Not Disturb is on now. I'll suggest yarn to Legal. Y'all have fun now, y'hear?"

She closed the door behind her and Gimlet stared up at it mournfully for a moment, then ran back into the main room and attacked her new weasel. Shal sighed and brought his arm around Tesla, hugging her while still holding the bottle and bag. He rested his chin on her shoulder and turned his head to kiss her on the neck.

"Well? How do you want to spend the remaining six days of our honeymoon? Karaoke?"

She laughed and slipped her hands down to squeeze his buttocks, partly so she wouldn't put pressure on his ribs, and partly because his ass was glorious. "Are you serious? I still owe you make-up sex."

"Well, in that case . . ." He led her back to their bedroom with the ginormous Martian king bed and set the Lunacy Gin on the sideboard. "So we don't have to get out of bed for the postcoital martinis."

"Ice?" She came up behind him and found the drawstring on his pajama trousers. "Vermouth?"

"Dammit." He turned in her arms and slipped his hands under the edge of her blouse. "I'm always forgetting something. Can we train Gimlet to make cocktails?"

"It depends on how much dog fur you want as a garnish." She raised her arms to let him pull her shirt up over her head.

He stopped, hissing. "Nope. Sorry."

"Ribs?"

"Rib. Singular." Shal grimaced as he lowered her shirt again. "It's just certain movements."

"Fortunately, I can take my own shirt off . . ." Tesla drew it up and over her head in a way that did wonderful things to her breasts and waist. Her back twinged, but nothing outside of tolerances. When she dropped her shirt on the floor, Shal was staring into her eyes with a crooked, goofy grin.

She closed the remaining distance between them, sliding her hands up his back and into his hair. His breath was warm on her neck, and she could feel every soft returning caress of his hands.

When he had suggested a cruise to Mars for their honeymoon, she had been, at best, dubious. Shal kissed her neck, lips warm and soft along her skin. "What about the martinis?"

"I suggest very"—Tesla Crane kissed her spouse's neck, tasting the sweet salt of his skin—"very"—she nipped his ear—"dirty."

ACKNOWLEDGMENTS

There are as always so many people to thank for getting this novel into your hands. This book was supposed to come out in 2021. Ahahahaha . . . My editor, Claire Eddy, was totally calm when I said that writing in 2020 and 2021 was hard because I was not the only author having that conversation with her. When I started this, there were no courtesy masks in it. I went back and wove them in to the early parts of the book because I can no longer imagine a future in which they aren't part of our lives. Not as constant, perhaps, but still present.

My agent, Seth Fishman, who always has my back, worked with Claire to take the novel off the schedule and told me to just take my time. That is . . . not easy for me. My assistants, Christine Sandquist and Alyshondra Meacham, kept things moving so that I had time to work on this novel even after I foolishly said "yes" to things like running a major convention. Christine also doubled as my sensitivity reader on trauma and gender. It turns out that I'm heavily programmed to write gender binaries even when I'm trying not to and they give excellent notes. Jordan Kurella was also a sensitivity reader on service dogs and was an invaluable help. For those listening to the audiobook, my engineer, Andrew Twiss, is a genius who makes me sound good and as if I can speak French. Lunar French at any rate.

The members of the Lady Astronaut Club have been an amazing addition to my life. Without our coworking sessions, I don't know that I would have kept writing at all during the pandemic. Special shout-outs to Anne Delekta, Stephanie Franklin, C. L. Polk, Jen Coster, Kate Montgomery, Kendra Zzyzwyck, Leane Parsons, Meagan Voss, Nathan Beittenmiller, Rachel Gutin, Dede, Stephen Rider, and Wen Wen.

The Whiskey Chicks have my heart. Thank you Eileen

Cook, Elizabeth Boyle, Susanna Kearsley, Kathy Chung, Nephele Tempest, Crystal Hunt, and Liza Palmer. You make me a better writer and a better person.

I also had help on some specific things, which are all kinda cool. Stuart Pluen-Calvo answered a call on Twitter to help me make the Lunar French nonbinary. Y'all . . . that ain't easy.

Speaking of difficult languages, I had the pleasure of attending IceCon in Reykjavík in one of the tiny gaps of normal. The last night there, a group of us sat around and filled in the Mad Libs where I'd left placeholders. Hildur Knútsdottir and Júlíus Árnason Kaaber, in particular, were greatly helpful with the Icelandic. One thing of interest is that Icelandic has historically had binary patronyms. So Captain Valdisardottir is literally Valdis's dottir. Valdis is a woman's name, which is allowed now. And in contemporary Iceland nonbinary folks can have "-bur" ("child of") instead of "-dottir" or "-son."

I need to thank Max Fagin, who made me the most amazing transit calculator to help me figure out the lag time as they went as well as brainstorming about how the wacky ship works. More about that in the About the Science portion.

I wrote parts of this while on a cruise with the *Writing Excuses* gang. We run a workshop every year and for six years it's been on a cruise ship. So thank you, Brandon, Dan, Howard, Marshall, Dawn, Sandra, and especially Erin Roberts for her karaoke expertise. Thank you to everyone on the 2021 WXR at Sea. That group of writers in the R-Bar? That's all of you. Shauna Hoffman and Lisa Harding introduced me to cruising and make my world a brighter place. Many thanks to Chef Calphus McDonald, the executive chef on Royal Caribbean's *Independence of the Seas,* for taking an hour out of his day to talk with me about how kitchens work on a cruise ship.

Gabriel Swiney, who is an actual space lawyer—and yes that's a real job—made both of my space lawyers better. Many thanks to my Patreon supporters and beta readers who read this and gave very helpful feedback, especially thanks to: Abigail Pankau, Alex

McKenzie, Amanda Joy, Anne Bingham, Annie Scribbles, Auriel Fournier, Bee Bube, Chanie Beckman, Christina Skelton, Deana, Debbie Lee, Francesca Kuehlers, J Zimmerman, J.A. Ironside, Jasmin Nyack, Jen Fiero, Jenn Mercer, Kimberly Savill, Kris Johnson, Lisa Pendragon, Lisa S, Marzie K, Megan Sohar, Meredith W, Mike Baltar, Natasha Gapinski, Nicole Murphy, Sarah Swarbrick, Susan Anne Kadlec, Vicky Hsu, and Victoria Winner.

My cats, Elsie and the late Sadie, who played tag across my notecards as I was working on the plot. Without them, the visit to the yoga studio would have been elsewhere in the novel.

And, of course, my family, who encourage me to vanish for long stretches of time. Mom and Dad, I love you so much.

Robert, you are the Nick to my Nora.

ABOUT THE SCIENCE

The *Lindgren* is a bonkers ship that no one would actually build. Except a cruise line. For the past seven years, I've been running writing workshops with the *Writing Excuses* podcast on cruise ships. Royal Caribbean, specifically. We held one on the *Oasis of the Seas,* which is also a bonkers ship that no one would build—I mean, it has a water show with three-story-tall diving platforms. Cruise lines build floating cities all the time, so why not a spacebound one? And if you are serving the populations of three different gravity wells, why not cater to them?

So the *Lindgren* is bonkers, but it would work in theory. Max Fagin, an actual rocket engineer, helped me work out the parameters of the ship to fit the needs of the story. Departure is on Tuesday, April 30, 2075, and is a twelve-day transit under constant thrust, which provides consistent Lunar gravity to the central column of the ship.

Extending from that are two centrifuge rings that allow the passengers to experience Martian or Terran gravity. I fudge a lot about distances between the rings because it's about fifty meters, which is about eleven stories. The theater makes no sense, really. I mean it works, but who would watch from the Lunar level twenty-two stories from the stage? I'm figuring there are massive screens up there. As I said, the ship is bonkers.

On the other hand, the Deep Brain Stimulator that Tesla uses is only barely science fiction. My mom has Parkinson's disease and has a DBS to help with symptom control. It took five different surgeries to install it, two of which were brain surgery. When she went it to have it activated for the first time she needed to use a walker and her speech was mushy. The doctor activated the DBS and the tremor just *stopped*.

I have never seen anything more miraculous in my life and it was a miracle made of science.

She walked out of there without assistance and her speech sounded like her again. It's adjustable, but you have to use a clunky device with direct skin contact to make changes. There are experimental DBS devices to control pain, but pain—it turns out—is so specific and so personal that doing a controlled study on this sort of management is really hard. There are also efforts to use DBS to help with various aspects of mental health like depression.

The other medical assistance that Tesla has is her service dog, Gimlet. Gimlet is based on two real dogs. There's an actual Westie named Gimlet, who belongs to my friend Eileen Cook. She is too cute to be real. There's also a service dog in our life named Captain, who is a stability dog for my mom. He's a chocolate Lab and is a very good boy and also very, very much a Lab. He's eaten a corncob and five nails. When we got him, the training center said, "He's a dog, not a robot."

The difference he's made in my mom's life is again, miraculous. The trouble with Parkinson's is that your brain starts to work slower and you'll freeze. A walker made my mom more of a fall risk because she'd freeze and couldn't squeeze the brakes, so the walker would keep going forward. Captain doesn't. He feels the freeze and stops. He can prompt her to move.

People with PTSD who have service dogs can go out into the world again because the dog can sense signals happening in their body before they do. I've talked to people and watched videos of dogs working with their handlers that are just heartbreakingly beautiful. In one, a person with a brain injury that caused random shutdowns was practicing crossing the street with the dog. The dog was doing an alert instead and the person was a little annoyed—then they had one of their shutdowns. The dog was in exactly the right place to catch them as they went down and stayed there until they recovered. If they had been crossing the street when that happened . . . All of which is to say that service dogs are amazing and can do so much more than you expect. They are highly trained and require maintenance, but can be liberating for their owners. When you see one, you can help their human by doing these things.

1. Don't make eye contact with the dog.
2. Don't touch the dog.
3. Don't talk to the dog.

The dog is working, so let them focus. They're a dog, not a robot.

And finally a thing that is just for funsies . . . the trivia game that's happening in the R-Bar is playable. All the answers are either in the book or in the real world. If you figure out the theme, email spareman@maryrobinettekowal.com for a bonus.

ABOUT THE COCKTAILS

Right up front I want to say that I think that everyone should be able to have a celebratory beverage and that it shouldn't require alcohol. I am interested in cocktails because I like flavors and alcohol affects the way flavors evaporate or change in your mouth. It's neat. I'm less excited about getting drunk so having zero-proof cocktails to switch to makes an evening more enjoyable. I prefer that term to virgin or mocktail because both of those seem like they are placing a value judgment on the drink.

As a culture we place a lot of stigma on people who don't drink. I'd rather we didn't. Did you know, by body weight, women can only metabolize a third of the alcohol that men can? So all the settings where drinking is expected place women at a disadvantage. If you're someone from a culture that doesn't drink or it's not healthy for you, doubly so.

I'm hoping that seeing the zero-proof drinks in here will give you things to order that are fun. My secret, if the bartender is not on the mixology god end of the scale, is to just ask for tonic and bitters with a lime.

But I also like a well-mixed, spirit-forward drink and can linger over it for ages. This is part of why I favor drinks served "up" because I don't have to worry about the flavor diminishing as the ice melts.

If you're new to cocktails, here are some terms that show up in the book that might be useful to know.

Serve up—Stir or shake it over ice to chill it, then strain it into a glass so there's no ice. This means that the cocktail doesn't dilute over time.

Rocks—Serve over ice.

Neat—No water or ice has touched this. It's room temperature and usually a single liqueur.

Dry shake—Shake without ice. You do this to emulsify ingredients.

To shake or stir—Shake if the beverage has fruit juice in it to emulsify it. Stir for pretty much everything else. Shaking breaks the ice up and causes it to melt faster so the drink will be slightly more diluted. If a cocktail is very "hot" you might want to ignore the shake/stir guidelines and go with shaking.

Flamed orange peel—Over the cocktail, hold the orange peel with one hand and a lighted match with the other. Squeeze the peel to express the oils over the glass so that the oil passes through the flame. It'll do flashy sparkles as the oil falls to the surface.

Cayenne salt—You can buy this, but if you want to make your own mix, use 1/4 cup kosher salt and 1/4 tsp cayenne pepper.

Also, hello, excuse me, but I made up these cocktails for this book.

Amal's Hospitality
Frisky Business
Orbital Decay
Reckless Generosity
Magician's Nibling
Dangerous Words

If you are interested in trying to create your own cocktails, take one of these and swap out an ingredient. Swap out two. Dangerous Words, for instance, is a Last Word with rye instead of gin and amaretto instead of maraschino.

The trick is that every cocktail has a base, a modifier, and an accent. Sometimes all of them are in equal parts. But you'll also often see cocktails structured as eight parts base, three parts modifier, two parts accent. This works regardless of what proof the cocktail is. Sometimes you'll want to adjust up or down depending on how strong a particular flavor is.

Flavors are fun and making something tasty doesn't have to be intimidating.